THE FIRST TASTE

CRYSTAL KASWELL

Copyright

This is a work of fiction. Similarities to real people, places, or events are entirely coincidental.

Also by Crystal Kaswell

Inked Love

The Best Friend Bargain - Forest

The First Taste - Holden

The Roomie Rulebook - Oliver

Inked Hearts

Tempting - Brendon

Hooking Up - Walker

Pretend You're Mine - Ryan

Hating You, Loving You - Dean

Breaking the Rules - Hunter

Losing It - Wes

Accidental Husband - Griffin

The Baby Bargain - Chase

Dirty Rich

Dirty Deal - Blake

Dirty Boss - Nick

Dirty Husband - Shep

Dirty Desires - Ian

Dirty Wedding - Ty

Dirty Secret - Cam

Pierce Family

Broken Beast - Adam

Playboy Prince - Liam

Ruthless Rival - Simon - coming soon

Sinful Serenade

Sing Your Heart Out - Miles

Strum Your Heart Out - Drew

Rock Your Heart Out - Tom

Play Your Heart Out - Pete

Sinful Ever After – series sequel

Just a Taste - Miles's POV

Dangerous Noise

Dangerous Kiss - Ethan

Dangerous Crush – Kit

Dangerous Rock – Joel

Dangerous Fling – Mal

Dangerous Encore - series sequel

Standalones

Broken - Trent & Delilah

Come Undone Trilogy

Come Undone

Come Apart

Come To Me

Sign up for the Crystal Kaswell mailing list

Chapter One

DAISY

I t's my birthday.

I can ask for anything.

A kiss is nothing. Less than nothing.

To a guy like Holden, who gives a whole lot more away for a whole lot less—

It's not a big deal.

At all.

My heart fails to accept my logic. It thuds against my chest. Echoes between my ears.

He's sitting right there, on the patio, fingers curled around a plastic cup.

Holden laughs—no doubt at something Oliver is saying—and holds up his drink.

They toast.

Holden takes a long sip.

Oliver swigs straight from the bottle.

Great. My brother is drinking heavily. And he's blocking access to my birthday wish.

I'm not thinking about it today.

Today is good.

A new leaf. A fresh start. A clean slate.

Any cliché works. No matter how I describe it, the situation is the same.

I'm starting my senior year at a new high school. Where no one knows me as *that* girl.

And I'm starting the year right. With a kiss from Holden.

I wait for my older brother to finish his bottle. Sure enough, he stands as he swallows his last sip of brown liquor.

I pretend as if I'm endlessly fascinated with the small talk of the group to my left.

For a party celebrating *my* birthday, the room is lacking in people I actually consider friends. Only Luna. And she's off somewhere. Probably flirting with a cute guy.

If I call her, she'll come running.

But she'll also push me to ask Holden for *everything*.

Maybe one day.

After many, many drinks.

But not today.

I nod along to a conversation about the weather, the school year, SATs, college applications.

Oliver steps into the main room. He looks to me. Smiles. "Happy birthday, kiddo." He pulls me into a tight hug. "You make a wish?" He motions to the cake on the table. To the blown-out candles.

I nod. "Of course."

"Don't tell me. Won't come true." He pats me on the shoulder. Releases me. Looks me dead in the eyes.

He has Mom's eyes. A deep shade of blue.

He has her hair too. Her skin tone. Her issues.

Or maybe I'm the one with her issues.

It's hard to say who inherited the worse hand. Not that

Oliver would have that conversation. As far as he's concerned, he drinks because it's fun.

Just like I—

No, I'm not going there. For one goddamn day, I'm not going there.

"I'm proud of you." His voice drops to his usual tone. Serious. Direct. *This is what I think, take it or leave it.* "I know it was hard, being away all summer, but you..." His voice cracks for a second. His eyes go to the ground. "I love you. Okay?"

I nod *okay*. "I love you too."

He hugs me one more time. Releases me. Goes in search of his next bottle. Fails to see the irony.

I guess I can't talk.

And now—

There's Holden, reclining on the patio chair, all long and lean and ready for me.

Not that I—

Oh my God, I can't even begin to think that.

Luna would say *go, get 'em tiger, tear off those jeans, pull out his ahem, and hop on.* Then she'd push me onto the patio.

Only she'd use much more explicit language.

Laugh at me for blushing.

God, I'm already blushing.

Which is silly. Holden is game for anything. I'm saying hi. Floating the idea. Asking for, uh, consideration.

Deep breath.

Slow exhale.

I smooth my dress—the pastel pink one from H&M— and take a step toward the patio. Then two. Three. Four.

There.

He turns as I slip through the space between the door and the wall.

"Hey." Holden sits up. Swings his leg to the side. Pats the spot next to him. "Happy birthday."

"Thank you." I take a seat.

God, he's so close. And so warm. And he smells so good. Like soap. Sandalwood, I think. It's that same soap he always uses.

He always smells like sandalwood.

Like heaven.

Like Holden.

He's so handsome and funny and dirty. God, he's so, so, so dirty. He thinks I don't overhear him and Oliver, but I do.

Holden offers me his drink.

My fingers brush his as I take it.

"Careful." His eyes meet mine. "It's strong."

I nod like I can handle it. Take a long sip. Cough. It burns. The sweetness of ginger ale and something else. Something overwhelming.

He chuckles. "Not your drink?"

I shake my head.

He smiles. "I can fix you something lighter."

"No, I just… wanted to say hey."

"Hey." He turns his body toward mine.

His jeans brush the bare skin of my knee. The fabric is in the way, but it still sets my body on fire.

It's like a match landing on a line of gasoline.

My toes curl.

My chest heaves.

My sex clenches.

Logic drifts to the back of my mind. What use is logic when the heat of his leg feels this good?

It's really possible to feel this good.

This at home in my body.

I need that. I need him to teach me that.

"You okay?" He nods to the drink. "You need another swig?"

I shake my head.

His eyes flit to the room. The party is mild, by Holden's standards. A dozen friends in a circle, playing one of those board games that rewards creativity.

A few of Oliver's friends.

A few cute women he and Holden invited.

My brother is talking to one of them. She's pretty. Short and curvy with bright pink hair and all black attire. I'd say she's his type, but he doesn't have one.

He sleeps with everything that moves.

Not that Holden is the picture of chastity.

More that—

Uh—

He's looking at me. Holden. His gorgeous grey-green eyes are fixed on me. The flecks of grey are glowing in the moonlight.

He's so beautiful. And handsome. And hot.

Attractive in every way a guy can be attractive.

"I guess you have a few minutes." Holden chuckles. "Oliver isn't going to go home with her tonight."

I shake my head. "Dad's here."

His eyes dart around the party.

"Upstairs. In his office. Just in case."

"In case?" Holden raises a brow. "What do you have planned, Daisy?"

"Nothing." My cheeks flush. "I'm—"

"You look sweet and innocent, but I know the truth." His smile widens. "You've got a troublemaker underneath the pretty pink dress."

My pulse races. "You think so?"

"I know so."

"I…"

"You…"

"It's my birthday." I just have to say it. It's the only way.

"It is."

"So you owe me a birthday wish."

"Do I?"

I nod. Take a deep breath. Exhale my nerves. This is no big deal. I'm flirting. Sure, Holden is three years older than I am, an adult with a job, an adult who is best friends with my brother, but, uh—

It's just flirting.

That's all.

No.

Big.

Deal.

"A birthday kiss." I swallow hard. "Just one."

"Daisy—"

"Don't say that I'm too young."

"Wasn't gonna say that."

"Oh."

His gaze shifts to the party—to Oliver—then it's back on me. "Usually, women ask for a birthday fuck."

My blush spreads to my chest.

"I guess you knew I'd say no."

"I, uh—"

He chuckles. "Is that really what you want?"

"To have sex with you?"

"No." His laugh is light. Easy. "A kiss?"

I nod.

"You could have anything. A free tattoo. A bottle of vodka. A wingman to find you a date for prom."

"Prom isn't until May."

He raises a brow.

I suck a breath through my teeth. "School hasn't even started."

6

"You want the best, you need to start early."

"You don't think I can find my own prom date?"

His eyes sparkle. Actually sparkle. "You're a beautiful girl. You're not going to have trouble."

My tongue slides over my lips. "You think I'm beautiful?"

"You know you're beautiful."

My stomach flutters. He's so smooth and sweet and suave and—

Oh my God. He's trying to let me down gently.

In his way.

He doesn't want to kiss me.

Because I'm a kid. Or because I'm his friend's sister. Or because I'm a certifiable mess.

No. He doesn't know that.

Oliver wouldn't.

Would he?

"Daisy?" He wraps his fingers around my wrist. "Are you okay?"

"Yeah, I just—"

"How many have you had?"

"How many?"

He motions to his red cup.

I shake my head. "Oliver has the only bottle."

Holden chuckles. "Has he really convinced you of that?"

"No," I lie.

"Fuck. He did. I shouldn't have said anything. I'm not a narc."

"Never?"

"Never ever."

"So you won't tell him about this?"

He shakes his head *of course not.*

For a moment, the sounds of the party drift into the

backyard. Laughter, conversation, the hum of Lorde.

The air gets charged.

Electric.

Then Holden's eyes meet mine. "Come here."

"Huh?"

"You want a birthday kiss, right?"

"Yeah."

"So come here." He pats the space next to his thigh. The space between us.

My heart thuds against my chest. "You'll do it?"

"It's your birthday. Like you said." His fingers dig into my wrist. "I can't deny a woman on her birthday."

"Oh."

His eyes meet mine. Then they travel down my body.

To my hand.

He lifts my arm. Leans down. Presses his lips to the back of my hand.

It's not the kiss I want.

Hell, it's as good as a rejection.

But it still sets me on fire.

I swear, somehow, someway, I'm going to kiss Holden Ballard properly.

Chapter Two

HOLDEN

Three Hundred Sixty Days Later

"**I**s it going to hurt?" My client looks up at me with wide eyes. Vulnerability. An intense need for comfort.

She should know better.

This isn't her first rodeo.

"Yeah." I shoot her my best *you know you want me* smile. (It's ace, if I do say so myself). "But I promise I'll kiss it and make it better."

"Really?" She lights up like a pinball machine. Her brown eyes brighten. Her red lips part. Her nails dig into her skirt. "Where exactly?"

"You're having second thoughts?" I motion to the trace paper on her wrist.

"Oh." Her eyes move over me slowly. She does nothing to hide her stare as she checks out my shoulders, chest, waist, crotch.

There's nothing to see at the moment.

If she keeps staring—

9

It won't be the world's most exciting lay. But she's cute enough. And she's certainly eager.

The type who will paw at my jeans and beg for my cock.

"I was thinking something more... personal." Her gaze stays fixed on my crotch.

Are my jeans really that interesting? They're nice, sure, and they fit well. But they're a pretty basic medium blue. Dark enough to hide excitement. Stretchy enough to make it bearable.

Not that I—

I may be a slut. Okay, there's no may about it. I sleep with a lot of women. But not clients.

Not in the middle of a tattoo.

Not at work.

This is the one place where I actually pay attention to shit. Where I actually give a shit. Where I actually try.

Not that I'd admit that.

If anyone asks, I'll deny it up and down. Say it's just a job. A way to pay the rent. A chance to hold a massive phallic symbol in my hand and paint women with my—

The damn thing writes itself.

"You have to earn that, sweetie." I snap my gloves. Pick up my gun. "I'm not easy."

"Really?" Incredulity streaks her expression.

"Hey." I feign offense. "I can't believe you see me that way."

Her lips curl into a smile. "You can't, huh?"

I shake my head. "You shouldn't stereotype."

"I shouldn't assume a guy who flirts with me every five minutes wants to sleep with me?"

"Wanting to do something and doing it are different things."

"True." She laughs.

"Now sit still. Maybe I'll forgive you."

"Maybe?"

"If I'm feeling generous." I wink. "You're lucky, I'm always generous."

She blushes as she shifts into the seat. Lays her arm on the chair.

I pin her with one hand. "You ready?"

She nods. "Count me down, okay?"

"Of course."

Her eyes close. Her expression shifts. All the fun and flirting fade into a mix of anticipation and anxiety.

Two sides of the same coin.

I need to keep her in the former.

Yeah, I'm not going to fuck her.

But there's no harm in letting her believe I am. It will get her through the tattoo. Keep her mind off the pain.

A lot of artists talk tough about how clients need to feel the pain. Because it makes them feel alive. Helps them earn it. Releases endorphins.

Whatever.

Sometimes, they act like it's for the client's good—they want the rush. Sometimes, they act like it's some price they have to pay—you want the ink, you suffer. But they're always self-righteous about it.

If this girl wants a pain-free tattoo, I'll do what I can.

"Three, two—" I bring the needle to her skin.

She yelps. "Bastard."

I chuckle. "You know me too well."

She smiles that same *please take me home* smile. It's quick this time. A few seconds. Then the pain takes over.

I understand why douchey tattoo artists get self-righteous about clients needing to feel the pain.

Tattoos hurt.

Like love. Or loss.

Of course, the trick to avoiding pain is the same.

No tattoo, no pain.

No love, no loss.

No loss, no heartache.

Simple. Not easy. But simple.

I flirt with my client as I trace the black lines. As I fill it in with orange, black, a hint of white.

A Monarch flapping its wings.

Classic.

Feminine.

Pretty.

It quite this girl I've got little touch of badass. The same reason she wants me.

Don't get me wrong. There's plenty to want. I'm tall, handsome, in great shape. Women go apeshit for my green eyes and my smile.

Then they see the ink on my sculpted shoulders and they lose their shit.

I'm not going to pretend I'm not hot. I work hard to look this good. And I've spent a fucking fortune on my tattoos—good work is expensive.

Lots of women are like my client. They want a taste of bad. One night on the wild side. Something with no strings and no commitment and no chance of heartbreak. For either of us.

It's perfect.

So, of course, I flirt as I finish, clean her up, check her out. And when she presses her card into my hand and smiles, I wink and ask her to call me.

Sure, she doesn't inspire me.

But she's cute and eager. She meets all my criteria.

"Poor girl." Forest shakes his head. "She could do better."

"Of course. But she knows what she wants." I

shrug. I'm not bothered by his insult. It's not like he means it.

Forest isn't just my coworker. He's also my older brother. He lives to keep me out of trouble. Or he did, when we were younger.

Of course, I lived to get into trouble.

And now—

Well, I guess not much has changed. "It's okay you're jealous."

He arches a brow *really*.

"You know the truth. That Skye has always wanted me." I wink as I mention his girlfriend. Forest and Skye were best friends forever. They *just* realized they want to bone each other.

I'm not sure what took them so long.

It was incredibly obvious.

But he's an idiot.

And she—

She's a curvy goth goddess. Too good for him.

That's it—"We both aim outside our league."

He chuckles. "True."

"And poor Ariel, dating down."

"Chase isn't here to hear you say that."

I shrug. "It will get back to him." Everything does. Everyone here gossips all the time. "You're going over tonight?"

He nods *of course*. Stares like it's the stupidest question in the world.

"Fuck." A loud voice interrupts us. Oliver's. He moves out from his suite. Looks to me. "Come here."

"Come here, please?" I offer.

He rolls his eyes *get real*. The guy is moody. He's in some sort of *who can brood the hardest* competition with my older brother.

Though, now that Forest is with Skye he's actually happy.

Which makes Oliver the most miserable guy at the shop. Not that he's miserable exactly. More standoffish.

He's a good friend, a good artist, a great brother.

And a moody motherfucker.

"What are you doing next week?" He crosses the room to us.

"World domination. Some light bondage. Maybe a threesome," I say.

Forest chuckles. "You need new material."

"Or at least a new routine." Oliver leans against the counter. He rolls his shoulders back. Digs his fingers into his cell screen.

"You have a problem there?" I ask.

"Yeah." He folds his arms. "It's Daisy's birthday."

Right. She's turning eighteen. I've been teasing him about it all summer. It drives him batshit, the thought of me kissing, touching, fucking his sister.

I wouldn't do it.

There aren't many things I appreciate. But loyalty is one of them. There's no way I'd ever fuck my friend's kid sister.

Even if there was, Daisy is a good kid. A sweet girl. She needs more than one and done. She needs someone who can love her with every bone in his body.

And I only have one bone—

Fuck, that joke is too lame. Even for me.

"We've been negotiating," Oliver says. "About her trip."

"The Mexico thing?" I guess it's a rite of passage, heading to Mexico to drink legally. Or maybe Oliver just wants the excuse to get trashed.

"She doesn't want me to come," he says.

"No shit. You're a buzzkill."

He flips me off.

I return the gesture. "She wants to get laid. She can't do it with you hulking around."

His smile gets wide. Knowing. Pure evil. "She's not getting laid."

"Are you going to stand outside her room, punching any guy who comes near?" Sure, I have no plans of sleeping with Daisy, but I'm not about to let Oliver know that.

"I talked her into Puerto Vallarta." His blue eyes shine with evil glee.

I don't follow. "Okay, you're going to Puerto Vallarta. And?"

"It's the San Francisco of Mexico." He taps his head *obviously*. "A huge spot for gay couples."

"So?"

"So?" He looks to Forest. "Is your brother really this dense?"

"Yeah." Forest nods. "He doesn't understand the concept of not wanting to fuck someone."

"You want to fuck guys now?" Oliver asks.

"Are you asking?" I wink at him.

Forest chuckles. "Even you can't sell that."

"Maybe we can find a girl who wants us both at the same time," I say. "That might sate your craving."

"I don't share." He shakes his head *isn't that obvious?*

It is, yeah, but Forest doesn't see it.

He shudders. "Too many details."

"Oh, do you have some better details?" I turn to my brother. "I bet there's a lot you could tell us about Skye. Does her lipstick leave a stain? How long does it take to wash that off?"

"None of your fucking business," Forest says.

"He probably has her lick it off," Oliver says.

Forest doesn't cringe or yell or even roll his eyes. He just turns and moves to the coffee maker on the other side of the room.

Oliver bursts into laughter. "He is so done with your shit."

"He left after your comment."

"I bet he does." Oliver raises a brow. "Fuck, how I bet her mouth is divine." His gaze flits to his cell. He slips from *dirty slut* mode to *protective older brother* mode without missing a beat. "We've been negotiating all week."

"Okay." What does he expect me to do here? I'm not going to help him cunt-block her.

"She's bringing a friend. You know that girl, Luna? Tall and leggy with the silver hair?"

"She's hot."

"Fuck yeah, she's hot." He says it without a hint of irony. It's cool for him to covet his sister's friend. But if anyone gets anywhere near his sister?

Fist to face.

Honestly, I don't blame him.

There's something about Daisy. I *need* to protect her. To make sure there aren't assholes taking advantage of her.

Yeah, she's a woman—or about to be one—with needs, desires, lust. I want her to experience that.

But only if she's with someone worthy.

With someone who won't hurt her.

"She says I can only come if I bring you," he says.

"Why is she considering letting you come?" If it was my eighteenth birthday, I'd tell my brother to fuck off. Then I'd get wasted, take home the nearest attractive stranger, demand eighteen birthday spankings. Or orgasms (for her, not me. Sadly, I don't have *that* much stamina. But I have two hands, a mouth, and access to plenty of toys).

"Dad's paying," he says.

"So? She should bring Gabe. He's more fun than you," I say.

He flips me off. "Don't call my dad Gabe."

"That's his name."

"He wants to go," Oliver says. "But Daisy would rather have me."

That's hard to believe.

"Something about how everyone thinks Dad is hot," Oliver says.

A laugh spills from my chest. "She thinks your dad will attract more women than you will?" She might be right. Mr. Flynn has this *knowledgeable older dude* vibe. He seems like someone who could teach a young woman many, many things.

Or maybe I watch too much porn.

Or listen to Ariel too much. She says she doesn't have a thing for older guys—Chase is only four years older—but she loves to mention how hot both Daisy's and Skye's dad are.

She's not wrong. But she brings it up a lot.

Oliver shakes his head. "No, she thinks I'll get drunk, fuck a stranger, forget I'm supposed to protect her. She knows he won't."

True enough. Their dad is practically a monk. Dude never dates. Even though their mom—

Well, that's a story for another time. An ugly one.

"Where the fuck is Puerto Vallarta?" I ask.

"It's a three-hour flight," he says.

"For her birthday?"

He nods *yeah*.

"Isn't that next week?"

"Yeah. That's why I need an answer now."

"What are you asking?"

17

"Will you come? Help me babysit her?"

"You trust me to babysit Daisy?" I need to step up my game. To tease him more about my intentions to show her porn, buy her sex toys, introduce her to bliss.

"You wouldn't fuck her," he says.

"I'm not making that promise."

He chuckles *okay, sure*. "She likes you, Holden. And not as a friend."

I'm well aware of that. Daisy's had a crush on me forever. But it's just a crush. Because I'm a cute, older guy. Not because she actually likes *me*. "So?"

"Don't break her heart. Please. If you're my friend, do me that one favor."

"Who said anything about heart break? Just one night of casual sex. To show her what she likes. She is a virgin, isn't she?"

He shrugs off my comments. "You want to come or not?"

"Only if she comes first."

"Seriously?" He rolls his eyes *get some new material*. "Will you do it? Will you help me babysit her?"

Chapter Three

HOLDEN

Will you help me babysit her?

It should be an easy answer.

Daisy is a good kid. If she needs help, I'm there. If Oliver needs help, I'm there.

Sure, I help in my way. But I get shit done. Just look at Forest and Skye. If it weren't for me, they'd still be dancing around their feelings.

"The trip's on me," he says. "Well, on me and Dad."

"Maybe I should buy her flights. Then she can ditch you." I try to make my voice light, but it doesn't get all the way there.

His expression is too dark. Too concerned.

Yeah, he's over-protective. And completely oblivious to his hypocrisy—the man drinks like a fish and fucks like a dolphin. But he's not usually this worried.

There's something else.

Something in the back of his head.

Fuck, if he wants *my* help protecting his sister's chastity—

He must be desperate, because he does know better. He knows I'm not going to buy into that retrograde bullshit.

I sure as hell didn't try to stop *my* sister from getting hers.

Yeah, she's older and a serial monogamist, but still. If she'd wanted to sleep with one of my friends, well, I would have told her she could do better.

But I wouldn't have stopped her.

Sure, there's something about Daisy. The thought of her with another guy makes me sick.

Some asshole who will go too fast, too rough, too hard.

Who won't appreciate her shy smile. Or her wide eyes. Or her sweet laugh.

Fuck.

There's the other problem.

I don't want to hurt Daisy. Which means I can't fuck Daisy. My head is on board with the plan.

My heart too.

My cock?

Not so much.

Removing her clothes from the mix—we're going to a beach town, not Antarctica—isn't going to help matters.

I know Daisy and Oliver. She's happy to hang with her brother for a while. Eventually, she makes an excuse to go off on her own.

He'll send me to go with her.

We'll be alone in some tiny pool.

She'll strip out of her sweet sundress. Blush as the sun hits her skin. As I fail to tear my eyes away from her perky tits.

And then—

Well, I hope I'm sober, because if I've been drinking—

It's a recipe for disaster.

"I'll sleep on it," I say.

His eyes fill with frustration. "If there's anything stopping you—"

"Just trying to figure out how I can help her ditch you completely." I shrug like it's not a big deal.

He doesn't buy it. "Seriously, Holden. It would mean a lot." His gaze shifts to the floor. "She trusts you."

She does.

There's no way I'm betraying that.

————

ALL AFTERNOON, I REASON WITH MYSELF. IT'S A TIMELESS conflict:

Brain versus dick.

For a while, I convince myself I'm above my impulses.

I finish work, do my leg routine at the gym, drive home, shower, fix dinner.

Brown rice, chicken breast, broccoli.

Healthy shit.

I'm not giving into the temptation of the couch. Or the ice cream in the freezer. Or the business card in my pocket.

I've mastered my routine.

Sure, my love of fitness is part vanity—I want to look good—but it's about more too. It's satisfying, getting stronger, bigger, more disciplined.

Most of the time, I follow my instincts. Do what feels right in the moment. Committing to a routine is funny. It pulls me to Earth. In a good way.

I finish dinner. Wash the dishes. Lie on the couch.

This apartment is tiny, but it's mine. Sure, I spend a lot of time at my dad's place when he's out of town—why not enjoy the basketball court and the seventy inch TV—but there's something about having my own place.

It's satisfying in a whole new way.

It's like working out, seeing my muscles get bigger and stronger. Or seeing my art get better.

My accomplishments are mine. And they're all the better for being fucking hard.

I put on one of those lawyer shows—what could be better than hot chicks in suits arguing?—but it fails to hold my attention.

My cell calls my name.

There's a text from today's client. I could reply. Invite her over. Clear my head by making her come.

But it doesn't appeal.

Not when I have a text from Daisy.

Daisy: I'm sorry about Oliver. He's being super pushy. I made a suggestion, not a demand. If you don't want to come, that's okay.

I want to come.

That's the problem.

Holden: What did he say?

Daisy: You know, Oliver. Always closed-lips. But I got the gist.

Holden: You want me to come?

Daisy: I'd appreciate it, yes.

Fuck, she's so sincere and honest. I don't know how to respond to it. I can't. I'm not physically capable.

Holden: You just want to see me naked.

Daisy: Why would you be naked?

Holden: Aren't there nude beaches?

Daisy: I don't think so.

Holden: Damn. You almost had me.

Daisy: Really?

Holden: Of course. I like to be free.

Daisy: You or your *ahem*?

Holden: Did you just type '*ahem*'

Daisy: Would you prefer an eggplant emoji?

A laugh spills from my lips. She doesn't realize it, but

she's funny. She's smart too. Way too smart to want anything to do with me.

I guess she's too young to know that.

My friends think I want to fuck Daisy. Okay, they're right about that. I want to fuck her. I have for a few months now.

Something clicked this summer. She stopped looking like a kid. Started looking like a woman.

Yes, I want her body under mine, over mine, in front of mine.

But I'm not trying to make it happen.

Holden: I'd prefer 'majestic cock.'

Daisy: Majestic, really?

Holden: Just wait until you see it.

Daisy: I thought I couldn't see it.

Holden: Damn, I forgot about that.

I know, if I don't plan on fucking her, I shouldn't flirt like this.

But the second I think about her adorable blush, I lose touch with my judgment. My fucking cock takes over. And it doesn't give a fuck about her being a sweet kid. Or my best friend's sister. Or unable to deal with casual sex.

Daisy: Would you really go to a nude beach?

Holden: You've never heard of skinny dipping?

Daisy: Of course, I've heard of it.

Holden: You've never done it?

Daisy: Never.

Holden: You're missing out.

Daisy: I have a dozen swim suits.

Holden: You bringing all of them?

Daisy: Only my favorites.

Holden: How do you narrow it down?

Daisy: Color, at first.

Holden: Let me guess, pastel pink?

Daisy: Am I that obvious?

Holden: No, it's your signature. It's a look.

Daisy: It's so girly. Sometimes people act like it means I'm not serious.

Holden: Fuck them.

Daisy: You probably would.

Holden: Probably.

Daisy: Isn't that weird?

Holden: Fucking people?

Daisy: Strangers?

Holden: Yeah. It's terrible. Don't do it. Stay a virgin forever.

Daisy: Why did I tell you that?

She's probably trying to keep me up all night.

Holden: Are you saying I'm not trustworthy?

Daisy: You won't tell anyone?

Holden: Cross my heart and hope to die.

I don't put stock in many things, but I am a man of my word.

Daisy: What's it like? Really?

Holden: Satisfying.

Daisy: You mean that you come?

Holden: Yeah, but more than that. You've wanted guys before?

Daisy: Of course.

Holden: You know that feeling, when you finally touch someone you really want?

Daisy: I haven't exactly done that much.

Holden: A small touch. Your hand on their wrist. Their lips on your neck. Their arms around you.

Daisy: That sounds romantic.

Shit, I need to pull this back. I need to sit in a tub of cold water every time I talk to her. I need to keep my head in the goddamn game.

Holden: It's terrible. Awful. The worst.

Daisy: That's why you do it all the time?

Holden: Masochism, yeah.

Daisy: And in Mexico?

Holden: Will I fuck someone?

Daisy: Will you?

Holden: I'm supposed to babysit you. That's why Oliver invited me.

Daisy: I invited you.

Holden: That's why he agreed.

Daisy: I know. But it's not why I invited you.

Holden: Why did you invite me?

Daisy: Because I like you. I trust you. I want you to help me celebrate my birthday. It's okay if you're busy or not interested or unwilling to get dragged into Flynn family drama. But I do want you there.

Holden: You sure about that? I'm known to cause trouble.

Daisy: Maybe that's why I want you.

Holden: You sure you know what you're getting into?

Daisy: No. But I still want you to come.

Fuck.

I need to say no.

To say hell no.

To say *I'm sorry, but I'm already hard picturing you in a pastel pink bikini, staring at me like you're desperate to tear off my jeans.*

Anything that will keep me from crossing the line.

But I don't say any of that.

I, once again, prove I have poor impulse control.

That I really, really do need to say no.

Holden: I'll do it.

Daisy: Really?

Holden: Really.

God help me.

Chapter Four

DAISY

I *'ll do it.*

He's coming with us. He's coming to Mexico.

The trip is no longer an exercise in Oliver babysitting me.

Or in Luna—

God, I don't know with her. I don't think she likes Oliver. But she certainly enjoys flirting with him.

It's harmless enough. She likes to flirt. It distracts him. Keeps him thinking with his *ahem*.

Ew.

I'm not thinking about my brother's sex life.

Not when I have the world's most perfect text.

I'll do it.

The three most beautiful words in the English language.

Sure, they aren't *I love you* or *I need you* or *please fuck me*, but they're still poetry.

Better than a strong cup of tea.

Or my favorite Lorde album.

Or a book that demands my entire night.

Better than anything.

I lay my cell on my chest. Let its weight sink into my skin.

My eyes close. My fingers brush my thighs. The bottoms of my cotton shorts.

I know Holden isn't going to touch me. That he isn't going to fuck me.

But I can still imagine it.

Him standing on the beach in some tiny speedo. Grey. Like his eyes.

Me tracing the ink on his chest. Then the lines of his muscles. All the way down his torso, below his belly button, to the low waist of his swimsuit.

Him whispering *I've always wanted to be your first.*

Stripping me out of my clothes, pinning me to the life-guard stand, burying himself in me.

It's all blurry. Dreamy. A vague idea, not a beautiful reality.

I don't know what that feels like. No one has ever been inside me. I've never touched myself that way.

I've certainly never let anyone else touch me that way.

Hell, for a long time I stopped thinking about being touched. Or touching anyone.

It's still new. Scary. Overwhelming.

But this is pure fantasy. A bright, gorgeous dream world where Holden wants me as much as I want him.

Where I'm completely without baggage.

Where there's no need to say *remember how I was away all summer last year? Well, the truth is…*

No. There's nothing in the way.

Just his lips on my lips. His hands on my chest. His body between my thighs.

That same feeling of warmth and hardness and weight I get when I hug him.

The smell of sandalwood and Holden and salt.

I push my shorts to my knees. Then my cotton panties.

My eyes close.

My hand slips between my legs.

It's still strange, touching myself, even after a year.

It's easier when it's him.

But it's not enough.

I need more.

I need him.

———

"What do you think you're doing?" Luna reaches for the mini-skirt sitting on top of the *no* pile. "This is coming."

She unfolds the skirt. Holds it against her hips. It's a little small for her—my friend is blessed with an hourglass figure—but she'd still make it work

She holds it up to the light. Marvels at the exact shade of blue.

"I'm bringing sexy stuff already." I'm still not used to revealing my body. Part of me wants to take Luna's advice. To pack only clothes that show off my legs, chest, waist. Part of me wants to step into that *desirable woman* role and find it comfortable.

But the other part—

I'm terrified just thinking about it.

I still avoid tight clothes. They still force my brain to ugly places.

I want to be healthy enough to wear a bodycon dress without wondering if the snug fabric will steal my mental energy.

But I'm not there yet.

I just… I have to find a way to be sexy. In my way.

Luna shakes her head. Taps the peach t-shirt folded in

my pastel pink suitcase. Then the white tank under it. The floral print wrap dress. "It's cute."

"Thank you."

"But you need more for your plan."

"My plan is to have fun."

"That's it?"

"Yes." Fun is already a big ask. There are only two things that really help me let go: books and music.

I've got reading all night, by myself covered.

I'm even good on rocking out at a concert. Or practicing salsa at a dance studio.

But hitting a club, drinking just enough, finding an attractive stranger—

That's way outside my comfort zone.

Whereas Holden—

He has that devil-may-care smile. The easy laugh. The gorgeous green eyes.

Okay, maybe I see him with rose-covered glasses. I'm not ashamed to admit I have a crush. At least, not to myself.

It feels good, holding onto that. Closing my eyes and letting desire flow through me.

It's a different kind of bliss than reading, dancing, listening to music.

Bigger, brighter, deeper.

He *does* know how to have a good time. And, more, he knows how to set me at ease, so I have a good time.

Somehow, he always knows exactly how much I can handle.

Everything is less scary when he's around. Even wearing a tiny bikini.

I can handle this pastel pink string bikini. I can handle feeling sexy.

If not—

Well, that's why I have a cover up.

I place it in my suitcase.

"Fuck, that's better." Luna rolls onto her side. "Holden is going to be into it."

My cheeks flush. "We're just…"

"Oliver might believe you invited Holden to keep him distracted, but I know."

It's true. Luna knows everything. And I mean *everything*. We've been best friends forever. She's seen every ugly phase in my life. And she's been my shoulder for many, many *why doesn't he like me* girl talk sessions. "I'm over it."

"Uh-huh." She laughs. "And I'm never eating chocolate again. In fact." She rolls off the bed, digs through her giant hot pink purse, brandishes a bar of eight-five percent.

The girl doesn't mess around.

When she wants something, she grabs it.

Her chocolate is the darkest, her coffee is the strongest, her taste in men—

Well, I try not to think about that. Lest she remind me how hot my brother is.

Or, God forbid, my dad.

"You want?" She breaks off a square. Cuts it in half with her teeth.

I shake my head. I can't go there right now.

"Because…" She raises a brow, inviting me to explain.

But there's nothing to say. She knows I carefully avoid triggers. Yes, I'd like to be a normal teenager who can eat a square of chocolate without contemplating deeper meanings. Maybe, one day, I'll be there.

Right now—

I'm at a healthy weight. I'm eating three meals a day. I'm focusing on college.

I'm not quite free, but I'm not trapped either.

For one fucking week, I want to forget about the cage,

about my history, about how hard I try to avoid calling foods good or bad.

I want to be normal.

Is that so much to ask?

"Can we please not?" I take a deep breath. "For one week?"

"Of course." Luna's eyes fill with regret. She blinks and shakes it off. "I know you get enough from Ollie."

"Thanks." I rearrange my suitcase. High-waisted blue shorts. White crop top. Peach wrap dress. Blue sundress. Pastel pink bikini. All stretchy. Thank God for elastic. I still can't handle clothes that pinch.

There. That's better. Neater.

There's something about organizing things. I take control of one small part of the universe. Turn chaos into order.

Prove I'm in control of something.

"Daisy?" Luna's voice is soft. "You okay?"

"Yeah." I *am* okay. Maybe I'm not better than okay, but I am okay. "I do like Holden. But—"

"You invited him to visit another country to celebrate your eighteenth birthday." She takes a square of chocolate. Bites off half. "Don't try to sell me this *oh, I just want my friend there, I'm not trying to offer him some barely legal action* thing."

"Oh my God."

"You've heard him and Oliver talk." She raises a brow. Tosses the rest of the chocolate into her mouth. "He's thinking it."

"He doesn't—"

"Sorry, Daisy, I know it makes you uncomfortable, but you're a hottie."

My cheeks flame red. It's hard to believe. No, impossible.

I can see the evidence—I'm tall, blonde, somewhere between slim and curvy—but I'm not there yet.

"You really… filled in." Luna laughs. She turns to the mirror. Combs her platinum blond hair behind her ear. "You could get some serious cleavage going." She leans over, checking out her cleavage potential. "And you have a butt now too."

"Oh my God."

"I'm not bringing it up—"

"Thank you."

"But the boobs suit you. And they're nice. You have any idea the shit I heard after you left my birthday party?" She refers to a party from last year.

I believe her, but I don't want to know what the guys from our old high school said about my body. At all. I clear my throat.

She laughs. "They were interested."

It's possible. I *have* filled in. A lot of the weight I gained went to my hips, thighs, butt, boobs.

Luna is much more gifted in this area. Incredibly gifted, actually.

I was jealous once. Now…

I'm just glad I'm healthy.

"If you're not ready, that's okay," she says.

"Good."

"But if you are ready, I'm going to make sure you get laid."

"Why do you care?"

"It's my birthday present to you."

I can't help but laugh. "Can I request a different present?"

"If you want to be super rude." She laughs. "And forgot all your manners."

"You don't care about manners."

"You do." She tosses a tight dress into my suitcase. "This trip, I'm yours. If you want to ditch the boys and get wasted, I'll make it happen. If you want to swim with dolphins, I'll make it happen."

"You'll find dolphins?" I ask.

She raises a brow. "You doubt me?"

"That you can find actual dolphins? Four years on swim team don't make you a dolphin finder."

"But they give me this." She motions to her broad shoulders. She used to complain about them. After last year... she's really good about keeping body talk to a minimum. "I can scour the entire Pacific finding you dolphins."

My smile spreads a little wider. "It takes up half the globe."

"I know."

She's ridiculous. It's part of why I love her. She's always all in. I wish I was better at that.

"Now," she says, "if you want to get laid. Or get some time alone with Holden. Or convince him to take your virginity..." She shoots me an *I know you do* look. "I can help."

I shake my head. "I don't need help."

She laughs *yeah right*. "You do need help. But that's what I love about you."

"My awkwardness?"

"Your Daisy-ness."

"And I'm the one who's full of it?" I raise a brow *really?*

"You admit you want to fuck Holden?"

"I can want that without—"

"That's where we disagree." She motions to the lacy bra sitting in the *no* column. "If you want him, you should go for him. Have him. Experience the perfect first."

I clear my throat.

"Don't tell me you don't think about it."

"I..."

"I know you do."

"That's—"

"I won't push."

I shoot her a *really* look.

"I won't push too much." She smiles. "But he's very—"

"Hey," a deep voice interrupts. Oliver knocks. "Can I come in?" He's very respectful of my privacy. More than I'd expect, given what happened last year.

"Come in," Luna calls. "We're... well, I'm never decent, but I am dressed."

He chuckles. Steps inside. Looks over the room.

It's not as neat as it usually is—there are clothes all over the bed—but otherwise, it's normal. Same clean white walls. Same framed posters of classic novels. Same stack of paperbacks on the desk.

Same Berkeley pennant on the wall.

Oliver bought it for me when we first visited the school.

When I got in, he and dad threw me a *huge* party. Bought me every single item of clothing in the store.

I'll never run out of navy and gold sweatshirts.

"Hey Luna." Oliver nods *hello*. "You packed?"

She shakes her head *no way*. "I'll do it morning of."

"We're leaving in two days." There are so many things to do. Sunscreen to buy, plans to make, summer assignments to finish.

"You'll make sure she has fun?" Oliver asks.

She returns a wicked smile. "Of course."

"Not too much?" he asks.

She shakes her head *no fucking way*.

Oliver chuckles *figures*. Turns to me. "You need anything? I'm going to the pharmacy." The implication hangs in the air. *Do you have your prescription?*

I appreciate the concern, I do, but I wish he'd give me space. "Only sunscreen."

"Condoms," Luna says.

His chuckle deepens. "You have a preference?"

Oh my God.

She laughs at my blush. "Ribbed. For her pleasure." She winks at me.

"Sure." He turns to me. "If you're going to be with someone, I want you to be safe."

"Did Dad tell you to say that?" I ask.

He nods. "He's got a whole talk planned."

"Oh God." Please no.

"It sounded pretty thorough." He pats me on the shoulder. "Good luck."

"Thanks." I'm going to need it.

Not just for the talk.

For this entire trip.

And the year after.

But, one thing at a time.

First, I survive a week away from home, with my brother, my best friend, and the guy I can't get out of my head.

Then, I figure out the rest of my life.

Chapter Five

HOLDEN

Between rearranging appointments and prepping for the trip, I stay busy.

Oliver stays worried and over-protective.

Daisy stays sweet and accommodating. In text, at least.

And my cock—

He stays a difficult motherfucker. No matter how much I reason *how about I go out tonight, find another woman, take off the pressure*, the damn thing refuses.

It's settled on Daisy.

Which isn't happening.

Sure, I imagine it every night before I fall asleep. And every morning. And in the shower.

But, that's just good sense.

———

"DON'T FUCK HER." FOREST SETS MY ELECTRIC BLUE suitcase on the curb. He pushes his trunk closed. Stares me dead in the eyes.

He uses his usual *I'm an older brother and I know best. I*

practically raised you, what with dad being despondent about mom's death stare.

He really does fit a lot into that stare.

I appreciate the effort. Not just the stare. But him picking up the slack. I'd never tell him—better to keep him guessing—but Forest is a great brother.

"Do you really think he's going to fuck her?" Skye rests her head on Forest's shoulder. She's considerably shorter than he is, but in her platform combat boots, she's in prime position for the gesture.

It's cute.

They're really cute.

She's hot as fuck—she squeezes her curvy figure into the world's sexiest black clothes—but I've never really seen her that way.

She's always been the girl Forest wanted, even when he didn't realize it.

And she's always had eyes for him.

"Are you jealous?" I wink at Skye. "I have room for you too."

"Uh-huh." She shakes her head *sure*. She knows I wouldn't actually fuck her. She still enjoys the teasing. Well, she enjoys how Forest gets all jealous and protective.

No doubt takes her home and fucks her senseless and growls *you're mine*.

"You want to come, Skye? I'll buy your ticket. We can get some great shots for your Insta." I offer her my hand. "Some dirty ones for just us."

Her cheeks flush. "I actually have plenty."

"Oh?" I raise a brow.

She and Forest exchange a look. One that's theirs.

They've always had the best friend mind-reading thing down, but now that they're actually together, they're at a whole other level.

He turns to me. "Seriously, Holden. Don't fuck her."

"Of course," I say.

For a second his brow relaxes. His shoulders drop. His eyes fill with relief.

"Saving myself for Skye," I say.

"You're going to be waiting awhile." She laughs. "Forever."

"That's okay. I'm saving the videos for you." I shoot her my flirtiest wink. It's not my best work—I'm too distracted by thoughts of Daisy—but it's good practice. Like attempting a poker face.

"The videos." Her eyes go wide. "Oh god."

"I can send them if you want," I say.

"Do you actually have videos?" Forest asks.

"What do you think?" I shrug. *I'll never tell*.

I do have videos. Many videos. Sometimes, women ask. And I aim to please.

It's exactly where I am.

There's nothing better than watching a woman come. Feeling her thighs against my cheeks. Or my hands. Or my hips.

The way her cunt pulses around my cock.

The way her eyes roll back in her head.

Daisy has such pretty blue eyes. What do they look like filled with pleasure?

Shit.

So much for fucking myself last night. And this morning. Some good it did.

"I hate to break it to you, Forest, but they're exclusively for Skye." I shrug my shoulders. Try to find all the *don't give a fuck* I have.

Skye laughs. "He's getting worse at pretending."

Forest nods. "He really is."

She moves in. Hugs me goodbye. "Take care of her, okay? She's a sweet kid."

"Of course." I keep my voice light. "I'll take care of every one of her needs."

"If I really thought you would, I'd..." She steps back. Bites her lip. "I guess she's going to be an adult. You're an adult. If it's all consensual..." She offers her hand. "Good luck."

"Good luck?" I ask.

Forest chuckles. "It's not fun for him if you give him permission."

"I appreciate that, Skye." I take her hand. "It's amazing you can step aside when you want me so badly."

"I know. I'm really the bigger woman," she says.

I make a show of staring at her chest. "Bigger something."

She blushes.

Forest shakes his head. "Seriously, Holden. Do what you're gonna do. But don't forget she's a sweet kid. And Oliver... He—"

"I know." No one has to say it. Oliver drinks too much. I need to make sure he doesn't cross the line. Whatever that means.

My brother pulls me into a hug. He pats my back. "You know, I'm proud of you."

"Yeah?"

"It's sweet that you're helping Daisy like this."

"Not the word I'd use, but thanks." I shoot him a wink. "I'll bring coffee back for you." I turn to Skye. "Chocolate?"

"Forest would appreciate it more," she says.

"Souvenir magnet?" I offer.

She nods *okay*.

"Chocolate for Ariel and Chase." I grab my suitcase. Nod goodbye to my family. Well, half of it. Ariel had a baby two weeks ago. With Forest's best friend Chase. That's a long story.

But the short version is I'm an uncle and Charlotte is the coolest kid in the world.

Fuck, I hate that I'm missing a week with her.

Even if she's too small—and she is tiny—to do anything but cry and eat.

But I get what a big ask this is. Oliver wouldn't invite me to come unless he needed me there.

I'm not sure why he needs me, but if he's willing to overlook how much Daisy wants me, and how little he trusts me to keep my hands off her—

Maybe he does trust me.

Or maybe there's some big, serious reason.

That's too much to contemplate. So I won't. I'm going to think about the sun, the cheap tequila, the torture of Daisy in a bikini.

The week I'm missing at home.

"Send me pics of Charlotte," I say.

Skye smiles. "You want pictures of your niece?" She slides her arm around Forest's waist. "You're softening."

Shit, I *am* softening. That can't happen. "Sweetie, I'll only soften after you squeeze every drop."

She shakes her head *yeah, right*. Turns to Forest. Offers him another *who is Holden trying to kid* look.

Fuck, I'm losing my touch.

I need to up my game. There's no way I'm living in this serious, sentimental world where people say things like *I love you and I'll miss you and you're the best thing that ever happened to me.*

"I don't have the time to do it right." I double down on teasing Skye. "I can't make it fireworks, but I'll still—"

"No thanks." She just smiles. Endeared. Endeared by my bullshit. "But I appreciate the offer."

"No problem," I say.

Forest nods his own goodbye.

Then, I turn and walk into battle.

Chapter Six

DAISY

"**B**e careful, baby girl." Dad squeezes me tightly. So tightly I can barely breathe.

It's sweet. But it's also a reminder of last summer. The year before it. The *broken* sign on my forehead. "I will."

"I'm proud of you." His voice stays strong. In control.

But I know better. He's trying not to cry. He's usually more... stoic. Like Oliver. But since last year—

I get that he's scared. That he and Oliver are scared. I'm scared too.

When they look at me like I'm fragile, I start to believe it. I start to worry I will break.

And then—

I just wish they believed I could handle this.

"I know," I say.

"You've been so strong." The wall drops. His voice cracks. It's right there, on the surface *please, Daisy, be careful. Tell me what I can do to make this okay. I can't watch you spiral again.* "You're such a good kid."

"Dad, please." I release the hug. "I'm okay. Really."

"I know." He looks down at me, his blue eyes filled with equal parts concern and love. As stoic as he is—was, I guess—he's never shy about telling us he's proud.

I've always known I was loved.

It's just, sometimes, I had trouble believing it.

"You're going to do so well at Berkeley." His smile is soft. Caring. "I'm so proud of you, baby girl. I really am." He pulls me into another hug.

I hug him back. I'm scared too. I'm overwhelmed too. And, historically, I don't do too well with those feelings.

But I can't tell anyone. They'll dote even more. Wrap me in even more bubble wrap.

"If you need anything, call. Okay?" he asks.

"Okay."

"Money. A ticket home. Advice. Anything." He releases me. Looks me in the eyes. "You have condoms?"

"Dad—"

"I know you don't want to hear it. But if you're going to have sex, you need to be safe."

"We already—"

"I know." He shifts his backpack off his shoulder. Pulls something from it. A box of condoms.

They're just there.

Not wrapped or in plastic or in another bag.

Here for everyone to see.

"Oh my God." My cheeks flame red. "I already—"

"Your brother has extra. I told him not to crowd you. You're an adult. If you want to experience sex, you should. It can be a beautiful thing. It doesn't have to be serious. You don't have to be in love. But you do need to trust your partner."

"Dad, we already—"

"Humor me." He presses the box into my hand. "Tell me you'll be safe."

44

"I will."

"That you won't drink too much."

"I won't."

"That you'll only be with someone if you trust them. If they respect you."

God, please kill me now. People are staring. They're staring at the box. At me. At the *awkward virgin* sign on my forehead.

"Daisy?"

"I promise." Why does everyone think I'm aiming to lose my virginity this trip? God, does Dad know I'm a virgin? Has word gotten to him and Oliver?

"If you need anything, I'll get on the next flight."

I shove the box into my purse. It's huge. Two dozen condoms. More than anyone could use in a week.

Well. I guess I shouldn't put it past Oliver.

Or Holden even.

Ahem.

"I will." I hug Dad one more time. "I promise."

"I love you so much, baby girl."

"I love you too."

He squeezes me tightly for a long moment, then he releases me. Turns to our right. Nods hello.

Shakes hands with Holden. "How are you doing, son?"

"Good, sir." Holden smiles, suddenly respectful. It's bizarre. He's never serious. Ever.

"Gabe," Dad says. "You know 'sir' makes me feel old."

"It suits you. You have a real *issuing orders* vibe," Holden teases.

Dad just laughs. No, he laughs knowingly. Like he—

Ew.

So gross.

So, so gross.

I don't care how hot Luna finds him; I don't want to picture that.

"Are you going to take care of my daughter?" Dad asks Holden.

Holden nods. "Of course." He turns to me. Holds up his boarding pass. "You ready to go?"

No. But I'm not sure I'll ever be ready. "Getting there."

He motions to the stairs, where Oliver and Luna are sipping iced drinks, watching.

Luna waves *hey*. Holds up my iced tea.

We have an audience.

I guess I should get used to it.

Chapter Seven

DAISY

Mmm. Tea number two.

English breakfast with a touch of honey and a dash of milk.

Sweet, creamy, rich caffeine.

From the Peet's Coffee in the terminal. The line is always shorter, even though their tea is so much better.

I'm still getting into tea. It feels safe. Easy.

There's something about the warmth filling my mouth, throat, stomach.

It's comforting. Like a hug.

This is a classic black tea. A robust blend of Assam and Ceylon. It lacks the nuance of something like Lapsang Souchang or Yunnan. But it's just tea, all tea. Not a tea flavored with oil or spices, like Earl Grey or Chai.

Not that I'd turn down either.

I love trying different blends. Different flavors. Lychee rose, chocolate chai, Market Spice. Anything. Everything. So long as it's warm and comforting.

I swallow another sip of English Breakfast. It isn't the finest drink in the world. It's hard to really brew tea right at a coffee shop. It always comes out too strong. Or not strong enough.

But it still tastes like safety.

Like comfort.

Like home.

At the moment, I need that. I need a space that's mine where I can lose myself in a book, where I can breathe without anyone else's expectations.

For now…

I'm going to have to make do with tea. And listening to Lorde during the flight. It's far from a consolation prize. I love music as much as I love reading or writing. It has the same appeal. It commands every one of my senses. Dissolves all my thoughts, my walls, my inhibitions.

It just feels good.

God, I wish it was easier to hold on to that. To find things that are just good. Period. End of sentence.

I take another sip. Lean back in my seat. Smooth my skirt.

I'm sure Luna thinks my wrap dress isn't cute or sexy enough, but I'm spending the next three hours on a plane. I look pretty good, considering.

It's not too crowded at the gate. Not yet. The people here are quiet. Reading, sipping coffee from take-out cups, typing on their laptops.

The sun—it's already bright, even this early—falls over the blue carpets and the cheap vinyl chairs.

Over checkered blue sneakers. Long jeans. Narrow hips. A bright muscle tank from one of those surf/skate shops.

Holden's smile.

He holds up his navy hoodie—the one he wears all winter—and offers it to me. "Oliver said you'd need this."

It is cold in here—the air-conditioning is so high—and

the plane will be worse. Why is it always freezing in planes? I'd say it's a conspiracy to sell blankets if airlines actually sold blankets. "He said I'd need your hoodie?"

"He said something about making sure you'd packed a sweater. But I thought this would be more fun." His fingers brush my neck as he drapes the hoodie over my shoulders. "Looks good on you."

"Oh?" I motion to the red and white floral print of my wrap dress. "Does it match?"

"Patriotic." He sits next to me. Offers me a sip of his milky drink.

I take a long sip. It's an iced chai. Not what I expect him to drink. Incredibly sweet. Way too sweet for me. "Thanks."

"What?"

"You drink chai?"

"You do too." He motions to my tea.

"It's English breakfast."

"Chai means tea."

My lips curl into a smile. "You're trying to out tea me?"

"Trying?" He turns his body toward mine. "My sister is obsessed with tea. And she spent nine months limited to two a day. It's all she talked about." His bright eyes light up. Well, more than usual. He loves his family. His sister. His niece—

God, she's so cute. I've only seen pictures, but there's something about those giant eyes. I don't even like babies and I still want to protect her.

"She knows a lot." I take a long sip of English breakfast. Let out a low sigh. It tastes so good. With him here, I feel it more. I can taste every note of caramel.

"She'd die if she saw me drinking this." He taps his iced chai. "It comes from a syrup."

"I know."

"She thinks it's sacrilege."

It kinda is. "But you?"

"It's not great. But I don't have her here to make me a fresh chai."

"Doesn't she live with Chase?"

He nods *true*. "I make them too."

"Really?" That's hard to imagine.

"You doubt me?" His voice lifts to a teasing tone. Well, a more teasing tone. "You think a guy like me isn't capable of fixing a fine chai latte?"

"Well." I try to match his tone. To tease back. There's something about Holden. He makes me feel good. He makes me forget all the stuff racing around my brain. Even with my heart thudding and my stomach fluttering, I just... I want to be around him. To drink up his smile. To watch joy fill his eyes. "I guess you'll have to show me."

"Oh?"

"When we get in."

"When we land and it's eighty degrees, you'll want a hot chai?"

"You can't do iced?"

His smile widens. "Demanding."

"You're the one insisting on your mastery."

He nods *true enough*. "And you're in a sweater now."

"You gave me this."

"You didn't take it off."

Because it smells like his soap. Not because... Okay, a little because it's cold. And I can't tell him I'm wearing it because it smells like his soap.

God it smells good.

He smells good.

How can he always smell so good?

"I'll try it hot first," I say. "Tea is better hot."

"It is."

"Then why are you drinking that sugary monstrosity?"

"You're a snob?"

"A little."

"A lot." He laughs. "I like it."

My heart thuds against my chest. It doesn't hear *I like
it*. It hears *I like you*. It jumps to all sorts of conclusions. *I
love you. Please marry me. But first, take off your clothes, I want to
make love to you.*

God, even in my head, my dirty talk is cheesy.

Holden is so smooth. And sexy. He probably dirty talks
like a pro.

God, just the thought of him laying me down and
whispering in my ear.

He could say *I want to ⸺⸺ love to you* and I'd still catch
flame.

I'm already burning up.

"You want more?" He offers me the drink.

I take a small sip. It is way too sweet. Not because it's
not what I'd normally allow myself. (Though it is). Because
the sugar overwhelms the spices. And the tea. It really does
taste like a syrup. "It's terrible." But I still linger on the
straw.

My lips are where his lips were.

God, he has such pretty lips.

He takes a long sip. Leans down to set his drink on the
floor. "You sure you don't want more?"

"Yeah." I lick my lips. They're sweet with this hint of
cinnamon. But all I can think is *I'm practically kissing him*.

He follows my gaze to the drink. "You're staring."

"No." I try to make eye contact. "I just… thought you'd
have more self-respect."

He chuckles. "Where'd you get that idea?"

"You're a smart guy."

"No, I'm not."

"But, you, uh—"

"No one thinks I have self-respect."

"You don't want them to think that. I mean, you do want them to think that." I take a long sip. My drink is better, much better, but I hate washing away the taste of his.

His lips must taste like that too sweet chai.

His lips must taste like heaven.

God, they're such pretty lips.

"You know what I mean." I swallow another sip. Try to direct my thoughts toward my tea.

He shakes his head. "What you see is what you get."

"I don't think so."

"You should."

"Well, I see a guy with self-respect."

"You need glasses?" His voice is light, teasing, but there's something in his eyes.

He blinks and it disappears.

Back to full-time trouble maker.

Or maybe it was never there. Maybe I'm imagining things.

"Good taste?" I ask.

"In what?"

"Clothes."

He laughs. "True."

"Women?"

"No one has ever accused me of that."

"Tea?"

"Apparently, not."

"See, I think you do. I think you'd prefer something like this." I hold up my drink. Offer it to him.

His fingers brush mine as he takes it. His lips close around the lid. He takes a long sip. Swallows hard. Lets out a soft moan. "Fuck, that is good."

"Better?"

"Yeah. I'm keeping it."

"You are not."

He nods *I am not.* "But I might insist you make *my* tea."

"You really drink tea?"

"Am I not allowed?"

"No. You just seem like... not like the type." Not just because he's a trouble making player. Because he's... normal. But normal people drink tea. It's the most consumed beverage in the world. It doesn't have to be about recovery. It can just be tea.

"Looks can be deceiving."

"I thought what I saw was what I got."

"Shit. Gotta work that one out." His laugh is light. Easy. He turns away from the gate. Scans the crowd.

For signs of Oliver? Or Luna?

Where is she anyway? She said she had to fix her makeup, but that was fifteen minutes ago. Maybe the Starbucks line is taking forever.

Maybe she's keeping Oliver distracted so I can talk to Holden.

Maybe—

His eyes catch mine. "You want good tea?"

"Always."

"What else?"

"In general?"

"For your trip." His knee brushes mine. Denim against my bare skin. "What, specifically, do you want?"

"Everyone is asking me that."

"It's for you."

True, but—"I want everyone to have fun."

"What kind of fun?"

"The normal kind. Swimming. Laying on the beach."

"Drinking until you throw up?"

I shake my head.

"It's a rite of passage."

"I'll save it for later."

His laugh is big. Easy. "Okay. Drinking until you're happy drunk and no more?"

"Okay."

"It's harder than it sounds."

Of course. Moderation isn't my strong suit. "But I have you to help me."

His smile lights up his eyes. "That's how you want my help?"

"It seems like where you'd excel."

"Okay. Swimming, sun, drinking just enough. Anything else?" He raises a brow. "Hot guys?"

"Which guys?"

"Ones who are hot."

"Maybe." My cheeks flush. "If something happens, it happens. But I'm not looking for it."

"So Oliver didn't slip that past you?"

"That Puerto Vallarta is a big gay destination?" I laugh. "No. I'm the one who suggested it."

"Oh?" Holden raises a brow. "Want to experiment? Can I watch?"

My blush deepens. "Would you really?"

"Not today. But tomorrow."

"So you're just waiting for me to turn eighteen?"

"If Oliver asks."

"You want him to believe that?"

He nods *of course*. "It keeps him guessing."

"And what do you… really want?" *Say you want me. That you want to touch me, kiss me, fuck me.*

"I want to show you a good time."

"How?"

"That's what I'm asking." His voice stays light. "I have a few ideas. But I need you to trust me."

"Trust you?"

"To plan your trip. Or, at least, your birthday."

"You plan?"

"It's a struggle." He taps his head. "Takes all the brain-power I have, but I can make it happen."

"Okay." My laugh eases the tension in my shoulders. He does that to me. Makes me feel relaxed. And in knots. It's weird. Addictive. "I trust you."

"You do?" His voice gets serious. Faux serious.

"I do."

"That's foolish."

"Is it?"

"Oh yeah. But I do appreciate it."

Chapter Eight

HOLDEN

Apparently, the premium economy seats offer free snacks and liquor. For those twenty-one plus.

Oliver vows to make the forty dollar upcharge "worth it." At eight bucks a cocktail, that's—

Well, let's just say I know he's good for it.

He flirts with the flight attendant as she drops off two tiny bottles of whiskey and two tiny glasses of ice. He pours one. Drinks it in three gulps.

Starts on the other.

Daisy averts her eyes.

Her friend Luna makes a show of pouting. Not over Oliver's drinking—I'm not sure she cares about that. Over the whole *we're not in Mexico yet, you can't drink yet* thing.

She's a tall, expressive girl with silver-blond hair, painted red lips, and trendy clothes. Between her curvy figure and her pouty lips, she's a certifiable babe.

I try to tell my cock to want her. I try to stare at her considerable cleavage—she's chesty yeah, but she's also making an effort to show off—and conjure images of her tits in my hands.

It wouldn't be that much better to want Daisy's best friend. If anything, it would break her heart faster.

But it would prove I'm capable of controlling my fucking cock.

I try, hard, to imagine her light hair in my hands, her round ass against my crotch, her red lips around my cock.

The images come.

But they shift to Daisy like *that*.

I'm only making the situation worse.

I steal Oliver's drink.

He shoots me a dirty look but he doesn't stop me. Just hails the flight attendant, flirts through a request for another.

I press my palm into the arm rest. I'm not getting out of my seat, crossing the aisle, comforting Daisy.

She's used to her brother drinking.

She has her friend by her side.

They're already onto another subject, sharing a pair of headphones, closing their eyes, losing themselves in the music.

"You need another?" Oliver taps my shoulder. Motions to his plastic cup full of ice and brown liquor.

"It's ten a.m."

"It's free." He shoots me an *obviously* look.

I turn to the flight attendant. She's still here. Still smiling at him.

"Could I get a black tea?" I ask.

She nods *of course*. "Cream and sugar?"

"Plain." My gaze shifts to the window. "Thanks." I'm in the window seat. Oliver's in the aisle. We got lucky. No one took the middle.

The girls are on the opposite side of the aisle. They're sitting aisle and middle. There's a stranger in the window seat with her eyes closed and her head on the window.

They chose to sit next to each other. To sit close enough to share headphones, coffee, blankets.

They're sharing a blanket.

Fuck, it's sweet.

She's sweet.

Way too sweet for me.

Not that it matters.

I'm showing her a good time. Making sure she has fun.

Whatever happens, I'm making her birthday something to remember.

Yeah, I'll have to find a way to ditch Oliver. I'll have to spend the whole day alone with her without touching her.

But I'm capable.

In theory.

———

THE FOUR OF US ARE GOOD FLIERS. NO COMPLAINTS OF boredom, hunger, thirst, coldness.

We keep to ourselves. Oliver reads one of those thrillers he loves. I don't know how he can concentrate on words after so many drinks, but he's a man of many talents.

Luna and Daisy share headphones the entire flight. They switch from talking to staring at screens—Daisy reads on her Kindle, Luna plays a game on her phone—but they stay in sync.

I lie back, close my eyes, focus on my playlist of eighties jams. They were Mom's favorite. Not that I remember, not really. I have the vaguest sense of sunny days, warm hugs, heaping scoops of whipped cream on hot chocolate.

A big smile—one exactly like Ariel's.

A soft laugh.

This look of love as grown-ups danced to a sappy song.

This song.

Just Like Heaven

I'm not sure how this music found its way into my head. Or my heart.

There isn't shit in my heart.

But there's something about the artsy electronic sound.

It takes me back to that feeling of love.

One big family. A house brimming with happiness. A mom with a warm smile.

I was a kid when mom died. I remember her in a hospital bed, tiny and frail, forcing a smile, promising she'd love us forever.

Dad falling apart. Spending every night in his room, alone, only emerging for work.

Forest forcing him to eat.

Taking Ariel to school.

Lecturing me about anything and everything. Then lecturing me again, for good measure.

My sister was always playing their songs. Mom's songs. They found their way into my head, my heart, my soul.

It's supposed to be empty.

There's not supposed to be anything there.

I'm not supposed to be in touch with this shit.

Maybe it's a good thing. To remember all this pain. The pain that comes with love.

I'm not feeling that again.

I'm not subjecting Daisy to that.

I listen until the flight attendant insists we turn off our electronic devices—a Mexican regulation, apparently— then I stare out the window, watch the clouds and blue sky fade into little houses, long stretches of ocean, sandy deserts.

Our landing is bumpy.

Nausea spreads over Oliver's face.

Daisy squeezes her friend's hand like it's a life raft.

I press my palms into my thighs. I want to be the one there, holding her hand, bringing her comfort.

It's ridiculous. That's not within my skill set. Yeah, I make things happen. But only when no one realizes I'm pulling strings.

Let me hold you, kiss you, love you is not in my vocabulary.

I push the thought as we taxi, collect our stuff, climb off the plane. Onto the concrete.

It's hot. Hotter than an August day in Venice and without the beach breeze. We're too far inland at the moment. Or maybe this is just the west coast of Mexico. Hot as fuck, always, all the time.

We squeeze into a bus, ride it to the terminal, break to piss and change, wait in a series of lines. Baggage. Customs. Immigration.

The other side of the airport is a zoo. Men and women hawking timeshare presentations and exclusive shows crowd us. They say hello in English and Spanish, offer deals, grab at hands.

I reach for Daisy reflexively. No one stops me from wrapping my arm around her waist, pulling her through the crowd, leading her out of the airport. Back to hot concrete.

Oliver's gaze goes straight to my hand, but he doesn't say anything. Just nods *drop it*. And I do.

"Fuck, it's hot." Luna shrugs her hoodie off her shoulders. Shoves it into her dark purple KanKen. She turns to Daisy. Holds out her hand.

Daisy nods. Slides my hoodie off her shoulders. Offers it to her friend.

Luna shoves the sweater into her backpack. Struggles with the zipper. Slings it over her shoulder.

Oliver gives her now exposed body a quick once over.

She's wearing a white crop top, charcoal high-waist shorts, bright pink high-tops.

She looks hip as fuck. And hot as fuck too. In that *cool girl, I don't care what you think* way.

If I didn't know better, I'd buy it. But I have a sister. Sure, Ariel doesn't know shit about fashion, but I've learned enough about women. That effortless look takes a lot of time and energy.

And, well—

I guess my effortless attitude isn't all that different.

"It is really hot." Daisy pulls out her reusable water bottle. Sucks the last drop. "Where's the Uber pickup?"

Oliver stares at his cell. "That way." He nods to the left. "You want me to find a vending machine?"

She shakes her head. "I'm okay. It's a fast ride, right?"

He checks the screen. "Twenty minutes."

She nods *okay*, takes her friend's hand, follows us around the corner.

The directions are incomprehensible. There are cars in front of us. Signs for pick up to our left.

Confused tourists heading right.

I follow a couple with a giant red suitcase to a bus stop.

There are half a dozen locals—the casual demeanor is a giveaway—standing under the shade.

Three sets of tourists stare at their cells. A car with a bright *Uber* sign stops. One of the couples gets into it.

This must be it.

We try to avoid the heat. Try to talk about anything else. But fuck, the sun is bright. I need to be in the water. Now.

After a five-minute wait—it feels like twenty—a car stops, asks for Oliver.

I open the door for the girls. Help my friend with their suitcases.

Oliver takes the seat next to the driver.

I take the one in the back.

Next to Daisy. Of course, she's in the middle. Her friend is an evil genius.

Or maybe it's just her accommodating nature. She's so fucking sweet. Always putting other people first.

I close my eyes. Will the air-conditioning to cool me off. Try to ignore the warmth of her skin.

I'm in my shorts now. Her bare skin is against mine. Her leg is against mine. I'm not as pale as my brother or sister—they inherited Dad's coloring, I inherited Mom's. I'm a shade darker than she is.

I always think of her as a beach babe, a California girl who belongs in the sand, but all her features are light. She probably burns as badly as Ariel does.

She probably needs sunscreen over every inch of her soft skin.

Fuck.

Not helping.

I press my palms to my thighs. Look out the window. Try to ignore the proximity of our bodies.

To ignore the way she glances at our limbs. Then stares.

Chain restaurants and local stores blur together. A boutique. A salon. A Cheesecake Factory. Strip malls, busy roads, bright sun. It's like we're in Orange County, not another country.

Sure, the signs are all in Spanish, but everything else is the same.

The radio booms with shitty pop music. Oliver makes small talk with the driver. A mix of Spanish—the one class he nailed in high school—and English.

Luna lies back and listens to her headphones.

Daisy turns toward my side of the car. She motions to my lap. Then the window. "You mind?"

No, baby, this is exactly where you belong. "Sure."

She leans over me to look out the window. The strip malls fade into a block of hotels. The ocean comes into view in all its deep blue brilliance.

The damn thing sparkles under the sunlight.

Her soft lips part with a gasp. It's a tiny thing. Barely audible. But it warms me all the same.

All the stupid shit in my head disappears. For a moment, all I want is the wonder in her eyes.

Then she leans a little farther, enough her dress falls down her chest and all I want is her groaning my name.

Her pastel pink bra demands my attention.

The floral lace spreading over the cup—

Fuck.

I turn to the window. Try to focus on the ocean. This is the Banderas Bay. Part of the Pacific. Of an ocean that connects continents.

It's not interesting compared to her.

I fold one leg over the other. Shift to the side. Recall my last tattoo. The pain of the needle against my skin. The places near the bone are the worst. They're agony.

Guys act all tough, like it doesn't hurt, but that's fucking ridiculous.

It's a needle. It always hurts.

Thankfully, I'm not into pain.

My cock cools it enough to survive three more minutes on the highway.

We turn onto a side street. Toward the Romantic Zone. It's part tourist trap, part quaint beach town, part party central, all cobblestone roads.

Daisy falls back into her seat.

I catch her reflexively.

She mouths *thanks*. Tries to hide her blush.

I try to focus on the bumpy road. On the sun-bleached buildings. On the tourists walking the narrow sidewalks.

My eyes keep drifting back to her thighs.

To our legs connecting.

The hem of her red and white dress.

The bright blue of my shorts.

My tan skin against hers.

Her dress sliding up her legs.

Higher and higher and—

Mercifully, we arrive before I come in my shorts.

The driver parks in front of a house on a hill. I get out of the car. Hold the door open for her.

Try to do anything except watch her hips sway as she walks into the house.

Fail completely.

Chapter Nine

HOLDEN

After we tour the four-story loft, we head to separate bedrooms (there are exactly four), unpack, change into beach gear.

This place is nice. Huge. Modern. Open. Yes, there are four separate bedrooms, but the outside walls are glass and the inside walls are thin.

No one is bringing home a fuck without the rest of the house knowing.

I'm half-impressed with Oliver, half irritated. A week without sex is a lot for him. But this attempt to protect his sister's chastity—

He needs to grow up.

His bedroom is next to mine. Under his sister's. We're on the third floor. Luna and Daisy are on the fourth.

They're next to the rooftop pool. And the amazing view of the town, the sky, the ocean. We're only a few blocks from town. Maybe a dozen from the beach.

I grab a towel from the linen closet in the hall. Head downstairs.

The first floor is just as gorgeous as the rest of the

house. Modern couch, huge TV, solid wood dining set, kitchen with stainless steel appliances and filtered water, fridge stocked with condiments and plastic bottles.

It's everywhere, the reminder to skip the tap water. Apparently, ice is okay. Freezing water kills the parasites that cause Montezuma's Revenge.

There's an unsexy thought.

The perfect focus for the afternoon.

I hold on to it as I down a glass of filtered water (the sink and the fridge have filters).

My thoughts dissolve as footsteps come closer.

Luna jumps off the second step. Tosses a towel over the chair. Stretches her arms over her head.

She's in a bikini top and those high-waisted shorts. She looks good. Like she's going to pop out of those triangles.

But my eyes still go to Daisy.

Gauzy white fabric drapes over her body. It's not quite see-through, but it's close. I can make out the shape of her figure—slim curves, round hips, long legs—and the pastel pink of her bikini.

Fuck.

I refill my glass. Offer it to Daisy.

She nods *thanks*, downs it in three sips, refills it, hands it to Luna.

"You hungry?" I nod to the fridge. "We can grab lunch. Pick up groceries on the way back."

Daisy's lips curl into a frown. It's a quick second, then she shakes it off. "I am, but beach first."

"Beach now." Luna calls up the stairs. "You have one minute, Oliver. Then we're leaving."

"I'm coming." His deep voice booms around the house. Reminds me of how well sound carries in the open space.

"Is that his line?" I tease. "Guess it's a classic."

Luna laughs.

Daisy turns bright red. "Please do not talk about my brother's sex life."

"Not sure there's much to say. He's probably too drunk to bring any skill to the table," I tease.

Oliver's footsteps move down the stairs. "It's sad." He moves into the staircase connecting the first and second floors. "How insecure you are about your sexual abilities."

"Oh?" I raise a brow.

"Always mocking everyone else, because you're not sure you have what it takes."

"Is that right?" I ask.

He nods *hell yeah*. "I know you ask him for advice about sex." He turns to Daisy.

Horror spreads over her expression. "Please stop."

"You do," Oliver says, suddenly in older brother mode. "He has some good advice."

"No one's ever said that," I say.

Oliver nods *it's true*. "He knows about condoms. And STDs. How many times have you had the clap?"

"Who says 'the clap'?" I ask.

"I do." He laughs. "That many times? You lost count?"

I can't help but laugh. "I'm always responsible."

"Now," he says.

Daisy's blush deepens.

Luna laughs. "It's never the sluts. It's always the good girls, who fall for some guy who isn't worthy of their trust."

Oliver turns to his sister. "He can help with condoms. But he doesn't know shit about technique. Last I heard, you're a two-pump chump."

"You shouldn't dare me like that," I say.

"You really shouldn't." Luna laughs. "He's going to threaten to whip it out and prove he isn't."

"Hey, don't steal my lines." I push her playfully.

She shoots Daisy a look that says *everything*.

Daisy clears her throat. "Well, um, I guess you could prove it."

"Oh?" I stare into her gorgeous blue eyes.

"Yeah." Her gaze travels down my body. Shoulders, chest, stomach, crotch.

It just stops there.

She does nothing to hide her stare.

It's not like the other day with my client.

The interest in her eyes sets me on fire.

At this rate…

I won't be a two-pump chump, but I won't last as long as I'd like. Not with her lips parting and her eyes wide.

"You could…" She looks to Luna for help.

Luna shakes her head *this is your battle*.

"Go upstairs." Daisy's gaze shifts to the floor. "Prove it."

"Uh-huh. Don't need to hear that." Oliver takes his sister's hand. "We have a town to explore." He leans in, lowers his voice to an almost whisper. "Did you get enough to eat?"

"I'm fine," she says.

"It's getting late," he says.

"A good reason to swim now." She shoots him a *please drop it* look. "Actually, I'm tired of waiting for you two." She motions to me and Oliver.

I press my hand to my chest. "I was here first."

"And you're wasting time with your *ahem* measuring contest." She stays bright red. "When you could be—"

"Swimming naked?" I offer.

"I don't need to see your dick." He motions to the door *let's go*. "Fuck knows I hear about it often enough."

"Oh?" Luna asks. "Is it really that interesting?"

"Don't bait him," Oliver says. "He won't stop."

It's true. Normally, I wouldn't stop. Right now… well, it's hard enough not taking orders from the fucker without making him the center of attention. "I'll give you some details later, sweetie." I wink at her. Then Daisy. "You too, of course."

Her expression gets shy. Well, more shy. "I appreciate that."

I motion *after you*, follow her and Luna out of the house, lock the door, try to pay attention to my small talk with Oliver.

To anything besides the back of Daisy's thighs.

———

FUCK ME.

This is worse torture than I imagined.

It's a beautiful day. Blue sky. Soft sand. Ocean sparkling in the sunlight.

Daisy pulling off her cover-up, laughing as she takes her friend's hand and runs into the ocean.

Oliver watches me watch for a second, then he plops in a deck chair, adjusts the umbrella for maximum shade. "You should go with her."

"Should I?"

"You stop liking swimming all of a sudden?"

I try to find the meaning in his expression. "You sitting there all day?"

"This is enough beach for me."

"Waste of a trip."

"It's for her." He motions to his sister. She laughs as a wave hits her calves. "She looks happy."

"Yeah." At peace. Free. Relaxed. It's rare for her.

"So, go. Have fun. I know you want to." He motions to the water. Then to the umbrella. "I'm good."

We're at a beach club. It's a few dollars an hour for a seat, an umbrella, a waiter offering icy beverages.

It's quiet. There are people walking along the boardwalk behind us, but it's nothing like a summer day in Venice. It's a trickle, not a tsunami.

The beach club itself—a dozen umbrellas spread out over a space the size of my dad's downstairs—is nearly empty. There's an older couple in the far corner. And us.

Fuck, the ocean does look tantalizing. And not just because Daisy's in it.

"Go. I can't watch this puppy dog shit." He presses his foot into my calf. Pushes me gently. "You know where you belong."

"I do?"

"You gonna pretend you didn't spend four years on the swim team?"

"Three." But no reason to bring up the way I flamed out senior year.

"Go." He pushes me a little harder. "I can't watch you yearn."

"I don't yearn."

"Yeah, you do." He motions *go* one more time.

So I do.

It's a dozen steps to the water. It's warm. Not like the beach at Venice. This time of year, that water is tolerable. Comfortable even.

The ocean here feels more like a pool. Just cool enough it's refreshing.

I dive under the waves.

The water envelops me.

I swim a little deeper. A little farther out. My lung capacity isn't what it used to be.

I surface early. Lick the taste of salt from my lips. Let my eyes drift to Daisy.

She swims toward me with steady strokes. "Hey." Her

lips curl into a smile. Her arms move back and forth. Her legs circle.

She knows how to tread water. Most people don't.

She dips beneath the surface. Emerges with her light hair sticking to her cheeks and chest. "You're fast."

"I have practice," I say.

Her gaze shifts to Luna. Even though the waves are small, a foot or two, she's reveling in diving under them. "Were you on the swim team?"

"For three years."

"Only three?"

"Yeah." I lower my foot. Find the sand. "Some shit happened senior year."

"Is it a secret?"

"You could say that."

Her eyes perk. "I didn't know you had secrets."

"They wouldn't be secrets if you knew."

Her smile stays soft. "True." She swims a little closer. Rests her hand on my shoulder. "You mind?"

"No." Fuck, her touch feels good. "You need the help floating?"

"For a second." Her body drifts toward mine. Her chest hits my side. Her arm slings around my shoulder. Her smile widens. "Flying always makes me tired."

"Me too." I pull her a little closer.

So she doesn't have to struggle to stay afloat.

Not because I want her closer.

Fuck, she smells good. Like salt and sunscreen.

She looks up at me like I'm going to save her.

It fills my chest with warmth. With a warmth I rarely feel. That I usually avoid.

But I like when it's from her.

"This is what I want." She licks her lips. "Quiet afternoons in the water."

"And loud nights at the clubs?"

She shakes her head. "Maybe a few drinks at a quiet restaurant."

"Then we ditch Oliver, dance all night, skinny dip at the sunrise."

Her laugh is light. Easy. "Quiet dancing?"

"A silent rave. You listen to your music. I listen to mine."

"So we're dancing to different songs?"

"Guess that won't work."

Her fingers dig into my shoulder. "How old were you?"

"Huh?"

"The secret. The thing that kept you off the swim team a year."

"My senior year," I say.

"My age?"

I nod. Fuck, that feels like it was a million years ago. Like I was a stupid kid who knew nothing. "You'll have to get me drunk if you want to find out."

"Really?" Her voice is soft. "You'll just tell me?"

"I have poor impulse control."

Her eyes travel down my body. She doesn't say it. But it's there. *You're doing fine not tearing off my bikini.*

Or maybe that's my head.

She's not the casual sex type. Sure, she likes me, but I doubt she's thinking about pushing my board shorts to my knees and mounting me.

Fuck, that's an idea.

"Isn't that everyone when they're drinking?" she asks.

"Yeah, but I'm gonna make you keep up with me."

Her eyes go wide.

"I do a shot, you do a shot."

"You're a lot bigger than I am."

You have no fucking idea. "I'll do two to start. Give you an advantage."

"I'll think about it." She leans into my chest. For a second, she looks me in the eyes. Looks at me like she's going to kiss me.

Then she releases her grip on my shoulders.

Pushes away from me.

"Tomorrow." She smiles. "When it's legal."

She means drinking, but that's not where my head goes.

Chapter Ten

DAISY

The water is perfect. Refreshing, calm, beautiful.

A brilliant blue that stretches over the horizon.

I glide around the surface. Dip my head. Press off the sand.

It's hard to breathe with Holden this close. I have to keep my back to him. To ignore the heat of his stare.

I'm imagining things.

There's no way he's looking at me like that.

He flirts a little, sure. He offers to show me porn, buy me condoms, help me find a boyfriend or a date or a one-night stand.

But it's always in a friendly *I'm just looking out for you* way. For some reason, he wants Oliver—and everyone else—to believe he has bad intentions. I know the truth.

I see past that whole *I'm a troublemaking bad boy* thing.

Sure, he has the mischievous eyes and the charming smile and the tattoos.

God, those tattoos. I fail to stop myself from turning around. From taking in the dark ink spreading over his shoulders. The same as the pattern his brother has. Flowers in grey.

His mom's favorite?

That Latin quote on his chest.

dulce periculum

Danger is sweet.

So Holden.

So irresistible.

What is it about him? It's more than his green eyes, his gorgeous smile, his strong body.

It's not just that he's hot.

That he curses like a sailor.

And flirts like a temptress... tempter... Whatever it's called.

I dive beneath the surface.

For a moment, the dark, cool space makes everything clear. I'm here. Enjoying the week in Mexico. Celebrating my birthday. My independence. The next phase of my life.

I want Holden. I want his incredibly attractive body. But I want more than that too.

I want to know him. And for him to know me.

It's out of the question—how could I ever tell him?—but it's nice fantasizing for a minute.

If only I was more like him.

If I was at one hundred percent perfect, able to forget my inhibitions, totally free of baggage.

Right now...

I've been in recovery for more than a year. I'm not sick anymore. But I'm not as free as I want to be.

I still hear that voice in the back of my head. The one that says *you aren't good enough the way you are. You're too much. You need to prove your worth by becoming smaller.*

When I started high school, I was normal enough. Sure, I felt compelled to organize everything. To get straight As. To never, ever upset my parents, lest I trigger another one of their fights.

Sure, I sometimes thought about my body, what I ate, if it was too much. What teenage girl doesn't?

I'm not sure how it started, really. My therapist thinks it was a reaction to my parents' fighting. To Mom's habit of self-medicating with anti-anxiety meds. Dad dropping an ultimatum—rehab or I'm taking the kids.

Mom calling him on it.

He said things would be calmer after their divorce, but they weren't. Everyone was further away. Both my parents were working more hours to cover the legal fees. Oliver was apprenticing. He was as desperate to get away from the chaos as I was.

He succeeded.

I didn't. I was alone. And the entire world was out of control.

I needed to take it back. To make one tiny part of the universe make sense.

I'm not sure how I got the idea. Eating disorders came up every so often in YA. And even in some of the *your body is changing, how to deal* books Dad bought me.

I knew how they worked, intellectually. But I didn't really know. I had no fucking idea.

At first, I starting skipping dessert. The candy Mom sent. Ice cream after one of Luna's swim meets. Cake at a party.

It was the only thing I could control. And it felt good. Comforting in a weird way.

Like I was proving my worth by denying myself pleasure.

For a while, that was enough. It was enough to lose a few pounds. Buy jeans one size smaller.

Then it wasn't.

I started skipping more.

Anything with added sugar.

Drinks with calories.

Bread.

Dinner.

Breakfast.

I wanted to be smaller, to be more worthy, to be enough. To prove I was stronger than my physical needs.

The more I had, the more I needed.

The more I denied myself, the harder I broke. I'd black out. Come to in my car, halfway through a quart of ice cream, desperate to fix my mistake.

That was always the worst. The panic that came with messing up. It was like I was crawling out of my skin. Like I needed to be anywhere else except my body.

Like anything would be better than sitting with that.

I always hated purging. But, at the time, it felt better than the alternative.

Even now—

I don't know.

I knew it wasn't healthy. But I needed that control. I would have done anything to hold onto it.

I thought I was good at hiding my behavior. I thought no one knew. I guess, for a while, that was true.

Eventually Dad and Oliver saw it. They were terrified. I knew they were terrified. I hate that they were terrified.

But I still needed my control. It was the only thing holding me together.

I didn't want to go to therapy, but I didn't have a choice. I was a minor.

After one session, the shrink recommended inpatient treatment. A week later, I was in a psychiatric facility, eating three meals a day, plus dessert, doing daily group therapy, individual therapy, art therapy.

It was so much about eating. About making sure I had enough.

I resisted for a long time. But eventually I saw it. That my head was a mess. That I didn't have to hate myself twenty-four hours a day.

Once I was coherent enough to start writing, I did better.

Then I was healthy enough to dance—starving yourself weakens your muscles, including the ones in your heart —and I…

It's hard to explain recovery. It's not like I had one moment of epiphany. I had a million moments. And a million moments of *no, that's not it* that followed.

It was a million steps forward and half a million steps backward.

Once I gained enough weight, and stayed stable enough on my anti-depressants, I was discharged. Sentenced to a fate of careful meal planning and therapy once a week, every week, for the rest of my life.

I follow my post-treatment plan now. The same thing for breakfast. Lunch and dinner every day. A small treat for dessert. Not enough to trigger panic.

I don't count calories in my head. Or stare at my stomach wondering why it's so soft. Or write odes to self-loathing.

But I don't live either.

I'm still trapped. Trapped by the fear that I'll slip.

Trapped by routine.

I scan the bright blue sky. Look to Holden—the wicked smile, the danger is sweet tattoo, the easy posture. My best friend. My brother.

The wide expanse of the Pacific Ocean.

Everyone keeps asking what I want from this trip.

I don't know how to explain it. Or how to achieve it.

I want to kill that voice.

I want to feel good.

To be alive.

To be free.

There has to be some way to do that. I just have to figure it out.

———

WHEN I EMERGE FROM THE WATER, OLIVER AND HOLDEN are lazing under an umbrella, sipping from tall glasses. Something clear. Water. Oliver doesn't do clear spirits if he has the option.

Luna squeezes my hand. Pulls me close enough to whisper. "He looks good, doesn't he?"

"He does." Tempting as hell, all casual and aloof, body spread out over the white chair.

"Are you going to—"

"Maybe."

"You want me to distract Oliver?"

"Depends how you're doing it," I say.

Her smile gets wicked. Her gaze travels over his body. Stops on his—

Gross. "You can do better."

She laughs. "I know. I wouldn't. He's your brother."

"Uh-huh."

"Really." She leads me up the sand. To the guys. "Hydrated?"

Oliver chuckles.

Holden offers her his glass. "We have more coming."

"We should eat." Oliver's gaze goes to me. "You must be starving after all that swimming."

My stomach growls at the thought of food. It's stronger

than usual. Way stronger. Even after a year, I'm not particularly in touch with my body's wants.

I eat because it's time for breakfast, lunch, dinner. Not because I'm craving satisfaction.

"Here?" I motion to the restaurant behind us. It's nice. Quiet.

"Sure." Oliver tosses me a towel. "Or we could grab street tacos on the way to the Airbnb."

I shake my head. "I want to stay out." To stay near the ocean. In the sun. "You can go."

He laughs *nice try*. Motions to the bathroom. "You want to change or—"

"They won't mind." I towel dry. Pull on my cover-up. Slip into my sandals.

Luna does the same.

Tragically, Holden pulls on his t-shirt. He offers his hand. Leads me into the restaurant.

The hostess nods *sit wherever*. We take a spot in the corner of the open space—there are no walls, only support beams—so we can look onto the beach.

Holden pulls out my chair for me.

I drape my towel over the back. Sit. Run my fingers over the menu.

It's the English menu. Familiar. Designed for tourists. One row of Mexican specialties. One of American favorites.

Hamburgers, French fries, mac and cheese.

Street tacos. Chicken, steak, carnitas, octopus.

I make the safe choice. Chicken tacos.

Luna orders extra guacamole.

Oliver gets some dish of meat and vegetables. (Binge drinking aside, he takes pretty good care of himself. Of course, there's always this implication when we eat together. Like he knows he's setting an example. Like he makes a point of eating what he wants, as much as he wants).

Holden gets the octopus tacos.

For a while, everyone makes small talk. Sips their waters. Nibbles on chips and salsa.

I watch Holden eat. He doesn't dive in like it's his last meal. He doesn't hold back like he's saving himself.

He dips a chip in the salsa. Takes a bite. Licks sauce off his fingers.

Catches me staring.

"You want some?" He offers his index finger. It's still dripping with salsa. A line of red over his tan skin.

My body screams *yes*. It's the same as my growling stomach. New. Unfamiliar. Impossible to ignore.

I should be used to wanting around Holden. But I'm not. Even after a year of "getting in touch with my desires."

No, that's bullshit. I haven't been getting in touch with my desires. I've been using routine to survive. To stay healthy but not recovered.

"I do. Thanks." I take a chip. Dip it in salsa. Break a piece on my tongue.

What is it my therapist says? Something about the experience. All five senses.

The smell of corn.

The taste of salt.

The sharp crunch.

The sting on my tongue. Tomato and chili. Spicy. Sweet too.

I chew. Swallow. Dip the other side.

Eat it just as slowly.

It takes two chips for the food to arrive. I focus carefully on my first bite. Tender chicken. Sharp cilantro. Tangy green salsa.

For a few bites, I focus on my food.

Then my attention goes to Holden. He's laughing at one of Oliver's jokes. Licking salsa from his fingers. Eating the way he does everything—with reckless abandon.

What's it like to be that free? That alive?

I want to know.

I have to know.

I have to convince him to teach me.

Chapter Eleven

DAISY

Thankfully, my best friend is a genius. She convinces Oliver to help her pick out liquor and mixers for tomorrow. Apparently, everything needs to be perfect for my birthday, and it needs to be a surprise.

I mouth *thank you* as she leads my brother into an open-air shop. Straight to the liquor section.

"He's really in his element." Holden offers me his hand. Motions to the path.

I take it. Follow him along the winding boardwalk.

The area is cute. A mix of authentic beach town and ridiculous tourist trap. Crystal blue ocean on one side. Souvenir shops, bars, restaurants on the other.

"I bet they won't card." He motions to a store selling blended cocktails.

My eyes go wide. Those drinks are huge. "Do people really drink all that?"

He nods *yeah*. "It's mostly sugar."

"Is that better?" It's totally out of the question.

"When you're drunk, yeah."

"You drink."

"It's true." His laugh is easy.

"Why?"

"Why?"

"What's the appeal? I get that people do it. That it's a social thing, but—"

"Your brother's always getting sloppy drunk?" he asks.

I swallow hard. It isn't just that. More that I'm afraid of losing control. "You think so too?"

"Yeah." His voice gets serious. More serious than normal. "Everyone does."

"Oh."

"It's normal. For his age."

Maybe. "He's the same age as you."

"Six months younger," he says.

"That makes you wiser?"

He nods *hell yeah*. "You disagree?"

No, actually. There's something about Holden. Unconventional methods, sure, but—"you seem to know what you're doing."

He stops in front of a tequila store. Open door. Dark room filled with bottles. Clear liquor. Amber ones. Honey ones. "You've drank before."

"Yeah." A few times. Mostly in his presence, actually.

"Remember that party?"

"You can remember a specific party?"

He chuckles. Taps his head. "I remember three things. Tattoos, parties, women. Everything else—" he makes that *whoosh* motion.

"Uh-huh."

He nods *uh-huh*. "You drank that whole cup of rum and diet. Then a second."

"It wasn't that strong."

"True." He leads me past the tequila shop. Along the boardwalk. "How did you feel?"

"Floaty."

"Specifically…"

Like I was going to blurt out *I need you* and climb on top of him. "Uh… More free, I guess."

"That's what people like. The loss of inhibitions."

It's what I want. I just have to ask him. Somehow. "You?"

"Oh, I don't need alcohol for that." His eyes pass over my body. "I don't have them."

"Never?"

He holds up his index finger and thumb *a little*. "You okay in that wet thing?"

"I'm pretty dry now." My gaze follows his body. He's still wearing that tank top, but it's low enough I can see the Latin quote.

I want to touch it.

Something is stopping me.

Sense. Reason. Fear of embarrassment.

If I was drunk, tipsy even, it would be different. Maybe I'd touch him. Maybe I'd know what it means to feel free and uninhibited.

Is that the solution?

It seems wrong. Like some kind of shortcut that will backfire.

"How do you do it?" I ask. "How do you live without inhibitions?"

"Just do."

"Could you teach me?"

He makes a show of scratching his head. "Teach you to forget your inhibitions?"

"Yeah." My teeth sink into my bottom lip. Maybe

there's a better way to ask this. One that doesn't give my secrets away. "Or is that stupid?"

"Not stupid." He runs his hand through his hair. "More… difficult."

"Are you saying you can't handle it?" I make it as teasing as I can.

He just barely chuckles. "Is that really what you want?"

"Yeah. I want to feel free. Like you."

He gives me a long, slow once-over. "You want to be like me?"

"Why shouldn't I?"

"You're going to Berkeley. You'll probably graduate with a 4.0, get a great job, marry some guy who can afford a house in Bel Air."

"Why can't I be the one who affords the house in Bel Air?"

"You'll afford it together. With your combined salaries. He'll wear a suit to work. Have paid paternity leave. Splurge on vacations to European cities with tons of history."

"Who says I like guys who wear suits and take fancy vacations?"

His eyes stop on my chest. For a second. Then he meets my gaze. "What kind of guys do you like?"

"I, uh…" I swallow hard.

"If you were me, you'd—fuck." He shakes his head. "I've already said too much."

"So?"

"So this is what you get when you drop your inhibitions."

"What?" I ask.

"Trouble."

"You're afraid of trouble?"

"No." His eyes pass over me again. But faster. "But I care about some things."

"My brother."

"Yeah."

"And how he'll kill you if you touch me."

His eyes meet mine. "I'm not going to touch you."

My stomach twists. He's so sure of that. And what am I going to do? It's not like I want to trick him, wear him down, somehow manipulate him into touching me.

I only want it if he wants it too.

If we're both lucid enough to decide.

"I know." I try to make my voice even. Easy. Like I don't care. "I'm not stupid."

"Good." His eyes move to the bar across the street. "If you were me, you wouldn't take that. You'd pin me to the wall, put your hand right here"—he places his hand on the waistband of his board shorts—"say some shit like *okay, I'll drop it if you can look me in the eyes right now, and tell me you don't want me.*"

"Are you advising me…" Is he telling me he wants me? He is. But then. "You want me?"

"Doesn't matter."

"But you… is that a dare?"

"No."

"It is."

He drops his hand. "If I wanted you to touch me, I'd ask."

"Say *please touch me, Daisy.*"

"Yeah. With different words."

I try to find the words. Something dirty enough to make an impression.

But I can't even think them.

How can I possibly hope to say them?

"Come on. Let's go somewhere." He looks to the bar

on our left. "I'll help you, Daisy, but I have to be honest. It would be easier if you just had two drinks."

"Okay."

"Is that a no?"

I nod.

His gaze shifts to the shops on our left. To one of the thin streets. Cobblestone sidewalk. Cobblestone road. Pretty. Bumpy in the car. But really pretty.

There's a restaurant. A swimsuit shop.

A chocolate store.

No, a chocolate museum.

Really?

An entire, three-story place dedicated to chocolate?

My tongue slides over my lips.

My stomach growls. Not with hunger. Not the kind that's an emptiness. With need for satisfaction.

For something delicious on my tongue.

I want to taste a piece of chocolate and enjoy it, period, end of sentence.

Like he does.

It must be possible. It's just one piece. It's not enough to scare me.

Holden nods *that's it*. "Come on."

"Huh?"

"You want me to teach you?"

"Yeah."

"This is our first lesson."

"What is—"

"No questions." He leads me toward the street. "You don't have to like them. But you do have to listen."

Chapter Twelve

DAISY

Air-conditioning greets me.

Then a friendly *hola*.

Holden presses his palm into the small of my back. He leads me farther into the shop. Away from the hot sun. Into the bliss of air-conditioning.

Or maybe his hand is the bliss.

Right now, I don't care what we're doing.

Only that there's a single layer of fabric between his hand and my skin.

Heat spreads through my body. Collects between my legs.

It's the strangest sensation—the cool air against my skin, the heat beneath it.

Intoxicating.

He's intoxicating.

I don't need alcohol. Just him. Can I ask for that? *Please, spend the next week near me. You can do anything, say anything, eat or drink or think anything.*

Just promise you won't go far.

That you won't have anyone else.

You don't have to kiss me. Or touch me. Or fuck me.

But I really hope you do.

"You're thinking something." His breath warms my ear.

"No." *Please keep touching me. Please keep distracting me. Please hold all of my attention.*

"Bullshit." His laugh is easy. "You sure you want to do this?"

I clear my throat.

"If you can't admit it to yourself—"

"It's a process."

"Don't tell me. Just think it. Close your eyes, and hold on to that thought."

My eyelids press together. Beautiful mental images crystalize in my brain. His hands under my cover-up. Tugging at my bikini strings. Tossing my swimsuit aside.

I wait for the usual shyness. Those lingering feelings of shame and disgust.

That *you're still untouchable* voice.

It doesn't come.

There's this vague sense in the back of my mind, a fear that I'm somehow not enough, but it's quiet. Out of focus.

I know, intellectually, that I'm attractive. That my body is perfectly normal.

I've even stopped hating it. Stopped picking at flaws. Stopped wanting to be less.

But I'm not at loving it yet.

I'm certainly not in touch with it.

Not usually.

He can teach me. Even if it's more leading by example.

"You got it?" He pushes my cover-up into my skin.

"I do."

"You want to tell me?"

I shake my head.

94

"Figured." There's a smile in his voice. More than usual. "This is still good."

"You have a plan?"

"Fuck no." He pushes me toward the counter on the right. It's past a shelf of chocolate bars. All kinds. White, milk, dark, even one hundred percent baking cocoa.

Sugar free. The kind of thing I'd have grabbed during the worst of it.

No, it would have still been too much. I would have found some manufactured chocolate flavor. Diet ice cream. Or a flavored yogurt. Rice cracker, maybe.

Not the real, sweet, rich chocolate that melts on the tongue.

When did I last savor chocolate? Really enjoy it?

When was the last time I ate without baggage?

Even now, there's so much effort to it. I have to try to enjoy. I have to focus on it.

He picks up a sample of milk chocolate. Fifty percent. "Everyone likes chocolate."

"True."

"And no one is ashamed to admit it."

I'm not sure about that. But I'd rather not dwell on it.

Holden places the piece on his tongue.

Pleasure spreads over his expression as the chocolate dissolves on his tongue.

He closes his mouth. Chews. Swallows. "Fuck, that's not bad. You try." He takes another square. Holds it up to me.

I nod *okay*. Open my mouth.

His fingers brush my lips as he places the piece on my tongue.

Fuck, his fingers taste good.

They're so firm. So… right.

It's strange. I've never wanted a digit in my mouth

before. Sure, I've had vague thoughts of *ahem* with guys. With Holden even.

But I've never thought about sucking on a finger.

Right now—

"You like it?" His eyes fix on mine. Fill with a mix of concentration and enthusiasm.

It matters to him.

He wants me to like it. Wants me to savor every drop of chocolate.

Okay. I close my eyes. So I won't stare at him. So I won't think of how much I'd prefer his skin.

The chocolate is good. A little too sweet, but rich. Fruity.

I lick my lips. "I do like it."

"Knew you would. You were staring."

"I wasn't staring." Okay, I was staring. But not for the reason he thinks.

He nods *yeah, you were*. "You can't admit it now. Can't admit what you want."

I swallow hard.

"Why is that?"

"It just is." There are too many asterisks. *I want some chocolate. But only a little. Not enough to push my thoughts to uncomfortable places.*

He arches a brow. "You don't have to tell me. But if you really do want less shit weighing you down, you should admit it to yourself."

"Are you a therapist?"

"Do I sound like one?" Horror streaks his expression. "Should I encourage more bad behavior?"

"Definitely." My lips curl into a smile. "Drunken orgies."

"You'd run a million miles from a drunken orgy." His

smile spreads. "But nice try." He turns back to the samples. "You like dark or light?"

"Dark." I used to daydream about it. It used to consume my mind. Wanting. Trying not to want.

Now, I'm trying to want.

Trying to be okay with wanting.

Trying to be okay with enjoying.

He picks up a piece of sixty percent. Offers it to me.

I part my lips.

Again, he places it on my tongue.

This time, I close my eyes immediately. Focus on the flavor.

"You like it?" he asks.

I nod. Mmm. This one is better. Sweet but not too sweet. I can taste the notes of cherry. The rich nuttiness. "A lot."

"Doesn't sound like it."

"Should I groan over it?"

"Fuck yeah."

"Really?"

"No. You'll make me hard."

My blush deepens.

"Fuck. Shouldn't have said that."

"But you—"

"You should do something to express your pleasure. It doesn't have to be a groan."

I chew. Swallow. Look him in the eyes. "Is that what you do?"

"I don't think about it."

"You're not... making an effort to make it known?"

His eyes travel over my body. For a second, they stop on my hips. My chest. My lips. "No." He does nothing to pull the conversation back. To suggest we aren't discussing sex. "I'm there, in the moment."

"Always?"

"I always try." He picks two pieces of seventy percent. Places one on his tongue. The other on his palm. "If you're not there, you can't feel it."

My fingers brush his hand as I take it.

"You can't taste it." His eyes flutter together. His brow softens. His teeth scrape his bottom lip.

My sex clenches.

My body buzzes.

My lips part.

It's so beautiful, watching bliss spread across his expression. Watching him savor every drop of it.

Not just because he's awake and alive and all in.

Because he's *there*.

Because we both know what this is really about.

Or at least I do.

"Fuck." A sigh falls from his lips. "That's perfect."

"Yeah?" My gaze stays fixed on his soft mouth.

"Forest only has super dark shit. Eighty-five percent. It's good in its own way, but this… Fuck." His fingers brush my palm. "That's melting."

"Oh."

"That's the risk of waiting."

"With chocolate, yeah."

He peels the half-melted slice from my hand. Brings it to his mouth. "With anything." He swallows the chocolate. Then he brings my hand to his mouth.

Sucks the melted treat from it.

He groans against my palm.

He's trying to kill me.

He's trying to drive me wild.

He's trying to wind me so tight I break.

It's agony.

But a good agony.

"Fuck." He releases my hand. "That's good. Try it."

"Uh-huh."

"Daisy." He turns me to the row of samples. "Pick one. Try it."

"Shouldn't I wash my hands?" I'm not sure how many samples I can have without the voice creeping in. I want to try. But I don't want to break.

His laugh is hearty. "Fuck it."

"Fuck spreading disease?"

"Shit, I did promise to teach you about that."

My cheeks flush.

"Speaking of." He picks up a piece of seventy percent. Holds it up.

I take it. Place it on my tongue. I can do this. I can enjoy it. It's no big deal.

Mmm.

It's darker. Richer. More earthy.

I let it melt.

Swallow the pieces.

I'm okay. I'm not panicking. I'm not worried I overdid it.

Sure, I'm not going to down an entire bar. But I am okay.

Holden turns to the counter. Bends to pick up something.

A white card with big pink hearts and gold text.

All You Need is Love and Chocolate.

There are others behind it. In English. And in Spanish. At least, I think that's what they say. I know a little Spanish —I do live in Southern California—but mostly stuff like *where's the bathroom* and *tacos please*.

Holden laughs as he opens the card.

Two chocolate flavored condoms.

Oh my God.

My blush deepens. "Does that... work?"

"They're still effective, yeah."

"Oh."

He hands me the card.

My fingers brush his. Stay pressed against his. "Do they really taste... like chocolate?"

"Haven't had them."

"But others..."

"Don't taste a lot of condoms," he says.

"Oh, right, you, uh..."

"Don't suck dick, yeah." His hand goes to his stomach. "Shit, that was loud."

Very loud.

The entire room is looking at us. Including the guy behind the counter.

"They do," he says. "Taste like chocolate."

Oh God.

He motions to the stairs. "We have a café upstairs."

Holden leans close enough to whisper. "He's telling us to stop scaring off business."

I shake my head. "He's checking out your ass."

"Must be disappointed I'm into women."

"Hard to blame him."

He pulls back with a smile. "Oh?"

My blush spreads to my chest. Oh my God. Did I really say that?

It's...

Okay, it's a little embarrassing. But the way Holden is looking at me.

God, I really like the way he's looking at me.

I clear my throat. "I just mean..."

"Go on."

"You're a very attractive man."

"And..."

"Lots of people want you. You know that."

"Maybe." He slides his arm around me. Holds up the card of condoms. "Can we bring this upstairs? Or should we pay first?"

The guy nods *go for it*.

Holden leads me up the stairs. He stays a pace behind me.

Checking out my ass.

I think.

I'm pretty sure.

He wants me. Even if he's not willing to act on it, he does want me.

He knows it.

I know it.

He knows I know it.

I know he knows it.

I just don't know what to do about it.

Chapter Thirteen

HOLDEN

I 'm an idiot.

Lacking self-control.

Unable to push my dick out of the driver's seat.

Fuck, this is going to kill me. I'm going to collapse at this table from pent-up frustration.

Is this how Daisy lives?

It's exhausting.

I try to pry my eyes from her soft pink lips. They're wrapped around a glass. She's sucking cocoa nib infused cold brew into her mouth.

Fuck, I want to be that cold brew.

I've never wanted to be coffee before.

An hour alone with her and I'm already going crazy.

An hour of failing to stop myself from blurting out the dirty thoughts in my head. Well, some of them.

You want to find out how those condoms taste, baby? Come here. As long as I can taste you first—— .

Goddammit.

Her throat quivers as she swallows. She pushes the drink across the table. Back to me. "It's a lot."

I nod *yeah*. "Good though."

"I knew you weren't a tea person."

"Didn't have a chance to make your chai." I take a long sip of cold brew. The addition of chocolate is subtle, but it's enough to make this drink fucking good. I'm not usually a coffee person. I've added enough cream and simple syrup to prove it—what can I say, I don't like bitter tastes?

But, fuck, there's something about the rich chocolate flavor.

The blue eyes fixed on me.

The flushing cheeks—

Not going there. Uh-huh. No way.

This icy drink is sending coolness through my body. It's calming my cock. That's a theoretical possibility.

Daisy picks up a chocolate-covered strawberry. Brings it to her lips. Takes a tiny bite.

Her eyelids flutter closed.

Her brow softens.

Her chest heaves.

I try to find coldness in the light brown of my milky coffee. I don't, but at least it keeps me from staring at her.

"These are good." She lets out a soft groan. "This was a good idea."

"I'm a genius."

Her eyes meet mine. Her lips curl into a smile. "It's… I really do appreciate your help."

"I aim to please."

Her smile gets wider. And somehow softer too. "You do."

"Oh?"

She nods *yeah*. "Are you going to pretend otherwise?"

"Fuck no."

"Not just with sex. Though I'm sure you do…" She brings the fruit to her mouth. Sinks her teeth into its flesh.

Red juice dribbles over her lips.

She sucks the berry into her mouth. Licks her lips. Wipes a drop with her thumb. Chews. Swallows. "Do you?"

"Do I what?"

She copies my easy tone. "Aim to please."

"When I fuck?"

Her eyes go wide. Her blush deepens. "Yeah." Her voice is quiet. Not timid exactly. More overwhelmed.

She is shy.

Uptight.

Completely and totally into me.

Which doesn't matter.

I'm looking out for her.

Helping her.

Even if it kills me.

No, I'm stronger than that. I can listen to her groan over chocolate without dying.

I can help her find someone else. If that's really what she wants. If she's here to punch her v-card—

I can't find a way to like it.

But I can do it.

"Holden?" Her fingers brush mine as she hands me a chocolate-covered strawberry. "If you don't want to talk about sex, I understand."

"Is that another dare?"

She shakes her head. "I know you better than that."

I arch a brow.

She lets out a soft laugh. "I could dare you all day." She leans back. Tries to copy my easy posture. Well, my usual easy posture.

At the moment, I'm tenser than she is.

Fuck, do people really live like this? With desire winding them so tight they could burst?

It fucking sucks.

No wonder Forest was so moody before he and Skye got together. I'm ready to hit someone, throw something, down the nearest bottle.

Fuck the nearest stranger.

Not that my heart will allow it.

Fucking A. It's just as unwilling to let my head in the driver's seat.

My cock keeps screaming *fuck her*.

My heart keeps screaming *whatever you do, don't hurt her*.

My head—

I can barely hear the damn thing.

She tries to imitate me. "Holden, it's okay if you can't handle talking about sex. I wouldn't want you to feel embarrassed." Her voice is halfway between her usual tone —straightforward and shy—and something light and teasing. "It's okay if you don't have the self-control."

Fuck, she makes a cute me. She's trying so hard to sell casual, but it's not in her nature.

It's so obvious she's trying.

That she's desperate for details.

Not that I blame her.

"Close." I sink my teeth into the strawberry. Focus on the sweetness of the fruit. The richness of the chocolate. "But I don't bait over my lack of self-control."

She presses her legs together. Leans toward the table. Places her hands on the wood. "What?"

"You don't know?"

Her brow furrows with concentration. "You like to be ridiculous."

I shrug like I don't try.

"You want people to think you don't care about anything."

"Maybe."

"Why?"

"Why?" I finish the rest of my strawberry. It's good—really fucking good—but I'd still rather taste her.

"Yeah." Her eyes fix on mine. "Why do you want everyone to believe you're ridiculous?"

"Why do you want to lose your inhibitions?"

"You need me to explain that?"

"Yeah." No, it's obvious she's wound tighter than a fishing line. But I need to keep this about her. Me helping her, sure. But still her. "Why not take a shot or two?"

"You know why." Her lips purse. The interest in her eyes turns to frustration.

My stomach churns. I hate it. I hate her joy turning to pain.

"Oliver… and I… well, I guess you could say I haven't been very good at moderation."

"When have you ever been immoderate?"

"In the past."

No fucking way. I don't believe that. Even if it's the kind of non-answer that suggests she's hiding something. I shake my head. "If anything, I should ask you to teach me a few lessons about self-control."

Her brow furrows. With concentration. "I can try." She wraps her fingers around the cold brew. "But I don't think you should take my advice."

"Why?"

"It's… personal." Her eyes go to the milky coffee. She takes a long sip. Swallows hard. "Maybe… I guess that's part of this. I wish I was free enough to just say. I wish I was free enough to have a few drinks and not worry I won't be able to stop. I wish it didn't feel like so much."

"What didn't?"

"I, uh…" Her eyes meet mine for a second. Then they're on the table.

"It's a secret?"

"Yeah."

"You don't want to tell me?"

She shakes her head. "I don't want to tell anyone. They act different. Look at me differently."

"Differently how?"

"Less like… I like the way you look at me. Even with the whole… Oliver issue. You… we're friends, yeah?"

That's a fair enough assessment. "We are."

"You want… well, for the sake of argument, let's say I believe that you're nothing but Mr. Party Boy."

"Let's."

"You are showing me a good time. And this… it's not the most conventional lesson, but it's helping."

"Really?" I arch a brow. I do want to help her, but she doesn't seem any more relaxed than she did an hour ago.

She doesn't seem freer.

Maybe she is.

Maybe I'm wound too tightly to assess her.

The Daisy I know isn't this direct.

"Really." Her lips curl into a half-smile. "You… what's step two?"

Fuck, that would mean I have a plan. And I don't.

How do I let loose?

I drink.

I fuck.

I focus on work.

That sounds like the opposite of letting loose, but it's not. There's a certain freedom that comes with sketching, drawing, perfecting a mock-up.

It's like my conscious self disappears.

Something deeper takes over.

Not that I can admit that. Or suggest it. I don't want to prove her right.

Not because I have to be right.

Because I don't want her thinking I'm this interesting guy with layers she needs to unpeel.

I saw that happen to Ariel. She thought there was more to some guy than met the eye, that he was mean because he was hurt, that he was standoffish because he was heartbroken.

It doesn't matter why they were assholes.

I don't care how much shit they'd been through.

They didn't treat her well. So they didn't deserve her. Period. End of sentence.

"Usually, I'd drink. Or fuck," I say. "But we're waiting on the first one."

She nods. "And you're… You know, if you really were just about tattoos, parties, and women, you'd have a different response."

I arch a brow.

"You wouldn't insist you aren't touching me."

"Maybe I'm just not into you." I completely fail to sell that possibility.

Her eyes turn down. For a second, she considers that possibility. Shrinks back, hurt. Then she shakes her head *no way* and returns my gaze. "You are."

"You're sure of yourself all of a sudden."

"Maybe you're not into me. But you do find me attractive."

"Yeah."

"And you don't exactly have discriminating criteria for your *ahem* friends."

I can't help but laugh. She's adorable. "So I fuck any hot woman who looks interested?"

"Do you not?"

Damn, this is a trap. Either I say *of course I do* and prove her point or say *of course not* and prove her point. "Only most of them."

"You are attracted to me."

There's really no arguing that point. "I value my life."

"Oliver wouldn't."

"He would." Hell, protecting Daisy is probably the only thing he cares about.

"He trusts you with me."

"I can't help that he's an idiot."

"Maybe."

"Is that what you want?" I ask.

"You?" Her blush deepens.

"Sex."

"Oh." Her eyes go to the almost empty cold brew. "Well… at some point, yeah."

There has to be some way I can work with that. That I can help her lower her guard without touching her.

It would be a hell of a lot more fun if I did touch her.

But that isn't happening. No sense in thinking about it.

"We can do that," I say.

Her eyes go wide. "We can have sex?"

"Not *we*. But I can help you find someone."

"You can?"

"Yeah." Fuck, that's it. "I have an idea."

"Yeah?"

"For tonight. But before that, I—" My ringing phone saves me from changing the subject.

Or steering my brain to some place besides making her come.

I grab my cell.

"Where the fuck are you two?" Oliver asks.

"Chocolate museum." I look to Daisy. "You ready to go?"

"Sure. I want to shower. Change." Her gaze shifts to the phone. "Tell him we'll meet him there."

I do.

He mutters something about how Luna's refusal to put anything over her bikini top is going to kill him. Hangs up. Tells me not to get home *too* quickly.

Like he thinks they're going to make out in his bedroom.

No, Oliver wouldn't do that to his sister. She's the only thing he cares about. In the entire fucking world.

All right, he's into his work—really into it—and he loves his dad. But that relationship is strained. Has been since their mom bailed.

Fuck, this girl has been through way too much. She needs someone like Forest. Who understands feelings, baggage, hurt.

Who knows how to be careful with her.

"You're right. I maintain a certain…" I slide my cell into my pocket.

"Persona?" she offers.

"It's real. That's all there is."

She shoots me a *really* look.

"Most of it." I stand. Pull my stack of pesos from my pocket. Count the money. "You're right, that I'm intentional in what I say. I like setting expectations. So I don't disappoint anyone."

"I hate that too."

"Who have you ever disappointed?"

Her smile gets sad. "You don't know?"

"Know what?"

Her eyes go to the table. "I won't argue I'm not an innocent good girl. It's probably as believable as your whole *I only think about boobs and tattoos* thing. But there's a lot you don't know about me. Enough to fill an ocean."

There is.

And I want to find out.

I want to know everything.
I can do that without touching her.
Without falling for her.
Without hurting her.

Chapter Fourteen

HOLDEN

I have to hand it to Oliver. The house is stocked. Not just with booze and mixers—though there are plenty of both—with enough food to feed an army.

Everything from frozen vegetables and milk to packaged Mexican candy.

The shower upstairs is running. Both of them, actually. I guess that explains where our co-vacationers are.

Daisy places her bag by the door. She moves through the modern living room, down the hallway, to the washer/dryer in the closet.

She places her towel in the washer, then she moves around the kitchen, grabbing the towels draping over the chairs—mine, Oliver's, Luna's—and puts them in the washer.

Fuck, she's deliberate. It's a good trait. But one that can—

Well, it's not hard to see why she's asking for my help. Besides the whole *she wants to fuck me* thing.

"You want to wash anything?" Her gaze flits to me. "Anything, sturdy, I guess. These need hot water."

I shake my head. I packed just enough. And I know how to do my own laundry. Forest, Ariel, and I have been taking care of shit forever. Sure, I always gave Forest hell for assigning me chores. But I did them. Eventually.

She nods *okay*, carefully measures detergent, sets the machine.

It whirs.

Sends my head to dirty places.

Have you ever fucked on top of a washing machine, baby? The vibration will drive you wild.

"You owe me something." She moves down the hallway. To me.

She's still in her bikini.

Yeah, the cover-up is over it. But it does a shit job of hiding her figure.

When did she get so curvy?

A year ago, she was a skinny kid—tiny even. She's still on the slim side, but her tits are full and her hips are round.

"Yeah?" I struggle to bring my gaze to her eyes. To push aside the shit running through my head. *Is it an orgasm, baby? Take off your bikini and sit on the table. You need to come on my face. Now.*

"A chai." She motions to the clean kitchen. "Unless you have some excuse."

"No." I shake my head. "But I have a better idea."

"Oh?" She rests her palms against the white tile counter. Then it's her ass. She's right across from me. Only three feet away.

It's different, being close in this space. Real. Domestic.

Weird, actually.

I don't invite women to my place. I always go to theirs. Sure, I fix them breakfast in the morning—if they don't shoot me that *hey, this was fun, but I have to go, so you have to go* look—but it's always their space, not mine.

This isn't mine either. It's a hotel. A temporary place to stay. No different than waking up after a one-night stand.

But it is different.

It's Daisy.

"Holden?" Her eyes meet mine. "Are you okay?"

"Sunstroke," I say.

"You supposedly have an idea."

"Doesn't sound like me."

Her smile spreads over her cheeks. She's a little flushed, but it's from the sun, not from anything I've said. "I was thinking the same thing." She motions to the fridge. "Oliver got milk?"

"Yeah."

"And you… brought chai?"

I nod. "Ariel's blend."

"So…"

Fuck, that's it. "We'll compete."

"We will?"

"Yeah. See who makes the best chai." I push off the table. Close the space between us.

She stays put for a moment. Stays pressed against the counter.

My body brushes hers, my crotch against hers, my hand against her wrist.

Then she turns sideways, so her chest brushes my chest, my arm.

She motions *it's all yours*.

I find the chai in the top cabinet. Place it on the counter. Fill the kettle with water.

"How are we competing here?" She takes two steps toward me. "We use the same hot water? See who gets the right ratio?"

"You have another idea?"

"Well, how can we make it fair? With only one kettle?

If I let you do everything first, your tea will be cold by the time mine is done."

"I trust you. To be honest."

"So you make yours, we taste it, decide how good it is."

I nod *yeah*.

"Then I make mine, we taste it, decide if it's better?"

"You don't like it?"

Her brow furrows with concentration. "I think at the same time is better. So both teas are fresh."

"And we'll vote ourselves?"

"Yeah. But blind." She rises to her tiptoes to open a cabinet and pull out two identical mugs. "Give me a second."

I nod *sure*.

She moves out of the kitchen. Goes to her bag. Pulls out a tiny notebook—pastel pink, of course—and a pen. She removes a sheet. Tears it in half. Scribbles something on each side.

"You took paper to the beach?" I ask.

She nods *yeah* as she hands me a paper with *Holden* in a neat cursive font. "I take paper everywhere."

"Why?"

"In case I have something I want to write down."

I can't help but laugh. "That's the kind of thing I would say."

"A non-answer?" She places her sheet—*Daisy* in that same neat handwriting—on the counter. Places the cup on top of it. Tries to slide both.

It works. Mostly.

I copy the gesture. It's not the neatest—the paper clearly drags—but it will do the trick.

Though—

I open one of the drawers. Find a roll of tape.

"Thanks. That's perfect." Her fingers brush mine as

she takes it. She's careful about taping the sheets of paper to the bottom of each mug.

It matters to her, this contest being fair.

Even though it's silly. A game. A way to set her at ease.

She's concentrating, but she isn't tense. I guess she is at ease. And she does love tea.

It's on the chocolate level of suppressed desire—less, probably, since there's all this cultural bullshit about chocolate being sinful—but it's something.

"What is it you want to write?" I finish filling the kettle. Place it on the stove. Turn the burner to high.

"Thoughts." Her eyes meet mine. "Ideas, I guess. I thought I wanted to be a writer for a while."

"But?"

"I hate everything I write."

"That's normal."

"Is it?" Her eyes flit to her bag then they're back on me. "It's never good enough."

"It never is. At first. You should see the shit I drew in high school." I shudder at the thought of my shitty comic book rip-offs. Not the place to learn anatomy. At least not female anatomy. "You can't imagine how bad it was."

"How did you get past it?"

I chuckle. "Well, at the time, I thought it was the tits."

Her cheeks flush. "Really?"

"For a while, yeah. At some point, I realized it sucked."

"Was it that bad?"

"Yeah."

Her eyes meet mine. "I don't believe you."

"You're trying to distract me from our tea."

She motions to the kettle. "I'm waiting."

Fair point. But—"I can prove it." Shit, I can, but I don't want to. There are things I prefer to keep to myself.

My art—not the stuff I do for clients, the stuff I do for me—is at the top of the list.

And that's the good shit I draw now.

The personal and terrible art from high school—

No way.

"Fuck, I need something in exchange," I say.

Her eyes fix on me. "You need something in exchange for proving your point?"

"Yeah."

"Maybe you should just admit you're wrong?" Her voice gets light. "It seems like you're capable. Usually."

"I'm wrong a lot. But not about this." It's weird. I want to show her. I want her to pore over my notebooks, to trace the lines with her fingertips, to somehow absorb what it means.

I want her to understand what it means. To accept it. To accept me.

I never want that.

It's not worth the risk. When you let someone in, you give them the chance to hurt you. And even if they don't, if they love you with their entire heart, they still leave.

Everyone leaves eventually.

All hearts break eventually.

I need to say *never mind, you're right*. To slide my hands into my pocket. Change the password on my cloud.

But I don't.

I pull my cell from my pocket. Login to my picture storage. Suck a breath through my teeth. "I'm gonna show you this. But, in exchange, I want to hear some of your supposedly shitty writing."

"No, it's terrible."

"This is worse. I guarantee it."

Her teeth sink into her lip. Her eyes turn down. She

sucks in a shaky breath. Pushes out a shallow exhale. "On one condition."

There it is. My last drawing.

A fallen angel, tugging at a locked heart, unable to take off because the weight is too much, and his wings are too worn.

It started as a riff off a client's request. They wanted a locked heart. I wanted to make it less cliché.

Eventually, it stopped being for her.

It's a solid drawing—a lot of emotion, clean lines—but it's too personal.

"It has to be as bad as you say."

"What if you have no taste and you think it's all right?" I scroll backward in time. Past last year's drawings. All the shit I did after Ariel told me she was a carrier for the gene that killed our mom.

All that shit about life, death, family.

Then before that.

Through years of training.

All the way back to high school.

This folder is all *my* drawings. But only stuff I deemed good enough to photograph. My sketchbooks are in a box in the closet.

They're full of real shit.

This is… well, it's not great. But it's better than the stuff that didn't make it.

"It has to be bad," she says. "I have to be able to see the badness."

"Fair." There. That's total crap. A self-portrait in shades of blue and black. All deep and dark, for my edgy teenage soul.

No, it was more than that. It wasn't pretense. Well, maybe it was. But that was still there.

That sense is still there. That part of me that wants

more. That wants love. That tires of parties, drinking, fucking strangers.

It wants to visit Mom's grave, to play her music for my niece, to send sentimental cards to family members.

To show Daisy all of these pictures.

But, unlike with my dick, I'm pretty good at silencing that voice. At distracting myself enough it doesn't nag.

"Can I?" Her fingers brush mine. "If you're right, and it's horrible, I'll pick something out tonight. Read it to you tomorrow."

I nod *okay*. Hand her the phone.

Her eyes go wide as she focuses on the picture.

My heart pounds. My stomach twists. My limbs get light. That same feeling I had when I was apprenticing. When I lived and died for a *good work, Holden* .

No one is ever proud of me. Not that I blame them. I make sure they don't have the chance.

Probably another sign of my fucked-up head, but it's working so far.

I'm happy. Life is good. Sure, there's shit that goes wrong, but that's true for everyone.

I get enough "realness" from my drawings.

This sense that I'm about to float to the ceiling—

I don't need that.

"It's not technically good." Her eyes meet mine for a second, then they're back on the screen. "But there is something about it. I can feel the mood of it. Were you really this... it's hard to imagine you drawing this."

"I was an edgy teenager."

"Oh?"

I nod *yeah*. "Listened to a lot of songs about how much no one understood me."

"Who didn't?" Her fingers brush mine as she hands the cell back. "It's not great, but—"

"Here." I scroll through the photos. Find something that's both shitty and empty. There. My Spider-Man phase. I drew a lot of bad fan art. "This is trash." I turn the cell to her. "Total shit."

She laughs. "You really thought it was great?"

"Fuck yeah, it's Spider-Man. I thought I nailed it."

Her laugh gets louder. "When did you realize it was crap?"

"A little after that. That's the thing with art. Your taste matures faster than your skill. You spend a lot of time making shit."

Her eyes fix on mine. "Oliver says the same thing."

"Yeah?" Thank fuck for the reminder of her brother's existence. My head is going to places it needs to avoid.

She nods *yeah*. "And then stuff about how I'm a perfectionist at heart. And I'll always be critical. Especially of myself."

"He's right."

"Yeah, but—" The steam of the kettle interrupts her. "I do make a mean tea latte. Chai is new, but—"

"You're going down, kid."

The nickname makes her smile. "No, you're the one going down."

I know she isn't talking about coming on my face, but that's exactly where my head goes.

Chapter Fifteen

HOLDEN

Daisy is meticulous in everything she does, including fixing chai lattes. She measures exactly two teaspoons of tea. Brews it in exactly eight ounces of water. Adds it to exactly eight ounces of warmed milk.

Sweetens with exactly one teaspoon of honey.

Adds exactly one shake of cinnamon.

I scoop leaves into an empty mug, brew until it feels done, strain, heat the tea and milk in the microwave, add the usual amount of cinnamon and cardamom.

We take our drinks to the kitchen table. Check that the labels are taped to the bottom. It's not really necessary— her mug is neat, mine is sprinkled with spice—but I play along anyway.

She takes the drinks. "Close your eyes."

I do.

She sets the drinks on the table. "Okay, now, I'll close my eyes, and you give me one of the drinks. I won't know which it was."

"You could just admit I'm better."

"No way." Her fingers brush my hand. "You ready?"

"Yeah."

"Open your eyes."

My gaze fixes on her immediately. Orange light falls over her blond hair, her wide eyes, her soft smile.

"Your turn." Her eyelids flutter closed. She holds out her hand, waiting for me.

I pick up one of the cups—it's obviously mine, but I don't call that out—and place it in her hand.

Her fingers curl around the cup. She brings it to her lips. Takes a long, slow sip.

Her brow softens. Her chest heaves. Her lips part with a sigh.

"That's good." She takes another sip. Stifles a groan.

"Don't do that."

"Huh?"

"Don't play it down."

"I'm not—"

"You don't have to play it up. But don't play it down either." My fingers brush hers. "Savor every fucking drop."

Her cheeks flush. "This one is yours, isn't it?"

"How could I know?"

"True." She brings the mug to her lips. Takes one more sip. "It is. There's more cardamom."

"More than what? Ariel puts extra cardamom in her blend."

She holds out the mug.

I take it. Replace it with the other cup. "I expect the truth."

"Of course."

Her fingers curl around the mug. She brings it to her lips faster this time. Takes a bigger sip. Lets out a louder sigh. "Damn, that's good too."

"Yeah?" I watch her chest heave with her inhale. Try to find the thread of my thoughts. Fail.

There's something I'm doing here. Some point to this. Something besides the chance to stare at her tits.

Let's face it. If I wanted to stare at her tits, all I'd have to do is ask.

She asked for a birthday kiss last year.

This year—

Fuck, I don't even have to wait. I could say I owe it to her. She'd say yes. Say *hell yes, let's go now*.

It could start with—

"It's really good." Her voice is soft. Easy. "But the other one was better." Her eyes blink open. "Which was it?" She holds the cup over her head. Reads the name on the bottom. "Dammit."

"I won?"

She nods *yeah*. "Your head is going to get even bigger."

"If that's possible."

Her smile spreads a little wider. "But, if you think about it, I'm the real winner."

"Oh?"

She nods *yeah*, moves into the dining room with the mug, takes a seat. "Now, I can ask you to fix my tea every morning."

"True."

"I get the better tea."

I take the other mug. Join her at the table. "You do."

"If I ask nicely, you might even teach me your secrets."

"No secrets."

Her eyes fix on mine. "No? There must be something. Some reason why yours came out better."

"Just practice. It's like everything, the more you do it, the better you get."

"Like sex?"

"Yeah." My eyes pass over her quickly. "Why? You gonna start practicing?"

"What would that even be?"

"I dunno. Something with bananas."

Her blush spreads to her chest. "Is that even… accurate?"

"Dunno. You have a banana handy? I can take it upstairs. Compare."

Her jaw drops.

Fuck, I'm so bad at controlling myself. "What do you want to do with the banana?"

"Well, uh… I'm not particularly interested in practicing moves on fruit." Her voice is shy. Shier than it's been all afternoon. "But I do… For some reason, everyone thinks I'm in Mexico to get laid."

"It's what people do."

"I guess. But I… I mean, I'd like to do that one day. With the right person. I would like to know what I'm doing. So I don't embarrass myself."

"You won't."

Her shyness fades enough for her to shoot me a *get real* look.

"Okay, yeah, maybe you'll go too hard or too soft or involve teeth some place you shouldn't." I shudder at a particularly painful memory. "But if you're with someone worth your time, they aren't going to make you feel bad about it."

"Yeah, but—"

"They'll show you what they want."

"What if they don't?"

"Ask."

She stares at me like I'm crazy. "Ask a guy what he wants?"

"Yeah."

"But that's… that's so awkward."

"So is sex."

"But…"

"But…?" I ask.

"You're uh…" She motions to my crotch.

"I'm…"

"Promiscuous."

I can't help but laugh. She's so fucking cute. "So? I have plenty of experience, yeah, but I'm not a mind reader. I have to pay attention to my partner if I want to figure out what she wants."

"Pay attention how?"

I need to steer the conversation to something else. To something that won't make me hard. At the very least, I need to grab a pillow for my lap.

But I want her to know this.

She needs to know this.

I don't want her with some idiotic college freshman who doesn't know where the clitoris is. Who thinks his dick is so magic he doesn't have to warm her up. Or finish her off.

Who treats her orgasm like an afterthought. Or an obligation.

Fuck, I hate this asshole so much and he doesn't even exist.

Daisy deserves the best.

She deserves a guy who asks her what she wants, who listens, who reads her like a fucking book.

The way her breath hitches as he goes left.

The way her nails punch as he goes right.

The way—

"Holden? Are you okay?"

Fuck me. There's no way to have this conversation

without getting explicit. And there's no way to get explicit without blood flowing south.

But fuck it.

There are worse things than my cock demanding attention.

"You groan when you like your drink," I say.

Her cheeks flush. "You do too."

"It's human nature. You like something, you make it known."

Her eyes fix on me. "That's it?"

"At the end of the day, yeah. I'm not gonna say it's hard, cause—"

Her gaze goes right to my crotch.

"—even for me, that's a shitty joke."

She laughs anyway.

"It's not easy. But it's simple. And fun." I reach for her hand.

She places it in my palm.

"It's like this." I run my finger over the back of her hand. A medium pressure. Then a little harder. Softer.

There. Her eyelids flutter together.

Her breath hitches as my fingers brushes the space between her knuckles.

I try not to think about the implications. "You—some women are loud. They know what they want. Demand it even. Some women climb on top of me, pull my jeans to my knees, take over."

"Is that what you like?"

"I like everything."

"Everything?"

"Most things." I force my eyes to her wrist. "It's not about coming for me. I have a hand. I can fuck myself anytime I want. I'm pretty good at it."

"A lot of practice?"

"Yeah."

"Do you..." She watches my finger glide over her skin. "What is it about, then?"

"It's about figuring out what someone likes. Making them come." My balls tighten. "Most women are like you. Shy. They don't know what they want. Or they aren't ready to say. So I read their bodies. Try different pressure." I make my touch lighter.

Her breath hitches.

"Different patterns." I try circles. Zigzags. Back and forth.

"Oh."

"Speeds." I do a faster circle. "Places." I run my fingers over her knuckles. "I watch her, to see what she likes, where she needs me."

"Oh."

"Most women know they touch themselves. But they don't know how to translate that into *put your head right here*."

Her eyes go wide. "You do that with—"

"Of course."

"Are you... with a lot of people?"

"Not a lot."

"You don't like it?" Her voice is nervous.

"Fuck no. I love it."

"Is it..." She looks toward the stairs. The showers are off now. There are footsteps. And some music. Oliver's. But the space is quiet. "Why don't you do it a lot?"

"It's personal."

"And women—" she nods to my crotch. "Do you have them—"

"I don't *have* women do anything. It's about what we both want."

"Oh."

"But you... want that?"

Fuck, her lips are pink. Her eyes are wide. Her hair is falling over her cheeks.

It's impossible to picture anything else.

Daisy sliding out of her chair. On her knees. Hands on my swimsuit, tongue sliding over her lips, eyes on fire.

Her mouth around my cock.

Me pinning her to the couch. Pushing her bikini bottom aside. Tasting every inch of her.

"What?" I blink. Stare at the sunset. Anything to distract me.

"Do you... of course you do. All guys do. The guys at my school, God the way they'd talk... it's like they expect women to just do that. Just because they're so amazing."

"They're just posturing," I say. "And stupid. Don't hang out with a guy like that."

"I know."

"Or a guy who... If you're into that, go for it. And if you like it rough, guys ordering you around, calling you awful things, whatever. It's cool if you like that. But if a guy does it without asking, he's a fucking asshole."

Surprise streaks her expression. "Being called... what?"

Fuck, that's a long list. "It's a wild world out there, kid."

"Yeah, but... specifically? The top three."

"Slut is a big one. Cum-slut too."

"But... why? How..."

"It's normal dirty talk."

She shakes her head *no way*.

"Yeah, *baby, on your knees. Take it. You're a slut for my cock, aren't you?*"

She goes pale. "People are into that?"

"Yeah." I bring the tea to her hands.

She stares at the mug, dumbstruck. Nods. Takes a sip. "I thought—"

"You don't watch porn?"

"Luna has shown me some stuff. But it's more… nice, I guess."

"It's okay to like nice. Or mean. Or dirty. Whatever. You'll figure it out once you meet someone you trust."

"Right."

"And, hey, if you want a guy to call you a cum-slut, I won't judge."

She shakes her head *no way*.

"Don't knock it till you try it."

Her laugh dissolves the tension in her shoulders. "I can cross that off the list."

"But what about *slut for my cock*?"

Her eyes light up with her smile. "I'll consider it."

"Could put it in your next—what do you write anyway?"

"Uh-uh. We're not talking about that."

"You'd rather talk about which degrading things you'd like to be called?"

"How about which… non-degrading things I'd like to be called?"

"I swear to fucking God," a loud voice interrupts us. "I did not just hear the words 'cum-slut.'" Oliver steps into the staircase. Looks down at us. "When did you get in?"

"Half an hour, maybe." Daisy nods *hey*. "We made tea. But, we drank it."

He laughs. "I'm good, thanks." He moves down the stairs.

She turns to me. "We can pick this up later."

I nod *yeah* even though I know the conversation is going to kill me.

Chapter Sixteen

DAISY

I cross and uncross my legs. Wrap my fingers around my chai latte. Take a long sip.

It's good. Sweet, spicy, robust. But it's not as good as the one Holden made.

He knows the steps by heart. Knows how to close his eyes and feel it. I guess that shouldn't be surprising. That's basically Holden.

My lipstick stains the mug. Pink on white. They fit. Two light colors. Ones that fade into the background.

I shouldn't complain about fair skin and blond hair. Yes, the whole *I burn if a ray of sun touches me* thing is troubling. As is increased melanoma risk. But there are plenty of advantages to my complexion.

Guys go apeshit for blondes. Especially for natural blondes. Luna's always been a knockout with plenty of male attention. But when she went platinum?

She's swimming in men. Not that it's a good thing. Half the guys are assholes. They're more aggressive. I guess that nearly white hair is a homing beacon. Light bounces off her beautiful locks. Makes her even more luminous.

She's just like that. So bright her darkness looks even darker. Or maybe her darkness is so dark her brightness looks even lighter.

She's been through a lot of shit. A lot of shit that made her disconnect, write off intimate attachments to men, push away anyone who hurt her.

But she's not always hard angles. She's soft with me. Sweet. Caring even.

And she's Luna. She's upstairs, blow drying her hair (she had to redo her toner, so it would stay silver-blond. She's not shy about discussing the great effort that goes into staying platinum. Sun, salt water, and chlorine are all her enemy).

I can't complain. She spent an hour fixing my hair and makeup. If she'd left me to fend for myself, she'd already be ready—the girl is a pro with makeup and a curling wand.

She did a great job too. I look beautiful. And like me. Like some version of me who's ready to dance with a handsome stranger.

Or at least leave my pink lipstick on a cocktail glass.

Not, a, uh…

Ahem.

I take another sip of chai. Close my eyes. Let thoughts of Holden fill my head.

He and Oliver are in the kitchen, fixing cocktails, laughing over something. They're always laughing. It's the only time Oliver is all smiles, actually.

I can't say I blame him.

There's something about the trouble making tattoo artist. He's just—

His laugh bounces around the room. It's different than my brother's. Light. Easy.

Full. So full it might burst.

I picture him next to me, looking up at me with those bright eyes, running his fingers over my hand. Then up my arm, along my shoulder, over the neckline of my dress.

Beneath it.

Fuck, I—

I hooked up with guys before my eating disorder took over. Freshman and sophomore year. When I still believed I could feel good. That my body was imperfect but worthy of pleasure. Before I realized I could seize control of my fucked-up life by controlling what I consumed.

My memories are fuzzy.

A kiss during a game of Truth or Dare.

A close dance at homecoming.

A make-out session on the couch, at a friend's party. Hands under my dress. The heat of fabric against my skin. The feeling of other people watching. The danger of getting caught.

The taste of rum and coke. Cold hands on my skin. Hardness between my thighs. Soft lips on my neck.

I always win games of Never Have I Ever. I've only been to second base. I'm so inexperienced I call it second base.

And that was all before.

I'm a different person now.

Sure, I'm not plagued by that same need to control every-thing that goes into my body. To prove my worth by eating less. By seeing smaller numbers on the scale. By shrinking.

I'm not in the throes anymore.

But I'm not brimming with self-worth. Or self-accep-tance. Or love.

I'm okay.

Just okay.

Always okay.

Not like Holden, with his hearty laugh and his bright eyes and his lust for making strangers come.

My sex clenches at the thought of his hands on my skin. His lips on my lips. His cock between my legs.

It's all I've been thinking about, honestly. Even as I ate a simple dinner with my brother—and Luna and Holden. As I touched myself in the shower. As I dressed. Chatted all through Luna fixing my hair and makeup.

This tea makes me think of him. The sweetness of cinnamon. Do his lips still taste like the spice?

God, I want to know.

I want to know everything.

"Hey." Holden's voice flows into my ears. His footsteps move closer.

My eyes flutter open.

"You look good." He gives me a slow once-over. Does nothing to hide his interest.

"Thanks."

"New dress?" He offers his hand. Motions *let's go*.

I motion to my chai. *Almost done*. "It is."

"Looks good. Short." His gaze flits to my thighs for a second, then it's back on my eyes. "Gonna irritate the fuck out of Oliver."

"Oliver can go fuck himself."

Holden chuckles. "Have you ever told him that?"

"Not in so many words."

"Have you ever told anyone to go fuck themselves?"

I shake my head.

"They might do it."

"Oh?"

"If you told me, I'd promise to do it."

My cheeks flush.

"Maybe offer to send you a picture. If you were interested." He sits next to me. "Well, sometime after midnight."

"Right." I wrap my fingers around my mug. Take a long sip. Let out a soft sigh. "It's not as good as yours but—"

"The time difference is fucking with me too." His fingers brush mine as he takes the mug. He takes a greedy sip. Lets out a deep moan. "Fuck, that is good."

"Yeah?"

He nods *hell yeah*.

"You know, I've heard you say that before. The thing about sending a picture of your *ahem* solo session. You've said that to Oliver a ton of times."

He chuckles. "Is my material stale?"

"It might be."

He turns his body toward mine. Offers something in his hand. "Got this for you." He places a bar of chocolate in my hands. It's seventy percent. The one I loved at the store.

"Thanks."

"Think it melted in my pocket."

"It was in your pants?"

"That a problem?"

God no. Just tell me how I can become this chocolate bar. I want to get in your pants. Do adults say that? Or does it make it even more obvious I'm a naïve virgin? "No."

"Still have this." He pulls the *All You Need is Love and Chocolate* card from his back pocket. "Want one for your purse?" He motions to my tiny silver bag.

It complements my tight red dress. Okay, it's actually Luna's tight red dress. An old one that doesn't fit her anymore.

But, hey, it fits me. And it has enough elastic it's comfortable. Comfortable enough it doesn't fill my head with *oh God, am I too much* thoughts.

And I—

Well, like I said. I'm okay. I'm healthy. But I'm not recovered.

I'm not sure how recovered anyone is, really. Society is diametrically opposed to recovery. Every other ad is for some diet product. Selling some idea that their yogurt, ice cream, cookie, whatever is guilt free. That "normal" dessert should be guilt-inducing.

Or it's an ad for the gym. Something about how people with enough willpower will push through the pain.

A diet product to help women shrink.

They work for men too, but it's always about women making themselves smaller, taking up less space, proving their worth and purity by eschewing things that bring them pleasure.

I understand all of that, intellectually. But I still panic when my jeans are too tight. Or when I can't control what goes on my plate. Or—

God, I'm tired just thinking about it.

I want a night where this isn't in my head. Where I let go.

Where I believe I'm enough.

How does anyone believe that?

I repeat the mantra every day. I have stickers on my mirror, reflecting the message back to me, but it doesn't sink into my head.

Despite the months of therapy, the anti-depressants, the attempts to embrace intuitive eating and body positivity—

It's always there, at the back of my head, this sense that

I could get back into control. That I'll lose control if I give in to too many temptations.

"Daisy?" Holden's fingers brush my wrist. "You want one of these?" He holds up the foil packet.

I shake my head. "I have some already." I unzip my purse. Show off the condoms inside. The ones Dad bought me. "Though… you saw my dad hand these over."

He chuckles. "Yeah. He's just worried about you."

"Why is everyone so fixated on my sex life?"

"You don't want me asking?"

"Well…"

"'Cause I can stop. If you don't want my—"

"No, I mean… um… thank you. I will take that, actually." My fingers brush his as I take the condom.

His eyes meet mine.

An electric current passes between us. It's like he's handing me a condom and ordering me to slide it over his cock.

Like he's about to pin me to the bed, slide my panties to my knees, drive deep into me.

Fuck, that's so hot.

He's so—

Ahem. "Thank you." I drop the foil packet in my purse. "That will be—"

"Delicious?"

"I guess we'll see." My gaze shifts toward the kitchen. Most of it is behind a wall. I can only see the open doorframe—there's no door, just a frame. The clean white fridge.

I can't see Oliver.

He can't see me.

Can't hear me over the music. The Bluetooth speaker is playing Lorde's latest album. My favorite. And Luna's favorite. She's the one who introduced me.

God, I love this song. Maybe if I focus all my attention on the chorus, I can ask this without dying of embarrassment.

I lean a little closer. So I can whisper. "Do people actually do that?"

"Do what?"

"Use condoms for—" I nod in the general direction of his thighs.

"For oral?"

"Yeah." My cheeks flame. "Luna told me... well, she says that it's safer to use a condom. But most people don't. Guys aren't into it. They'd rather just... not."

Holden chuckles. "Don't know about that."

"Oh?"

"Don't know if many guys would turn down a blow job, condom or no condom."

"Oh." I try to focus on Lorde's vocals, but all I can hear is Holden's steady breath.

"But women have told me they don't like using them. They don't like the taste of latex. Even if it's chocolate flavored."

"Right." I nod like I know this.

"What did your dad say?"

I shake my head. "It was too horrifying to remember."

"I know what you mean. When I was thirteen, my dad sat me down, gave me the talk."

"Really?"

"Yeah. Forest had been lecturing me for years. Before I had any interest in sex. When I still thought girls had cooties."

"I guess they do. It's just they're actually STDs," I say.

He laughs. "Yeah, he used that one."

"Do you worry about it?"

"No. I'm religious about using condoms now. And I get tested regularly."

"Have you ever—"

"Yeah. When I was younger. And more casual about using protection." His eyes meet mine. "There's nothing to be embarrassed about."

"I'm not."

"It *is* awkward. It's weird, asking a stranger about their STD status. Or telling someone to slow down, because there's no fucking way you're doing this without a condom."

"But you… do oral without a condom?" Oh my God, I'm going to die of embarrassment.

"Only if I'm in a more monogamous thing."

"You do monogamous things?" That's hard to believe. Encouraging. And horrible. It's awful, imagining Holden with a stranger. Imagining her hands on his skin and her name on his lips.

But him keeping someone around? Needing her? Loving her?

My stomach twists.

I force my gaze to the kitchen. It's still quiet. I guess Oliver is still fixing cocktails.

He has this idea that I'll taste all the classics. Or at least all the ones he can make here. So I know what I like.

It's not a bad idea.

Not that different than what Holden is—

Well, he's not offering it. But maybe if I ask…

God, there's no way I can ask. Even if I wouldn't die of embarrassment—and I would—he's right. It would ruin his friendship with Oliver. And I'm not doing that to either of them.

"Fuck buddies," he says. "If I'm with a girl who gets that I'm not going to fall for her."

"How can you be sure?"

"That she gets it?"

"That you won't fall for her?" I press my lips together. I don't know why I'm asking. I can't go for him. It doesn't matter if he'll fall for me.

But maybe… maybe I can have a taste.

A birthday kiss.

That isn't so bad.

My brother doesn't have to know.

"I just do," he says.

"But how?"

"Some things you just know. Like how you love to read. Or how Luna loves red lipstick."

"She does." I laugh.

"Hey!" Oliver's voice booms. "You ready for this?"

No, but I guess I can't say *I'd rather keep flirting with Holden. Am I even flirting with Holden? Or is this more of a conversation.*

"We'll be there in a sec," Holden calls.

Oliver makes that *mm-hmm* noise.

Holden stands. Offers me his hand. "Your lipstick is going to wear off."

"Huh?"

"On the cocktail glass."

"Right." I take his hand.

"Did Luna do your makeup?"

I nod *yeah*. Take his hand. Let him pull me up. "Is it too much?"

"No. You look beautiful. Grown-up."

"Yeah?"

He nods *yeah*.

I know he isn't saying *you look old enough to be in my bed.* But I let the thought linger anyway.

Chapter Seventeen

DAISY

The white counter top is covered in booze.

Rows of liquor in the back. Liqueurs and mixers in the middle. A bowl of citrus, a jar of maraschino cherries, a peeler, three bottles of bitters, five pounds of ice.

And, sitting in the front, a dozen cocktails. Some light, almost clear. Some fizzy. Some a deep amber. And one artificially green concoction.

"Where do you want to start?" Oliver slides his arm around my shoulder. Adopts his usual paternal stance. *I've got this. Don't argue.*

And, well, I can't. My brother is very good at a few things. Tattoos. Avoiding honest conversations with our father. And drinking.

"Fuck." Holden shoots my brother a *really* look. "Are you trying to give her alcohol poisoning?"

"Taste as many as you want, Daisy." Oliver releases me. Motions to the left side of the row. "I arranged them most bitter, to most sweet."

"Give me the one on the right." Holden laughs. "You know I can't take bitterness."

"How'd you deal with your brother for so long?" he teases.

Holden just laughs. "That was easy. It was being friends with Chase—"

"He and Ariel seem really happy." I turn to Holden. "What's it like, having a niece? She's so cute."

"Don't get ideas," Oliver says. "You're too young."

Does he really think I'm going to jump to getting pregnant because I saw a cute kid? I'm not sure I ever want kids. I certainly don't want any now. It's hard enough taking care of myself. "I'm not even—what time is it?"

Oliver pulls out his cell. Brandishes the time. A quarter to eleven.

God is it really that late? My mind is racing—from the caffeine and the proximity of the guy who drives me wild.

My body is buzzing. But there's an exhaustion under all that energy.

An incoming crash.

It's something, that I can feel that. That I'm in touch with my body enough to know. That I'm not running on caffeine and self-loathing.

More caffeine and desire.

It's a lot better than self-loathing.

It's so much better.

"All you need is a sip," Oliver says.

"Really? I'm allowed even though it's not midnight?" I ask.

"I'll make an exception. For your birthday." He picks up the drink on the right. Hands it to me. "You're already eighteen in London."

Holden chuckles *okay, sure*.

Neither of us calls out my brother's hypocrisy. He

drinks—and fucks—constantly, but he tries to shield me from that.

If he's going to let up on the over-protective thing for one night, I'm not going to call him on it.

I take the drink. It's something clear, in a martini glass, with a lemon rind hanging off the edge.

All these drinks are presented well.

I guess Oliver *is* an artist. Maybe it's not about his love of alcohol. Maybe he's going all out. For my birthday.

It's possible.

"Dry martini," he says. "With lemon. Not olive." He turns to Holden. "She hates olives. Ironic, huh?"

"Dunno. She's not crazy about you," Holden says.

Oliver pushes him playfully.

He pushes back.

They laugh. It's big. Hearty. Happy. Real.

Okay, here goes nothing. I hold up the glass. Toast to no one. Take a small sip.

Oh my God.

It's so strong. Almost all alcohol. Gin, I think. Rubbing alcohol and something with pine.

Then lemon.

It's astringent. Like over steeped tea.

Holden laughs. "It's too much, huh?"

It's not terrible. And, no doubt, it's light in sugar. A good choice if panic hits me. If that voice starts whispering *are you really going to drink all those calories? You have to fix that.*

I'm not letting that voice in tonight.

Either, I'm knocking her out with booze. Or I'm sticking with drinks that won't send me into panic mode.

Rum and diet really isn't that bad.

I set the drink down. "Not my favorite."

Oliver takes the glass. Takes a sip. "You can't toast alone."

I guess that's reasonable.

"Should I call Luna?" he asks.

"No." I shake my head. "If she's doing her makeup—"

Oliver chuckles knowingly. "Can't complain about the results." His eyes fill with something—

Ew. "Don't," I say.

He nods *of course not*. Takes another sip. Motions to the second drink. "This is a gimlet. Lime and vodka. A lot like that first drink. But a little sweeter."

"Okay," I say.

"If you want something different." He taps the third glass. "An old-fashioned. Quality varies. It can be fucking bliss or total shit."

Holden nods *true*. "Since you made it, I'm sure it's the latter."

"Never get it as a well drink. Fuck, the places we're going tonight, you're gonna want to keep it simple. Straight booze or booze and one mixer." He picks up the drink. Places it in my hands. "I made it pretty dry. But I can add some simple syrup if it's too much."

"When did you—" I take the drink. Swallow my question. Do I really want details about Oliver's skill in fixing drinks? He did work as a bartender for a hot second. Right after he turned twenty-one.

It wasn't that long ago, but—

Tonight isn't about that anyway. I know, better than anyone, that you can't help someone until they're ready to accept it.

I hold up my drink to toast.

Oliver clinks glasses with me.

I take a long sip. Swallow hard. This one is strong too. A little less strong. With more sweetness, more richness, a hint of orange. "Shit."

"You like it?" His eyes light up. "Yeah?"

"I do. But it's... a lot." I take another sip. A smaller one. There's something appealing about the rich flavor. It's almost spicy. Like tea.

"Try this." He finishes his martini. Places the glass on the counter. Picks up another drink.

It's a shade darker, and it's in a different glass. One with a round bottom. Like something a super villain sips as he recounts an evil plan.

It looks grown-up. Sophisticated even.

Good.

It has a cherry too. Only the cherry is on top. The cherry is waiting for me.

Oliver hands me the drink. Takes the other. Gives it to Holden.

Holden slips his finger into the glass. Pulls out the cherry. Tosses it into his mouth.

Fuck, I know it doesn't mean anything, that it's just his sweet tooth. But my head still screams *Holden wants a cherry. He wants to pop my cherry. He wants to take my virginity.*

He wants to be my first.

He could be my first time.

The perfect first time.

What a beautiful thought. His hands on my thighs. His nails on my skin. His lips on my clit.

Woah.

I don't think about *that*. Not usually. Even when I touch myself, it's vague thoughts of our bodies joining. Or memories of hands on my chest. A scene in a sexy movie. (I don't really like the porn Luna sends me. It's just sooo much. Not that she pushes. I ask).

Maybe these drinks are working.

Or maybe it's Holden.

I hold up my glass.

Oliver and Holden clink.

147

I take a long sip.

Mmm. That's good. It has the faint taste of booze, but it's mostly a perfect blend of sweet richness, spice, and cherry.

I take another sip. Let the drink warm my throat and chest.

"I like this one," I say.

Oliver nods *I know*.

Holden reaches for my hand. "Slow down, kid. You've got more."

"If you know what you like, you know." He picks up another drink. A fizzy one with honey. "Never thought you were a Manhattan girl."

"Does that mean something?" I ask.

"No. Just thought you'd stick to clear spirits." He offers me the glass. "You can stick with what you like. Or try this."

"What is it?" I ask.

"Kentucky mule. Bourbon and ginger beer. I have one with vodka too," he says.

I take the glass. Take a small sip. It is good. Like an even sweeter, even spicier ginger ale. I can't taste the booze. At all. "This one is dangerous." I offer it to Holden.

"He's not gonna give that back," Oliver says. "It's his drink."

"Oh." Suddenly, I want every sip. I want to taste like his lips. But I already know it's a bad idea. Not just because it's so sweet and rich I can't taste the alcohol.

Because my head is saying *are you really drinking all that sugar?*

"Go for it." My fingers brush his as I hand it over.

Holden takes a sip. Lets out a loud sigh. "You're gonna kill someone with this." He turns to the sound of footsteps. Toasts to Luna as she steps into the kitchen.

"Fuck, you look good." Oliver's jaw nearly drops.

She does. She's channeling Marilyn Monroe, with her hair in pin curls, her lips painted red, her white halter dress showing off her strong shoulders.

She's wearing hot pink sandals, and she's way taller than the late icon, but she's still rocking the vibe.

Though—

I guess I worry about her too. The actual Marilyn Monroe wasn't a carefree fashion slash sex goddess. She was a troubled woman who died of a drug overdose.

My best friend does well. She certainly doesn't drink as much as my brother does. But still...

I guess worrying is in my nature.

"I know." She blows him a kiss. Shoots Holden a wink. "Is that for me?"

"You have a favorite cocktail?" he asks.

"A strong one. Oliver made all these, so—" *of course they all fit the bill.*

"What do you think, kid?" Holden turns to me. "Which one are you holding onto?" He holds up the Kentucky mule. "This one is dangerous. Sweet enough you'll blink and be drunk."

"Now, I have to try." She shoots me an *are you okay* look.

I nod *yeah*.

She takes the drink. Takes a long sip. Lets out a soft moan. "That is good. Should we rock, paper, scissors for who keeps it?" She turns her back to the boys. Mouths *give me a sec*.

I nod *sure*. "Let's see."

We set our drinks on the counter.

She pulls me to the edge of the room. Holds her hand into a fist. Pretends to go through the whole *one, two, three* count. "You're blushing."

"I am not."

She nods *you are too*. "You want me to reapply your lipstick now?" She says it loudly, so the guys will hear.

They make that guy *are you really taking more time for makeup* groan, but they nod *sure*. Go back to laughing over something.

God, I can't remember the last time Oliver laughed this much. Is it because he's drunk? Or is it having his best friend around?

"Did I give you enough time alone with him?" She pulls a tube of lipstick from her purse. Checks the shade. Tosses it back.

"You took forever on purpose?"

"Of course." She tests another tube. Nods *ahhah*. "You're beaming."

"I'm not."

She nods *you are*. Motions for me to close my mouth and pout.

I do.

She takes advantage of my temporary silence. "If you want, I can keep Oliver distracted. Make sure you get some time to dance. To… do more than dance, maybe?"

"Oh my—"

"Mouth closed." She applies the lipstick carefully. "I'm not saying you need to drag him to your bed. Though you should. But it would be nice, if you had an hour here, alone with him." She studies her work. "Press together."

I do. "It would be nice."

"Text me if you need more time."

"More time for what—"

"You'll know what." She applies one more coat of lipstick. Drops the tube in her purse. "Is it okay?" She motions to the drinks.

I'm not sure if she's asking about my tolerance for alcohol or my tolerance for going off my routine.

Either way, it is.

It has to be.

I nod.

She smiles *good*. Turns back to the guys. "Where's our next drink?"

"Who's getting that one?" Holden asks.

"You." She hands it to him. "Daisy wants a taste of everything." Her voice gets low. Heady.

I guess Oliver is distracted enough by the thought of sex with Luna. He doesn't notice the implication.

Maybe it's something about the forbidden. He wouldn't touch her. He knows it would mess things up.

Knowing you can't have something—

There is something about letting desire consume you.

I want that again. To have that in a healthy way. I want a craving I can sate.

I want Holden. "She's right. I want a taste of everything."

"You sure?" he asks. "I'm buying you a drink tonight."

"Me too," Holden says.

"You know I am," Luna says. "But I won't cry if you want one that's non-alcoholic. Even though it totally defeats the point of this trip."

"I'm not here for that," I say.

"Really?" She raises a brow. "Because I remember you wrote off my idea of Hawaii. Even though the weather is perfect this time of year."

"Is weather ever bad in Hawaii?" It's like Southern California. Always nice.

"It rains," she says. Like a light drizzle is going to ruin the bliss of seventy-five and slightly humid. Or make the ocean less inviting.

"It was because of price, I swear." Really. I'd love to be in Hawaii. But one night in Hawaii, in two hotel rooms, would be nearly as much as our entire stay in this Airbnb.

She nods *uhuh*. "Lie to your brother, but I know the truth. You're here so you can finally have your fix." She winks. *And by fix, I totally mean Holden's dick.*

No comment.

We move on to the next drink. A not at all sweet mix of gin, lime, and soda water.

Then a refreshing mix of grapefruit, soda, tequila, and lime.

A similar drink, only with Mezcal. Apparently, that's some super strong version of tequila.

The final drink is a margarita. A real one, with scratch lime and a hint of agave.

Thank God Oliver is fixing all these. He uses as little sugar as possible.

But, fuck, this is tart. Way too tart for me. I let Oliver drink that one.

Sip the mix of grapefruit, soda, and lime. It's such a perfect blend that I forget the tequila is there.

I barely taste it.

We all hold up our glasses. Clink them together.

"To Daisy's birthday," Oliver says.

"To finally being legal," Luna says.

I laugh as I tap my glass to hers. "To finally being legal."

Chapter Eighteen

HOLDEN

We spend fifteen minutes on the beach, watching the waves crash into the sand, joking about nothing, counting down the minutes to Daisy's birthday.

She looks gorgeous in her red dress. It's bright for her. Tighter than what she normally wears.

She doesn't look quite like herself.

No, that's not it.

She looks like a different version of herself.

A grown-up.

It's impossible to see anything else.

Between the soft waves falling at her shoulders, the snug dress, the subtle makeup—

She looks so much the girl I saw this morning. Fuck, the dress is the same color. But there's something else. Some change.

Something that screams *I'm an adult woman with desires of my own.*

Maybe it's the moonlight—it casts her in an angelic glow, bounces off her light hair and fair skin.

Maybe it's the booze—I had most of three cocktails and those are Oliver pours. They're strong.

Maybe it's my cock getting demanding.

Or maybe it's something else. Something we shared today. Something that's all her.

She squeezes my hand as she climbs the rocks to the sand.

Oliver pulls out his cell. Opens the clock app. Counts down the seconds to her birthday.

Ten, nine, eight—

She moves closer.

Seven, six, five—

He readies a bottle of champagne.

Four, three, two—

Luna squeals.

One.

At once, we all say, "happy birthday."

The cork goes flying. Foam spills from the bottle. Fills my head with way too many ideas.

Luna holds up the champagne flutes. Helps Oliver fill them.

Then we all toast again.

Now, it's official.

It's possible.

I'm no longer a sick fuck for wanting her.

Just a guy who knows a beautiful woman when he sees one.

Who wants a sweet, innocent angel who asks him questions about using condoms during blow jobs.

Fuck, the thought of some asshole ordering her onto her knees—

I hate that fucker.

I have to keep her away from him.

Sure, it's not going to be me. But it's not going to be

some jerk who doesn't deserve her either.

———

THERE'S NO LINE AT OUR DESTINATION—THE ONLY straight club in town. We sail through the ID check. The bouncer even nods *happy birthday* to Daisy.

Inside, it's crowded. Loud. Packed with dancing people. It's too dark. I can't tell if this place is for tourists or locals. I guess it doesn't matter.

A warm body is a warm body.

A good song is a good song.

A fuck is a fuck.

Oliver motions to me. "Usual?"

I nod *yeah*.

Luna whispers her drink in his ear.

He nearly blushes. Fuck, he's so into her. Which is such a bad idea. But it's not like I can talk.

He takes Daisy straight to the bar.

Luna wraps her fingers around my wrist. Leads me to a booth in the corner.

It's not quiet, but it's a little more private.

She sits. Motions for me to sit. When I do, she leans close enough to whisper. "You want to get her alone?"

"Huh?"

"Tonight. I can distract Ollie."

"You call him Ollie?"

"Do you want it or not?"

I pull back so I can look her in the eyes.

Her expression is serious. Not upset. Just to the point. "You want to bone him?"

"No comment." Her laugh brightens her light eyes.

"Would you?"

"No." She looks to the bar. It's hard to see Daisy and

Oliver through the crowd, but he's tall enough he stands out. "She's my best friend." Her gaze shifts to me. "You?"

"Same."

"Too bad."

I arch a brow.

"What? Am I supposed to care more about your friend-ship than my best friend?"

"You really—"

"You know that she likes you. You're obvious about it," she says. "And, well… I don't know why, but I trust you."

"You do?"

"With her." She nods. "She's been through a lot."

"I know."

Her brow furrows. "No… you don't. But that's not mine to tell." Her red lips press together. "Be careful with her."

"Of course."

"Really, Holden. I know you're normally with girls who get your whole player thing. I know how that works. I get it. But no matter what Daisy says, she won't. She's too into you. She'll tell you she understands, but… don't break her heart, okay?"

"I wouldn't."

Incredulity spreads over her expression. "I just…"

"Make sure he doesn't get too drunk, okay?"

She shoots me a *really*.

"If you're gonna hang out with him, you have to know—"

"I'm not an idiot." Her eyes fix on me. Examine me. Like she's looking for some deep truth about the situation. She must find it, because she relaxes. Turns to the bar. "He can hold his liquor."

"Normally."

"I'll make sure he gets home."

"Thanks." I offer my hand.

She looks at me funny, but she still shakes.

Oliver and Daisy cut through the crowd.

"You two conspiring?" Oliver asks.

"We are." She turns to Daisy. "On who gets to dance with you first." She offers her hand. "I called dibs."

Daisy smiles. Takes her best friend's hand. "After you."

"What about——" Oliver motions to her drink.

"Hold it for me." She hands him the cocktail.

He shakes his head *what a waste*. "She barely had a sip." He sits on the bench, next to me. "Fuck, this music is bad."

"It is." I take my Kentucky mule. Watch Luna lead Daisy into the crowd.

They get close, but only friend close.

Daisy shifts her hips. Throws her arms over her head. Loses herself in the music.

It's fucking beautiful.

It's fucking everything.

Chapter Nineteen

DAISY

The music booms with a steady bass. *Thump. Thump. Thump.*

At this point, I'm pretty damn good at finding the beat. I've always loved music. Loved letting it wash over me, letting the melody pluck my heartstrings, letting the bass sink into my bones.

I don't know anything about scales, half-steps, keys, rhythms. But I know feeling a song in my heart.

I know poring over lyrics, dissecting every ounce of meaning.

During inpatient treatment, music was one of the only things that stayed mine. There was no privacy. I shared a room, a room with a window in the door. I had to spill my thoughts in group therapy sessions.

I had to stare at my family during visiting hours, trying to hold my tongue. To keep the *fuck you for putting me here* to myself.

Even once I accepted it, that I needed to be there, I hated seeing them. Their eyes were so full of pity. They spoke with such hushed tones. Like they were afraid anything above a whisper would break me.

My eating disorder was the one thing that was mine.

And I lost that.

All I had was music.

Sure, I poured every thought into my journal. But I never trusted it to keep my secrets hidden. Someone could find it. Rip it away from me. Use it as evidence that I needed to stay locked away longer.

Music was different.

I lost my control. I felt it in my heart, my body, my soul.

It was the only thing I felt in my body.

Even now—

God, it feels so right, letting a song wash over me. Letting my hips find the beat. Letting my body tune into the rhythm.

I understood the lyrics. I knew how to pick them apart. Hell, I willed them to wash over me. To save me. To help me understand and feel understood.

And, sometimes, I coveted the pain on display. I wished my hurt could be that pretty.

It's practically a cliché at this point, listening to Amy Winehouse, simultaneously wishing for her ability to bare her soul. And her predisposition for self-destruction. Bulimia and alcoholism. And an early death via alcohol poisoning.

The chanteuse had it all. At least according to my still sick brain.

I don't know when it switched. There wasn't one day, really. There wasn't a carrot dangling on a stick. It wasn't even the fear of disappointing my family. I wasn't there yet. I couldn't see that they loved me. That they wanted me to be okay. That I deserved that love.

I can't even say why I was so sick.

It just got easier. I hated myself less. Saw more of the ugliness for what it was.

I was so fucking tired. But it's not like there was any way to rest. Healing was hard. Staying sick was hard.

Everything was hard.

Now—

"You need another drink?" Luna leans close enough to whisper. She turns me around. Looks into my eyes. "Or we can talk."

No. I'm good. I can be good.

I just have to focus on the music.

I shake my head. Close my eyes. Let the rhythm wash over me.

My hips catch the beat. Then my chest. Shoulders. Arms.

"I'm good." I can be good. I can be normal. For one fucking night, I can be normal.

Her expression streaks with concern for a moment, then she blinks and it's gone. "Okay. Then it's dancing." She takes my hand. "Are you up to finding a hottie?"

"I have you."

She laughs. "Flattering. But you know what I mean."

"I'm up to it." That was always a part of it. My therapist thinks I starved myself so I could stay a girl forever. So I could deny my curves, my sexuality, my desire for satisfaction.

I guess she's part right. It was always about denying myself satisfaction. About proving myself worthy. Worthy of what, I'm not sure. Existing, I guess.

She says that was all my depression talking. Now that I'm medicated and talking through my problems, I feel okay. Not great. Not amazing. Okay.

I'm not trying to disappear.

I'm not trying to shrink myself.

I'm not worried I'm not worthy.

But I'm still scared of that voice. Of relapsing. Of going into the world and finding it too much and running back to easy comfort.

I'm so tired of being tired. Of being scared. Of being chained.

Maybe my best friend is right. Maybe I need another drink. Maybe I'm too sober.

"Okay." I take her hand. "Drink first."

"Let's go." She cuts through the crowd to lead me to the bar. She bumps into a tall guy with sandy hair.

My brother. "Hey." He gives Luna a quick once-over. Looks to me. "You two good?"

"We're finding Daisy a dance partner," Luna says. "After another round."

Oliver nods *of course*. Hails the bartender. Orders four more drinks.

He turns back to the wall.

To Holden.

Motions *come here*.

The troublemaker jumps to his feet. He practically skips to us.

My heart thuds against my chest.

It means something, that I want him. That I'm actually thinking about taking him.

If I'm really ready to take off my clothes in front of him. To let him touch me. To feel all that pleasure.

That satisfaction in my body.

God, what is it like to feel that way without effort? To lose yourself in a kiss? A touch? A fuck?

I want that.

For one goddamn night, I want that.

My heartbeat picks up as he comes closer.

He stops at the bar just in time to pay for our drinks. He takes his. And mine.

His fingers brush mine as he hands it to me. "You're not venturing past your usual?"

Same rum and diet. "I know what I like.

He nods *fair enough*.

It's still strong. And cheap.

My throat burns.

My face flushes.

My chest warms.

It's not terrible. Just not great.

I take another sip. Then another.

Holden was right. I just need a few shots. Maybe I need his lessons too, but a few shots can't hurt.

Anything to make it easier to touch him. To feel this. To feel every ounce of my desire.

"We're trying to find a dance partner for Daisy." Luna motions to the room full of sweaty dancers. "Help us?"

His eyes meet mine. He raises a brow *you sure*.

I nod.

"What do you think?" Luna asks. "More cute? Or more sexy?"

"What's the difference?" I ask.

"Cute is the guy who will cuddle with you and watch Netflix," she says. "Sexy is a guy who will slip his hand under your dress."

"No," Oliver growls.

She laughs *okay, sure*. "It's just an example. But, sure, cute it is. If that's what you want, Daisy."

"Cute is good." Holden is good. But I can't say that in front of my brother.

She scans the room. Taps her chin like she's using every bit of her concentration. Stops on a guy at the other end of the bar.

He *is* cute. Dark hair. Blue eyes. Strong shoulders.

He's sitting with a tall, blond friend, drinking a beer, laughing over something.

Luna offers her hand. "I'll go with you. Be your wingman."

"I'm a better wingman," Holden says.

"You'll scare him." She takes my hand. Motions *let's go*.

I finish my drink. Place it in my brother's hand. Follow my best friend to the other side of the bar.

"You do think he's cute?" she asks.

"He is." He's muscular and tan. No tattoos. Not nearly as appealing as Holden. But still incredibly attractive.

"Follow my lead." She stops in front of the pair. Flashes both guys a million-dollar smile. "Hi."

Both of them turn toward her. Like she's the sun and they're a plant desperate for nourishment.

"My friend and I are looking to dance." She turns to the guy with dark hair. "Her name is Daisy."

"Hi." I offer my hand.

He hesitates. Offers his. "Mark."

I shake. It's not like with Holden. My body doesn't buzz. My heart doesn't pound. My sex doesn't clench.

But when I turn back to the troublemaker, when I watch his eyes fix on me—

Is he already jealous?

God, I want him jealous. It's ridiculous. I don't want that. I never want that. But I do.

"I have to be honest," Luna says. "I bet her a drink that you'd want to dance with me."

Mark's laugh is awkward.

"But here's the thing. It's her birthday. And she won't let me buy her a drink." Luna places her hand on my shoulder. Shoots these guys a sweet *please help my friend* look. "But she lives to gamble."

The other guy smiles. "You don't seem like the type."

"I know. That's how she wins. Sweet innocent blond on the outside, card shark on the inside." Luna nudges me toward the dark-haired guy. "Help me buy her a drink. Please?"

"Yeah. Sure." Mark offers his hand. "Want to dance?"

"Okay." I take his hand. Follow him onto the dance floor. Watch as Luna sits at the bar. Flirts with the tall guy.

He buys her a drink.

Of course.

She's an evil genius. And super charming. Guys are always into her.

She says that I'm no different. That guys are always looking at me. That, one day, I'll see it. And it will mean I'm at a hundred percent.

It's weird, her knowing. Better than when I kept it secret. It was such a heavy secret. It made the walls between me and everyone else so thick. So high. So impossible to scale.

I felt so alone.

But it needed to be mine. When I realized people knew—

I was so ashamed. So scared. It took a long time to realize that was okay. That it didn't mean I was fundamentally broken. Well, no more broken than anyone else.

We're all a little fucked up.

That's what Luna says.

She's not like Oliver. She doesn't hover. Or bring it up. Or watch me eat.

She makes sure we don't skip meals or listen to negative body-talk.

But she doesn't make it a thing.

She just… is.

And now I just am. Tonight, I just am. For one night, I just am.

I turn to the dark-haired guy. Mark. I sling my arms around his neck. Move in time with the music.

This is one place where my brain doesn't step in. Where I'm one with my body.

I focus on Mark. He's a little shorter than Holden. His eyes are darker. Less luminous.

He's not nearly as handsome. And he's completely without charm.

But he's cute enough.

Safe enough.

At least when it comes to heartbreak. Maybe he's an ax-murderer. But he's certainly not interesting enough to hurt my feelings.

"Is it just you and your friend?" he asks.

"And a few other friends." That's close enough to true.

He places his hands on my waist.

For a second, I cringe. Not because I'm worried I'm off somehow, that I'm unworthy of touch. Because it's weird, having a stranger's hand on my body.

It's not like in salsa class. It's different. More… presumptuous.

We dance through the song.

The next one is faster.

He leans closer.

His hands slip lower.

His breath hits my ear. "Is it really your birthday?"

"Yeah."

"What are you doing to celebrate?"

"Uh. This." I suck a breath through my nose. Focus on the rhythm. Try to ignore how foreign his hands feel.

It's not him. It's me.

This is normal dancing.

I can enjoy normal dancing.

I can enjoy one night of fun without being the girl who's still broken.

"We're going to a party after this," he says. "Good drinks. Nice view. A couple of poker games."

"Poker games?"

"You're a gambler, right?"

"Right." That's our story.

His laugh flows into my ear. "You're cute."

"Thanks." I think.

"There's privacy too." He pulls my body into his. "If that's what you're looking for."

"Oh."

His hands drip over my hips.

Then lower.

To my ass.

It's too much. Too far.

I jump back.

A hand curls around my upper arm. A strong one.

The grip is rough. Possessive.

"Hey." Holden's voice is just as rough as his touch. "Having fun?" He loosens his grip. Runs his thumb over my skin. It's like he's saying *I've got you*.

His body is right behind mine. So, so close to mine. So, so close to where it needs to be.

And this—

He's jealous.

He's rushing in to save me. Or maybe it's more than that. Maybe he's rushing in to stop someone else from touching me.

My heart thuds against my chest.

My veins buzz.

My sex clenches.

"Yeah." The dark-haired guy looks at Holden strangely.

"You one of Daisy's friends?"

"Yeah," he says. "We were gonna head out, actually."

"Us too," the dark-haired guy says, totally oblivious to the tension. "We're heading to a party. Good view. Free drinks. Poker."

Holden turns my body toward his. Stares into my eyes. "What do you think, kid? Want to go?"

God, there's something about the protective look in his eyes.

It sets me on fire.

I don't think.

I just nod *yes*.

Chapter Twenty

DAISY

"They're on their way." Holden slips his cell into his back pocket. He turns toward Mark—that's the dark-haired guy's name—and his friend Steve. Not the tall guy from inside. A different guy.

Steve is in board shorts and a tank top. Not club attire. But then every other person who steps out of the club is dressed for the beach.

Mmm, the beach. That's an idea.

Holden and I skinny dipping at the beach.

Holden and I naked.

Right now.

Holden—the actual dressed guy, not the one naked in my fantasies—moves closer. "You guys met in college, huh?"

Mark starts going on and on about their business 101 class. And how they all ended up at different companies with the same finance job.

He goes into great detail about his very uninteresting job.

"Sounds like what Ariel does." He turns to me. "Are you good at math, kid?"

"God no." I can't help but laugh. "It's my worst subject."

"What did you take last year?" He arches a brow *yeah right*.

"Calculus."

"You're bad at math but you took Calculus?"

I nod *yeah*.

"And you got, what, an A minus?"

"A B plus," I say.

He looks to the guys. *Ridiculous, huh?*

They just shrug.

"It was my worst grade." I ignore the guys. Focus on Holden. "And uh, I had to study a lot for that B plus. All the time."

"Calc was hard," Steve says. "I don't blame you."

"You in college?" Mark asks.

"Yeah." I will be. Soon. "Berkeley."

Holden looks at me curiously. Like he's examining my half-truth. But he doesn't call me on it.

"You too?" Mark asks.

"No." Holden shakes his head. He points to his arm.

The other guys stare at him with confusion. "You're an… arm model?"

I laugh. "You could be."

"Maybe Skye can help." He refers to his brother's girlfriend, who's a plus-sized model. And a photographer. She has a bajillion Instagram followers, and it's easy to see why.

She's really pretty. And she has perfect boobs. They're amazing and she's always showing them off in black lingerie. Or a black bikini. Or a black corset dress. (She wears a lot of black. And a lot of black makeup).

I guess that's a lot. Progress. I envy her body. There

isn't a single part of me squirming over the thought of being too much.

See.

Tonight is a good night. A night of freedom. Freedom from my brain.

"I can help." I pull my cell from my purse. Open the camera. Turn it toward him. It's too dark to see anything. I take a picture anyway.

He blinks at the flash. "Dammit, kid, warn me about that."

I show off the photos. It's terrible. He's squinting, his face twisted with discomfort.

But those tattooed arms.

Mmm. He's so sexy. I want him. And I want him to want me.

I want all the things. All the normal things. Not to prove a point. Because he's the sexiest man in the history of the world.

And I'm a woman. It's official.

"Want one of me?" One of the guys strikes a pose.

"Sure." I snap a picture of him. Then his friend.

They move closer to look at the photos. Stand behind me. Right behind me.

Holden's fingers curl around my wrist. He pulls my body into his.

My shoulder brushes his chest.

His arm slides around my waist.

My eyes meet his. God, he has such pretty eyes. That gorgeous shade of green. Those flecks of grey.

I stare up at him.

He stares down at me.

Mark and Steve talk about something.

A car horn honks.

"That's our ride," one of the guys says. "You two ready?"

"Yeah." Holden steps backward. Turns toward the car. An Uber. A normal sedan.

Small for the four of us.

No room for Oliver and Luna.

Where are they anyway?

"Give me a sec," Holden says.

The guys nod *sure*. One of them goes to catch the driver.

Holden taps a text. Looks up at me. "You sure you want to go?"

No. I want to stay here, on the boardwalk with him all night. It's beautiful. Warm. Romantic.

Private.

But that's not an option.

He isn't going to kiss me under the stars.

Or lay me on the sand.

Or slide his hand under my dress.

I have to soak this up while I have it. "We can leave if it's not fun."

He looks at me funny. "Since when do you go to strange parties?"

"Didn't you hear? I'm a card shark," I say.

He chuckles. "A what?"

"A gambler. According to Luna. Supposedly, I bet her that the guy would rather dance with me."

"And?"

"I guess she owes me a drink."

"Is that what we're betting?" His phone buzzes with a reply. "Oliver said he'll meet us there."

"Yeah?" I ask.

He nods *yeah*. "He's into Luna."

"I know."

"She into him?"

"She thinks he's hot, but she knows…"

"That it can't happen?"

"Well…" Yeah, but it's more—"he's not really good for her."

"Who said anything about good for her? Maybe she just wants his cock?"

My cheeks flame. "Please do not talk about my brother's cock."

"I won't. But you should know, he's supposed to be—"

"Oh my God—"

"Massive."

Please kill me now. "Stop."

"Not as big as me though."

My blush deepens. "How do you even know?"

"Rumors." He taps a reply. Returns his cell to his back pocket. "They're gonna get a 'snack' first."

"Oh." Maybe they are going to get a snack. Luna and Oliver both love street tacos. And this is the place to get them.

But what the hell is open this late? Besides the clubs, the Romantic Zone is quiet. A sleepy beach town.

Well, a sleepy beach town with a ton of bars. Some of them must have food.

"If you're sure—" He motions to the car *shall we*.

I take his hand. Let him lead me to the Uber.

The other guys climb in.

Holden insists on taking the middle seat. He's impossibly cramped in the tiny car.

His leg brushes mine. His jeans against my bare thigh.

God, it feels good. Like heaven.

And I…

I try to think of something else. Of anything else. But my head screams with *Holden's cock is massive*.

"It's fifteen minutes," one of the guys says.

I nod *okay*.

We ride over a bump.

Holden reaches out. Places his arm over my chest. To protect me.

He pulls it back. Looks at it like he's not sure how that happened. Like he's not sure what he's doing.

"Fuck." He presses one hand to the roof. "Think I had too many of Oliver's pours. These bumps are a lot."

"Yeah, it's tough. We've been here two weeks," one of the guys says. "We have a trick for it though."

"Oh?" I ask.

"Yeah, we play a game. I'm thinking… truth or dare," he says.

"Are you kidding?" Holden asks.

"No way." The guy shakes his head. "It's great."

"What kind of dares can you do in a moving car?" Holden asks.

"This." Steve motions to his friend. "Mark, truth or dare."

"Dare." Mark plays along.

"At the stoplight, roll down your window, tell the first cute girl you see you want to fuck her," he says.

"Creative." Holden rolls his eyes.

The other guys don't notice his sarcasm. They watch the car slow. Watch another car pull up next to it.

Lucky them, it's a car full of girls. Well, besides the male Uber driver. Is everyone here in an Uber?

He rolls down the window. Makes that *roll down, I have to talk* motion.

A cute Hispanic girl laughs. Rolls down the window. Blows him a kiss. "*Hola*."

"*Hola*." He winks at her then says something to her in Spanish.

She laughs.

He motions to the street. Then our car.

I don't catch his flirtation. Only the Spanish word for car.

"He's inviting her to the party," Holden says.

"You know Spanish?" I ask.

"Poco." He smiles, proud of himself.

God, his smile is so beautiful. And that pride. I want more of it. All of it. I want it directed at me. "Was that your best class in school?"

He shakes his head. "Art."

"Oh. Of course."

"You'd be surprised." He places his hand over mine. "I didn't like taking orders for a while."

"You?"

"Hard to believe, I know." His smile widens. "My first year, I'd do the opposite of the assignment. But my teacher loved it. The harder I tried to piss her off, the more she loved it." He chuckles. "She'd say *a real artist innovates. I'm proud of you, Mr. Ballard*."

"She called you Mr. Ballard?"

He nods. "You didn't have teachers who called you Ms. Flynn?"

"One. My creative writing teacher. But I, uh… I did the assignment and then some. She'd tell me, *Ms. Flynn, I understand you're able to write two thousand words, but I want you to write to the prompt. I want you to try doing more with less. Sometimes, you have to do less*."

"Was she right?"

"I don't know." It makes sense, if I think about it. But it's hard to get over my instinct to do more. To do better. To achieve. "Sometimes. Other times… I had those moments. Where I lost myself in the words. That always felt good."

"Better than anything." He nods.

"Than sex?"

"Okay, better than almost anything." His eyes find mine. "You've been asking a lot."

"Maybe you're offering a lot."

He shakes his head *uh-uh*. "And you have a look."

"What look?"

His eyes travel my body. Slowly.

For a second, I forget we're in a crowded car. That we have an audience. I feel nothing but his gaze. His breath. His heat.

Then the car jerks to a stop.

And one of the guys complains, "Hey, it's my turn."

"Go for it," the other says.

"Daisy was it?" he asks.

"Yeah." My gaze stays on Holden.

"Truth or dare?" he asks.

Both are scary in their own way. There are so many secrets I can't share. I don't want Holden looking at me differently. I love the way he looks at me.

He doesn't think I'm broken.

He's the only one who doesn't think I'm broken.

No, that's not true. No one at school knew. No one at work knows. But they don't know me either.

Holden does.

The way he looks at me… It's different. Better.

I need to keep it that beautiful and pure.

"Dare," I say.

"Flash the next car," he says.

"Fuck no." Holden's nostrils flare. He turns to the guy. Shakes his head. "She's not doing that."

"You her keeper or something?" The guy shakes his head *what's this guy's problem?*

Holden's jaw cricks.

He's so pissed. And jealous.

God, I've never seen him this jealous. Or this serious.

"Maybe just my bra," I say.

He turns to me. "Daisy—"

"I want to." I want him to watch. I want him to see. I want to keep pushing aside my inhibitions. To feel as free as he is all the time.

Most of all, I want him.

I wait for our car to speed. Then I roll my window down. Let the fresh air fill my nose, mouth, throat.

It's warm outside. Humid. It's not like August in Venice. The temperature isn't dropping to something cool and comfortable.

It feels cooler with the sun gone, but it's still balmy.

Warm enough for a dip.

Warm enough for this.

The front of our car aligns with the back of the car in the right lane.

I suck a deep breath through my teeth.

Close my eyes.

Repeat a mantra of confidence.

I can do this. I can do anything.

I'm beautiful and sexy and desirable.

I'm enough.

I'm spending tonight driving Holden crazy.

Even if I can't have him.

At least I can have that.

I roll my dress down my chest.

A horn honks. A guy hoots. Yells something about going back to his place.

Holden's arms slide around my waist. He pulls me into my seat. Almost all the way into his lap.

His fingers brush my shoulder. My collarbone. The lace of my bra.

Fuck, that feels good.

I need it everywhere.

I really do.

"Should we catch them, Daisy?" one of the guys asks. "We could invite them."

"No, that's okay." I readjust my dress.

"It's your turn now," the guy says.

"Right." I try to think of some way to use the game to my advantage. A dare for Holden. *Kiss me, touch me, fuck me.* A truth. *Do you like me? Do you want me? Do you think about me when you touch yourself?*

His eyes stay fixed on me.

Even as we pull off the main road. Into a neighborhood. A marina.

The car stops in front of a massive condo building.

"We're here." The guy in front gets out of the car. "You can take your dare upstairs."

Holden's tongue slides over his lips. It's a quick thing. He barely notices.

He doesn't say anything.

But he pulls me closer as we move into the lobby. As we step into the elevator.

As we ride to the penthouse floor.

He stays close enough to kiss me, touch me, fuck me.

Chapter Twenty-One

HOLDEN

Daisy's eyes go wide as we step into the apartment. It's a massive space. The penthouse.

The opposite of the quaint Romantic Zone.

Gold fixtures. Lux couches. Booming music.

People everywhere.

A dozen gathered around a card table. A dozen at the bar. A dozen dancing.

A normal party. More or less.

If I was alone, I'd run inside, fix a drink, find a cute girl.

Hell, if I was with a different girl, I'd whisk her inside, pour her a drink, find a private spot to talk. Or to not talk.

The thought is already filling my head.

There's a balcony.

Is it empty? Could I take her out there, roll her dress to her waist, marvel at her lacy pink bra?

My cock whines at the thought of her perky tits. How does she like to be touched? Soft and slow? Or hard and fast?

Does she even know?

Fuck, to be the person who helps her find out—

"Another drink?" one of the guys asks.

"Sure." Daisy squeezes my hand. She looks back to me, asking something, but I'm not sure what it is.

Only that she trusts me.

That it matters.

But I've had too many fucking drinks. I can't stop my eyes from traveling her body.

She's beautiful. So fucking beautiful.

I need to make her come. To lay her on a bed, pull her panties to her knees—

"Your usual?" she asks.

"Yeah, sure." Probably a bad idea, but I don't really care at the moment.

"Help me fix it." She breaks away from the guys. Whatever their names are. Heads straight to the bar.

I grab two red plastic cups.

She fills both with ice. Fills one with diet. The other with ginger ale.

There's no bourbon, so I grab the rum. Pour something light. I think. It's hard to tell with these wide cups.

She holds up her drink. "To truth or dare." Her cheeks flush. "I can't believe I did that."

"Me either." I tap my glass against hers. Take a long sip. It's shitty rum and worse ginger ale, but it's not terrible.

She takes a long sip. Swallows hard.

"How many is that?" I ask.

"What if I lost count?"

I can't really talk. "Let's get you water after this."

She nods *okay*. "What do you think?" She motions to the makeshift dance floor. Then to the poker table.

"Aren't you a card shark?"

"I'm not sure I know the rules."

"Follow my lead," I say.

She nods *sure*. Takes my hand. Follows me through the crowd.

To the table.

Her gaze goes to the game on the green felt. A deck. Three face up cards. Ace of spades. Eight of spades. Eight of diamonds.

People throw their chips in. Raise. Call.

The table jumps.

What the—

A guy on the other side pulls at something. Something in his lap.

He groans.

The table jumps again.

Oh fuck.

"Let's go," I say.

Daisy looks up at me *what do you mean?*

"Hey, Eduardo, take it somewhere else," a guy says. He motions *hold the cards*. Pulls the table aside.

I push Daisy backward reflexively.

But it doesn't do shit.

The guys still pull the table out of the way.

And it's exactly as I expected. There's a topless woman on her knees, bobbing her head up and down this Eduardo guy's dick.

"Oh my God." Daisy's eyes go wide.

The guy looks at me. Nods *yeah, that's what's up*. His gaze shifts to Daisy. "You could go next, baby."

"Fuck off." I take another step backward. Scan the room for our hosts. They're on the couch, a girl between them, flirting like there's no tomorrow.

It's not that big a deal. A rowdy party. It happens all the time.

Usually, I'd stay and watch. Hell, there's a topless girl sucking cock. And she's hot.

It's free porn.

But so not where Daisy needs to be.

I don't wait for her response. I turn her around, march her out of the party, to the elevator.

The shiny silver doors close.

She looks up at me with wide eyes. "Was she really?"

"Yeah."

"Is it really… like that?"

"Like what?"

"So…" Her gaze travels down my body. Stops on my crotch. "I don't know. I… Uh…" She hides behind her drink. "I should finish this." She takes a long sip. Then another.

"Sure." I finish my drink. Swallow the dirty talk that rises in my throat. *How about we go back to your room so I can show you exactly what it's like? I promise I'll be gentle. I have to see those pretty lips around my cock. After you come on my face.*

We stop at the ground floor. Step into the lobby. Then into the parking lot of a marina.

"I should text Oliver," I say.

"It's just a party. I can handle it," she says.

"I don't want to be there." I pull out my cell. Shoot him a *we're turning around* text. "Let's take a walk for a minute."

"Here?" She looks around the empty parking lot.

"There." I motion to the marina. It's a nice size. A dozen shops on three sides, a bridge over the fourth, a bunch of boats on the docks, calm blue water.

"Sure." She takes our cups. Drops them in a trash can. Follows me.

Her movements aren't messy, exactly. More swaying. I'm not sure if she's drunk or tipsy. But she's definitely not sober.

Not that I can talk.

Fuck, she looks cute strutting around the sidewalk, half nervous, half turned on.

She can't hide it. At all.

She liked watching.

Not that I can talk about that either.

If circumstances were different—

I pull her closer. Fuck, she feels good. And she smells good too. Like lavender and citrus and rum.

I'm drunk enough that appeals.

Or maybe it always does.

We step into the marina. A square of shops around a tiny harbor. Yachts tied to the dock. Stars reflecting off the deep blue water.

Daisy crosses the sidewalk. Moves toward the water. A rocky decline leads to the marina.

But it's blocked off with a temporary metal railing.

She moves closer to the railing.

Toward—

"Slower." I pull her body into mine.

She looks up at me with a curious expression then she looks back to the water. "Holy shit." She pushes back. "Is that a—"

"Yeah."

"Oh my God." Her eyes go to the metal railing. The rocks. The crocodile sleeping in the water. "That's an alligator."

"A crocodile."

"What the hell is it doing?"

"It's normal." I pull her back. Motion to a sign on the light post. *Watch out for alligators*. Even though it's a crocodile (they live in salt water). Mistranslation, I guess. "There are two that live in the marina."

"Oh."

"It's a big tourist draw. We're lucky to see him."

"Lucky to see a giant crocodile?" Her eyes go to the animal. "He's huge."

"Yeah." Normal size for a crocodile, but that is huge. Seven feet long, easy. Big enough to eat tourists for breakfast.

"People want to be this close?"

"He can't get up here." Crocs don't usually attack people. Only if they're threatened. But we're safe here. He can't get up the steep rocks.

If someone fell in—

I really don't know. Maybe I should ask someone in Florida. They deal with this shit all the time.

Daisy turns to me. "What if he gets up here?"

"I'll protect you."

"Yeah?"

"Yeah." I pull her backward. Until we're all the way on the other side of the sidewalk. And there's no chance she'll trip and tumble into the water.

Instead, she trips on a step. Falls right into my arms. Looks up at me with wide eyes. "Hey."

"Hey."

"I, uh… It's still my turn."

"Huh?"

"Truth or dare."

"You're too old for that."

"Yeah. But it's still my turn." Her fingers curl into my neck. My shoulder. "And, you, uh… you're the only one here."

"I am."

"So… um… truth or dare?"

Dare me to fuck you, baby. I'll go right here. Against this wall. Just grab that condom I gave you.

You can see if it tastes like chocolate.

"Holden?" she asks.

"I, uh—" My phone buzzes, saving me from an answer. A reply from Oliver. "Oliver and Luna are heading to a bar. It's quiet. Good drinks. We can meet them."

"Oh, right."

"Or go somewhere else."

"Back to the house, maybe." She rests her head on my chest. "I'm kinda tired."

"Sure." I force my gaze to my phone. "I'll call a ride."

"Thanks. I, uh… I'm going to get a water." She motions to a liquor store that's still open. "You want one too?"

"Thanks."

I let her go. Watch her until she's in the store. Then I call our ride.

Five minutes.

Five minutes to figure out what the fuck I'm doing.

Chapter Twenty-Two

DAISY

Between the bumpy ride and the rum, my stomach is all butterflies. I press one hand into the car's window. Place the other on Holden's thigh.

It's instinct.

It feels right. Like my body is taking over. Like there's some Daisy who understands desire. Who knows exactly what she wants and makes no qualms about getting it.

The heat of his thigh, the softness of his jeans, the quiet sigh.

We hit another bump.

My fingers curl into his skin reflexively.

His gaze focuses on my hand. He stares, rapt, but he doesn't say anything.

He doesn't move my hand away.

Or closer.

We hit another bump.

He slides his arm around my waist. Holds me steady through our next string of bumps.

We're almost there.

The last part is the worst.

I press my eyelids together. Focus on the safety of his touch. The heat of his skin.

All this fabric in the way.

My dress. His jeans.

It's so close to being perfect.

I want it to be perfect. For one night.

One moment even.

His fingers curl into my skin as we turn onto the main road.

The car makes a sharp right.

His body presses into mine.

He's sitting in the middle seat. It's just us and he's sitting in the middle seat. That means something.

My body melts into his as we take a sharp left into the driveway.

The car stops.

My chest caves with my exhale.

I'm still buzzing. Still antsy. Still impossibly on edge.

"Thanks." Holden nods *goodbye* to the driver. He undoes his seatbelt, gets out of the car, moves around it to open my door.

"You're a gentleman?" I take his hand.

He pulls me up. "Always."

"Always?" My voice is light. Easy. That's where I am. Happy drunk. No desire to confess ugly things. Only this beautiful buzz in my veins.

"Yeah." His voice is light too. In that Holden kind of way. That *I'm a troublemaker and I can prove it* way.

"Opening doors, kissing hands, bringing young ladies home by curfew?"

He chuckles *of course*, slides his arm around my waist, helps me to the door. "Not usually what I mean."

"What do you mean?"

"A gentleman makes sure a lady comes first." He fishes

his keys from his back pocket. Slides them into the door. Motions *after you*.

"You mean... sex?"

"Yeah."

My body buzzes. I suck in a deep breath. Step inside.

My wedges teeter, but I stay upright. Sure, I sway, but it's a sexy sway. It's practically on purpose.

Totally.

"Hey." Holden wraps his arms around my waist. He pulls my body into his. "Be careful."

"Inside?"

He nods *yeah*. "This is a very breakable condo." He motions to the glass table. The floor to ceiling window. The narrow staircase. "Come on, I'll help you to bed."

"Help how?"

He chuckles. "Is that your come on?"

"Is it working?"

He says nothing. Just motions to the kitchen. "Water first."

"Water first?" Does that mean he's joining me in bed second?

"Yeah." He leads me through the living room.

I slip on the tile floor, but he catches me.

He moves to the sink. Pours two glasses. Hands one to me.

I hold it up to toast.

"To?" he asks.

"Uh... birthday wishes."

"To birthday wishes." He taps my glass. "You didn't blow out a candle."

"I don't have one."

He shakes his head. Motions *one second*. Moves to the drawer next to the sink.

The sink full of cocktail glasses.

The mixers and bottles are still sitting there, in a neat row, beckoning anyone who wants a shortcut to relaxation.

No wonder my brother drinks all the time.

This is nice.

That voice in my head *is* gone.

Is it the same for him? How many drinks does it take?

No, I'm not going there. Tonight is good. Tonight is already perfect.

I down half my water in three sips.

Holden turns to me. He holds up a candle. A lighter. A bar of chocolate.

"That isn't going to work," I say.

He raises a brow *just watch me.*

"Upstairs," I say. "By the pool. I haven't gone in yet."

For a second, his green eyes fill with desire. Then, he blinks and his expression is confused. Conflicted even.

He's not sure if he wants to sleep with me. If he will.

But I'm not asking that.

Not yet, at least.

"I, uh, I'm going up." I finish my water. Brush against him as I take three steps to the counter. Pick up the bottle of tequila.

He shakes his head.

"*Are* you my keeper?"

"No. But I'm not letting you drink tequila with choco-late. At least not blanca." He places his body behind mine. His chest against my back, his crotch against my ass.

Slowly, he peels my fingers from the bottle. Places said bottle on the counter. Picks up the bourbon.

"Fuck, I can't believe there's this much left." He sets the bottle in my hands. "We can get the ginger beer if you want that too."

"No." I can handle this straight. "This is good."

"Is it?" His breath warms my ear.

"Yeah." I rock my hips, rubbing against him.

He lets out a soft groan. Releases me. Steps to the side.

My body whines. It wants him. All of him.

It overtakes my senses. Swallows me whole. It's a familiar want. So much like the want that used to own me all day, every day. That part of me that screamed for pleasure. For nourishment. For food.

The part of me I tried to deny. That I hated. That I called all sorts of names.

No wonder she's shy.

No wonder she needs half a dozen drinks and the sexiest man in the world.

No wonder I'm completely out of my depth.

"Shall we?" I hold up the bourbon.

He gives me a curious look, but he still nods *sure*.

I move to the stairs.

He grabs a water bottle from the fridge. Follows close behind me.

It takes every bit of my concentration to climb without slipping. These stairs are narrow. And they're long. Three flights.

There. I step onto the top floor. Cross the hallway to the sliding glass.

Warm air greets me as I pull the door open. It fights the air-conditioning. Then I move outside and the warm air wins.

I sit on one of the cream lounge chairs. Slide out of my shoes. Set the bottle on the glass table.

Holden sits next to me. Between me and the table.

He unwraps the chocolate. Lays the paper over his thigh. Places the bar on top of it.

"You're going to stain your pants," I say.

"Should I take them off?" He arches a brow.

"Definitely."

"Nice try." He lets out an easy laugh. Turns his body toward mine. Enough that his jeans brush my thigh. "I like this side of you."

"Which is that?"

"Happy."

"I'm happy all the time."

He shakes his head *you're not*. "I wish you were."

"Why?"

"I don't know. It does something to me. Makes the world into someplace beautiful."

"When I'm happy?"

"Yeah."

My heart thuds against my chest. That's so sweet. Romantic even. Or maybe he's about to say something like *but only as a friend*. Or the more horrible *you're like a sister to me*. "I like it too."

"When you're happy?"

"When you are."

"I'm always happy."

"You always act happy."

He breaks off a row of squares. Holds them up to the lighter.

Flick. Flick.

There.

The tiny flame glows against the dark sky. Casts highlights over his beautiful face.

It melts the chocolate a little at a time. Then enough the cocoa drips onto the paper.

"Here." He places the candle in my hand. "Hold it there."

I nod *sure*. "It's going to taste like gas."

"It's the thought that counts." He laughs as he melts the top of the bar.

Then the bottom of the candle.

He presses the chocolate to the tiny candle.

Turns them sideways, so he can hold the flame against both.

Slowly, they melt into each other. Into some inedible mix of wax and chocolate.

"Perfect." He turns off the lighter. Blows on the birthday candle.

"That's my job."

"You could bring up something about blowing."

"I have my own style," I say.

"You have a seduction style?"

"Yeah." I laugh. "I like to call it awkward virgin." I try to make eye contact, but I can't. It's too much. "Is it working?"

His gaze darts to my exposed thighs. My chest. My eyes. "You can't tell?"

"You're hard to read."

"True."

"And I'm a little..." Something. "I do like it. When you're happy. It's not like other people. It fills me in a different way."

"Thanks."

"It's weird, talking to you like this."

"Like how?"

"You're being sincere."

"I'm always sincere." He tries to hold his poker face, but it cracks immediately. "All that bullshit is the real Holden."

"You, uh... you were right."

"About?" He holds up the birthday chocolate. *Are you ready?*

I'm not. But I'm not sure I'll ever be ready. I nod *yeah*. "The drinks."

"Oh?"

"It's a much easier way to drop inhibitions."

"Too easy sometimes."

"Yeah." My laugh is awkward. "I, uh…"

The lighter flickers on. He holds it to the candle. Lights it. Brings it toward me. "Make a wish."

I close my eyes. Hold tightly to my usual wish. Then I let that dissolve into something more urgent.

I blow.

Open my eyes.

He's staring at me, those gorgeous green eyes filled with curiosity and concern.

It's not like him. Or maybe it is like him. Maybe I just don't know him.

Sure, Holden and I have been friendly for a long time. He's always been around. In Oliver's life. He's always looked out for me, more or less.

But we've only been talking for the last few months.

And he… well, he's right. He's not usually sincere. He's not usually letting anyone in.

"You make a wish?" he asks.

I nod *yeah*. "I can't tell you. Or it won't come true."

"You believe that?"

"A little."

He breaks off a piece of chocolate. Brings it to his lips. Takes a tiny bite. "No wax." He offers the rest to me.

My fingers brush his as I take it. Mmm, it is good. Rich and sweet. Then the faint taste of gas. Ick. I cough. Reach for the bottle.

He grabs it. Uncaps it. Shoots me this *are you sure?* look.

I nod *of course*.

Holden takes a swig. Passes the bottle to me. "Fuck, that's strong."

I wrap my fingers around the glass. Bring it to my lips. I can take a drink without making a fool of myself.

I've drank and eaten way more disgusting things than alcohol.

So many, honestly.

Eyes closed.

I tip my head back. Then the bottle.

Fuck. The taste of alcohol overwhelms me. It burns my throat as I swallow. I vaguely recognize the rich, spicy flavor of the Manhattan. But only vaguely.

Holden laughs as I cough. "Anyone ever tell you that you're adorable?"

"Too many people."

"You are." He takes the bottle. Sets it on the table. "Fuck, Daisy, you have no idea what you do to me."

"What do I do?"

He shakes his head *not going there*.

But I need him to go there. I need this tonight. I need him tonight.

His eyes travel down my body.

My gaze follows his. God, there's something about watching him look at me. It should make me shy or insecure.

But it doesn't.

It sets me on fire.

I really do feel like some sort of sex goddess. Like I'm beautiful, like I'm desirable, like I'm enough.

"I… Uh…" My fingers brush his jeans. "I, uh… want to…"

"Yeah?" His breath is heady.

Kiss you. Touch you. Fuck you.

Anything.

Everything.

I want to taste the chocolate on your lips. And on that condom. Will you show me how to do it?

Will you ease into me? Make sure I enjoy it?

Please, Holden. Please kiss me, touch me, fuck me.

"Swim," I say. "You had a good idea before."

"I did?"

I nod *yeah*. "Skinny dipping."

His pupils dilate.

I muster all the confidence I can. "You want to join me?"

Chapter Twenty-Three

HOLDEN

Y*es.*

Fuck yes.

Take your dress off. And your underwear.

Then come here and sit in my lap.

I'm going to make you come until you can't stop. You think we can get to eighteen orgasms?

I've never managed before, but I'm game to try.

I swallow hard. Reach for some semblance of judgment. That voice in my head that tells me not to do stupid things.

It's there. Somewhere. But it's too fuzzy. Too quiet. Too overwhelmed by bourbon and ginger beer.

And beautiful baby blues.

Fuck, the vulnerability in Daisy's eyes. Like she'll die if I say no. Like she'll die if I don't fuck her now.

Or maybe I'm the one who will die.

Is it possible to die of blue balls? At the moment, it feels like it. Like I'm going to burst if I don't carry her to my bed.

"Is that your birthday wish?" I ask.

She shakes her head. "Just something I'm doing." Her fingers brush my thigh. "You don't want to?"

Fuck yes, I want to. I want to strip her naked, lay her on this lounge chair, lick her until she begs me to stop.

It's stronger than usual.

I'm a generous fuck. I enjoy making women come. Enjoy the feeling of thighs against my cheeks. The way a woman—

Shit.

Not helping.

Not even a little.

Her eyes travel up my thighs. Stop on my hard-on.

Her chest heaves. Her tongue slides over her lips. She stares like she's about to drop to her knees, pull out my cock, demand to see if that condom really tastes like chocolate.

For the first time ever, I curse my high tolerance for alcohol. I need to drink more. To drink until I have whiskey dick.

Thank fuck Daisy is too shy to ask.

"Well… you can stay here." Her eyes travel up my body. "But I'm going in the water."

"Go for it."

Her eyes meet mine. She stares at me, stares through me. "You're not going to join?"

"I can get your swimsuit."

"Is that what you want?"

I should say *yes*. Or *this is a bad idea*. Or some sensible alternative.

Something I won't regret tomorrow.

Something that won't fuck up shit with Oliver.

Or lead to her getting hurt.

I reach for an excuse, but it's too fuzzy, too far away.

The words spill from my lips.

"No." Fuck, I'm already hard enough to burst out of my jeans. This is going to kill me. To actually kill me.

"Then help me." She turns her back to me. Motions to her zipper.

My hand brushes her shoulder.

She groans as my fingers glide over her dress. I pull the zipper down her back.

My hand acts on its own. It traces a line up her spine.

Fuck, her skin is soft.

And the way she's shaking—

I'm going to come in my jeans if I keep this up. Which is probably for the best. I won't rebound fast enough to fuck her.

God, I want to fuck her.

To taste her.

To fill her.

To be the first person to fill her. I don't usually care about that shit. I don't have some virgin fetish.

But Daisy—

"Thank you." She shifts her hips, turns her body toward me. Stands. Peels her dress off her shoulders. Over her chest, stomach, hips, knees.

She bends to step out of it. Folds it and sets it on the chair behind us.

Her underwear isn't any skimpier than her bikini. But the implication is so fucking different.

This is private.

For her.

For her and anyone she invites to watch her, touch her, kiss her, fuck her.

I try to meet her gaze, but my eyes refuse. They trace a line down her body. Then back up again.

She's not the skinny kid she used to be. She's still long and slim, yeah, but she's curvy too.

The pale pink lace hugs her chest. Her hips.

"Holden?" Her voice drips with sex. "Are you okay?"

"Yeah. I, uh… I'll look away."

"Don't."

"Daisy—"

"Please. I've never… No one has ever seen me. Not like this."

My balls tighten. "No one?"

She nods *yeah*. "I know you… just… I'm going to lose my nerve if I wait. So don't ask me to stop. It doesn't have to be more than this. But let me have this."

She's asking me to watch her strip.

I fell asleep and woke up in a porno.

I'm dreaming.

This isn't reality.

Only when I pinch myself, I see the same sky full of stars, the same glowing aqua pool, the same gorgeous girl standing on the concrete.

"Is it okay?" she asks.

She's asking me if it's okay for her to take off her clothes.

Either her dad really focused on the consent part of "the talk," or there's something I'm not seeing. Something about her.

Maybe I don't get women. Don't get what a big deal this is.

Or maybe I—

"Holden? Is it okay?" She straightens as she meets my gaze.

"You want me to watch?"

"Yeah."

Fuck me. I can't say no. I can't do that to her. I don't want to. "Okay."

Her cheeks flush immediately. Slowly, she reaches

behind her back. Unhooks her bra. Peels it off her shoulders.

Then off her chest.

She places it on top of her dress.

Her arms fall to her sides.

Her eyes meet mine.

She's perfect. But then she'd be perfect if she was bigger or smaller or rounder or straighter.

She's perfect because she's Daisy.

And, okay—

I'm not going to bullshit.

She's perfect in all the usual ways too.

Her tits are on the smaller side, but they're perky.

Her nipples are hard.

That's for me. The blush, the heaving chest, the shaking—

It's all for me. It's how much she wants me.

And I'm sitting here, on this bench, like an asshole at a strip club. An asshole who can't even bother to tip.

Her hands go to her hips.

This time, she manages to hold my gaze as she pushes her panties to her thighs.

Her blush deepens.

Her limbs shake.

She lets the underwear fall at her feet. Kicks it aside.

Looks to me.

Her lips part. She starts to say something. Stops herself.

Takes a step closer.

Then another.

"Daisy—" I don't know how to finish the sentence. I can't tell her I don't want her. I'm not going to lie to her.

And that whole *we shouldn't. Your brother would kill me* thing doesn't matter at the moment.

At the moment—

Fuck, I can't remember the last time I was this hard.

Her gaze travels over my body. Holds on my eyes.

Something passes between us.

Something different.

New.

It's not the usual *I want you, you want me.*

It's deeper.

A lot deeper.

Like she's seeing into my soul.

Her throat quivers as she swallows. She turns on her heels. Slowly. Carefully.

Fuck, her ass is divine.

"Am I okay?" she asks.

"What?" Okay? Okay doesn't begin to describe it.

I need that ass in my lap. In my hands. Against my pelvis as I fuck her from behind.

I need her bending over.

I need her begging me to split her in half.

"Do you want me?" She turns, so we're face-to-face. "Do you want to fuck me?"

"Yes."

"Would you?"

"Would I?"

"If I asked?"

My cock whines for attention. It steals all the blood from my brain. Steals the last bit of judgment I have left. "I might."

"I don't want to manipulate you." Her tongue slides over her lips. "I just want… I want to want, I guess. To feel wanted. To feel normal. For one night."

"How are you not—"

She takes another step toward me. "Can I?"

Conscious thought flees my brain at an alarming rate. Whatever it is she wants to do, the answer is yes. I nod.

She places her hands on my shoulders. Slides into my lap.

Slowly, her body sinks into mine.

"Fuck." Her breath is heavy. Needy. "That feels so good."

I wrap my arms around her.

"You... uh... you're hard."

"You're naked." I need to defuse the tension. To pull this back to humor. But it's not enough. I still want her so much I can't stand it.

Her laugh is awkward. "I, uh... it's been a long time. I haven't... I haven't felt that since—"

"Since when?" Whoever he is, I'm going to kill him.

"This guy sophomore year." Her fingers curl into my neck. "It feels good. I forgot."

"Daisy—"

"You're the only person who helps me remember." Her eyes bore into mine. "You're just... I really like you, Holden."

"I like you too."

"I mean... *like* you like you."

"I know."

Her fingers curl into my neck. She stares into my eyes, stares all the way to my fucking soul. "I know you don't do relationships. I just want... I want whatever you're willing to give me." She shifts her hips.

Fuck, that feels good. My hands go to her hips reflexively.

Her chest heaves with her exhale. "I don't know if I'll ask again. I can barely ask now. But, I, uh—if you want me to stop—"

"Fuck no."

"So you..."

"Come here." One hand slides to her lower back. The other goes to the back of her head.

Her arms hook around my neck.

Her eyelids flutter together.

I pull her into a slow, deep kiss.

Her lips brush mine.

Softly.

Then harder.

She tastes good. Like chocolate and bourbon.

Like heaven.

Like Daisy.

I wait for my brain to argue. For judgment to kick in. For some part of me to want anything other than her mouth against mine.

But it doesn't.

Chapter Twenty-Four

DAISY

Kissing Holden isn't like kissing other guys.

He's more steady. More sure.

He leads and I follow.

He scrapes his teeth against my bottom lip.

He presses his palm into my lower back.

He holds my body against his.

Fuck, I'm naked in his lap.

It's a neon sign in my head.

Naked. In. His. Lap.

I've never been naked with a guy before.

But I'm not scared. I'm nervous as all hell, but I'm not scared.

I trust him. Probably more than I should.

God, he tastes good.

He pulls back enough to look up at me.

It's too much. I can't hold his gaze.

My eyes go to his chest. The tattoo peeking out from his t-shirt.

"Fuck, Daisy." He cups the back of my head with his hand. "Are you sure?"

"Sure of what?"

"This." He shifts his hips so his hard-on presses against my sex. "I don't trust myself to stop if you keep going." His voice is honest. Sincere. The most sincere I've ever heard it.

I nod. "Please." I dig my fingers into his neck. "I need you."

"Fuck." His pupils dilate. "Daisy—"

"I love that you're being a gentleman. But I don't want that. I want to feel you, Holden. Please. Give me this."

"You know how this ends?" His breath is strained, like he's struggling to hold on to conscious thought.

"I'm leaving for college in less than two weeks. I just want… this trip."

"Are you sure?"

No. Not even a little. "Yeah."

"Fuck." His hand slides to my hip. "I really want to make you come."

My response is a groan.

"You have no idea how much I think about it."

"When?"

"Every fucking night. And every morning. Every shower." He runs his fingers over my hips. "You've been wearing me out for weeks."

My sex clenches. "I think about you too."

His fingers trail around my neck, over my shoulders, down my collarbone.

To my chest.

He cups my breast with his palm. "You touch yourself?"

My cheeks flame. "Yes."

"Show me."

"Here?"

"Yeah."

"This first." I'm not sure what *this* is. Only that I need it desperately.

He looks up at me with every ounce of desire in the world. It's crystal clear. He wants me. Holden Ballard, the sexiest man in the universe, a man who can attract the attention of any woman, wants me.

His eyelids flutter together.

Mine follow.

He kisses me hard. Like he needs every ounce of me.

Maybe he does. Maybe he needs this as much as I do. Maybe he's as empty as I am. Maybe he's just better at hiding it.

My desire to contemplate his mental state fades as he runs his thumb over my nipple.

The friction of his digit sends desire straight to my core.

It's been a long, long time since anyone has touched me like this. There was only my not-really-a-boyfriend sophomore year. We made out a lot. But never like this.

This is something else.

This is everything.

He draws slow circles around my nipple. Again and again and again.

I groan into his mouth.

Rock my hips against his.

He brings his other hand to my breast. Toys with my other nipple just as mercilessly.

Slow circles. So soft I barely feel them.

I pull back to moan.

He looks up at me with rapt attention. Like I'm the best thing he's ever seen.

It's intoxicating. A million times better than alcohol.

A million times better than anything.

"Fuck, Daisy. You're responsive."

"Is that bad?"

"Fuck no." He presses his lips to my neck. A soft kiss. Then another. He draws a trail of them down my neck, collarbone, chest. "I wish I had the patience to toy with you properly."

The demanding tone to his voice makes my sex clench.

"You've never been with anyone?"

"Never." My cheeks flush. Which is ridiculous. I'm naked in his lap. And he knows I'm a virgin. But it still makes me shy. I'd say I need more bourbon, but there's no way I'm moving off him.

"Nothing?"

"Just… above the waist."

He lets out a groan that's half agony, half ecstasy. Brings his hands to my hips. In one swift motion, he pulls my body up, bringing my nipple to his mouth. "This?" His lips brush my flesh.

"A little."

"You're gonna kill me, baby."

The term of endearment makes my sex clench. "Holden—"

"Can't think of a better way to die." He takes my nipple into his mouth.

It's different than his hand. Softer. Wetter. All-encompassing.

He flicks his tongue against me. Softly. Then harder. Then so softly I barely feel it.

I reach for him. For whatever I can get.

My nails scrape his neck. His chest.

I slip my hand under his t-shirt. Press my palm to his bare skin. There's something about the feeling of his flesh against my hand.

He takes my nipple into his mouth. Sucks hard.

I have to tug at his hair to stay upright.

"Tell me if I go too fast," he groans.

"Okay."

"If anything is too much."

I nod.

"Don't hold back. Whatever you're feeling, I want to hear it. Good or bad." He moves to my other nipple.

I yelp as he takes my flesh into his mouth. Then it's the soft scrape of his teeth. "Oh my God."

"Like that." He does it again, but harder.

"Fuck." My eyes press together. My fingers dig into his skin. It's so much. It's all so much. My world is already upside down and all I have are his hands and lips. How am I going to survive more?

How am I going to survive without more?

I'm so empty. I've never felt that before. But I do. I need to be full. "Holden——"

"Yeah, baby?"

I can say it. I can. "I... uh..."

"Too much?"

"No."

"More?"

"Perfect."

He does it again. That hard scrape of his teeth. Just enough to hurt in the best possible way.

Just enough to send desire racing through my veins.

My sex clenches. I'm already wound so tight. I need release. I need him. "I... I need you inside me."

"Fuck." He looks up at me, his eyes hazy with lust. "Daisy..." His breath is heady. Needy. "Show me."

"What?"

"How you touch yourself."

"Oh." My eyes go wide. I... I can't. That's different than being naked in his lap. It's too much. Too intimate. Too mine.

But then, there's something about the need in his eyes.

And the ache between my legs.

I nod *okay*. Hold his gaze as I slip my hand between my legs. "Hold me steady."

He brings his hands to my hips.

I run my index finger over my clit. Then the middle. Ring.

A little lower. To the left.

There.

I start with a slow stroke right where I need it. Then a little faster.

A little harder.

He watches with rapt attention. Like I'm the Mona Lisa. Like I'm his favorite scene in his favorite movie.

It's new. But good.

It makes my entire body buzz.

I move a little faster. A little harder. Until I'm right at the pressure I need.

"Fuck." My eyes close. My nails dig into his shoulders.

It's so much. More than when I'm alone.

Almost too much.

But somehow not enough too.

"You're so fucking beautiful." His fingers dig into my hips. "You close, baby?"

"Yes," I breathe.

"Show me." His nails scrape my skin. "Come for me."

Fuck, that's the hottest thing I've ever heard. I… He… Oh my God…

I stare back at him for a moment. Until it's too much.

My eyes close.

My finger glides over my skin.

It's a familiar rhythm. But it's different with him watching.

I wind tighter.

Tighter.

Tighter than I ever have before.

So tight I'm about to burst.

I tug at his shoulder.

Groan his name as I push myself over the edge.

My sex pulses as I come.

I rub myself through my orgasm.

Then I open my eyes. Stare back at him.

He takes my hand. Brings my fingers to his mouth. Sucks the taste of me off them.

I lower my body onto his. So my crotch is against his. He's still hard. And I still want that so fucking badly.

I'm still so fucking empty.

So in need of filling.

"Fuck me." My cheeks flush. "Please."

He nods *hell yeah*, wraps his arms around my waist, pulls my body into his.

In one swift motion, he lifts me, lays me down on the lounge chair next to ours.

He does away with his t-shirt. Pulls something from the back pocket of his jeans.

A condom.

I watch closely as he slides his jeans off his hips and kicks them aside.

Then it's the boxers.

And it's just him.

Oh my God.

That's… a lot.

And I—

"Come here." He tosses the packet on the table. Sits next to me. "Spread your legs—"

I'm staring. But I just… oh my God. "You're…"

"Yeah."

"And that's… wow."

"Come here." He takes his first two fingers. Slips them into my mouth.

I suck hard.

But I only get him for a second. He pulls his hand from my mouth. Slips it between my legs.

Fuck, there's something about the feeling of his hand between my legs. It's different than mine. Different than him watching.

More intense.

Just more.

He teases me with two fingers. "Tell me if it's too much."

I nod *okay*.

He holds my gaze as he slips both fingers inside me.

Fuck. It's a lot.

Intense.

But not painful.

His eyes fix on me. He studies my expression. Waits until my shoulders sink into the chair and my eyes close.

Then he pushes his fingers deeper.

"Holden—" I reach for him. Get his chest. No shirt in the way. Just his soft skin. His hard muscles. His flesh against mine. "That's... fuck."

He pushes a little deeper.

My fingers curl into his skin. "More." My eyes blink open. Meet his.

Somehow, he's lost and found at the same time.

Somehow, he's exactly where he needs to be.

We're both exactly where we need to be.

This is why people talk about making love, becoming one, feeling another person's soul.

It's just right.

It's perfect.

He watches my expression as he drives his fingers

into me.

He does it slowly at first.

Then a little faster.

A little harder.

It's intense. In a good way. Like jumping into the ocean.

Too much.

Then exactly enough.

He pulls his hand back. Reaches for something. The condom.

He tears the packet with his teeth. Slides the rubber over his cock.

Fuck, there's something about the gesture. It's not like the girl from my homeroom said. It's not some bummer that takes me out of the moment.

It's really sexy.

He's so sexy. It's impossible. It's impossible to believe that he's about to—

"Breathe for me, baby." He wraps his arms around my waist. Places his body between my legs.

Slowly, he lowers his body onto mine.

There's something about the weight of him, the pressure.

Holden looks down at me as he brings his hands to my hips.

He tilts my pelvis. Holds me steady as he brings our bodies together.

I hook my legs around his waist.

He stares into my eyes as he moves closer, closer—

There.

A sharp tug of rubber.

Then pressure.

So much pressure.

And this overwhelming sense of being full.

My eyes close.

My nails dig into his back.

My legs squeeze his thighs.

"Breathe, baby." He runs his lips over my neck.

I nod though my inhale.

He brings his lips into my skin. A kiss. Then the soft scrape of his teeth.

Harder.

So hard it hurts. But only barely. And in the best possible way.

"Fuck. That's…" I reach for words. Find nothing. "More."

He shifts a little deeper as he scrapes his teeth against my neck.

Then deeper.

Deeper.

Mmm.

He nips at the curve of my neck.

A groan falls off my lips.

"Inhale." He scrapes his teeth against my skin again.

I suck in a deep breath.

"Exhale."

I push the air from my lungs.

Then I do it again. Again.

Slowly, the pain fades to discomfort.

Then pressure. So much pressure. Almost too much, but, somehow, I need more.

"More," I breathe.

He looks down at me for a second, then he shifts back and fills me with a slow, steady thrust.

"Fuck." I dig my nails into his back. Suck a breath through my teeth.

"Too much?" He holds my body against his.

"No. A lot. But not too much."

"Just breathe, baby. I'll take care of the rest."

I nod an *okay*.

His eyes stay trained on me. He pulls back. Fills me with another steady thrust.

It's a lot. It hurts.

I let my eyes close.

Let my nails dig into his back.

Let my thighs squeeze his hips.

Deep breath.

Slow inhale.

His next thrust is deeper. It stretches me. Stretches me further than I've ever gone.

It's a lot.

So much pressure I might burst.

But no pain.

He fills me again.

A little faster. A little deeper.

I stretch a little further.

My nails scrape a little harder.

He brings his lips to my neck. His hand to my chest.

He toys with my nipple, drawing soft circles, as he nips at my neck.

We stay locked together, him inside me, so deep inside me I might burst.

Bit by bit, I get used to the pressure.

To the sensation of him inside me.

It's different. Really different.

But in a good way. In a fucking great way.

He drags his lips down my collarbone. Over my chest.

He takes my nipple into his mouth. Sucks softly. Then harder. Then it's that gentle scrape of his teeth.

"Fuck. Holden."

He pulls back. Drives into me again.

Then again.

I bring one hand to his head. Dig my fingers into his hair. Tug just hard enough.

He looks up at me, his green eyes filled with bliss.

It's so beautiful.

It's perfect.

It's everything.

He brings his lips to mine. Kisses me hard.

His tongue slides into my mouth.

His hands dig into my hips.

With each thrust, he moves a little faster, a little harder, a little deeper.

Until he finds a rhythm.

Fuck.

It's too much.

It hurts.

Then it doesn't. It's just a lot. So fucking much.

I dig my nails into his back.

Suck a breath through my teeth. Force an exhale.

He slows for a moment. For long enough I catch my breath.

He looks down at me, waits for my nod. When he starts again, the pain is gone.

It's still a lot of pressure.

But a good pressure.

A fucking great pressure.

He drives into me with those steady strokes.

His body stays pressed against mine.

The rest of the world disappears as we move together.

Bit by bit, that sense of too much fades. The pressure is just right.

It's fucking perfect.

It's so fucking good.

He drives into me again and again.

Then his posture changes. His kiss gets more aggressive. His nails dig into my skin.

He pulls back to groan my name.

Then he's there.

Pleasure spills over his expression as he comes.

He thrusts through his orgasm.

It feels so good, the pulsing of his cock. So different but so fucking good.

When he's finished, he untangles our bodies. Presses his lips to mine. "Give me a minute."

I nod *okay*.

He stands. Moves inside. Straight to the bathroom.

The water runs.

Then it turns off.

A moment later he returns. No longer hard. Or sheathed in a condom.

But still naked.

Still incredibly inviting.

"You have another one in you?" He offers me his hand.

"You can go again?"

"No." His laugh is soft. "But I have a hand."

"You—"

"Want you to come on my hand." He pulls me up. "Or my face."

Oh. My cheeks flame. "Later."

"Later?"

"I'm kinda… spent."

His smile is easy. "Tomorrow."

"Tomorrow." We're going to do this again tomorrow.

Best day ever.

Best year ever.

Best birthday ever.

Holden pulls my body into his. "You still want to skinny dip?"

My lips curl into a smile. "Definitely."

Chapter Twenty-Five

HOLDEN

I blink my eyes open. Roll over. Away from the brightness.

It's not enough. The blinds are up. The wall is all windows. I'm in an east facing room.

Sunlight floods the space.

Casts shadows over the opposite wall.

I reach out to the other side of the bed, but it's cold. Empty.

I slept here alone. Daisy insisted. She's right—there's no reason to start a fight with Oliver—but it still feels off.

Sure, we aren't doing anything wrong. But he won't see it that way.

And I—

Fuck, I've gone insane.

Officially lost touch with logic.

Not that it was my strong suit to begin with.

I toss off the covers. Head to the bathroom. Piss. Wash my hands. Brush my teeth.

Toss an extra four tissues on the trash can. To cover the condom sitting at the bottom.

It's out of sight, more so now, but it feels like it's shining.

Like it's screaming *Holden Ballard has no concept of loyalty*.

I know it's bullshit, that whole bros before hoes, I won't sleep with your sister just because you say so thing.

But I did agree. I meant it. And now—

I can't say I regret last night. I don't. Fuck, the thought of Daisy's blue eyes brimming with pleasure—

Of her thighs squeezing my hips—

Her nails digging into my back—

I'm never going to regret that.

Fuck, if it somehow got erased, if she came to me right now, the two of us sober…

I don't know what I'd say.

My cock answers for me. Fuck, her groan is melted into my brain. I need to step into the shower. Fuck myself now.

It's the only way I'm going to survive today.

But there's music downstairs. One of Oliver's favorites. Some moody, mumbly shit that wants to be grunge even though it's half as good.

He's awake.

I need to be somewhere else.

I pull on running shorts. Head downstairs.

My best friend is lying on the couch, half-awake, t-shirt pulled over his eyes.

"Drink too much?" I don't wait for an answer. I head straight to the kitchen. Fill two glasses with water. Bring him one.

He tosses his shirt aside. Squints just enough to reach for the glass. "Why's it so bright?"

"It's almost noon."

"No fucking way."

I nod *way*. "Time difference."

"Yeah." He finishes his glass in one go. Drops it on the coffee table. Leans back. "What the hell are you wearing?"

"What about you?"

He groans as he grabs a pillow, holds it over his eyes. "Didn't make it to my bed."

"Too drunk?"

"Fuck off." He holds the pillow over his head, blocking the light from the windows—the ones that face the ocean. "Where the fuck did you guys go? We waited for you for… that place poured them strong."

What is strong to Oliver? I've seen him enter a party with a full bottle of bourbon and leave with an empty one. Sure, he's not downing every drop.

He does share.

Makes a point of it even.

And where the fuck do I get off pointing out his lapses in judgment?

I fucked his sister last night.

I took her virginity.

My balls tighten at the thought.

Blood rushes to my cock.

So not the time. I grab his glass. Mutter something about a refill. Move into the kitchen.

"Holden?" Oliver mumbles. "You drink too much?"

"Did *I* drink too much?" My chuckle eases the tension in my shoulders. This is fine. Normal.

It can be normal.

That's possible.

I move into the living room.

Oliver sits up enough to take his glass. He nods *thanks*. Swallows a sip. "Where'd you get the scratch marks?"

"Huh?"

He motions to my chest. Then my back. "You fuck a cat or something?"

"How would I fuck a cat?"

"It's called a metaphor."

"No. I fucked your sister."

He rolls his eyes *get real*. "Get some new material. Seriously, Holden. Your stuff is getting stale."

My stomach churns. That's how little he thinks it's possible. That's how much he trusts me.

"Who was she?" He swallows another sip. Sits up straighter. "Hot?"

"Of course."

"What was she into?"

Fuck, this is so messed up. No way am I telling him what his sister liked. Even if he thinks I'm talking about some random chick.

Even if he trusts me so much he can't fathom me breaking my promise.

"She was into, uh… none of your business." I finish my water. Move into the kitchen. Drop the glass in the sink.

"Seriously, Holden," Oliver calls. "I'm worried about you. With all these bad jokes. You need to see a shrink or something?"

"Do you?"

"Daisy thinks so. Dad too." His voice shifts back to his usual aloof tone. Like he can't possibly be bothered to contemplate that. Like he's so above mortal concerns. "You picked up some chick while you were watching her?"

"After I took her home," I say. "She was tired."

"Oh." He clears his throat. "You gonna stay in there?"

Yeah. It's easier if I don't have to look him in the eyes. I feel less like a piece of shit.

"You're not gonna give me the dirt?" he asks.

"Going for a run." I move to the dining table. Grab my cell. My keys.

Oliver looks at me funny for a second. "You're really holding out?"

"Later," I say.

"Fuck, you should have heard the shit Luna said last night." His eyes light up. "Girl is trying to kill me."

"Yeah?"

He nods *yeah*. "She has a fucking mouth on her."

"And you experienced it?"

He shoots me that same *get real*. "Had to stay down here. So I wouldn't get ideas."

"You really wouldn't?" I ask.

He stares like he doesn't understand the question.

"Really?"

"I think about it, yeah. I'm going to think about it in the shower in about... as soon as you leave. But I like her too much."

"You do?" I swallow hard.

"Even if she wasn't Daisy's best friend... I know her too well. It would be different."

"Maybe that's good."

"Maybe you're getting soft."

If only. "Maybe you're too old for this shit."

"Maybe—" He flips me off. Chuckles as I return the gesture. "Get me Tylenol."

"Your liver is already fucked."

"Aspirin then."

"You don't have any?"

"Loaned it to Luna."

"You're not gonna go in her room? Climb into her bed? Wake her up by eating her out?"

His chuckle is low. Dirty. "Fuck, that will keep me going for a while."

"You're gonna end up thinking of me."

He shakes his head *hell no*. "Spent most of yesterday

looking at her thighs." Something spreads over his expression. Something carnal.

Too much information.

But at least he's distracted.

"I'll get it. But you owe me." I motion to the door *later*.

He nods *sure*. Falls back onto the couch as I move outside.

I close the door. Start down the hill.

It's way too bright and I don't have my sunglasses. I make it across the main drag, down the cobblestone streets, all the way to the boardwalk.

I face away from the sun. But after a few minutes, it's too much. My head screams. For water. Coffee. Advil.

The ability to reconcile my loyalty to my best friend and my desire to hold Daisy all night.

Even right now, I want to climb into her bed, hold her close.

It's not just that I want to make her come. That I want to taste her cunt. Watch her eyes fill with bliss.

Feel her thighs pressed against my hips.

Shit. I'm already getting hard.

I stop. Duck into a pharmacy—there's one every other block. They sell all sorts of common prescriptions. Plus the usual over the counter stuff, water, soda, snacks.

I grab water, aspirin, ibuprofen, a box of condoms, cheap sunglasses.

The saleswoman looks at me funny, but she still takes my cash and places my change on the counter.

I don the shades, sling the plastic bag around my wrist, grab my cell.

It's still too bright. I can barely see the screen. I have to stop under an awning to make out the texts from last night.

Nothing important. A lot of *where are you? Are you coming?*

For fuck's sake, tell me if you're not, so I can go home and fuck myself. Luna is driving me insane.

You think she's as good with that pretty mouth as she looks?

I bet she is.

I bet she's greedy.

She's tall enough we could sixty-nine. Haven't done that in forever. Kinda miss it.

God, my best friend really is a dirty bastard.

If Daisy was any other girl, he'd cream himself over the story. Taking a virgin home on her eighteenth birthday, warming her up slowly, filling her—

No.

Even if she was another girl, it would be weird telling him. Wrong.

It's not like me. Usually, I replay all my fucks.

It's fun. Kills time between appointments. Keeps the day interesting.

With Daisy, there's something different. Personal.

I like her.

A lot.

I need to talk to her. To make sure I don't hurt her.

However the fuck I do that.

I call my sister—she isn't a relationship expert, but she is honest to a fault. Leave a message.

"Hey Ariel. I hope I didn't wake you. Call me when you get a sec. Need to ask you something. Give Charlotte a kiss for me. And tell her that no one ever made headlines playing it safe. Love you." I end the call. Slide my cell into my pocket.

Climb the streets back to the house.

Oliver is MIA—no doubt fucking himself in the shower.

Daisy is sitting at the kitchen table, across from her best friend, picking at a bowl of oatmeal.

She smiles as her eyes catch mine.

I melt.

I completely forget what I'm trying to accomplish.

I forget everything but how badly I want to make her smile again.

Chapter Twenty-Six

DAISY

"Hey." Holden tosses his sunglasses on the table. His green eyes meet mine. His cheeks just barely flush.

"Hey." I press my thighs together. It's not enough to contain the ache between them. I'm sore in a way I've never been sore before.

And now I'm acutely aware of this emptiness in my core.

And how good it feels to fill it.

If I can even handle him, ahem, filling me.

Right now.

I mean, because last night—

God, I'm already red.

"I made a chai." I hold up my mug. "You want a sip?"

"Sure, yeah." He leans over the table. Takes the mug from my hand. Brings it to his lips. "Morning, Luna."

"Morning." Her eyes go straight to his chest. Not the Latin tattoo. Or the tan skin.

The red marks. In the spot where I was—

Fuck, I did that to him.

I branded him.

It shouldn't be so hot, but it is.

When I saw my hickeys in the mirror this morning—

Shit. I comb my hair over my neck. So Oliver won't notice.

"That's good." He takes another sip. Swallows hard. "Really fucking good."

"Thanks." It's torture doing anything besides touching him.

Which is ridiculous. This is good oatmeal. Spicy from the cinnamon, chewy from the raisins, just sweet enough.

The same breakfast I have every day.

Nourishing. Delicious. So much less appealing than Holden.

"You making me one too?" Luna teases.

"If you want," I say.

"No, Holden. You're the master of chai lattes, right?" Her gaze moves down his body, then back up it. It's not an *I want you* look. More like she's assessing him as worthy or not.

"You could say that." He places my mug on the glass table. "Daisy is good too."

"Are you?" She turns to me. Raises a brow. "How good are we talking?"

"Oh." Realization spreads over his face. "You…"

"No." My cheeks flame. I shake my head, sending my hair in every direction. "I, uh…"

"You should probably practice your lines." Luna takes a long sip of her coffee. "Oliver is hung over, but he's not blind."

"We didn't." I clear my throat.

Holden just shrugs. "I'm gonna shower."

"Right," I say.

His eyes meet mine. "You good?"

"Yeah." My blush deepens. There's so much I want to say. But not in front of Luna. Not in front of anyone.

He places a plastic bag on the table. "Aspirin in here. As your brother requested." He looks to Luna. "Whatever you're doing with him, it's driving him insane."

"Oh?" Satisfaction spreads over her face.

"Supposedly he's in the shower, fucking himself to thoughts of your thighs," I say.

"Are you supposed to share that?" Her laugh is easy.

Holden shakes his head. "He'd be glad I did. If he could see your face right now."

"What about it?" she asks.

"You're thinking it too." He winks at her. Then his eyes meet mine. His expression gets shy. It's not like him. Which makes it super hot. "We're doing something cool today."

"We are?" I know everyone wanted to make my birthday special, but there's no way we're topping last night. We might as well just…

I don't know. All I want to do is climb into the shower with Holden.

Drag him to the couch.

Or my bed.

The pool.

Anywhere. Everywhere.

"Yeah. We're already late. So you should get dressed. Pack snacks, sunscreen, cash." He picks up the mug. Takes another sip. "Should probably make another chai."

"You're stealing mine?" My eyes meet his.

He nods *yeah*. "I need the taste of it on my lips."

"Oh." My chest heaves with my inhale.

"Need to savor every drop." He holds my gaze for a moment, then he turns, moves up the stairs.

Luna watches, slack-jawed and wide eyed. "Oh my God."

"What?" I take another bite. Chew. Swallow.

"You fucked him."

I clear my throat.

"You fucked him and you didn't tell me."

"I, uh… I am going to make more tea. But English Breakfast. You want some?"

"Fuck no. I want details."

"Tea first." I stand. Move into the kitchen. Fill the kettle.

She follows me into the space. "He wants the taste on his lips?"

"I, uh…"

"He wants to eat you out."

"That, uh…"

"Oh my God, Daisy…" She presses her palms into the counter. "That was so hot."

"Yeah?"

"Like he was about to fuck you right there, in front of me."

"You think so?" My stomach flutters at the thought. I like Holden. And I want him. A lot. All the time.

She nods *hell yeah*. "He's really into you."

My teeth sink into my lip. "It's just… we're just…"

"Did he?"

"Huh?" I rise to my tiptoes to grab my tin of English breakfast.

"Eat you out?"

"Oh." My blush deepens. I try to push it aside. Focus on scooping tea into my strainer ball. "No. But he, uh…"

"Did he make sure you were ready?"

"Yeah." My chest warms at the memory of his touch. The weight of his body. The pressure of his hands. The softness of his lips. "He was insistent."

She nods *go on*.

"I kinda… invited him to skinny dip. Then took off my dress."

Her eyes go wide.

"I was a little drunk." Maybe a medium amount drunk. But I *was* lucid. I knew what I was doing. I just wasn't as afraid as I normally am.

"You came on to him?"

I nod.

"Damn." Her eyes go wide. "I didn't think you had it in you." She moves closer. Pulls me into a tight hug. "I'm proud of you."

"For fucking a guy?"

"For all of it." She squeezes me. "You're all grown up."

"Oh my God."

She laughs. "A confident minx."

I shake my head.

Her laugh gets louder. "You're getting there."

"More than yesterday."

She claps her hands together *hell yes*. She moves closer. Close enough to whisper. "How was it?"

"The sex or the stripping?"

"All of it." She releases me. Stays close enough to whisper. "Was it okay? Him seeing you? Or did you get—"

"I didn't."

"Yeah?"

"I don't know, Luna. I can't explain it. Maybe it was all the rum. I was scared. And I needed him to see me. To see me and want me and think I was enough—"

"You are."

"I know."

"Even if you were bigger, you'd be enough."

I swallow hard. "I…" Want to believe that. That I'll love myself no matter what my body looks like. That I'll accept gaining weight without blinking an eye. That it won't send me spiraling back to full-blown obsession.

"It's so fucked up. I'm telling you that. And I believe it about you. I love you, Daisy. I'd die if something happened to you. Really. You're my favorite person in the world."

"The entire world?"

She nods *yeah*. "I hate that we're not going to be in the same space anymore."

"At least we're not that far apart."

"Only half the state of California."

"At least it's not a long state." Only the longest state in the country.

"Not at all." Her smile is sad. "I hate that everything is changing. I'm excited too. And terrified. I just… don't show it."

"I know."

She nods. "I want you to have this… if you want to spend the week with Holden, don't let me stop you."

"I want to spend it with you too."

"Good." Her smile is soft. "It really is fucked up, because I'm saying all that shit to you, trying to believe it. And I do believe it about you. That you'd be worthy no matter what you looked like. Even if you were completely hideous."

"Hey."

"I know you don't realize you're gorgeous yet, but it's going to change when you get to school. You're going to need a baseball bat to keep guys away."

"Not as much as you."

"I don't know." She motions to her light hair. "Guys assume I'm a slut. That I'll blow them if they ask nicely. Maybe I need to cut it shorter. Give off more of a *don't fuck with me, asshole* vibe."

"Would you not?" I tease.

She chuckles. "What do I get out of it?"

"You don't… enjoy that."

"You haven't?" She motions to the upstairs. The shower is running. But only one of them.

Luna holds up her finger *one second*. She moves to the table, grabs her phone, pairs it with the Bluetooth speaker.

It takes a while. Long enough for the kettle to steam. For me to fill my mug.

"There." She sighs with relief as our usual soundtrack fills the room. Lorde. Like this is any other day, and not my eighteenth birthday.

Not the day I slept with Holden.

That I lost my virginity.

God, it's still hard to believe.

She grabs her coffee, returns to the room, stays close enough to whisper. "You didn't?"

"No, we uh… weren't you saying something?"

"Fuck that. I want details."

"This is how he and Oliver talk."

"And?"

"Aren't we supposed to be… better than that?"

She looks at me like I'm crazy. "Why?"

"I don't know. Dad would—"

"Tell you that as long as you trust him and you're safe, it's all good."

I cringe at the thought of my dad's sex talk.

"God, Gabe is so hot. You think Oliver will look like that in twenty years?"

"I think please no to the rest of this conversation."

"Don't worry. I think Oliver is hotter. But there's something about Gabe. A real daddy vibe."

"Please. Stop."

She laughs. Takes a sip of her coffee. Laughs more. "Neither of you did oral?"

"No. I, uh… I wanted to. To touch him. Taste him. Feel him. He's really—" My blush deepens. "Big."

She holds her hands about six inches apart. "Or?" She pulls them wider, wider—

"There."

"Damn." She looks at her spread hands. "That is a lot."

"Yeah."

"Did it hurt?"

"A little."

"He made you come?"

I nod. "He asked me to touch myself."

"Damn." She makes a show of fanning herself. "I didn't think he had it in him."

"You didn't?"

She shakes her head. "He's hot, yeah, but in a… I guess I just prefer the brooding ones."

"I swear to God, one more word about a Flynn male being hot and I'm leaving."

She laughs. "It was good?"

"Really good. Different. Not just physically but emotionally too."

"Intimate?"

"Yeah."

"And now…" Her expression softens. "Do you know what you're doing?"

"We're just… hanging out. For the rest of the trip."

"That's it?"

"Yeah."

"Four days then you part ways? You go to college? Find some educated guy to satisfy you?"

"Yeah."

"You're okay with that?"

"It was my idea." And it's fine. It's totally fine. I mean,

it's the only reasonable course of action. So it has to be fine.

Her eyes narrow. "Daisy... I love you. I say this with all the love in the world. Okay?"

I nod *go for it.*

"There's no way you believe you're okay with that."

I bite my lip.

"Maybe it's just... how it has to be. But if that's really what you're doing, be honest with yourself about how it's going to break you."

"It won't—"

"And if it's not how it has to be... be honest with him about what you really want?"

"This is what I want."

"Look me in the eyes when you say it."

I try. But as soon as my gaze meets hers, the words dissolve.

My best friend is right. It's bullshit. I can't stand the thought of kissing him goodbye.

But it's a problem for later.

I'm enjoying my stay in Mexico.

Even if it means spending my first night home crying myself to sleep.

Chapter Twenty-Seven

DAISY

As usual, Oliver emerges from his shower slightly grumpy. He chugs a milky cup of lukewarm coffee. Chases it with two aspirin. Transforms from Oscar the Grouch to mildly brooding and aloof.

"You ready?" He nods *good morning* to me and Luna.

She pats her tote bag. "Water, snacks, towels." She shoots him a knowing look. "Advil."

He chuckles. Reaches for something on the counter. The bottle of tequila. "If the birthday girl requests it."

"Can I request you actually swimming for once?" I ask.

His nose scrunches in distaste. "I'll think about it."

"Bring it if you want." Not thinking about my brother's drinking. Not today.

He nods *sure*, crosses the room, hands the bottle to Luna.

He gets as close as possible. Well, as close as he can get without making it clear he's trying to fuck her. Then he gets closer.

Whispers in her ear.

She laughs. Nods a yes. Watches as he releases her,

moves down the hall to the bathroom, slams the door closed.

I raise a brow.

"Birthday surprise," she says.

"Not your desire to mount him?"

She mimes pulling her lips zipped. "I promised not to discuss matters of Flynn hotness."

"Would you?" I ask.

"Sleep with your brother?"

I nod *yeah*.

"Sisters before misters."

"If you really think he'll make you happy…" I love Luna. I love Oliver. I almost love the thought of them together. If they got married, she'd be my sister. She'd be in my life forever.

But I know them both.

And they—

It's not a good idea. Maybe if he was sober it would be different, but he's not.

"I think… I need more coffee." She squeezes me. Moves into the kitchen. Fills a cup with what's left in the coffee maker. "He's usually better than this."

Footsteps move down the stairs.

The hall door opens.

Like they're working in unison, Holden and Oliver approach from opposite sides of the house.

My blush deepens as my eyes meet Holden's.

His cheeks flush. His smile gets goofy.

It's not like him.

It's intoxicating.

He shifts back to careless troublemaker. Clears his throat, dons his sunglasses, turns to my brother. "You bringing bourbon?"

There's something in his voice, like he's reminding me

of last night on purpose, like he wants me to recall the taste of his lips.

God, I bet he tastes good right now. Like toothpaste and Holden.

How much would it ruin everything if I kissed him right now?

If I tore his clothes off and fucked him right here on the floor?

"Tequila," Oliver says.

Holden raises a brow. "Doesn't sound like you."

"Trying new things." He slides his backpack over his shoulder. Steps into his flip-flops. "You ready, Daisy?"

"Yeah. Thanks." I pick up my tote bag and follow my brother out of the house.

———

IT'S ALREADY HOT. TOO HOT FOR ANY SERIOUS conversation. We walk in silence. Toward town, then down the boardwalk, to a docked boat.

Oliver talks to the, uh, seaman. Pays him for something. Turns back to us *come here*.

"We're going on a boat?" I appreciate the thought, I guess, but what the hell?

Holden presses his palm into my lower back. My cover-up brushes my skin, but I can still feel the heat of his hand. The pressure. The friction.

He leans in to whisper. "We're going to a hidden beach."

"We are?" My heartbeat picks up. That's incredibly, amazingly perfect.

"Yeah, but I didn't say anything. It's a surprise." He winks and follows my brother onto the boat.

Then it's Luna.

Me.

It's a small boat. Or maybe it's big, by boat standards. I'm not really sure. It's the size of my bedroom, with seats along three edges and a steering wheel up front.

The, uh, sailor motions to a cooler under one of the benches. He says something in Spanish, but I only catch half the words.

"It will be an hour." Oliver sits on one edge of the bench. He slides his backpack off. Bends to dig through the cooler.

Water.

He actually removes waters. One for each of us.

He hands them out, then he returns to his seat, dons his headphones, pulls out his Kindle.

"Good idea." Luna sits on the same bench. Dons her headphones and sunglasses. Leans back to soak up the sun.

I sit on the bench next to theirs, the one opposite the steering wheel, at the back of the boat.

Holden sits next to me. Offers his hand. "It might be rocky."

I nod *thanks*.

Then the sailor gets into position. Takes off.

The ride is slow, but it's fast enough it's choppy.

Thankfully, I have provisions. I pull a non-drowsy Dramamine from my bag, take one, offer it to Holden.

"Thanks." He takes one. Holds it up, offering it to Luna and Oliver.

Oliver nods yeah.

Holden tosses it over.

He turns back to me. "Doesn't it take an hour to kick in?"

"Someone should have warned me we're going on a boat."

"Damn." He leans back. Lets his legs splay open. "If only I wasn't distracted last night."

"Yeah?"

He nods *yeah*. "How do you feel?"

"Good." I fight a blush. "Sore."

Pride spreads over his expression. "You sleep okay?"

"Barely slept."

"Here." He reaches into his backpack. Pulls out something. A bottle of tea. "It's not a Holden latte, but it's not bad."

"Thanks. Really." I take the glass container.

He holds up his water to toast. "To your official birthday."

"I'm not sure I'm topping last night."

"You don't have faith in me?"

My stomach flutters. "Do you really think…"

"Maybe." He taps his bottle with mine. "At least, I hope so."

Fuck, there's something about his tone.

It's so hot.

I take a long sip of my iced tea. It's rich, with this hint of lemon, but it does nothing to cool me down.

"We have an hour here," he says.

"Are you going to offer me your headphones?"

"Sure. You like eighties music?"

"The stuff on the radio."

"You have a favorite?"

"Hmm." That's an excellent question. "I guess I'm partial to that one about dying in someone's arms."

He sings the chorus.

"That's it."

"Romantic."

I nod. "I like that idea. Of loving someone so much you could collapse in their arms. That you just… feel safe."

"It's sweet."

"Do you believe in that?"

"I don't know. It happens for some people." His voice trails off, but the implication stays clear. *But not for me.*

Ahem. "What's your favorite?"

"*Come on Eileen.*"

My laugh gets louder. "You like a guy pestering a woman to sleep with him?"

"Of course. That singer knows what he wants."

"Really?"

He shakes his head *of course not*. "It's a fucked-up song, but it's catchy."

"You like that sound?"

"Yeah. All the new wave stuff. Guess, in today's terms… it's kind of like Lorde. Only eighties."

"Like Lorde only eighties?"

"Is that not clear?"

I shake my head.

He smiles. "Pop. Electronic. A little weird. A little goth. My mom's favorite band was The Cure. Well, top five."

"*Lovesong?*"

He sings the chorus. He hits every note, and he sells the emotion too.

It's so not what I expect from him. But then I didn't expect last night. I'm not sure what I expect from him anymore.

His cheeks flush as he finishes.

"It's really earnest," I say.

"I told you. I'm earnest."

"I believe you."

He arches a brow *really*.

"Really."

"Good. That means you're more likely to agree to this."

"To?"

"The bad writing." He pulls out his cell. Goes straight to his shitty drawing, the one he showed me yesterday.

Though it's not all that bad. The technique is decent. As far as I can tell. "I, uh…"

"A promise is a promise."

"I don't…"

"I see that pink notebook." He motions to my tote bag. "You keep all your secrets in there?"

Yes, actually. Too many. Things he absolutely, positively can't see.

Although…

What if he could? What if I showed him? If I told him and he still wanted me?

What if someone else believed I was okay?

If he knew I was a mess and he still wanted me…

My heart thuds against my chest. My fingers curl into my thighs. My eyes press together.

I want it too much. So much I can barely breathe. And I… I don't want that ruining this.

Yes, I want to show him my scars. Yes, I want him to understand. To hold me and kiss me and whisper *I love you the way you are*.

But that…

Is it even possible?

"Daisy?" His fingers brush my wrist. It's a soft touch. Tender. Loving even. "If you really don't—"

"No, I do." I bend. Pick up my notebook. Run my finger over the edges. "But give me a minute to pick something out."

He nods *sure*.

I flip to something in the middle. Recent enough it won't give away anything. Old enough it's not raw.

There are so many ugly thoughts. Even a few months ago.

I skim a page about how I missed the comfort of my eating disorder.

Another about graduation. How scared and excited I was.

That fight I had with Mom over where to spend my summer.

The night Oliver passed out on the couch.

The first time Holden answered one of my questions. God, that was so embarrassing. I was so excited. Thrilled to have any hint of his attention.

I still am.

I want him to know.

But more than that, I want him to know the rest of this. To know and accept me.

Is it really possible?

Maybe… I mean, this isn't a good poem. It's impossible for anyone else to understand. I wrote it and I barely understand.

I trace the words with my fingers. Repeat them to myself.

My chest gets heavy. Shame rises in my throat, but I swallow it down.

Maybe I'm not sharing this with the world. Maybe it's ugly, but I…

No, I can't even say *it's a part of me and I accept it*. I'm not there yet. One day.

One day I'll be brave enough to tell him.

Today…

This is as good as I can do.

"It's really bad." I cover the poem with my hand.

"And this?" He holds up his drawing. The moody self-portrait in blue and black.

But I can't see the design flaws. Only the scared, lonely boy inside the troublemaker.

I want to see that side of him.
I want him to see this side of me.
"I'll read it once," I say. "But that's it."
He nods *okay*.
I take a deep breath. Exhale slowly.
Here goes nothing.

Chapter Twenty-Eight

HOLDEN

Daisy's brow furrows with concentration. He eyes fix on the paper. Fill with focus. Purpose. Determination.

Her chest heaves with her inhale. Caves with her exhale.

She opens her mouth to speak. Pauses. Like she's mustering up the courage.

Her finger traces the first word. A doodle next to it. A heart covered in thorns.

It's good. Every line has a purpose. The meaning is clear.

I don't know words, but I know images. And that one—

Is that really how she feels?

Fuck, I'm not supposed to be diving that deep. Everyone's warning me she's been through a lot. That I'm the last thing she needs.

I don't want it to be true. But I know better than to buy into my own hype.

She clears her throat. Begins.

I never find the right note
the hard angle
the perfect phrase
only two tiny words
not promise, or plea, or apology
but something in between
I'm sorry
I repeat the refrain
again and again
but only in my head
to the chains that used to bind me
and hold me together
I push them away
then they're too far
and I reach higher
and higher
closer
and closer
Until I can touch, taste, feel
that sweet sick comfort
of falling together
by falling apart
I'm sorry
I say it again
sit here empty
caving from the weight on my chest
those two words
the heaviness of everything unsaid
I'm sorry
but not for the reasons
I should be

Her posture shifts as she speaks. It's like she's melting into the words. Like they're coming straight from her soul.

She speaks every line with purpose and clarity.

Then she finishes, shrinks back, looks up at me with a nervous expression. "It's…"

I don't know what to say. I have no idea if it's well-written. That's way beyond my paygrade.

Hell, I don't even know what the words are.

But that ache in her voice.

I want every ounce of it. I want to know where she hurts. To kiss it better.

To hold her until—

I don't even know.

But then it doesn't matter. I can't have that. It's not within the realm of possibility.

"I, uh…" She presses the book closed, slips it into her tote bag, crosses her legs. "Bad, like I said."

"I liked it."

Her eyes fix on mine. "Yeah?"

"Maybe it's not good. I don't know. I couldn't tell Shakespeare from a cereal box. But it's raw. Real."

"Yeah."

"You, uh…" I reach for the right thing to say. Fail to find it. "That's a talent in its own right."

"Writing angsty poetry?"

"I'm not saying it will pay the bills. Or that you need to pursue it. But if it makes you happy—"

"It's not that exactly."

"What?"

Her eyes meet mine for a moment, then they drift to my hands. To the drawing on my cell. "It's more that if I don't write, my head gets too full. All my thoughts jumble."

"What do you write?"

"Besides bad poems?"

"Yeah."

"Mostly, I journal, I guess. I pour my thoughts onto the

page. It's like that old expression. Writing is easy. Just cut yourself and bleed onto the page."

Fuck, that's heavy. "Does it feel like that?"

"Yeah, but…" She wraps her fingers around her wrist. "In a good way. It's painful sometimes, but I always feel better after."

"Always?"

She nods.

"I get that." I turn to my cell, flip through my sketches. There's no Wi-Fi here. No data either. But I have some stuff on my phone. "When I can't figure something out, I draw."

"There are things you can't figure out?"

"A lot of them."

Her laugh is easy. "Like what?"

"How to help the people I love." I clear my throat. "Other stuff too. There's this voice in the back of my head. I usually move too fast to hear it. I try to stay busy. With work. Or the gym. Stupid TV shows. Sex."

She nods with understanding.

"It keeps that voice quiet. But when I sit with it… I start to ask myself what the fuck I'm doing with my life."

"You don't want to be a tattoo artist?"

"No." I swallow hard. I don't talk about this with anyone. I've never told anyone. But I want her to know. "I love my job. It's more… the rest of my life. I try not to get too attached to anyone. Or anything. Because that's more pain. There's no way to love without losing. And when you lose someone…" My gaze shifts to the ocean. "I don't want to be like my dad. He's not the same. He's never going to be the same."

"After your mom?"

I nod.

"Do you think he'd trade that time?"

"What do you mean?"

"That he'd give up the years he had with her to take all the pain away."

"No. He says it's worth it." But I don't see how. How can anything be worth two years of not getting out of bed? Of looking at the world like it's a dark place? "But he has to say that. He wouldn't have kids if—"

"Maybe he means it."

"Maybe."

"I've only met him a few times, but he seems more like Forest than you."

My laugh breaks up the tension in my shoulders. "What's that supposed to mean, kid?"

"Hmm." She plays dumb. "What could it mean? Could it have anything to do with both of them being sincere and you being—"

"Full of shit?"

"I was going to say… having a persona. But yeah," she says. "I don't know if it's worth it." Her gaze flits to her brother. "I wonder sometimes. I have nightmares about Oliver dying in a car crash. Or aspirating in the middle of the night. And I think… I don't know if I could live with that."

"What's the alternative?"

Her gaze shifts to the floor. "I just… I know what you mean. Who wants to open themselves up to that hurt? To let someone else reject them?"

"Yeah."

"I… I don't. But then…" Her eyes meet mine. "I really do like you."

"I like you too."

"And I… well, if you wanted to let your guard down, show me the real guy under the… uh, persona. I liked him last night."

"That was—"

"Sweet."

"Yeah."

"I, uh… I hope you do. Even though… it's a risk."

"Yeah."

Her smile is soft. "I always had you pegged as a risk taker."

"Some are scarier than others."

She nods *true*. "I, uh, I can't really talk. I'm still shaking, thinking about you reading the other stuff in there."

"It's not as bad as you think."

"No, it's more… what it says about me. Things you don't know. I think about telling you. I… I guess this is a start."

"You can tell me anything."

"But it might change the way you look at me. The way you think of me. Some things do. And I… I like the way you look at me."

"Me too." God, I really like the way she looks at me.

She leans back. Rests her head on my shoulder. "I promised myself I'd only think good thoughts today."

"This isn't good?"

"I don't know… but I… I want to have fun. Can we do that?"

"Of course." That's the one place where I excel.

That's what she wants from me.

What everyone wants from me.

———

DESPITE THE DRUGS, DAISY IS TOO MOTION SICK TO READ. We spend the rest of the ride sharing my headphones, listening to my mom's favorite The Cure album.

Daisy rests her head on my shoulder, closes her eyes, taps her fingers along with the music.

She's there. Free. Relaxed. Happy.

Usually, I try to set people at ease with... alternate means. It works, more or less.

This is different.

Like she can see some part of me no one else can.

Thankfully, Oliver doesn't think anything of us sharing music. He says nothing as we dock.

The beach is beautiful. A stretch of beige sand, nestled between high cliffs. Clear blue water. A cave roof stretching over half the water.

A dozen people on the sand. Another dozen in the water.

It's as picturesque as it gets, right down to the lemon sun and the bright sky.

Daisy rouses. Turns her attention to the beach.

Even though she's wearing her sunglasses, I can tell her eyes are going wide.

Fuck, the curve to her smile. The heave of her chest. The tug of her nails.

"Oh my God." She stands, which tugs at the headphones.

They fall out of her ear. She mouths *sorry*. Turns back to the beach. Takes in all its glory.

It is glorious. Clear water disappears into a cave roof. Sun falls through a hole in the roof, turns a circle of ocean into sparkling turquoise.

There's a sand bank past that, though it's out of sight at the moment.

Daisy turns to her brother. "Thank you."

He stands. Pulls her into a tight hug. Whispers something in her ear.

She looks to me with a smile. "Thank you, Holden." Her attention turns to her brother. "Swim to the bank. With us. At least for a while. Then you can hang out on the boat." She slides off her sunglasses. Places them on the dock.

Oliver's face scrunches in distaste.

But he nods *okay, fine*. Motions to his waterproof backpack.

She nods *good thinking*, moves some of her stuff into his bag.

Luna does the same. Then she does away with her sundress, slips out of her sandals, moves to the edge of the boat. "You coming?" She looks back to Daisy and raises a brow.

Daisy nods *hell yes*.

I try not to stare as she takes off her cover-up.

I fail completely.

Fuck, she's beautiful. And she's wearing that same pastel pink bikini.

It's perfect against her pale skin.

It's—

Fuck, I need to stop this line of thinking or I'm going to fuck her right here.

I force my gaze to the ocean.

Daisy takes her best friend's hand and jumps off the boat.

They shriek as they hit the water.

The sailor says something about how the boat will return in two hours.

Oliver looks to me *what the fuck am I doing?* He shakes his head. "Might as well get this over with."

"Is it that bad?"

He looks at the ocean like it did him wrong. Then he shrugs *here goes nothing* and jumps in.

I dive into the water. Take in the comfort of the warm, salty ocean.

Then I surface and try to keep my eyes off Daisy.

She and Luna swim around like they're part mermaid.

Oliver heads straight for shore. Despite his hatred of the beach, he's a strong swimmer. Even with the backpack, he's fast. And fuck knows that backpack must be heavy. There's at least a gallon of water in there.

He surprises me. He finds a spot on the sand, drops his backpack, returns to the water.

Goes straight to his sister.

She shrieks as he splashes her. Then she splashes him back.

They're so close. Like best friends.

They've been through a lot of shit together and they're still standing. Helping each other stand.

And here I am, threatening to fuck that up.

But I won't.

Whatever happens, I won't fuck that up.

Chapter Twenty-Nine

HOLDEN

"This is perfect." Daisy looks up from her spot in the middle of the cave. She takes in the wide hole letting in the sun, the brilliant sky, the greenery covering the rock. "How did it get so round?"

"Supposedly, it was from some kind of artillery," I say. "A cannon or something."

"Damn." Her eyes stay fixed to the opening. "That should be horrible. But it's so pretty." She swims into a ray of sunlight.

Fuck, she looks like an angel.

Light covers her in a warm glow. It bounces off her pale skin, her wet hair, her pink bikini top.

The purple bruise on her neck.

She catches me staring. Fights a blush. "I should have warned you."

"Yeah?"

"I bruise easily. But… uh…" She looks around the cave. There are other people here. A young couple on our right. A family on our left. But no sign of Oliver or Luna.

They're on the beach. Out of view.

More or less.

Daisy turns to me. She moves closer. Closer.

Her fingers brush my chest. "I'm glad I didn't." She slings her arm around my neck. "Is this okay?"

I nod. "I'm glad you didn't too."

Her smile spreads a little wider. "It was… I just… Can we do it again?"

My laugh is easy. "Here?"

"Is that even possible?"

"You don't think I'm up for it?"

She wraps her legs around my waist. "I'm not sure I am. That's a lot of athleticism."

"You're a strong swimmer."

"Maybe closer to the sand. But, that's—"

"Yeah."

"And, uh, there are a lot of people here."

"There are."

"Wouldn't be appropriate."

"You're only encouraging me."

She smiles. Presses off my chest. Treads water a foot away. "I guess I have to save you from yourself."

"Someone should."

"So, uh…" She motions to the greenery covering the roof. "You love the beach too?"

"Always have. But I have a new appreciation."

"Oh." Her cheeks flush. "There's something about it. This freedom."

"Yeah."

"Being in the water is safe. Comfortable. Like it's holding your body."

"It is."

"It's one of the few places where I stop thinking. Where I sink into the moment and feel."

"What else?"

Her eyes meet mine. "Besides writing shitty poems?"

"Isn't that thinking?"

"At first. But after a few minutes, I fall into it. I'm one with my pen. It sounds silly. But it's magic."

"When you fall into something?"

"Yeah." Her cheeks flush. "It does sound stupid. I can see it in your eyes."

"No." I shake my head. That's not it. Not even close. "It's more… you really think you need to tell me about the merits of turning off your brain?"

"It's not that, exactly. More that my thoughts aren't in the way anymore. There's no voice saying *this isn't good enough*. Or *watch out for your brother*. Or *is this really a productive use of your time?* I'm there, in the moment."

"Writing in your journal?"

"Yeah." Her gaze shifts to the sky. "Someplace like this… it's beautiful. Not inspiring exactly. But there's a feeling. I want to hold on to it. So I can capture it. But if I try to do it analytically, it doesn't work. It has to come from—"

"Instinct?"

"Something like that, yeah."

"Isn't that what you want from me?"

"Huh?" Her eyes fill with confusion.

"You asked me to help you drop your inhibitions."

She nods.

"Or were you just trying to get in my pants?"

Her cheeks flame red. "A little."

My laugh is easy. "Glad to help." I swim to her. So I'm close enough to slide my arm around her waist.

It's under the water. Our secret.

No one around us can see.

If I slip my hand into her bikini bottoms—

That could be our secret too.

Ahem.

"I meant what I said before. You're high-strung." I run my fingers over the curve of her waist. "It's good in some ways. It's why you have straight As and admission to Berkeley."

She nods.

"But I'm guessing it's tiring."

"Very."

"When else? Do you let go? Lose yourself?"

"Well… there were moments. Last night." Her blush deepens. "Is it normally like that?"

"Sex?"

"Yeah."

"That's always my goal. I want to be there, in that moment, every ounce of my attention focused on my partner. On the pleasure in her eyes. The part of her lips. The scrape of her nails against my back."

She hangs on every word.

"I want to watch her shudder. To see the moment where she falls over the edge. To feel her cunt pulsing around me."

Her eyes widen. "You, uh…"

Shit, I need to ease her into this. "I'm already doing it. Falling into the moment. Tuning into you."

"So you uh—"

"You don't like it?"

"I like it."

"The word?"

"Oh." Her teeth sink into her lip. "I haven't heard a lot of people say it."

"Try it."

She shakes her head *no way*.

"Why not?"

"I just…"

"You appreciate the power of words."

"Oh." Her brow knits with epiphany. "That is true."

"It's a strong word."

"Yeah."

"So try it."

Her blush deepens. "Maybe."

"If you're not ready—"

"It's not that—"

"Listen to it." I bring my lips to her ear. "I want to taste your cunt."

Under the water, her nails scrape my skin.

"I want to feel your cunt pulsing around my cock as you come."

"Fuck."

"I want to come inside your pretty pink cunt."

Her response is a groan.

She runs her fingers over my chest. Then down my stomach. Beneath my bellybutton.

Over my swimsuit.

"You're hard," she breathes.

"Yeah."

"You… we… I want to do that. Later."

Whatever it is she wants to do, the answer's yes. "Say it."

She clears her throat.

"Say: baby, I want you to taste my cunt."

She shakes her head *no way*.

All right. I'll let her off easy. This time. "Baby, I want to come on your face."

She rubs me over my swimsuit. "This instead."

It's tempting. But also a terrible idea. "That later."

Her sigh is a whine. She pulls back enough to look me in the eyes. But only for a second.

Her gaze goes right to my chest. "So, uh, we were

talking about sex. And how it's a place where you can let go."

"That's the goal."

"And, uh…"

"Say it, baby."

Her cheeks flush.

"Say it."

She sucks in a deep breath. Pushes out a shaky exhale.

Then she moves closer. Melts into my body. Warms my ear with her breath. "I want… to come on your face."

Fuck, that's hot. Even with her nervous. "Again. Like you mean it."

This time, her breath is easier. "I want to come on your face."

"One more time."

Her nails scrape my chest. "I want to come on your face."

My balls tighten. Fuck, this water isn't cold enough. It's not doing shit to cool me down.

It's filling my head with all sorts of bad ideas. Like dragging her to the beach and fucking her right there, in front of everyone.

"I do." She pushes off me. "But, uh… not here."

"That's good."

"Yeah?"

"I can't breathe underwater."

Her laugh breaks the sexual tension. "Well… um… in that case, maybe—"

"You ever feel that?"

"That state where I let go and lose myself in the moment?"

"Yeah."

"It's only been the one time." Her blush spreads to her chest.

"When you're alone?"

"Touching myself?"

I nod.

"Sometimes. Other times, I'm kinda stuck in my head. I'll try so hard to focus on the sensations, but thoughts keep intruding."

"Maybe you need to try less hard."

"Maybe." She motions to the other side of the cave. The one that leads to the open ocean.

She doesn't wait for my reply. She just swims.

There's something about seeing her in the water. She belongs here.

It fits the image I have of her—beautiful, blond beach girl—but it clashes too. Sure, I often imagine Daisy in a tiny bikini. Or sprawled out naked on the sand.

But when I really think of her, I see a girl reading at home. Sipping tea on the couch. Obsessing over her homework.

We move past the cave. Then around it. All the way to the other side of the beach.

She climbs onto the sand.

I follow. Scan the beach for a quiet spot. There are people to our right. A dozen or so, including Oliver and Luna.

But to our left—

It's not exactly private, but it's hidden. A cave. Tiny. But out of view.

I take her hand. Lead her into the shady spot.

Her fingers brush my wrist.

I slide my arm around her waist. "Where else?"

"Hmm?"

"Do you feel that? Lose yourself?"

"Oh. When I listen to music I love. I can feel it in my

bones. And when I dance." She rocks her hips to one side. "That's my favorite."

"You're there, in your body?"

"Sometimes." Her eyes meet mine. "You?"

"I'm always in my body."

"But you... I don't know, Holden. You're *there* a lot of the time. But, sometimes, you're more like me. You're hanging out on the sidelines, cracking wise so you don't have to engage."

Fuck, that's true.

"It's not a judgment. I get it. I really get it. But I... I guess I'd like to help you too."

"Oh?"

She nods *yeah*. "Help you get over that fear of letting your guard down."

"I'm afraid?"

"Aren't you?"

I can't deny that. I swallow hard. "I..."

"I am too." She runs her thumb over my forearm. "I, uh... I have a lot of things I want to ask you. About art. And how you got into it. How you started this—" she traces a tattoo up my forearm. "It's a lot of work. I'm sure you have some bullshit answer—"

"About how I love having a huge phallic symbol I can use to paint women with my—"

"Oh my God." She laughs so hard she doubles over. "It's... oh my God."

"It's good, yeah?"

"And true... I mean, that has to be part of it? All these guys leaving their mark on people. Especially pretty women."

"You're into that?"

"Into..."

"Me leaving a mark on you." I like talking to her. I

really do. But, right now, I need this. "Here maybe." I press my palm into her lower back.

"How would you—" Her eyes light up. "Oh."

"Maybe here." I place my hand on her chest. Above her heart. So I don't start stripping her out of her bikini.

She nods *yes*.

"Oh maybe—" I drag my fingers up her neck, over her chin, along her lower lip. "Maybe you want me to come in that pretty mouth."

"Holden—"

"Yeah, baby?"

"I know you're trying to distract me."

"Am I?"

"Yeah. And it, uh… it is working."

"Good."

Her chest heaves with her inhale. "But, uh… I just I have to say… that I'm not going to forget this conversation."

"Me either."

"And I do want to hear more."

"Me too."

"But, I also—"

"Want to come on my face?"

"Yeah." Her cheeks flush. "Is it…? Will someone see?"

"Maybe."

"Oh." She looks to the beach to our right. Then she moves farther into the cave. Stares at the dark wall. "I…"

"It's up to you."

Her eyes meet mine. Her tongue slides over her lips. "Okay."

"Okay?"

"Hell yes."

"Good." I pull her body into mine. "I've been dreaming about this for way too fucking long."

Chapter Thirty

HOLDEN

Daisy's eyes flutter closed.

She rises to her tiptoes. Brings her lips to mine.

I press one hand into her lower back. Bring the other to the back of her neck.

Fuck, she tastes good. Like salt and like Daisy.

I need more of that. Every drop of it.

It's not like kissing other girls. It goes deeper. It sinks into my bones.

I don't know how to handle that.

So I focus on her soft lips. The way she groans against my mouth. The way she tugs at my hair as I scrape my teeth against her bottom lip.

I need to show her how to do this. How to lose herself in the moment.

I kiss her harder. I pull her closer. I claim her mouth with my tongue.

It's ridiculous. She can't be mine. It's completely out of the question.

Right now—

This moment is ours. In this moment, she's mine.

I'm not thinking about anything but how much I want to make her come.

I trace the strings of her halter top. Down her neck and chest. Over that tiny triangle.

I push the fabric aside.

Her breast spills from the top. I cup her with my palm. Run my thumb over her nipple.

She groans into my mouth. Rocks her hips against me. Claws at my back like she needs more. Like she needs everything.

She does.

And I need to give it to her.

And that's fucking magic.

I make my pressure harder. It's different, with us still wet from the beach. There's less friction, but we're stickier too.

She tastes like salt.

Fuck, I need to taste her everywhere.

I bring my lips to her neck. I kiss her softly to start.

Then harder.

Harder.

The scrape of my teeth.

Enough she feels it.

Enough it hurts.

"Fuck." She sinks her nails into my back. "Holden—"

"Yeah, baby?"

The pet name makes her shake.

"You want more?" I bite her again, a little lower.

"Yeah-"

"You want me to suck on those gorgeous tits?"

"Mmmm."

"They drive me insane, baby. You know that?" I take her free hand. Bring it to my cock.

She cups me over my swimsuit. "I love this."

"Yeah?"

"This." She rubs me over my swimsuit. "Knowing I make you hard."

"You do."

"And you… I want to make you come."

"After."

"You promise?"

"Fuck yeah." I nip at the soft skin of her neck.

She lets out a heavy sigh.

I do it again. And again.

Until her sighs run together.

Slowly, I bring my lips to her chest. I tease her with light flicks of my tongue.

She scrapes her nails against my back.

My balls tighten. I should tell her to stop—this is going to show, and it's going to be hard to explain—but I can't.

Right now, none of that shit matters.

This is all that matters.

This is fucking everything.

I flick my tongue against her nipple a little harder.

Then harder.

Hard enough she shakes.

I toy with her nipple. With slow circles, fast flicks, zigzags.

The soft pressure of my mouth.

Then more. Harder. Until I'm sucking so hard her groan is agony as much as it's ecstasy.

I move to her other nipple. Toy with her just as mercilessly.

When she's panting, I scrape my teeth against her flesh.

"Fuck, Holden." She rocks her hips against me. "Don't stop."

I scoop her into my arms. Help her onto the sand. Push her legs apart.

She looks up at me as I place my body between her legs. She pushes her other triangle aside.

I lower my body onto hers.

She groans as my hard-on brushes her cunt.

I kiss her hard and deep. Then I work my way down her neck.

To her breast.

I toy with her right nipple.

Then the left.

Then it's my teeth against her flesh until she's shaking.

Slowly, I move lower.

My lips between her breast.

On her stomach.

Above her bellybutton.

Below it.

At the low waist of her bikini bottoms.

I undo the right strap.

The left.

I peel the garment off her body. Lay it beneath her.

Her fingers dig into the sand.

Her chest heaves with her inhale.

"Holden," she breathes.

"Yeah, baby?"

"I… uh…"

"Remember what I said last night?"

"Just breathe?"

"Yeah. Can you do that for me?"

She nods *okay*.

"If it's too much." I take her hand. Bring it to the back of my head.

Her fingers curl into my hair. She tugs softly. Then harder.

"Perfect." I pry her thighs apart.

She groans as I pin her legs to the sand.

I want to tease her for hours. To keep her on the edge. To stay the only thing in her brain.

God, if this was different, if we were in my apartment with no plans.

If I could spend the entire week making her come.

Learning every nook and cranny of her body.

Exactly where to press to make her purr—

Fuck, what am I saying?

So what if I don't have all afternoon?

I have this.

And this is fucking magic.

I press my lips to the inside of her thigh.

Then higher.

Higher.

Higher—

So, so close to where I need to be—

There.

She groans as I bring my lips to her clit.

I lick her up and down. Slowly.

Not to tease her or toy with her or push her toward the edge.

Because I want to taste every inch of her.

The salt from the ocean. And a sweetness that's all her.

I run my tongue over her one more time. Then I bring my mouth to her clit.

Brush my lips against her softly.

Then a little harder.

Harder.

"Fuck." Her toes curl. "That's... fuck."

I match the pressure with my tongue. Try a little harder, a little lighter, until I find exactly what she needs.

She rocks her hips as I lick her.

There.

I explore her. Higher. Lower. Right. Left.

Her nails scrape my skin.

Her thighs fight my hands.

Her hips rock to meet me.

I lick her up and down one more time—for me, because I want every fucking drop of her—then I bring my tongue to exactly where she needs me.

I work her with steady strokes.

"Holden." She tugs at my hair, holding me in place.

I scoop her hips into my hands. Hold her against me.

Her thighs press into my cheeks.

Her nails dig into my skin.

I work her with those perfect steady strokes.

Again.

And again.

Until she's right at the edge.

Until she's panting and shaking and writhing.

One more flick of my tongue and I push her over the edge.

She groans my name as she comes.

She squeezes me with her soft thighs.

I work her through her orgasm. But I don't release her. I hold her in place. Work her a little harder.

A little more to the right.

"Fuck." She rocks her lips into my mouth again and again.

Until she comes on my lips again.

Fuck, she tastes good.

I never want to stop.

She has to pull me away.

She *does* pull me away.

Her palm brushes my chest. Stomach. Crotch. "Can I?"

"Can you?"

She pushes me onto my back. Climbs into my lap.

"I don't have a condom."

She nods with understanding. Brings her lips to my neck. Then my chest. "I've never done it before."

Fuck.

"Will you show me?"

I nod *yeah*. Hell yeah.

She kisses her way down my stomach.

I lift my hips so she can pull my swimsuit to my thighs.

Fuck, now I really am dreaming.

There's no way this is possible.

I've officially lost it.

But I haven't.

Daisy Flynn is straddling my thighs, staring at my cock like it's the best thing she's ever seen.

This is actually happening.

Fuck, I'm supposed to be instructing her.

"Wrap your hand around me." I curl my fingers around her wrist. Bring her into position.

Slowly, she wraps her hand around my cock.

"Harder."

She grips me tighter.

Fuck, that already feels so good. I'm going to come too fast. "Run your hand up and down."

She pumps me with a soft stroke.

"Harder."

She does it a little harder.

My eyelids flutter closed. "A little harder."

"Really?"

"Yeah."

She pumps me harder.

"Fuck." I reach for some more specific instruction, but she's too fast. She runs her hand over my cock again.

273

Again.

Again.

"You're gonna make me come," I groan.

"How do I…" Her cheeks flush as her eyes meet mine. "I haven't—"

Jesus Christ, she wants me to tell her how to suck my cock.

This is going to kill me.

It's actually going to kill me.

"Wrap your lips around me."

She looks at my cock like it's an ice cream cone she's desperate to taste.

She leans down. Brings her mouth to my flesh.

Her lips brush my tip.

Then it's her soft, wet tongue.

I reach for her. One hand on the back of her head. The other on her chest.

I nod *go on*.

Slowly, she takes me into her mouth.

"It's the same motion." I run my thumb over her nipple. "But with your mouth."

She takes me deeper.

Deeper.

Deep enough she gags.

She pulls away. Sits back on her heels. "Sorry, I—"

"It happens. Should have warned you."

"Oh."

"You don't have to go that deep. You can—" I take her hand. Bring it to the base of my cock. "Keep it here."

She runs her thumb over me.

Fuck. "If you want to make it happen faster—" I draw circles around her nipple. "One here—" I repeat the motion on my tip.

She watches with rapt attention. "Would you?"

"Would I?"

"Touch yourself? If I asked?"

"Yeah. But I'll come too fast. Won't have—"

"I want to be the one." Her cheeks flush. "Like you said. I want you to... to come in my mouth."

My balls tighten.

"Please."

"You're gonna kill me."

"Good." She holds my gaze for a moment, then she watches herself work.

One steady stroke.

Her thumb against my tip.

A slow circle.

Fuck.

She lowers herself. Brushes her lips against my cock. Around my tip.

I knot my hand in her hair as she takes me into her mouth.

She runs her mouth over me again.

Again.

"Harder, baby."

She follows the instruction immediately.

Works me harder.

And harder.

Until my eyes close.

And my body takes over.

I toy with her nipple.

She sucks on my tip.

I tug at her hair.

She flicks her tongue against me.

Swirls it around me.

Then it's the soft pressure of her entire mouth.

Harder.

Harder.

"Fuck." My hips buck of their own accord.

She jumps back for a second. Goes right back to that same pressure.

I toy with her as she toys with me.

Harder.

Harder.

That same perfect pressure again and again.

"Fuck." I tug at her hair. "I'm gonna come."

She keeps her hold on me.

Works me though my orgasm.

I groan her name as I come in her pretty mouth.

She waits until I've spilled every drop. Then she sits up. Swallows hard.

She beams with pride for a moment. Then her eyes catch mine and her cheeks flush.

She's shy after that.

It defies explanation.

But then that's Daisy.

She's something else.

She helps me into my swimsuit.

I help her into hers.

"We should probably—" she motions to the beach opposite us.

I nod *yeah*. It's getting late. The boat is due back soon.

"That was uh…"

"Educational?"

"Really hot. But also educational. Thanks."

"Anytime."

"Later?"

"Later?" I'm too disconnected from conscious thought to follow this conversation.

"Can we do that again? Later?"

Oh. "Yeah. But not until after you come on my cock again."

Chapter Thirty-One

DAISY

W e barely make it to the boat.

I spend the ride back to town sharing Luna's headphones, whispering a replay I really shouldn't share.

Not with Oliver ten feet away.

But then I don't care.

For once, I'm relaxed. Easy. Free.

Totally and completely spent.

The ride passes quickly. Then it's dinner at a restaurant downtown. A quiet place with fresh fish and homemade cocktails.

Mine is delicious—some mix of tequila and tropical fruit—but it's also enough to push my exhaustion over the edge.

Genius that she is, Luna insists she wants to stay out for one more drink.

Holden agrees to take me home.

We have the place to ourselves. For long enough. But I'm too out of energy.

Even so, I invite him to shower with me.

It's strange, being naked with him in the tiny space, under the bright lights.

There's a part of me that's scared and insecure, but it's tiny. Barely there.

Even as he soaps his hands and runs them over my body.

Even as he holds me close.

Even as he whispers, "I want to watch you come," in my ear and slips his hand between my legs.

My insecurities disappear.

All my thoughts disappear.

I surrender to the sensations in my body.

He makes me come quickly. Then he helps me out of the shower, into my pajamas, into bed.

He holds me close.

I know he'll leave as soon as I fall asleep.

I know he's too good at this to get caught.

But I don't care.

I only care about how good his body feels against mine.

Chapter Thirty-Two

DAISY

I wake to the orange light of sunrise. I'm alone—Holden must have left my bed hours ago—but I don't feel abandoned.

Yes, I want him here. I want him closer. I want every inch of him pressed against every inch of me.

But I'm also a reasonable woman. Even if Oliver wasn't an issue, Holden is…

Not a commitment guy.

And I don't need a commitment. No matter how much I like him. Or how good he makes me feel. Or how much easier it is to let go around him.

It's a fresh start. Another one, I guess. No whispered secrets about last summer (they followed me to my new school). No comments on how uptight I am. Or how I need to let my hair down. (I wear it down, thank you very much.)

Yes, I feel free around Holden now. But starting school with a long-term boyfriend, one who's never had a girl-friend before, who usually sleeps with a different person every three days.

I don't need that headache.

I just don't.

No matter how much I want it. Or want him. Or want this to last forever.

Ahem.

I fix a cup of English breakfast with extra milk. Then my usual oatmeal. Raisins, cinnamon, milk.

It's nice, eating alone, at the big table. It's nice to finally have some space that's all mine.

When I'm finished, I check my cell messages. One from each of my parents. A sweet *happy birthday, honey, call me if you need anything* from Dad. And an *I miss you so much, please call* plea from Mom.

She sounds lucid, but it's hard to tell with her.

I listen twice, make a mental note to call back later—it's really early in California—then I fix another cup of tea and head to the pool deck.

It's already warm—too warm for a hot beverage—so I slip my feet into the pool. Watch the sunrise as I sip.

Slowly, the orange fades from the sky.

The sun falls over the pool deck.

Over me.

I close my eyes and soak in the feeling of warmth. It's comfortable. Safe. There's no other way to describe it.

It's perfect.

This—dipping my feet in the water, feeling the sun on my face, listening to the quiet sounds of the quaint town beneath us—is perfect.

It's peace.

It's the thing I've been failing to achieve for the last... ever.

Footsteps interrupt the quiet.

I turn, expecting Holden.

But Oliver is the one sliding through the glass door. He holds up a water bottle. *You want some?*

"Sure." I turn my back to him. Focus on the brilliant blue sky.

My brother sits next to me. Dips his feet in the water. Hands me the bottle. "You're up early."

"I was going to say the same."

"Couldn't sleep."

"Why not?" I take a long sip. Then another. Fuck, I *am* thirsty. Thirsty enough to down this entire thing.

"Just couldn't."

"Drink too much?"

He shakes his head *no*. Says nothing about the comment. Or his lack of desire to have this conversation again.

Honestly, I don't want to have it either.

I'd like to never have it again.

But it's not like I can talk about avoiding getting better.

"I'm glad no one else is up." He takes the water back. Tilts his head back to swig. The same motion he makes when he drinks bourbon. "We only have three more days."

"Yeah."

"Then, what, a week, at home? And you leave for Berkley."

"That's still three days."

"Yeah, but you're not here to hang with me."

"True." I can't help but laugh. Maybe this can be an easy conversation. Maybe we don't need to discuss his drinking. Or Holden. Or my eating habits.

"You having fun?"

"A lot, yeah."

"And Holden's taking good care of you?"

So much for that. I look to the water. Try to steel my expression. "Yeah. He's... fun."

"He's good at that."

I nod.

"Nothing inappropriate?" Oliver's voice is matter-of-fact. Like he's asking what kind of tea I'd like. Not like he's trying to figure out if I've fucked his friend.

I match his vibe. "It's Holden."

"True." Oliver chuckles. He turns just a little. Just enough to look me in the eyes. "You know what I mean."

Yeah. I'm not answering that question. Or lying. I just have to word this right... "He's not crossing any of my boundaries."

"Fuck, you sound like a shrink."

"I feel like one. After all those appointments." So many during inpatient treatment. Then one a week, every week, for the rest of my life.

"You talk to the therapist your shrink recommended?"

"The one in Berkley?"

"Yeah."

"Well... only in email." I've been putting off all my thoughts about moving. About leaving my life. And especially about needing constant therapy. But I have scheduled my first appointment. "I'm going to see her the week after classes start."

"You promise you'll stick with it?"

"Yeah." What's the alternative? I don't want to be a mess. I just am.

His voice drops to a whisper. "And you've been eating enough."

I try to swallow my irritation. "Can we not?"

He shoots me that typical Oliver look. *Are you gonna make me drag out this conversation?*

"Seriously, Oliver."

"Say yes, and I'll drop it."

"What if I asked, 'are you drinking too much'?"

"How's that different than the look you give me every time I order a fucking drink?" His voice barely raises. Frustration barely seeps in.

But it does.

Am I that obvious?

Back when I was in the middle of it, when I was still trying to lose enough weight I'd disappear—

I didn't think anyone could tell.

I didn't think anyone cared enough to notice.

They certainly didn't call me on it.

"I'm not going to feel guilty for worrying about you," I say.

He shrugs *fine*.

"What if I gave you an ultimatum?" I leave the *like you did to me* as subtext. "If I said I won't talk to you until you stop drinking?"

"Are you saying that?"

"No, but what if I did?"

His brow furrows.

"How is it different? Than last year? How would it be different?" So much for subtext.

"I have it under control."

"I thought that too."

His eyes fill with frustration. He shrinks back for a second. Then he nods like he's realized something. "Are you trying to avoid a real conversation?"

"No."

"Are you skipping meals again?"

"No."

"Purging."

I want to say *fuck you*, but it doesn't help my case. "No."

"Is that why you left dinner so early?" His expression is equal parts anger and concern.

"No. I'm good. I've been good for a long time."

"Then it's about Holden?"

"No… I just… I worry about you."

"What did he do?"

"He didn't do anything."

Oliver scoffs *yeah right*. "If he touched you, I'll kill him."

"Grow up."

"I will."

I… am so not having this conversation. There's nowhere to go. No way to avoid it.

My brother is right there.

Only.

Okay, that's it.

I slip into the pool. In my pajamas. They're nothing special. A tank top and shorts. Easy to replace.

"I need to grow up?" he asks.

I keep my back to him as I swim to the other end of the pool.

"Fuck it," he mutters.

Splash.

My brother jumps into the pool.

He crosses it quickly. Stops at the wall, next to me. "You are trying to avoid something."

"My brother dictating my sex life, yeah."

His eyes turn down. "Did he—"

"Seriously, don't."

"I will kill him, Daisy. I will. If he hurts you, it will be the last thing he ever does."

I focus on the blue sky. It's almost sweet, how much Oliver is willing to kill to defend me. Even if he's overly fixated on the whole *he better not touch you* part of that. "Noted."

His voice softens. "Does he know?"

"Know what?"

He shoots me a *get real* expression.

Oh. I guess it's always there. Like his drinking. There's no hiding it. No changing the subject. No feigning ignorance. "No, he doesn't know."

"Are you going to tell him?"

"Maybe… we're just friends. I don't know if he—"

"Me either."

I turn toward my brother.

His blue eyes are filled with sympathy.

"You don't have faith in him?" I dig my fingers into the concrete. The water is still cool and supportive, but that safety and peace is gone.

"You have to accept people for who they are."

Understatement of the year.

"Not everyone can handle heavy shit."

"Yeah." I suck a breath through my nose. "You think… how do you think he'd react?"

"Honestly, Daisy, I don't know."

"You've never mentioned anything—"

"I'd die first."

"Really?"

He nods *of course*. "I'd do anything to protect you."

I turn back to the house. It's still quiet. The hallway is still empty. "I know."

"Are you two…"

"We're friends."

"If you are—"

"Are you going to threaten to kill him again?"

He matches my position. "Probably, yeah."

"Why?"

"What else can I do?"

"Talk to me like we're both adults."

"Dunno. Sounds impossible."

I can't help but laugh. "You've done it before."

He makes that *sorta* motion. "Are you okay?"

"Yeah, just…"

"Tired of my bullshit?"

"Kinda, yeah."

His laugh is easy. "Okay, I won't ask again. On one condition."

"What?"

"You'll tell me if something happens between you two."

"If I do?"

"I'll try my hardest to act like a reasonable adult."

"And not a drunk caveman?"

He nods *yeah* and offers me his hand.

I shouldn't shake. It's a lie of omission. A promise to lie in the future.

But I do.

He pulls me into a hug. Pats my back. "I'm glad you're willing to tell me off."

"Yeah?"

"You wouldn't have done that two years ago."

True.

"You… fuck, I know you hate when I say this, but I'm so fucking proud of you, Daisy."

I nod *okay*.

"I was so fucking scared… I thought I'd lose you forever."

"I know."

"You can't do that to me. I know it's not fair to ask, but I don't care."

"Okay."

"And you promise you'll tell me if you need anything? If school is too much and you need to come home?"

I should say no. That I'm sure I'm ready to be on my own. That I'm sure I'm strong enough to survive that. But I'm not. I'm terrified. And I want to know my brother will do whatever it takes to make sure I'm okay. "I promise."

"I'm really gonna miss you."

"I'll miss you too."

"How about this. You stop asking about my drinking, I'll stop asking if you're eating."

"Always or for the next three days."

He shoots me that *get real* look.

I guess that's fair. It's not like I'm going to stop worrying. "Okay."

I offer my hand.

He shakes.

This time, I'm not sure which one of us is lying.

Chapter Thirty-Three

DAISY

T he tension of our fight diffuses. By the time the house is dressed, fed, and ready to hit town, it's gone.

I let our agreement swallow every bit of concern in my head. I stop asking myself about Oliver's habits. Stop worrying about him watching me eat.

I just... live.

We spend the morning walking around town, then hanging out in Starbucks for the beautiful air-conditioning. Oliver and Luna complain about the shitty coffee. Insist on going somewhere else to find the "good stuff."

Genius that he is, Holden claims he wants another tea. Here.

I follow his lead.

We linger in the blissfully air-conditioned shop talking about nothing and everything forever.

Touching more than we should.

Kissing way more than we should.

Sneaking out of the store, finding a quiet spot on the beach, kissing until we're out of breath.

———

Eventually, I answer one of Luna's texts. We meet for lunch. Spend the afternoon at the beach, the four of us together. Eat dinner together. Drink just enough together. (Oliver doesn't overdo it, for once).

Holden and I linger in the pool together, but we don't touch or kiss or fuck. It's too risky.

The next day, I hang out with my best friend. We swim and walk and shop and talk. And we even drink a little.

I'm running out of time with her. After this trip, we'll be hundreds of miles apart. Too far apart for quick visits.

Sure, we have chats and texts and emails and Face-Time. But it's not the same. It's never the same.

We stay out late. Get home to the boys asleep. Barely make it to our beds.

She promises to leave the last full day for me and Holden. To keep Oliver distracted—and out of the house —all day.

Because it's my last day with him too.

I'm not sure if it's the end of us.

But it's the end of something.

Chapter Thirty-Four

DAISY

Except for the hum of an eighties rock song, the house is quiet.

Oliver and Luna are already gone. Off on some all-day tour of a Mexican coffee roaster. Apparently, the country had a rich tradition of growing beans—it has a lot of land in the "coffee belt"—but it's suffering from a bad reputation because of a shortage a dozen or so years ago.

Our resident coffee addicts are excited to learn more. No doubt they'll educate us tonight.

It's interesting enough, but I can't say I'm craving the information. Coffee is in a weird place for me. Firmly in sickland. I drank it all the time when I was sick. To fill my stomach with warmth. Distract my taste buds with artificial sweetness. Speed my heart with caffeine.

It was bad coffee too. Instant stuff.

Now I...

The taste is too strong, too bitter, too much like mud. I'm not sure if it's something about the coffee itself or if it's the memory.

Either way—

I have tea.

I have today.

I can hang out on the couch with Holden.

Or drag him to my bed.

Or jump into the ocean.

Or whisper my secrets in his ear.

The world is full of possibilities.

After I go through my morning routine, I change into a cute sundress and I head downstairs.

He's in the kitchen, fixing a mug of tea, one eye on the pot of oatmeal on the stove.

"Hey." He turns to me with a megawatt smile. It's pure Holden. The guy I've known for… it feels like it's been forever. Maybe it has. Since he and Oliver started at the same high school. How long was that? Six years? Seven? Eight?

"Hey." My chest warms. This is just so… easy. How can anything be this easy? "Is there one for me?" I motion to his mug.

"Not yet." He takes a sip. Lets out an over-the-top sigh. Makes a point of holding the tea close to his chest.

"Cruel."

"Is it?"

I nod.

"How's that?"

"You're showing me this perfect, beautiful thing I could have. Then denying me."

"Sounds kinky."

My cheeks flush.

"You into that?"

"Into…" I want to play coy. To convince him I'm less clueless than I am. But I'm really not sure what he means.

"Edging?"

"Edging?"

He chuckles *fuck, you're adorable*. "If I pushed you against the wall, slipped my hand between your legs, and worked you until you were right. On. The. Brink."

I swallow hard.

"Then kept you there until you were begging me."

"Oh."

"Then kept you there a little longer."

"That... uh..."

"Not usually my thing." His eyes pass over me slowly. They stop on the sweetheart neckline of my dress. My waist. My hips. My thighs. "I don't get off on... well, I guess you could say I get off on getting you off."

"How can something sound so hot and so cheesy at the same time?"

"It's pure skill."

"It must be."

He motions *come here*.

I close the distance between us.

He sets the mug on the counter behind me. Wraps his arms around me. Pulls me into a slow, deep kiss.

Mmm, he tastes good. Like cinnamon and honey and Holden.

My hands go to his waist reflexively. The soft fabric of his t-shirt. Then under it.

Soft skin over hard muscles.

All the warmth of him.

The feel of his heart pounding against his chest.

The soft pressure of his palm against my lower back.

His hands in my hair.

This is better than a chai latte. Than a perfect English Breakfast.

Hell, it's better than discovering the perfect book. Or listening to my favorite album. Or dancing all night.

He pulls back with a sigh. Cups my face with his palm. Stares into my eyes. "You need to go easy on me, kid."

"I do?"

He nods *yeah*. "I have the best of intentions."

"To…"

"Show you a great last day. Whatever you want."

"What if I want to take you to my bedroom?"

"Keep doing what you're doing."

My smile spreads a little wider. "Maybe we… uh… Can we do that?"

"Can we do what?" He plays dumb. Reaches behind his back. Grabs the mug of tea. "Fix chai lattes?"

I shake my head.

He motions to the pot on the stove. "Eat cinnamon raisin oatmeal?"

"No."

"Hmm…" He makes a show of pushing his lips to one side. Tapping his forehead. Looking to the ceiling for answers. "Listen to eighties music?"

"Well… that could be part of it."

"Read our poetry?"

"God no."

"Read someone else's poetry. I asked Luna for recs."

"No, you didn't."

"I did." His eyes meet mine. "I had to write the names down. I only recognized two of them."

"She knows my favorites."

"It's quite a list."

"I'm really not… that pretentious."

He raises a brow *you sure about that?*

"Honestly, I'd rather listen to a Lorde song than recite Adrienne Rich."

"Who?"

"She's a… Oh, that's your point."

He nods *yeah*.

"I mean, I did have to study all that stuff last year. For AP Language. We did a poem analysis every week."

"How did that go?"

"We'd copy the poem on one side of the paper." I fold an invisible piece of paper. Draw a line over the left side. "Then we'd write our thoughts on the right. It was short and sweet. The first thing that came to mind. And I... I loved it. It was my favorite thing we did."

"More than—what the fuck do you do in—" He raises his voice to something prim and proper. "Advanced Placement Language."

"Advanced Placement Language and Composition. If you want to get technical." My laugh is light. Easy. "We read a lot of books. Wrote a lot of essays about them. Then more essays. Essay tests. Short answer tests. More short passages. More novels."

"You love reading?"

"Is that not obvious?"

He holds up his thumb and forefinger *a little*. "You don't talk about it."

"Well, uh... no offense, Holden, but you don't seem like the literary type."

He feigns insult. "How dare you."

"Oh? You finished *Catch-22* last night? *Heart of Darkness* the night before? Writing a blog series about war in literature?"

"Fuck yeah."

"Can I read it?"

"Of course. But it's all about *The Hunger Games*."

My laugh gets bigger. "*The Hunger Games*?"

"You think *Catch-22* is a better example of war in literature?"

"Well..." I study his expression, trying to figure out

how serious he is. Normal Holden level of serious. Which is mostly kidding. "They deal with the themes very differently. *Catch-22* is all about the absurdity of war. How you can't really wrap your head around what's happening. Whereas *The Hunger Games* is… it's really more like *Heart of Darkness*. About the horror of war. Or maybe more like *The Things They Carried* or *All Quiet on the Western Front*. You know, now that I think about it, the series belongs in any English literature class. At least when it comes to war." Fuck, I'm rambling.

And he's just staring back at me, smiling. "You like it?"

"*The Hunger Games*? Of course. Who doesn't?"

"Just thought you'd…"

"Be too pretentious to appreciate it."

He makes that same *a little* motion.

But I don't take offense. "Is that how I come across?"

"Sometimes. It's not a bad thing."

"What if I don't want to come across like that?"

"Talk more about *The Hunger Games*."

"I've read it three times."

"There you go."

"Well, uh, that's not necessarily a lot for me."

"What is?"

"There's this one YA romance I've read ten times. Once a year, since I first discovered it." My fingers brush his as I steal his mug. "But, uh… I guess I'm still in school mode. I spent last week finishing my summer assignments."

"You have summer assignments in college?"

"One of my classes, yeah. Summer reading."

"What bullshit."

"Kinda." I take a long sip. Mmm, rich, sweet, spicy chai. And it tastes like his lips. Chai is always going to taste like his lips, now and forever.

"Be honest."

"Okay."

He steals the mug back. "You prefer the highbrow stuff, don't you?"

"Not exactly. I do like reading stuff for class. I love analyzing the themes and motifs and character arcs. But I love *The Hunger Games*. And the movies I watch with Luna. And even some of Oliver's thrillers. There's gold in all fiction. It can offer so much, tell you so much about life. It doesn't always do that. Sometimes the low-brow stuff is empty. Sometimes, it has nothing to say. But, other times... there's something magical about when a book clicks, when I really understand it, when I see something in it... I love that."

"All books?"

"Anything. Songs, poems, books, TV, movies, art. Though, I'm not great with visual art. More words. I, uh, I love thinking about it, figuring it out as much as I love experiencing it."

"You're always thinking."

"I guess. But it's not like I'm doing it for the brownie points. I enjoy digging into the themes of a TV show after I watch it."

"Any recent ones?"

My cheeks flush. "It's embarrassing."

"Why?"

"You'll think it's stupid."

"I'm sure it's a better use of your time than the shit I do."

"What do you do?"

He shakes his head. "You're not distracting me."

I motion to the tea. "I could steal that."

"You could... only." He swallows the last sip. Shows me the empty mug.

"Cruel."

He nods *hell yeah*. "I'll start another one."

"Will you show me how you make it?"

"Yeah, but I'm not sure that will help."

"Even so."

He nods *okay*. "After you tell me."

Damn.

He fills the kettle with water. Sets it on the stove. Pulls the tea from the shelf.

He turns back to me and raises a brow *I can go all day*.

I nod *uh-huh*.

He holds my gaze for a moment, then he moves to the fridge, gets out the milk, warms it in the microwave.

"It's really not that interesting," I say. "Now, I've hyped it up and it's going to seem like a big deal. But it's just the last thing I watched."

"You can just say it."

I swallow hard. "You won't laugh?"

"Why would I laugh?"

"*Dawson's Creek*."

"What's wrong with *Dawson's Creek*?"

"It's, well… how much time do you have?"

He laughs. "I really like you, Daisy."

"I like you too."

Chapter Thirty-Five

DAISY

After a short latte lesson where we discuss the merits of various teen shows—*Dawson's Creek, Degrassi, Riverdale, Gilmore Girls, Gossip Girl, Skins, 13 Reasons Why*—we move on to breakfast.

Holden has seen his fair share of TV. He does have a sister, even if she's a little older and more into sci-fi and comic book stuff.

I mostly watch with Luna.

She enjoys popcorn fare. Not that I hate it, exactly. I mean, some of those shows are really thematically rich. Some are great soaps. And some are... total garbage.

Honestly, that one show especially.

Ahem.

"I feel like I always sound so critical." I finish my last bite of oatmeal. It's cold—we've been sitting here forever—but I don't mind. "I'm always picking apart the flaws. Thinking things aren't good enough."

"You don't sound like that."

"At all?"

"Maybe a little." His eyes meet mine. "But why does that have to be a bad thing?"

Everyone acts like it is. Like I'm too hard to please. Or unable to see the merits of anything. Or just a critical bitch. "This guy in my creative writing class… every week, after I gave him my critique—we always swapped critiques. The whole class. He'd look at me like I cut his heart out and mutter something about how I needed to get laid."

"Really?"

"Yeah."

"Fuck, where is this guy?" Holden's fingers brush my wrist. "I'm gonna punch him in the face."

"He was—"

"Who the fuck does he think he is, saying that to you?"

"But—"

He shrugs his shoulders, and the tension is his jaw dissolves. "I wish it was different, kid, but the truth is, men can't handle it when women don't like the things they like."

"Yeah?"

He nods *yeah*. "In high school, I had this friend. Dude was a total nerd. I think he only hung out with me for access to my mom's comic collection. One time, we were hanging at my dad's place, reading some comic. I don't even remember what it was. Ariel came downstairs. And he looked at her like he was a cartoon character with his eyes bugging out of his head."

"She's cute."

"And awkward. She had no idea. Poor Ariel…" He shakes his head knowingly. "You've talked to her. You know she hasn't got a hint of tact."

"True."

"So when she saw the comic, she offered her opinion. It was harsh. Fair, but not at all sugarcoated."

"And?"

Holden shakes his head in distaste. "The guy lost it. He started going off on how she didn't appreciate quality. And she couldn't see it. Because it was too important for girls to understand. And maybe she was just not as smart as she seemed." His eyes meet mine. "Fuck, you have no idea how many women have told me their ex lost it when they didn't like their favorite band or TV show or book or whatever. And some of the guys in my art classes... most of them were okay. But there were always one or two like that asshole."

"Who couldn't take criticism?"

"Yeah. And especially not from women. Men are just... they're used to being right. Sometimes they can't handle being wrong."

"Not you."

"No." He laughs. "I'm wrong a lot. I'm used to it."

"You're smarter than you look though."

"I don't know about that." His gaze shifts to my empty bowl. My almost empty mug of tea. He motions *you want some?*

I nod. Take a long sip. The chai I made. Not as good as the one he made, but closer. I'm getting there. "Maybe... deeper than you look."

"Maybe." He sips his tea. Sighs with his exhale. "Fuck, kid, you're too good at distracting me."

"Yeah?"

He nods *yeah.* "Lost track of my point." His eyes meet mine. "There's nothing wrong with being critical. Or having high standards. Or being hard to please."

"You think so?"

"Not when it comes to work. Or life. Fuck, if you want the best tea, demand it. If you want a guy who treats you like a princess, demand it. If you want a boyfriend who calls every night and—"

God, I do. "I was thinking about work. School. Books."

"It's a good quality, being critical. Even if it means most people won't get your opinions."

"Maybe." My eyes flit to the windows for a minute. It's a beautiful day. Blue sky. Ocean for miles. But I'd rather stay inside with him than go anywhere.

"It is. Fuck, when I was apprenticing... At first, it killed me, hearing that my work was shit. But I needed to hear it. I needed the feedback, and I needed it to be honest. That was the only way to get better."

"You're skilled now." It's beautiful here too. Clean tile, white walls, glass table. Holden's pretty green eyes. At the moment, it's hard to believe I see fault in anything. That there's any fault in anything. Life is just... good.

"Exactly." He draws doodles on my wrist. "And... shit, don't tell anyone I said this."

"Never."

"But that's the only thing I take seriously. If I hadn't had the most brutally honest criticism possible—"

"Am I that bad?" I don't mind the comment coming from him. There's something about the way he says it. The way he looks at me. Everything feels like a compliment.

"I don't know." He slides his arms around my waist. Pulls me into his lap. "Critique something for me?"

"What?"

"This—" He turns his shoulder to me. Motions to the tattoo running over it.

"I don't know much about visual art."

"Just your gut instinct."

"Maybe..." I trace the lines over his skin. God, it feels so good touching him, feeling his pulse, hearing his breath. "I... uh... I'm not sure I can be critical of something on your body."

"What if it said *I hate Daisy*?"

"It doesn't." I trace the lines back down his skin. "It's beautiful. And it suits you. It's just… right."

"Gotta be honest, kid, you're not bringing it on the criticism front." He knots his hand in my hair. Pulls me into a kiss.

Mmm, he tastes so good.

Our kiss breaks with a sigh.

He looks up at me like I'm heaven-sent for a moment. Then he blinks and he's back to the thread of our conversation.

"How about something more your vibe… Ruin my favorite movie," he says.

"What's your favorite movie?"

"Fuck, I have to decide my favorite movie?" His laugh lights up his eyes. "I'm not a list guy."

"It was your idea."

"Can't think right now." He places one hand on my thigh. Runs his thumb over my skin. "Something is distracting me."

My eyes flutter closed as he drags his thumb higher and higher—

Fuck.

More.

Yes.

Please.

"Holden—"

"I love the way you say my name."

"I do too."

"Fuck, Daisy—" He pulls me into another kiss. A faster one this time.

His tongue slips into my mouth. Dances with mine.

I lean into his touch.

He pulls back with a sigh. "I'm gonna fuck you senseless—"

"Now."

"After this conversation." He brings his hands to my hips. Helps me off his thighs. Onto the chair next to him. "I... I really fucking like talking to you."

"Me too."

"No, it's... I've never felt like that before. Don't get me wrong. I love shooting the shit. With anyone. But I've never wanted to talk to a girl as much as I wanted to fuck her."

"Is that a compliment?"

"Absolutely." His eyes meet mine. They fill with something I can't quite place. Something between *I really like fucking you* and *I really fucking love you*. "How about this? You tell me about the last book you read. What you liked and what you didn't. And I'll tell you if it sounds too harsh."

"Okay." I recall my last read. A YA book. A romance. It was pretty good. Entertaining. Sweet. But too manufactured. The characters never seemed real. They were inconsistent. And not in a moody teenager kind of way.

I look to Holden.

Then I string together the best summary I can. Everything I liked. Everything I hated. Ways the book could have been better. If the author had only cut that chapter about the ex-boyfriend. And given the best friend a real motive.

I mean, why would the best friend try to fuck things up for no reason? Who does that? Who stays friends with someone like that?

He hangs on every word.

When I finish, I bring my eyes to his. Brace for the usual commentary about my high standards.

But he doesn't say that.

He looks me in the eyes and says, "I bet you'd be a great editor."

"What?" That's... not what I expected.

"I haven't read that book, but I can tell... that's dead on. Honest. Helpful. Insightful. I don't know shit about books or writing or editing. Maybe the industry is dead. Maybe you're better off learning to love programming."

"Please no."

He chuckles. "But I do know... that was smart. Really smart."

"You think so?"

"I know so." He squeezes my palm. "And maybe I'm distracted by your pretty eyes. Or your perfect tits. Or how much I want to hear my name roll off your lips. But I don't think it's too much. I don't think you're too harsh or critical or negative. Yeah, you're still a little high strung. But, Daisy, when you relax, when you lose yourself—you're so fucking full of joy. I... I really love it."

"Yeah?"

"Yeah." He leans in. Brings his lips to mine.

I kiss him back with everything I've got.

There's more in it this time. Things neither of us are saying.

Promises we shouldn't make.

I let my body make them anyway.

After our kiss breaks, he stands and pulls me out of my chair. "I want to talk to you all day."

"Yeah?"

"But, first, I have to make you come."

Chapter Thirty-Six

DAISY

The sun fills the bedroom with a soft glow. It's beautiful. Like we really are in heaven.

We are.

This whole trip is a slice of paradise.

I don't know what happens tomorrow, but I have today. I have this.

God, I want so much of this.

Holden presses me against the wall. He takes one of my hands. Brings it over my head. Looks down at me. *Is this okay?*

Hell yes. I nod with everything I've got.

He locks eyes with me as he brings my other arm over my head. He presses his palm into my wrists, holding me in place.

Then his eyelids flutter closed.

He brings his lips to mine.

There's no patience in his kiss. Only pure, raw need. It pours from him to me. It swallows me whole.

Does he need me that much?

As much as I need him?

Does he also want this to go forever?

Well, maybe not forever. But for… for longer than today. Longer than next week. Longer than my first semester and my second and—

My thoughts dissolve as his tongue slips into my mouth.

I asked him to show me how to get out of my head. How to drop my inhibitions. How to just let go and feel it.

I meant it.

I still mean it.

He's still showing me. I just have to follow his lead.

I really, really want to follow his lead. To soak up every second of this.

Because, really, anything could happen tomorrow. Even if today were a normal day. Even if we were a normal couple. If we'd exchanged I love yous or promises of forever or goddamn wedding vows.

Nothing is guaranteed.

Not ever.

And this—

Fuck, he really is a good kisser.

I rock my hips against his. There's still too much fabric in the way—my dress and panties, his jeans and boxers— but I can feel him.

He's already hard.

I lift one leg. Hook it around his waist.

He drops one of his arms. Slings it under my thigh. Holds my legs against him.

I pull back with a sigh. "More."

He presses his palm into my wrist, holding my arms over my head. "Not yet."

"But—"

"Not until I say."

The bossy tone to his voice makes me shake. I'm hot everywhere. And I'm buzzing everywhere.

Holden is already the sexiest guy alive.

When he gets demanding?

Mmm.

My body melts into his.

I wrap my lips around his lower lip. Suck softly. Then harder. Then I scrape my teeth against him, the way he does to me.

He pins me tighter. Rocks his hips against me again and again.

He takes over our kiss. Sucks on my bottom lip. Then the top. Then it's that scrape of his teeth.

Again and again—

He drags his hand up my thigh. Higher, higher, higher—

There. His fingers skim my panties.

There's barely anything between us, but it's too much.

I rock my hips against him.

He kisses me harder.

Deeper.

He claims my mouth as he runs his fingers over my sex. Again and again, until I'm panting and shaking.

When I'm sure I can't take it anymore he releases me. Steps backward.

"Take off your dress." He doesn't wait. He tosses his t-shirt over his head.

Mmm, Holden in only his jeans. That soft shade of blue against his tan skin. The waistband dropping below his hips.

Begging for my hands.

I want to touch him. Taste him. Tease him. Fuck him senseless.

It overwhelms me, how much I want him.

It's not like our drunken fuck. It's not fuzzy from the alcohol. I'm not rushing past my dissolved inhibitions.

I'm standing here, feeling everything.

The hint of fear in my stomach. The insecurity in my chest. The nerves in my—

Everywhere.

I feel all that.

But I feel the desire too.

I close my eyes for a moment. I soak in every ounce of it.

The buzz in my veins. The ache between my legs. The sense—the sense that's everywhere—that I'll die if I don't have him every way I can have him.

Any way I can have him.

Is sex always like this?

Or is it just Holden?

Am I finally free? Finally normal?

Maybe I'm there. In touch with my body. Living in my body. Embracing every single pang, want, craving.

Right now—

He lifts me into his arms. Carries me to the bed. Lays me down flat.

Holden nudges my knees apart with his legs. Then he places his body between them.

The weight of him sinks into me.

I reach for my dress. Roll it up my hips. To my waist.

He slips his hand under my thigh. Wraps my leg around his torso. Then the other.

He looks down at me, his green eyes filled with desire. "Too fast?"

"Not fast enough."

His laugh is soft. "I created a monster."

"You really did."

"Good." He presses his lips to my neck. "I like you needy."

"Mmm."

"Demanding." He drags his lips a little lower.

"Holden—"

"Begging." He places a kiss on my chest, just above the neckline of my dress. "Fuck, I love your groan so much. Tempted to tease you all day."

"Mmm."

"You're lucky I love the taste of your cunt more."

My response is all vowels. He's right. The way he says that—

It's so fucking hot.

It's too fucking hot.

It's just wrong.

He presses his palms into my thighs, pinning my legs to the ground. Then he shifts down my body.

Until his mouth is against the inside of my knee.

He teases me with a soft kiss. Then he moves higher, higher, higher—

Up my thigh.

So, so close to where I need him.

Almost.

Almost.

He pulls away. Brings his mouth to my other leg. The inside of my knee.

He teases me the same way. Up, higher and higher, until he's almost there—

Then down my other leg.

Again and again.

Until I'm shaking.

Until I'm dizzy.

Until I'm clawing at his hair.

And again.

Again.

There—

His mouth brushes my sex. Over my panties.

Then it's the heat of his breath.

It's strange, with the fabric in the way, but the friction is still divine.

He teases me with another hot breath.

Then it's his lips against my panties.

Fuck, the feeling of the cotton against my skin. His warm mouth so, so close.

But so, so far.

He keeps me pinned to the bed as he pulls my panties aside.

His fingers brush my sex.

My clit.

Then it's his soft, wet mouth.

Sensation overwhelms me. It's so much, so different than his hand, so different than anything.

I reach for something to grab onto. Get the soft sheets.

They're practically my sheets at this point.

We're practically in my bed.

Fuck, maybe we can do this in my bed.

Maybe this can be—

No, maybe doesn't matter. Tomorrow doesn't matter. This is all that matters.

He works me with soft strokes. Then hard ones. Fast. Slow. Circles. Zigzags.

He winds the tension inside me tighter and tighter. Until I'm ready to burst.

Then he pins my legs to the bed, and he goes right where I need him.

He already knows where I need him.

I already know where I need him.

He—

I—

Fuck.

With the next flick of his tongue, I fall over the edge. I tug at the soft sheets, groaning his name as I come.

Holden places a kiss on my inner thigh. Then he climbs up my body. "You have a—"

"Yeah." I reach for the bedside dresser but it's way too far away.

He shifts off the bed. Opens the drawer. Pulls out an entire pack of condoms. "Ambitious."

"Thanks."

He pulls out a foil packet. "Greedy even."

"Is that a compliment?"

"Absolutely." He unzips his jeans. Pushes them off his hips.

Then the boxers.

God, he really is beautiful.

All of him.

I never thought I'd consider a cock beautiful but he's so—

"Panties off." He kicks his clothes aside. Tears the wrapper.

"Can I?" I push my panties to my ankles.

He nods *yeah*. "Clothes off first."

"Or?"

"Clothes off now."

Yes. I want to be naked with him. To feel all his skin against mine.

To see his eyes light up as he takes me in.

I love the way his eyes light up.

I love his eyes.

Not just the perfect shade of green. The joy. The fullness.

The desire.

I pull down the zipper of my dress. Then I toss it over my head.

I'm not wearing a bra today.

I'm naked, splayed out in front of him.

For a moment, nerves rise up in my stomach.

Then he looks down at me with wide eyes. "Fuck." He climbs onto the bed. "You're so fucking beautiful."

"You too."

"No more talking." He presses the foil packet into my hand.

I do away with the packaging. Then I slide the condom over his cock.

It's different than touching him properly, but it's still really fucking hot.

I look up at him. Motion *come here*.

He climbs on top of me.

His hands go to my hips.

Slowly, he pulls our bodies together. His tip strains against me. That sharp pull of rubber.

Then a slow, steady slide—

Fuck.

It's just as overwhelming. He makes me feel so full, so whole, so complete, so—

"Fuck, Holden." I dig my nails into his back.

He wraps one arm around me. Holds my body against his as he shifts inside me.

Then he pulls back and does it again.

He takes his time easing me into it. Warming me up.

Then he brings his hands to my hips. He flips us over, so I'm on top of him.

So I'm straddling him.

Fuck, this is the perfect view. I want to take a mental snapshot. Paint him. Hang him in a fucking museum.

But, more than that, I want to have *my* way with *him*.

I'm not exactly sure what I'm doing, but I don't feel shy or scared.

"Fuck me, baby." He digs his fingers into my hips. "Come on my cock."

Fuck, that's so hot.

I press my palms into his chest for support, then I lift my hips, sliding over him, then back down.

Mmm. I do it again and again.

I drive him deeper.

Deeper.

"Fuck, Daisy—" A groan falls off his hips.

My nails dig into his chest.

My eyes flutter closed.

I work him with those same steady motions.

He brings one hand to my chest. Toys with my nipple as I work him.

Fuck, he feels so good.

My hips move of their own accord. They go faster. Drive him deeper.

His groans get lower.

Louder.

His touch gets harder.

It spurs me on.

I move with that same rhythm. Again and again.

Until I'm wound so, so tight—

And he's toying with me harder and harder—

And—

He slips his hand between my legs. Presses his thumb to my clit. Works me with slow, steady strokes.

It pushes me over the edge.

I claw at his chest, rocking my hips as I come.

Pleasure spills through my body, all the way to my fingers and toes.

Too much.

And not enough.

I sink my nails into his chest. Lift myself up. Drive

myself down again.

His groans run together as I work him.

His thumb stays that same perfect pressure.

My sex winds tighter and tighter—

Then I'm there again, pulsing around him, pulling him closer.

And he's there, groaning my name as he comes.

I work him through his orgasm.

Then I press off him. Collapse next to him.

He pulls my body into his. "Fuck, you're a fast learner."

"Thanks."

"You're... fuck."

He's speechless.

Holden Ballard is speechless because I fucked him that properly.

It's...

Fuck is right.

Chapter Thirty-Seven

HOLDEN

W e've been naked for most of the morning—since we finished breakfast, really—but it's still thrilling.

Not just sexy as fuck.

More too.

Like we're peeling back the walls around our hearts as much as we're peeling off our clothes.

Daisy squeals as she jumps in the pool.

She's so full of joy. I don't see that side of her a lot. She doesn't share it with many people.

Getting it now—

Fuck, it's amazing.

There's no other way to describe it.

She pushes off the bottom. Turns to me with a wide, wet smile. "Are you coming in?"

"Not sure. The view is nice here."

Her eyes travel down my body. "It is." Her blue eyes fill with desire. And something else too. This excitement she doesn't usually have.

Like she's about to take the world by storm.

She is.

This is—

Fuck, why am I so far away?

I dive into the pool. The cool water is a sharp contrast to the hot air. It's not New York humid here, but it's not as dry as Southern California either.

Mexico is supposed to be a desert, as arid as Los Angeles, but fuck if I know shit about climate.

I meet Daisy at the other end of the pool. Wrap my arms around her. Pull her into a tight embrace.

She groans as my lips skim her neck. "Holden…"

"Is that a *Holden, stop* or a *Holden, keep going*?"

"Hmm…" She reaches back for me. Gets my hips. "Can it be both?"

"No."

"Damn." She shifts, turning around in my arms. "I, uh… do you think we're good?"

"Good?"

"With Oliver and Luna? She'll warn me if they're heading back, but, uh—"

"Our phones are downstairs?"

"Yeah."

"We'll hear them come in."

"You're fast enough to get to the shower."

I nod *hell yeah*.

She arches a brow. "And I explain my skinny dipping by…"

"What's to explain?"

She stifles a laugh. "It's not what people—"

"You love the water. Why let clothes get in your way?"

"Doesn't sound like me."

"You're a new person."

"Am I?"

"Are you?" Under the water I squeeze her hand.

She looks up at me. "I've wanted that, so many times. When I started a new school last year. When I got off the plane. After we *ahem*. And when I start school…"

"Are you excited?"

"Yeah. Berkley is amazing. With all my extra credits, I got to enroll earlier than most freshmen."

"What are you taking?"

"Two requirements. A science class"—she sticks her tongue out *ugh*—"and an English one. I can already take these amazing English classes. One on the history of criticism. Another on Shakespeare."

"Are you majoring in English?"

"I don't know. I want to, but…"

"But?"

She presses her lips together. "People always tell me it's impractical. A waste of time. A surefire way to unemployment forever."

"People are assholes."

"But they might be right." She turns, takes in the view of the town, the bright blue sky, the sparkling ocean. "I love reading. I love writing. I love tearing things apart. But… things are already hard for me. If I can't find a job or a job that pays enough… that's not going to make them easier."

"Shit's hard to everyone."

"Yeah." Her fingers curl into the railing. "But, uh… I guess I appreciate stability."

"It's a big world. There's a lot of stuff out there."

She nods *true*. "That's why you're supposed to wait to declare your major at the end of sophomore year. You're supposed to take different classes, expose yourself to new things."

"It's a good idea."

"Probably."

"But?" I place my body next to hers. Fuck, this really is a beautiful view. And there's something about taking it in with her. Something I can't explain.

"No, it is."

"You should take an art class."

"Art History?"

I shake my head. "A studio class. Painting. Drawing. Fucking ceramics."

"Clay?"

"Why not?"

Her laugh is easy. "Because... I guess that's not a good reason."

"It's not."

"I'll consider that." Her eyes meet mine. "I was thinking more along the lines of psychology—"

"Isn't that a science class?"

She nods *yeah*. "Or maybe business. Marketing. Stuff that's more employable."

"I'm not gonna tell you that shit isn't helpful."

"You get by pretty well without it."

"Even with my gig, there's a lot of that shit. I have to attract new clients. Retain the old ones. Keep track of my schedule, make sure my rates are in line with my skill—"

"Are you saying you aren't the best of the best?"

"Not quite."

She shoots me an easy smile. "It's hard to believe you're admitting that."

"I know."

"But then I..." Her fingers go to the Latin quote on my chest. "I love all of these."

"That's your expert opinion?"

She traces the words with her index finger. "It's possible, I'm distracted by your body."

"Plus, I didn't do these."

"That would be tough." She traces the lines again. "It always seemed so you. *Danger is sweet*. But I'm not as sure."

"You still think I'm scared?"

"Well... we all are. But then I... I always wanted one."

"A tattoo?"

She nods. "As soon as Oliver got his first one. But it's scary, the permanence. How do you know you'll want something on your body forever?"

"You don't."

Her eyes go wide. "You're not sure you'll love this in thirty years?" Her fingers brush the Latin phrase. "What if you hate it?"

"What if?"

She bites her lip. "No offense, Holden, but you don't really strike me as the commitment type."

"Me?"

She nods *yeah*.

"Maybe that's the appeal. Taking the way you feel in one moment and making it forever."

"Even though you might feel differently later?"

"Because you might feel differently later. Because you want to remember the person you were. The things that mattered to you."

"Has that happened yet?"

"Have I grown out of anything?" I ask.

She nods *yeah*.

"I don't know. I don't really think about it like that. Sure, some of my early work isn't great. But if I didn't get that, I wouldn't have the stuff that is great. I needed to build off something."

"Like with writing?"

"Yeah. Kinda." It's hard to explain. "It's not like that's required. If you know what you want, get a good artist, you can get great work right away."

"Hmm... a good tattoo artist. Where can I find one of those?"

"No idea," I tease.

Her smile spreads a little wider.

"What do you want?"

"I don't know. I guess I just like that idea. The permanence. But I... I don't know." Her gaze goes to the tattoo on my chest. "I love this."

"Danger is sweet?"

"Yeah. I... maybe it's not who I am now. But I want to get there. I want to absorb the words."

It would be perfect for her. "Right here maybe." My fingers brush her chest. The curve of her breast. High enough she could show it off without getting arrested. Low enough she could keep it to herself.

Her cheeks flush. "Maybe... here." She turns. Motions to her ribs.

"Gotta be honest with you, kid."

The pet name still makes her light up. "Yeah?"

"That's gonna hurt like a bitch."

"Oh."

"Ribs are awful."

"You don't think I can handle it?"

"You can. But it's a lot for your first time out." Fuck, it would look perfect. Thin words over the curve of her side. It suits her too. Something secret. Just for her. "Can I do it?"

"The tattoo?"

"Yeah." Fuck, I need her to say yes. I don't know why. I'm not usually territorial. But the thought of someone else marking her skin—"Whenever you decide you want it. If it's tomorrow. Or three years from now."

"Even if it's later and we're... not."

"Yeah."

She swallows hard. "Okay."

"You promise?"

"I do." She holds my gaze for a moment. Stares into my eyes, looking for something. She must find it, because she turns. Looks to the sky. "How did you get into tattoos anyway?"

"You don't know?"

She shakes her head.

Okay, this is a fun story. And it's easy to talk about. Mostly. "My mom was an animator. She loved all kinds of visual art. I don't have that many vivid memories of her. Half of them are watching a movie or reading a graphic novel or wandering around a museum. When she took us to New York, she took us to the Met then MoMA. She'd ask us to stand there and stare at paintings forever. Even though we didn't get it. Well, I didn't get it. I was probably six at the time."

"Yeah?"

I nod. "I was this tiny kid, staring at a blue canvas, wondering why it meant anything, thinking *damn, that looks like the sky, how about we go outside?* Though, fuck, kids probably have the most honest reaction to art of anyone."

"How's that?"

"They don't get deeper themes. They don't understand religion or love or sex. But they don't have any mental baggage either. It's not that kids can't be fucked up. Or troubled. Or whatever. But they don't have that voice that says *this is important* or *you need to find an important meaning* or *if it's in a museum, it must matter.* They see a painting, they feel something. Always."

"I don't know." Her gaze softens, like she's diving into her head, looking for a memory. "The first time we went to the Met, I was just… tired."

I can't help but laugh. "When you looked at the paintings?"

"Every moment."

"How old were you?"

"Nine or ten."

"You're a fast learner. Pretentious early."

"Hey." She play swats me. "That's cruel."

"Only if it's not true."

Her smile gets shy. She makes that *a little* gesture with her thumb and forefinger. "Do I have to go back further?"

"Yeah. To the drawings you did in kindergarten?"

"Mom and Dad with a big line between them."

"Yeah?"

"Yeah." Her voice softens. "They fought all the time. It was obvious they were only staying together for us, though I'm not sure I got that at the time. Only that it wasn't right. That it was such an ugly relationship. When they finally got a divorce… I thought that would be better, but it wasn't. My world was even more upside down."

"That's hard."

"Not compared to losing your mom."

I run my hand through my hair. Fuck, I really don't know how to talk about this.

"You were so young."

"Yeah."

"Do you miss her?"

"I try not to think about it."

"But you must." Her eyes meet mine. "You followed in her footsteps." She runs her fingers over the tattoo going down my shoulder. "You've given parts of your body to her."

"That's not—"

"Isn't it?"

Maybe. I don't usually talk about it. Better to avoid

dwelling. Bad shit happens. So what? I can pick myself up and dust myself off. But maybe…

Maybe that's just another excuse.

A way to avoid it.

I suck a breath through my teeth. "I remember the day it happened."

Her eyes meet mine. They fill with something. Sympathy. And this expectation. Like I'm going to say something that matters.

It's weird. I should hate it. On anyone else, I'd hate it. But I like it on Daisy. "She was in hospice care. At home. It was a normal day. Dad took me into her room after dinner. We read a book together. Said good night. She kissed me on the forehead and gave me this look… I still remember it. I'll always remember it. It was like she knew it was over."

"Did she?"

"Maybe. Or maybe she felt like that every night. She was weak for a while."

"That's hard."

It was. Even though I was a kid. Even though I didn't quite understand what was happening. "I… I couldn't sleep that night. Then, when I woke up, Dad was sitting at the breakfast table, staring at the wood. He didn't move for hours. All day even. Forest had to tell me."

"How old was he?"

"Too young for that." I turn to the sky. "I know what everyone says. That it's better to have loved and lost. Dad would say that too. And it's not like you get a choice about loving your family?"

"If only." Her smile is sad.

"I always thought that was bullshit. Maybe I decided that day. Or maybe it came later, as I watched my dad fall apart, as I watched Forest lose himself picking up the pieces. It seemed easier to not get invested. To not care."

"To take nothing seriously?"

"Yeah."

"Do you?" Her fingers brush my wrist. "Do you take nothing seriously?"

"Our secret?"

"Of course." Her smile is soft. Loving.

"I'm serious about my work."

"Your family?"

"I—"

"Your methods are strange, but you try. You were obsessed with getting Forest and Skye together."

My laugh breaks up the tension in my chest. "They were idiots about it."

"It took them awhile."

"And you kept pushing."

"Yeah, 'cause—"

"You did care."

I nod. I did. I still do. I want my family to be happy. I want Daisy to be happy. Fuck, I want Daisy to soar.

"Just… you didn't want to admit it."

"Where's the fun in that?"

She runs her fingers over my forearm. "I like that you're so fun. That you value that so much. You always make me laugh. But this… you're better at this than you think."

"At?"

"Sharing. Real conversations. Slowing down and listening to that voice."

"Maybe."

"You are." Her lips curl into a smile. "You don't have to like it. But I do."

Part of me does. It's easier staying on the surface, but only for so long. Eventually, that voice in my head catches up with me.

Right now—

My chest is heavy, but it's getting lighter. The weight is lifting. Maybe that's possible.

Sometimes.

Fuck knows I only have so much sincerity in me.

With her, it's not so bad. Nice even.

I wrap my arms around her. Pull her into a tight embrace. "I'll consider that."

"Good." She looks up at me with those big, blue eyes. "You didn't finish your story about how you got into tattoos."

"We could do something more interesting than talking?"

"We could do that after the talking."

"Is that a promise?"

Her nod is shy.

Which is so fucking sexy.

Is it really possible this is our last day together?

I hate it. But it's the only thing that makes sense. It's certainly what's best for her.

There aren't many things that matter to me. Daisy's well-being is top of the list.

Whatever it takes.

Chapter Thirty-Eight

DAISY

Holden's story is funny. And completely Holden. He got into art because it irritated his brother. He worked hard at it because it *really* irritated Forest that art came more naturally to Holden.

He almost dropped it. Almost dropped everything.

That was his senior year flame out.

He got caught with alcohol at school. Almost got expelled. Only his art teacher came to his defense.

She basically convinced him to try. To actually, sincerely try.

And the whole tattoo apprentice thing—

It was equal parts *I want a cool career because I'm cool* and *fuck, this will really annoy Forest.*

It did, at first. Then, Holden realized Forest appreciated having him around. They were both adults. Able to finally communicate like adults. Except that Holden was… well, Holden.

Always starting shit, refusing to take things seriously, helping in his way.

He really does help in his way.

It's an awesome way.

And I'm totally not falling in love with him.

Totally.

It's just.

Uh…

Yeah.

After he finishes the story, he makes good on his promise to satisfy. He rubs me to orgasm right there in the pool.

We linger in that perfect space forever.

Well, almost forever.

Eventually, we rinse in the shower, dress, move downstairs.

My stomach growls. I'm starving. But it's not threatening to consume me. Or push my thoughts to dark places.

It's just there.

I'm hungry.

I haven't eaten since breakfast, so I'm hungry.

It's time for lunch. Like what any normal person does.

"Do we have any food?" I move into the clean, white kitchen. Fill a glass with water. Swallow in three gulps.

Holden pulls open the fridge. He scans the shelves. Milk. Cheese. Bread. Salad. Mango. Avocado. Tomato.

No leftovers.

No normal ingredients. We ran out of chicken and rice last night.

This is, uh… God, I'm not really a great cook. I should probably learn. So I can feed myself in school.

It's just a reasonable thing to do.

Only I can't.

Before my time in inpatient treatment, Dad worked late most nights. I could skip dinner without notice. Or fill my stomach with salad, celery sticks, rice cakes, whatever.

A million years before that, before I could control what

went into my body, before I realized it was the only thing that made me feel in control—

Well, he still worked late. (I don't blame him. He does what he has to do to keep us comfortable. God knows I would have been fucked if he had a worse job with worse insurance). Oliver made sure I ate. He's a great cook. But once I was old enough to feed myself, I convinced him I was capable.

The days he went out, I made microwave meals, mac n cheese, sandwiches.

I guess I still know how to do that.

"You want to go out? Get something?" Holden asks.

"You don't cook?"

He pulls out a loaf of bread. A half-used block of cheese. Sets both on the counter. "This is the extent of my skills."

"Me too. Well—" I bend, grab the tomato, place it next to the bread.

"Gourmet."

"Very." My laugh is easy. My entire body is easy. I'm thinking about *that* and I'm not getting lost in it. I'm not scared he'll read it on my face. I'm just okay…

And I—

God, I really do want to tell him.

But what if he runs away? If he looks at me like I'm a freak? If he realizes just how precarious this whole thing is and ends it early?

We only have four or five hours alone.

Then Oliver and Luna get back.

Then…

Who knows?

I don't want to waste those hours. They might be all I get with him.

This might be my last chance.

My only chance.

I swallow hard. "You want to lead?"

"How confident are you?"

"A little."

He chuckles. "Maybe practice is good. You're heading to college."

"In a dorm. I don't have a kitchen."

"We should eat the bread and cheese plain. Get you ready for next year."

"The dining hall is supposed to be… open most hours."

"Complimentary." His laugh is easy. The usual Holden laugh.

He's an easygoing guy. But there's more too. This whole other side of him that I love.

I…

No, I can't love him. Sure, he's sweet and caring and protective in a Holden kind of way. And his green eyes are the most beautiful thing in the world. And his laugh is better than any music.

And his groan is better than the best cup of tea in the world.

Is this how it feels to love someone?

My entire body is warm. My chest is light. My stomach is fluttering. It's not like the nerves of a crush. It's deeper but easier too.

Better.

I trust him to catch me if I fall.

Which is proof I'm out of my mind. Holden is a lot of things. A troublemaker. A talented artist. A skilled lover. A beautiful man.

He is not a boyfriend.

He doesn't do that. And, well, my brother was right. You have to accept people for who they are.

I accept that.

I just, uh…

I'm focusing on this moment. On making lunch. On breathing. "I'm not that picky, really."

"No?" He raises a brow.

"Not usually." Not anymore.

"Is there anything you can't get enough of?"

Besides you? "Tea."

He chuckles. "Food."

That's harder. Tea is easy. No risk of triggers. "Chocolate."

His eyes meet mine. "Any meals."

"You can have chocolate for a meal."

"A whole bar?"

"Mole."

His laugh is easy. "You're making mole?"

"No, but I, uh… I order it sometimes."

"And you like it?"

"It's just okay."

"That ruins your argument."

"Yeah." I bite my lip. There's so much I want to say. But I don't know where to start. If I'm capable of starting. "It kinda does."

"Not everyone is into food."

"No, that's not it." Not exactly.

He raises a brow *then what?*

I can tell him. Here. Now. I can just say it. *The thing is, I used to be too into food. Into not eating food. Though there's really nothing that makes you obsess about food like not eating it.*

It wasn't about the food, exactly, more a way to take control of my life.

To prove myself worthy.

To end the day with a feeling of accomplishment.

Even after six weeks of inpatient treatment and a year of recovery, I'm not there yet. Not back to normal. To a person who eats what she wants, when she's hungry, stops when she's full, stops thinking about it after she's done eating.

I eat as I should. Reasonable portions of healthy things. Smaller, still reasonable portions of less healthy things.

I don't even describe foods as good or bad anymore.

But I don't dive in with abandon.

It's too scary.

What if I go back to that?

What if an extra slice of cake triggers a self-loathing black out and I come to on the bathroom floor, with my fingers down my throat?

"Daisy?" His hand brushes my forearm. "You okay?"

"Oh, I was just… thinking." This is an easier conversation away from food. In theory.

I'm cooking first.

Then…

I don't know if I'm telling him.

But I am cooking first.

I grab a pan. Place it on the stove. Turn the burner to high. "I do like grilled cheese."

"Yeah?"

I nod *yeah*. "It's one of the few things I make for myself."

"What else?"

"Spaghetti with broccoli and jarred marinara."

"Classic." He laughs. "That was one of my go-tos for a while."

"You cook for yourself?"

He motions *a little*. "Eventually I started adding Parm. And frozen meatballs. Fuck, I ate that every night for a while."

"You should make it for me sometime."

"Sure." He moves closer to me. "But don't expect gourmet."

"Are you kidding? With the Parmesan cheese on top?"

He nods *yeah*.

"That *is* gourmet."

"I make garlic bread too."

"Yeah?"

"In the toaster oven."

"Fancy." It almost is. It's so Holden, actually. Taking something that could be an ordeal and making it small and easy.

Or maybe it is easy to make garlic bread.

Maybe I'm blinded by… everything.

"As fancy as I get." He reaches for a container of olive oil. Hands it to me. Nods *go for it*.

I warm the oil on the stove.

He pulls out a cutting board. Slices cheese and tomato. Lays the former over bread. "What do I do with these?" He taps the sliced tomato.

My laugh breaks up the tension in my chest. This can be easy. No, it is easy. I place the slices on top of the bread. "Voila."

"That's it?"

I nod. "That's it."

"I don't know." He shakes his head with exaggerated disbelief. "A vegetable on a cheese sandwich?"

"It's a fruit."

"In that case——" He places the other slice of bread over the first sandwich. Then the second.

I laugh as I bring them to the pan.

Shit, that really sizzles. I jump back.

Holden wraps his arms around me. He brings his lips to my neck. Kisses me softly. Then harder.

"We, uh…"

"Yeah." He pulls back. Makes a show of holding up his hands. "Stop distracting me."

"I'm distracting you?"

"Yeah. All this talk about sandwiches. You know guys are obsessed with hot chicks making them sandwiches."

"Are they?"

He nods *of course*, completely full of it. "It's a full-on fetish. A guy—"

"Laying back on a La-Z-Boy, waiting for a naked chick to bring him a hunk of meat and bread, drop to her knees, blow him while he's chowing down."

"Fuck, girl." He makes a show of fanning himself. "You're making me hard."

"I am not."

"Nothing hotter than—"

"Patriarchal fantasies."

"Wow, slow down with the SAT words."

I arch a brow. "You know what I mean."

"Maybe." He shrugs. Holds his poker face. "I mean, it would say something, if I thought the stereotypical sexist request from a man to a woman—a joke that was old ten years ago—was actually hot."

"It would."

"Not anything good."

"No, but you'd get away with it. Because of this." I run my fingers over his chest. His t-shirt is in the way, but it still feels good, touching him.

"Same for you." The back of his hand brushes my chest. It's high enough it's decent.

Which is terrible. "I always thought… I mean, I don't think about it a lot anymore. But I used to think they were too small."

"No." He shakes his head. "Fuck no."

"They are—"

"Perfect. And I won't let you say another word about them."

"But they're smaller. I mean, it's not a bad thing. Just a thing."

"Don't like where this is going."

"I just, I uh…" Fuck, that's a long conversation. But maybe I can… I want to. I really do.

The smell of burning bread interrupts me.

"Shit." I turn to the pan. Grab a spatula. Flip the grilled cheese as fast as possible.

It's not too bad. A little charred on the edges, but otherwise toasted.

I focus on cooking for long enough to melt the cheese, cook the tomato, toast the other side of the bread.

Holden gets out plates.

I scoop the sandwiches onto them.

He holds the plates up like he's a waiter at a fancy restaurant. He motions *after you*. Follows me to the dining table.

We sit. Hold up our sandwiches to toast.

He laughs as he brings the grilled cheese to his lips. "Here's the test."

"If it's edible?"

"Was gonna say good. Can't believe your standards are lower than mine."

My lips curl into a smile. "I'm not much of a cook."

He shrugs *we'll see*. His eyelids flutter closed. He chews. Swallows. Lets out a low groan. "Fucking delicious."

"Yeah?"

He motions *try it*. "I hate to say that the tomato works, but—" He takes another bite. Lets out another groan.

Maybe he's showing off. Or trying to drive me insane. He's probably trying to drive me insane.

Even so—

I take a small bite.

Toasted bread, melty cheese, soft, juicy tomato. Rich and creamy. Not too dry.

Just good.

No other baggage.

No other… anything.

I chew. Swallow.

He looks to my barely touched sandwich. "You don't like it?"

"No, I do." I really do.

"You're not—"

"That's not it."

"What?" he asks with his mouthful. "What's up?"

"I…" I can't say it here. Now. No, I have to. I need him to know.

Even though my heart is thudding against my chest.

It's pounding so loudly it's drowning my other thoughts.

I just—

Here goes nothing. "I had an eating disorder. Maybe had is too strong a word. I'm not sure it will ever be completely in the past. I was… last summer. When I disappeared. I wasn't visiting my mom. I was in inpatient treatment. I—"

He swallows.

"I, um, I don't need you to say anything. Or do anything. Or think anything. I just wanted you to know. I want someone to know. Someone who didn't see it up close. Someone who doesn't think I'm broken."

He stares back at me for a minute.

Then he does the very last thing I expect.

He kisses me.

Chapter Thirty-Nine

HOLDEN

This is not the appropriate reaction.

Even I understand that.

Hell, there's a voice in my head, screaming *what the fuck are you doing?*

I can hear it.

But I still can't stop myself.

I wrap my arms around Daisy. Pull her closer. Try, as hard as I can, to feel every inch of her.

She—

I—

Fuck.

My body hums. Not just desire but something deeper. Purer. Something in that part of myself I ignore.

That part that nags at the back of my head. Begs me to slow down. To stop. To feel.

She pulls back with a sigh.

Her eyes blink open. They meet mine for a moment, then they flit to the ground. Her expression gets shy. Nervous. "I, uh…"

"Yeah."

"You don't have to say anything."

"Okay."

"I just—"

I kiss her again.

That same voice screams *what the hell is wrong with you?*

This time, I have control of my limbs. I *can* move them. But I don't cede to the logic in my brain.

I *know* that I should let go, give her space, formulate some sort of verbal response.

But I don't care.

She groans against my lips. Digs her fingers into my skin. Parts her lips to make way for my tongue.

It hits me a little at a time.

Then she pulls back and looks at me with those big, blue eyes and it hits me all at once.

I'm in love with her.

I'm crazy, stupid in love with her.

But I'm not crazy or stupid enough to think now's the time. That ever is the time.

I just—

Fuck.

Her chest heaves with her inhale. "I, uh… I didn't expect that."

"Yeah."

"You, uh… I'm gonna, uh…"

Fuck, I have to say something. "For how long?"

"Oh." Her eyes turn down. "How long was I sick?"

"Yeah?"

"I guess it depends how you define it. If I had to give it a number… two years. Really bad for one. And since treatment ended last July… I'm getting better. I don't have the horrible thoughts anymore. I don't have a self-loathing voice in my head, telling me I'm not worthy. But I… I'm not all the way recovered either. I'm not even sure what that means. If it's possible. Or if I'll always be a little broken."

I want to tell her she's wrong. That she's not broken. That even if she is, I don't fucking care. Because who isn't?

But I need to give her space.

To let her talk.

Her voice stays soft. Scared. "This trip has been different. I guess it's my first time away from my life. From my dad. And Oliver... well, he's hovering. But still. It's nice, not thinking about it as much. Not feeling like the broken girl who has to be handled carefully. You... seeing me as a normal person."

"No one is normal."

"You know what I mean."

I do.

"But I... I guess I just want someone to see all of me. I thought the other night... I thought that was what I needed. And I did. I really did. But I need this too."

"Okay."

"It's okay if you want to ask questions. Or run. Or just not talk about it. Or—"

"No."

"No?"

"You..." Fuck, how do I explain this to her? I don't even understand it. It means so fucking much, that she's trusting me with this. That she's willing to share her burden with me. It means the fucking world.

"You don't have to..." Her voice gets surer. "It's okay if it freaks you out. It freaks me out sometimes too."

"No. It doesn't."

"At all?"

Maybe it should, but it doesn't. "I won't pretend I understand it. But I want to... if you want to share that with me."

Her eyes fix on mine. "Yeah?"

"Yeah. It means the world to me, Daisy. That you trust me with this."

"I do."

"I..." It's not the time. And it's not the thing to say. She's been clear about what she wants. I'm not about to stand in her way. "Thank you."

"Thank me?"

I nod.

She blinks and a tear catches on her lashes. "But..."

"But what, baby?"

"I..." Her fingers brush my wrist. My forearm. My waist. "You don't think I'm a freak?"

"No."

"You don't want to run?"

"Do you want me to?"

"No." She rests her head on my chest. "Maybe. I don't know."

"I don't want to."

"You promise?"

"Yeah."

I pull her closer.

Her fingers dig into my t-shirt.

Slowly but surely, her body melts into mine.

———

WE LINGER AT THE TABLE, TALKING, EATING, SIPPING TEA.

She lays her heart bare for me. It's beautiful. And terrifying. But not for the reasons she thinks.

She's halfway through a story about her brother when her phone buzzes. Luna and Oliver are on their way back to the house.

At the moment, I don't care. I want to sit here with her and soak up every second.

I want to pin her to the wall and kiss her senseless.

Make her come until she begs me to stop.

Hell, I want to rip open my chest, tear my heart out, and offer it to her.

I don't know how to do that.

But I know this:

Family first.

I can take the hit from her brother. I can take him punching me in the face, never talking to me again, getting me fired.

I can't take fucking up her most important relationship.

So when she looks at me with those big blue eyes, I nod *of course we should clean up the scene*.

I kiss her hard.

I kiss her like it's goodbye.

Because it is. Whatever happens in California, this is the end of something.

I just hope it's not the end of everything.

Chapter Forty

DAISY

The four of us spend the night together. Dinner at our favorite taco joint—we already have a favorite. Karaoke at a run-down dive of a karaoke joint. Drinks on the beach.

Walking in the sand.

In the water.

I want to kiss, touch, fuck Holden, but I manage to keep my hands to myself.

All night.

I head to bed the second we get home. I pack, shower, slip into my pajamas. Into my room.

I cross my fingers, hoping he'll sneak in to kiss, touch, fuck me.

But he doesn't.

———

Sixteen hours later, Holden and I hug goodbye. Then Luna and me.

Dad is waiting at baggage claim. He holds me tightly. Like he can't believe I didn't break.

Honestly, sometimes I can't believe it either.

I let him have the moment. Let him gush about how tan I look, how much he missed me, how little he'll be able to stand this year.

Then I wave one last goodbye to my friends, follow my family to the parking garage, slip into the passenger seat of Dad's car—it's my birthday trip, so I deserve it—and watch as we pull into the chaos that is LAX.

I wait until I'm home to check my texts.

Sure enough, there's something from Holden. A picture from the beach. Me in the water, looking up at the sky like it's a thing of beauty and wonder.

And three little words.

I'll miss you.

Chapter Forty-One

HOLDEN

I'm a wreck. At work, the gym, home, walks to the nearest coffee shop.

No matter what I do, I'm miserable.

Every so often, I pick up my phone. Stare at my text from Daisy.

I'll miss you too.

The four words that say everything.

That turn my stomach to acid.

And turn my limbs to lead.

Somehow, those are the four worst words in the English language. And there's no one else I want to tell.

Only her.

Who else would appreciate a comment about language?

Maybe Skye. She does have a BFA, even if it's in Film History. Or Criticism.

I'm not sure how it applies to her current gig taking pictures of her massive tits for a bazillion Instagram followers (supposedly, she's advertising clothes, but she certainly isn't wearing a lot of them).

Hell, I try focusing on my brother's girlfriend. I send him taunting texts. Tease him all day at work.

It doesn't fill the empty spot in my gut.

It doesn't soothe my soul.

It doesn't quiet the voice in the back of my head.

The damn thing keeps screaming.

You're never going to find someone else like her.

It's right.

But that doesn't change anything.

Chapter Forty-Two

HOLDEN

The pastel pink notebook looks exactly like the one Daisy keeps in her bag.

It's probably the same as the one she keeps in her bag. Same size, shape, shade of pink.

Not that it's all that different than the five notebooks in my car. None of them are right. None of the dozen shops I've visited had the right notebook.

I need something better for her going away present.

Something that explains—

Fuck.

I place the notebook in the red basket. Reach into my pocket. Feel the weight of the tiny jewelry box.

It's still there.

But is it enough?

Is it really going to say—

Fuck, I'm not sure what I want to say to her. Besides *do you really want this to be the end? Because I sure as fuck don't. And this sure as hell sucks. Tell me you want something else, that you're as miserable as I am, that this is as impossible for you.*

That's not happening.

This is what she wants. I have to learn to live with it.

I check the shelf again. For a thinner notebook. A different color. Something with unlined pages.

For the art class she's probably not going to take.

"Mr. Ballard," a familiar voice interrupts. Daisy and Oliver's dad.

I turn to the sound. To Mr. Flynn pushing a cart full of notebooks, pens, organizers. Shit I haven't used since high school. Hell, I never used most of that stuff. "Mr. Flynn."

"Gabe," he reminds me.

Fluorescent lights bounce off the cart. Bring out the shades of light pink and purple. Daisy's stuff.

And she—

"Dad, did you get the—" She steps into the aisle. Stops as her eyes fall on me. "Hey. Holden." She pulls her arm over her chest. "You, uh—"

"Yeah." I run my hand through my hair. There's so much I want to say. So much I shouldn't say. For once, I'm going to keep my mouth shut.

It's not my strong suit.

But I can try.

"We were just…" She takes two steps toward us. She's closer, but there's still half an aisle between us. It still feels like she's a million miles away. "Picking up a few things."

"Will we see you tomorrow?" Gabe asks.

Daisy clears her throat.

Her dad turns back to her. I'm not sure what he communicates, but it must be something, because she nods *okay*.

He steps away from the cart. "I have a hot date with a coffee maker." He nods a goodbye. "I'll see you tomorrow?"

"Yeah." I nod back.

He moves away from the cart. Stops to whisper something to Daisy.

She nods. Waits for him to turn the corner. Closes the space between us.

Fifteen feet. Ten. Five.

One.

"You uh…" She presses her lips together. They're soft. The same shade of pink as always. She's in that same red wrap dress and matching Keds.

Fuck, she looks adorable.

And sexy as hell.

I swallow hard. "Buying stuff for school?"

"Yeah." Her eyes flit to the pastel pink notebook in my basket. They trace a line up my body. To my eyes. "I guess you're—"

"Yeah."

"It's nice. I like it."

"Good."

She nods in agreement. Smooths her dress. "Are you good?"

No. But I don't need to put that on her. "Yeah. Are you?"

She stares into my eyes for a long moment. She must find whatever she's looking for, because she nods. "I am." She steps backward. Places her body behind the cart. Wraps her fingers around the handle. "I changed my schedule."

"Yeah?"

She nods *yeah*. "Added a studio art class."

Does that mean she's taking an extra class? That's the last thing she needs. But *I* need to keep it to myself. "Ceramics?"

She shakes her head. "No. I still can't get into clay."

"Too tactile?"

"Maybe. Maybe that means I should do it. Because it would challenge me. Force me out of my head. But I think

—" She motions to the yellow sketchbook sitting in the cart. The metal tin of pencils. From the soft, dark 2b to the hard, light 6h. "After I survive drawing… maybe I'll give clay a shot."

"You might like it."

She nods *I might*. Her gaze shifts to the sketchbook. "Holden I… I really appreciate last week."

"Me too."

"You… I don't know what we're… but I… I'm always going to remember it."

I swallow hard. "I will too."

Her eyes meet mine. They ask for something. Something I desperately want to give her.

Something I absolutely can't give her.

I suck a breath through my teeth. Extend my hand. "I should go. Early appointment."

"Right." She offers her hand.

"Take care, kid."

"I'll see you tomorrow?"

"Of course."

She shakes my hand. "We uh—" She releases my hand. Opens her arms. "You have to do better than that."

"You cribbing my lines?"

"Only the good ones." Her smile is sad.

I take it at face value anyway.

Chapter Forty-Three

DAISY

"Will your brother drink this?" Dad holds up a box of coffee pods. He holds a poker face for a moment.

"Really?" It's a ridiculous question, and he knows it. Mom sent Oliver an instant coffee maker a few birthdays ago. He complained about it nonstop. *This isn't real coffee. This is an abomination.*

"Really." He places the dark roast pods in the cart. "He's always sleeping in."

I stifle a laugh.

Dad's poker face cracks. He lets out a hearty laugh. It's so much like Oliver's laugh. A little higher. A little easier. But otherwise, the spitting image. "He should know his limits."

"Should he?"

Dad nods *true*. "That was his friend."

"Yeah." I so don't want to have this conversation. I'm still shaking. My legs are still threatening to buckle. I want to run to the parking lot, pound on Holden's car, beg him to comfort me.

Please, come to my room. Come to Berkeley with me. Stay in my dorm. In my bed.

Stay with me forever.

That's not within the realm of possibility.

There's no us. No future. No relationship.

I don't need Dad warning me not to date my brother's friend. Because I'm not.

It's over.

No matter how much I hate it.

"The one who comes over all the time," Dad says.

"You know it is."

"That's why I didn't pose it as a question."

I clear my throat.

He motions to the next aisle. Pens. "Your brother only stays in the house because you're there."

"I know."

"He'd rather—"

"Drink without judgment?"

Dad nods *yes*. He doesn't add anything about how I should let it go. That I should wait for Oliver to realize he needs to quit. That pushing him is going to push him away. Like what happened with Mom.

We've had that conversation before.

It never goes well.

Even if it's true, it's bullshit. That didn't stop them from pushing me. They always say it's different, but it's not.

It's the same.

It's just…

Life isn't fair.

I'm not upset about that anymore. It happened. It sucked, but it was for the best. I'm… better. I am better. Maybe I'm not all the way, but who is?

Holden is right.

We're all a little fucked up.

We're all a little broken.

One day I'm going to find someone who accepts that. Who loves me anyway. Who wants me anyway.

Someone else.

Not that he—

God, it's hard to breathe in here.

Dad grabs a box of gel roller pens. His favorite brand. Blue. Of course. "Does he know?"

"What?"

"Does your brother know you slept with his friend?"

"Dad!"

"Should I pretend it isn't obvious?" He chuckles *because it's very obvious*.

"Oh my God." Please stop this conversation. Somehow.

"Were you safe?"

"Yes."

"With everything?"

"I'm not—"

"You can get STDs from—"

"I know." My face flushes. My chest too. My dad is lecturing me about STDs in an office supply store. A week before the district's classes resume.

God knows who could be here.

Maybe someone I knew in high school is listening. They're probably sending out a mass text *oh my gosh, can you believe it? Daisy Flynn finally got laid.*

"They have testing at the school's medical center," he says.

"Yes." I do not need to have this conversation.

"You should make an appointment. Just in case."

I clear my throat.

"Or would you rather find a gynecologist who can see

you outside of school? In case you stay in Berkeley. I'm sure your mother—"

"Can we please not?"

"No." His voice stays matter-of-fact. "If you don't promise to make an appointment, I'll have to call your mother and—"

"I promise." Anything but that.

He nods *good*. Grabs another box of pens. Tosses it in the cart. "Unless you prefer black."

I shake my head. "Blue is good."

He motions to the red pens.

I nod *yeah*.

"Are you going to tell Oliver?" He grabs two boxes.

Oliver. Not *your brother*. That means something, but I'm not sure what. "It was just a… fling."

"Really?" His voice is incredulous.

"Dad, please. Can we at least have this conversation later?"

"When, baby girl? You're booked all day tomorrow. We leave the next morning."

"Well…"

"I know you'd rather talk to Luna about these things. She's a good friend. But she's so young. She doesn't always have the perspective."

"What perspective do you have? You date less often than I do." I try to say it in a teasing way, but I only get halfway there.

He chuckles anyway. "Are you sure?"

"That you—"

"About it being a fling?"

"Oh." My chest pangs. It already hurts. But it will get easier with time. That's what people say.

"He might want more."

"It doesn't make sense."

"Maybe. But sometimes that doesn't matter." He's quiet for a moment. Then he pushes the cart forward. "What do you want?"

"More pens." I grab a multi-colored set. Pink, purple, red, green. A bright green and a teal closer to Holden's eyes. His eyes are softer. Greyer. A million times more beautiful.

Dad makes that *hmmm* noise that means *why are you lying to yourself?*

At least, it does when he makes it.

"Don't *hmmm* me."

"I won't."

"You are."

"I said nothing." He shrugs, feigning innocence.

"You're thinking it."

Dad mimes zipping his lips. He turns to the cart. Guides it to the next aisle. Organizers.

We have plenty, but I don't want to call it yet. I don't want to step outside and breathe in the cool night air and realize that I might never hug, kiss, touch Holden again.

"He seems like a nice boy," Dad says.

"Is that reverse psychology?" I ask.

"Approve so you'll lose interest?"

"Yeah."

"No." His laugh is soft. "You never went through that phase."

"Maybe I'm due."

He makes that same *hmmm* noise.

I clear my throat.

"Okay. No *hmmm*." His gaze shifts to the glass doors. "Isn't that his car? In the parking lot?"

It is his silver sedan. But I'm not thinking about that.

"You could talk to him."

I shake my head. "It's too hard."

He nods with understanding. "Love isn't always enough."

"It's not… We're not…" Maybe we are. I don't know. "Does it always suck this bad?"

"Yeah. But the first cut is the deepest."

"When does it stop hurting?"

"I don't know. Soon, I hope."

"Me too." But I have a feeling it won't.

Chapter Forty-Four

HOLDEN

I suck a breath through my nose as I step into the Flynn house.

It's decked in blue and gold streamers. A giant cut out of a bear.

A circular table filled with every mixer imaginable.

And not a single drop of booze.

Or so it seems.

I know better. The off-brand cola on the left—no one would drink it when there's actual Coke and Pepsi available —is half bourbon.

God knows what's in the off-brand lemon-lime soda.

Or the ginger ale.

I nod hello to the eighteen-year-old who greets me. Some guy from Daisy's school. He's vaguely familiar in an over eager kid kind of way.

Not that I can talk.

I was the same when I was his age.

He is her age.

The age of a guy who should be dating her.

Another reason why I should back the fuck off.

But, hey, I'm just here to say goodbye. To drop off this present. To… whatever.

I cut through the room—it's not all that crowded, four or five of Daisy's friends plus most of the guys from Inked Love—and pour a glass of ginger ale.

No luck. It's just shitty soda. I hold my red plastic cup up to whoever wants to toast.

Oliver pulls away from a conversation with Patrick and Dare. He motions *come here* to me.

I join him on the couch.

He pulls something from the side, something wedged between the arm rest and the cushion.

A silver flask.

He doesn't ask if I want any. Just uncaps and pours. Into my drink.

Then his.

He holds up the cup to toast. "To the end of an era."

"To the end of an era." I tap my plastic cup against his. Take a long sip. Fuck, that's better. It's still shitty ginger ale, but the bourbon makes it rich and sweet.

It warms my throat and chest.

Makes my face flush.

"Fuck." I cough. "Could you have bought cheaper shit?"

Oliver chuckles that low, deep chuckle of his. Like we're still best friends. Like I didn't fuck his sister a week ago. Like she's not leaving first thing in the morning. "You know how old this is?"

"You've been aging it in the leather?"

His laugh gets louder. "That's good."

It's really not.

He uncaps the flask. Takes a swig. Grimaces. "Found this bottle in the back of my closet. Got it senior year.

From that weird homeless guy who used to hang out in front of Rosewater."

"You drank something he gave you?" I ask.

"You just did." He taps my cup with his.

Fuck it. I take another swig. This time, I swallow my cough.

"I saw him buy it."

"Bourbon from 7-Eleven?"

"Trader Joe's."

"No fucking way." I swallow another sip. Then two. "They don't sell to shady dudes at Trader Joe's."

"He cleaned up nice," Oliver says.

"Probably bought you apple juice and put it in an old bottle," I say.

Oliver chuckles *maybe*. "It's alcoholic now."

It is. And it's as strong as it's awful. I swallow another sip.

Let him top me off.

Toast with my friends.

Patrick takes a long swig. Lets out a much too illicit sigh. "That's terrible."

Dare nods *it is*.

"Like you know shit." Oliver chuckles. "You drink Bud."

"Bud light." Patrick's smile is slight. He's usually a fun guy. The life of the party. But other times, he pulls away. Hangs out on the sidelines. Or avoids people entirely.

Maybe he's just sick of our bullshit.

He and Darren—who tries to go by Dare, because he thinks it's badass—work at Inked Love. They're newer to the family, I guess. They weren't at Oddball with me, Forest, and Oliver.

They're good artists. They show up on time. They bring drinks to parties.

Usually, I'd love hanging out. Shooting the shit. Teasing them about how hard they try to be cool.

Not that Patrick really tries. He got the nickname Trick a million years ago. Alternates between loving it and hating it.

It has something to do with his ex-girlfriend. The one he insists he's over.

The one he's totally not over.

Dare holds up his cup. "Bet I can drink it faster?"

"Than Oliver?" Patrick's chuckle is low. Just like Oliver's. "I doubt that."

Oliver nods *it's true*. "What are the stakes here?"

"Why do we need stakes?" Dare asks.

"'Cause otherwise it's not a bet." Oliver nods *obviously*.

Patrick shakes his head. "He knows he's going to lose."

Dare flips him off.

Oliver holds up his glass. "Loser buys coffee for a week."

"You buy expensive shit," Dare says.

"Exactly." Oliver holds his glass a little higher. He raises a brow. *Let's go. Unless you can't handle it.*

Dare shakes his head *fuck that*. He taps his glass with Oliver's. "On three."

"Make sure they're even." Patrick looks to me. He's expecting me to do it.

To participate in this idiotic pissing contest.

Usually, I would.

Usually, I'd tease my best friend and my coworkers for hours.

Tonight, I can't bring myself to care.

I nod *sure* anyway. Grab the bottle. Fill their glasses to the top.

Patrick holds up three fingers. "Glass upside down when you're done." He motions to the coffee table. "Right here." He looks to the contestants. When they nod *sure*, he shakes his hand. "Three, two, one."

They go.

Oliver drinks like it's nothing.

Dare's more ambitious. Tries to chug. Struggles through his third swallow.

Oliver tilts his head back.

Drinks a little faster.

A little—

There.

He wipes his mouth as he places the cup on the coffee table. Raises a brow *I told you*.

Dare finishes two seconds later. He pouts *fuck this*. Reaches for the bottle anyway.

"Not sure why you thought you had a chance." Patrick shakes his head.

"Flew too close to the sun." Dare shrugs *no big deal*. He turns to Oliver. "That homeless guy? You bought from him a lot."

"Oh yeah." Oliver holds up the flask like it's his finest possession. "You should have seen this dude when I met him. I was hanging out at Rosewater, hoping one of the artists would take pity on me, teach me *something*. Or do some free ink. And this guy comes in with a wallet. Says he found it outside. That he just wants to do the right thing and return it. And if there's a reward on the way…" He raises a brow, copying the guy's posture.

I let him go off on the story.

I've heard it a million times, but it's still good. Funny. Punctuated.

Bullshit.

Parts are true. Oliver did pay a homeless guy to buy him booze every so often. But the details—

Let's just say he's spinning a yarn.

I try to listen, to laugh at the proper places, *no fucking way* at the right moments, give him hell every so often.

Then I see her.

It's like the fucking sky parts.

Daisy descends in a cobalt blue dress and bright yellow flats.

She looks at the shoes and raises a brow *these are hideous*.

"It's called theme!" Luna squeals loud enough for everyone to hear. "Besides, you're a spring. It suits you."

"Please don't start with that." She slides her arm around her best friend. Smiles back at her.

Then her eyes meet mine and her smile disappears.

She stares back for a long moment, then she mouths "Outside." Holds up her hands *five minutes*.

I nod an *okay*.

Fail to do anything except watch her.

––––––

IT'S A NICE NIGHT. WARM AND CLEAR.

The big silver moon casts highlights over the backyard.

The stars try to shine. We're close to the beach—there's a faint smell of salt in the air—but the peace of the Pacific Ocean can't compete with the light pollution of the city.

They're dull spots on the indigo sky.

I'm sure it means something to Daisy. That she could make it into something beautiful. Set the mood in a dozen words.

But I—

Well, that's another thing outside my skill set.

I swallow another sip of ginger ale. Set the mug on the cement. Move around the corner. To the brick edge of the flower bed.

It's a nice sized backyard—the size of my dad's down-stairs. Succulent garden. Bed of roses. Glowing aqua pool.

Patio chairs on a patch of gravel.

Daisy pulls the sliding door closed behind her.

She forces a smile. Steps onto the gravel path that cuts through the succulent garden.

Sits next to me.

"Hey." She pulls her arms over her chest. Rubs her upper arms with her palms. "You, uh… I didn't think you'd come."

Me either. "You invited me."

"A long time ago."

"Even so." I unzip my hoodie. Shrug it off my shoulders. Sling it over hers.

She brings her hands to the soft fabric. "You don't mind."

"Clashes with my outfit." I motion to my light jeans.

She laughs as she slips her arms into the sweater. "Of course. Navy doesn't go with light blue."

"It's ridiculous. Like some cool color convention. Who needs that?"

"No one."

"Besides." I motion to her blue wrap dress. Her yellow flats. "Now, you're *really* rocking the Bear's colors."

"These are ridiculous." She holds up her foot. "But Luna… she was so excited when she brought them over. I can't remember the last time I saw her that happy."

"After she sang *Like A Virgin*."

Her laugh is soft. "Yeah. She, uh, she has passion."

"Not a lot of pitch."

"I don't either."

"You do all right."

Her cheeks flush. "You, uh… I meant to call you."

"Oh?"

She presses her palms into her thighs. "I just… I got so busy, with packing and preparing everything. And… I was scared too."

"Nothing to be scared of."

"Yeah, maybe. I guess I just… wasn't ready to say goodbye." Her eyes meet mine. "I had a lot of fun in Mexico."

"It was something else."

Her smile is soft. Honest. "You're a good guy, Holden. I'm glad I got to see that side of you. I really like it."

"Thanks." I do too.

"Do you think you'll… stay in touch with him?"

"Maybe."

"I hope you do." She turns her body toward mine. She opens her mouth like she's going to say something, then she stops.

"It must be scary."

"Huh?" Her back snaps upright.

"Leaving tomorrow. Starting this new phase in your life. With almost nothing from home."

"Yeah." Her sigh is heavy. "I, uh, I do know a few people who are going to Berkley. Two dozen, between my last school and the one before. Though I… I kinda hope I don't see them."

"You want to start fresh?"

"Yeah."

"Without baggage?"

Her lips press together. "Is it that obvious?"

No. Just human nature. "It must be hard."

"It is."

"I like that you say that. You admit it. You don't come back with some sarcastic bullshit."

"That would be stealing your thing."

I smile, even though she's doing exactly that.

"I know… that's the same thing. But it's true. It's your thing."

"It is."

"And I, uh… I guess I am scared. Living alone, making new friends, being far from home. And the rest too… Last time I was left on my own, it didn't go so well."

You don't have to be on your own. Be with me. I don't have a fucking clue how to do this. Much less do it long distance. But I don't care.

Be with me.

I love you.

I love you so fucking much.

I swallow hard. "You can always call."

Her smile is soft. "Thanks, I… I do appreciate that."

"Really. I mean it. Anytime, day or night. If you need to talk. It doesn't have to be more than that. It doesn't have to mean anything."

"So you'll be… waiting for me?"

Is that what she wants? I try to read her expression, but I can't figure it out. "We're friends."

"We are."

I suck in a shallow breath. "Do you want something else?"

Her eyes meet mine. "Oh. Well… it's for the best. Like we talked about."

"Right." My stomach twists. "We'll always be friends."

"I hope so."

"And I'll always be there. I can't promise I'll be lucid. Or sober. Or smart. I might tell you to go get wasted and fuck the nearest hot guy—"

She shrinks back, wounded. "Yeah."

"Can't promise good advice. But I will try." I run my hand through my hair. Fuck, this is not what I'm supposed to say. But I can't say what's in my head.

This is what's best for her.

It's probably best for me too.

I'll see that eventually.

It just has to suck for a while.

I can't stand in her way.

I can't clip her wings.

"If you ever need an ear… I can do that." I force a smile. "I, uh… I got you something."

"The notebook?"

"Yeah. I left that on the table. This is… more personal." I pull the jewelry box from my pocket. Offer it to her.

"Oh." Her fingers brush mine as she takes it. "Can I—"

"Later." I can't watch her open it. I won't be able to leave.

"Sure."

I can't take another moment of goodbye. I already miss you so fucking much. "I have an early morning, so—"

Her eyes turn down. "Of course." She stands.

I do too.

She opens her arms.

I pull her into a close hug.

She melts into my chest. Just like she did that day in Mexico.

Like it's where she belongs.

Like this is where both of us belong.

But it's not. It just feels like that right now.

I release her.

She looks up at me with a soft smile. "You could come by tomorrow. If you want. We're leaving at eleven."

"That early?" I tease.

"Yeah, Oliver figured it was the best way to beat traffic. But I think he just wants to sleep in."

"Probably."

"We're stopping in Monterey for the night. To see the aquarium. So, uh… we don't get into Berkley until the day after tomorrow."

"Say hi to the octopus for me."

"Sure, yeah." Her fingers brush my wrist. "You could come by… in the morning… if you want."

I can't. I can barely stand here. "I have an appointment."

"I'll be up early."

"I'll see what I can do." My eyes meet hers. There's so much in those gorgeous blue eyes. Pain, longing, determination.

This hurts her too.

But she's sure.

As sure as she was when she set these terms.

She's the one with her life in flux. I can't tempt her with an offer of something steady. No matter how badly I want to.

"Well, just in case…" She wraps her arms around me again. "I'll miss you, Holden. I really will."

"I'll miss you too, kid."

Chapter Forty-Five

HOLDEN

I don't drive home. I go to my brother's place.

He answers the door with a raised brow and a knowing smirk. "You finally gonna admit you're miserable?"

"No, just looking for a good Moscow Mule. Know anyone who makes one?"

He pulls the door wider. Motions *come in*. "I might."

I follow him into the apartment.

Skye's on the couch in some gorgeous black dress. She's sitting there like a curvy goddess—not that my body cares.

But she's not alone.

Ariel is next to her.

And my sister is holding my niece.

"You left the house?" I ask.

Ariel shoots me a *get real* look. "You're not ruining my first night talking to another adult in—"

"What about Chase?" I ask.

"What about me?" The brooding tattoo artist steps out of the bedroom with a raised brow. "You looking for some tips? Not inspiring enough women?"

Forest chuckles.

Skye laughs too. "You know that only encourages him."

"Why are you in his bedroom?" Either there's something weird and kinky going on or—

"Too much attention for Charlotte." He crosses the room to his daughter. Pulls her out of Ariel's arms.

Ariel squeezes her tiny hand. Kisses her tiny nose. "Sleep tight, baby." She waves Charlotte's tiny hand. "Say good night to your uncle."

"You mind if I help?" I ask Chase.

He raises a brow. "You want to help? Period? End of sentence?"

"What's wrong with that?" I ask.

Chase shoots Forest a look. Then Ariel. Skye.

"I can be sincere if I want," I say.

"Can you?" Forest asks.

I flip my brother off.

He just laughs. "See. It only lasted a minute."

"Come on, Mr. Sincere." Chase nods *follow me*. Holds his daughter to his chest. "I'll show you how to do it. Then I have some tips that might help you keep a woman around for—"

"Do I need to explain how many times I made—" Fuck, I can't say it. It hurts too much. "What's there to say? Growl *like this, baby*. Or *you'll come when I say so, baby*. Then you hold her arm down until she's screaming."

"It won't disturb you if I say 'yeah,' will it?" Chase asks.

"No, but it will disturb Forest," I say.

"Seriously, TMI," Forest whispers.

Skye just laughs.

They get quieter as we move into the bedroom.

Chase lays Charlotte down on a tiny foam mattress that's sitting inside a mesh crib.

I kiss her goodbye.

Give him his moment.

He lingers with her forever—and I thought the guy loved Ariel—then he turns to me, slides his arm around my shoulder, shakes his head. "Are you going to admit you're miserable? Or do I have to—"

"What, hit it out of me?"

He arches a brow *really*.

"You ever hit someone?" I ask.

He shakes his head *no*. "I was going to offer you a drink."

"You're offering me a drink?"

"Yeah."

"It's that bad?" I ask.

"It's way worse."

Chapter Forty-Six

DAISY

I mingle. I chat. I even flirt with the guy from my AP Chemistry class.

I don't avoid or overdo it on the cupcakes (decorated with bright blue icing and gold candy, of course).

I wait until the party dies down. I make it all the way through my shower. All the way until I'm in my bedroom alone, Holden's present resting on my sheets.

It shouldn't be the present.

It should be him.

His body against mine, his sweet nothings in my ears, his hands on my skin.

It should be a million things.

But it's not. And I know...

This is what he wants.

It's what makes sense.

Sure, it's horrible and miserable and awful. And it's only going to hurt more when he's an extra few hundred miles away.

But—

It's logical.

There's no reason to go to college with a boyfriend.
With a boyfriend who's never even been a boyfriend.
With baggage.
With a tether.
With an inability to truly lose myself in the moment.
I pull the covers over my head.
I tell myself I won't open the present.
But I do it anyway.

Chapter Forty-Seven

DAISY

There's a soft knock on my door.

I swallow a sob. Pull my cover over my head. Press my eyes together. *Please go away. Please don't force me to face this. Please—*

"Daisy." Oliver's voice is understanding. "I'm coming in."

"Don't."

Yellow light floods the room as he opens the door.

He steps inside. Presses the door shut. Sits on the bed.

"I'm fine."

"Yeah?"

I nod *yeah*.

"Crying in your bed, alone, at ten p.m. because you're fine?"

"That's what fine people do." I press the silver key chain between my palms. It's mine. I want it to stay mine.

To stay ours.

If Oliver sees it—

Sure, it's under the blanket, but... I don't know.

I just need it to be mine. All mine.

"You need to know something, Daisy," he says.

"That you refuse to believe simple facts? Like me being fine?"

He turns so he's looking me in the eyes. "If he hurt you, I'm going to kill him."

"Oliver—"

"Don't tell me you didn't. I'm not a fucking idiot."

I swallow hard.

"And don't say *I thought you wouldn't notice 'cause you're so drunk all the time* or some shit like that. You aren't changing the subject."

"I'm an adult."

"I know."

"I can sleep with anyone I want."

He stands. Flips on the light.

Fuck, that's bright. I pull the cover over my head.

He tugs it back. Sits at my desk. Shakes his head at the sorry sight that is my life. "What? Did it get too real for him?"

"No, I… it was my idea. Or his. I don't know."

"It your idea to…"

I clear my throat. "Can we not?"

"Sure."

"Thank you."

"As long as you look me in the eyes and convince me you're actually okay."

"I'm just…" I meet my brother's gaze.

He stares back with those penetrating blue eyes.

It's way too much. Honestly, I don't get why Luna is into him or his eyes. She's always going off on how pretty and penetrating they are. *Yours are pretty too, but his are just mmmmm.*

"I'm gonna kill him."

"Can you not?"

"No."

"Just… stop at hurting him."

"I'll consider that."

"Please."

"Eh." He shrugs like he's considering it.

"Pretty please."

"Pretty please?"

"Yeah."

"Fuck. That's it. That's the code word." He holds a poker face for a moment. Then he cracks. Lets out a soft chuckle. "I gotta do it if you say pretty please."

"You could not hurt him at all."

"I don't know… sounds like we agreed on me hurting him." He raises a brow *I gotta do it*. "Look how miserable you are. And he's the cause of that."

"It's not like that."

"Isn't it?"

"No." I shake my head. "I… it's the logical decision. No tethers, right? That's what everyone says. And I… I just…" I blink back tears. "Why do I have to do all this? Leave? It's too far from home. It's too much on my own."

"It's a lot. I know."

"Too much." A tear rolls down my cheeks. "I can't do this. I just can't, Ollie. I can't be that far away from you or Luna or Holden—"

"Daisy—"

"And it's not just because I like him. Or love him. Or want him. Or whatever it is. It's all too much. What if I relapse? I'll be all alone, with no one to notice the signs. I'll come home for Thanksgiving and be—"

"You won't."

"You don't know that." I shake my head. "I can talk to Dad in the morning. I can skip this semester. Start in the winter. Or transfer to UCLA." I suck a breath through my teeth. It's not enough oxygen. I need more. "I can't do this all on my own, Ollie."

"I know." He offers me his hand.

I take it. Squeeze tightly. "I can't do it."

He nods *okay*, squeezes back.

I push out a heavy exhale.

He stays silent.

Which is wrong. He's supposed to argue, tell me I'm wrong, that I'm silly, that I can do this.

Why isn't he saying this?

Does he not believe it?

Maybe that's why Holden isn't here. Maybe it has nothing to do with what I asked, with practicalities, with any of that.

Maybe he is scared.

Maybe I am too much.

Maybe he just can't handle that.

I let go of my brother's hand. Turn over. Bury my face in the covers.

Oliver waits until my breath slows.

Then in a low, even tone, he asks, "Is that really what you want?"

"Huh?"

"Do you really want to skip a semester?"

"I don't know."

"To stay here? Live in dad's house? Go to UCLA. Or SMC."

"It's just… it's too much."

"You can do it."

"That doesn't mean anything."

His voice is even. "You really believe you can't?"

"I don't know."

"All right. Maybe you can't. But if you go and you fail, at least you tried."

"That's stupid. If I go and I fail, I'll have shitty grades.
Or get 'withdraws.' Or—"

"So?"

"So? That will be—"

"A bad first semester. And maybe you'll need to be
here. At UCLA. Maybe you'll need us nearby. But last time
I checked, you got into UCLA."

"Yeah." That is true.

"And UCSB and UCI and USCD and USC and—"

"I know where I got in."

"We visited all those schools."

We did.

"And some on the East Coast."

Yeah.

"But you choose Berkley."

"But—"

"You said, as soon as you stepped onto campus, you
knew. It felt right. And you felt happy. Every time you
thought about it, you felt happy. You felt like you were
home."

"Well—"

"If it's too much and you're scared and you need
someone from home, then you'll have to fight to keep me
away."

"But—"

"They have tattoo shops in Berkeley, don't they?"

"Probably." I push out a shallow exhale. "But it's
expensive."

"Yeah, but I'll have you as my roomie."

I shake my head.

"I'm gonna cunt-block for four years straight."

A laugh breaks up the tension in my chest. "You will
not." I roll over so I can look him in the eyes. "Will you?"

He shrugs *maybe, maybe not.* "You think I'm letting some punk football player fuck with my baby sister?"

"Oh my God."

"Bad enough I missed you sleeping with the biggest slut in the state."

"That isn't you?"

"All right, top two." His smile is soft. "I know it's scary. Really fucking scary. But you can do it. And I'm not saying that because it's what you need to hear. I'm saying it because I know you. And I know you've been through a lot harder shit than this."

"Okay."

"So trust me when I say, you can do it. You don't have to believe me. Hell, you don't have to try. If you really want to pull out of school, I'm not going to stop you."

"You're not?"

"No." He stares into my eyes. "I will kill Holden though."

"But—"

"Don't try to tell me it's not about him. I'm not that oblivious."

"But—"

"What did he give you?"

"That's kinda—"

"Is it a picture of his dick?" Oliver asks.

"Why would it—"

"Then it's not that personal." He motions *give it.*

I push myself up. Swallow hard. "Well, it's…" I hold up the silver key chain. It's inscribed with the quote on his chest.

dulce periculum

Danger is sweet.

Until you get the real thing on the other side.

The First Taste

Oliver holds it up. Shakes his head *of course*. "If you drop out of school for him, I'll kill both of you."

"Oliver—"

"You think that's gonna stop me?"

"How about 'pretty please'?"

He shakes his head. "You used yours."

"I only get one?"

"Per day." He places the key chain in my palms. "You can have another tomorrow. If you want to waste it on Holden's life..." He shakes his head *I won't stop you*. He stands. Flips off the light. "You need anything?"

"No. Just—"

"Yeah." He pulls the door open. "I'm proud of you."

"I know."

"Do you? 'Cause sometimes, I'm not sure you have any idea how fucking proud I am." His voice cracks for a moment. Then he swallows it. "Get some sleep. It's gonna be a long day."

"Okay."

"Don't let him do your first tattoo."

"I already—"

"I'm a better artist."

"Maybe we can negotiate."

"For his life? Don't count on it," Oliver says.

"Maybe you could... think about... drinking less."

He swallows hard. "I'll think about it."

"Really?"

"Yeah. Now go to bed." He nods *good night*, steps into the hallway, closes the door behind him.

Chapter Forty-Eight

DAISY

The next morning is quiet. Breakfast, tea, last-minute packing.

A goodbye from Luna.

Absolutely no sign of Holden.

We pile my stuff into Dad's car. Drive to my music.

Oliver barely complains about the auto-tune.

Dad insists it's a jam. He's pretty up to date on the latest. Or maybe he's trying to connect with me.

The road stretches forever. It feels like it takes a million miles to arrive in Monterey, park, check into our hotel, head to the aquarium.

Sure enough, there's a giant octopus in a cylindrical tank.

He's pressed to the glass. Suctioned to it, I guess. The poor guy just can't let go.

Or maybe he doesn't want to.

Maybe he doesn't need to.

What's the difference?

I snap a dozen photos. Open my texts from Holden. Tap a message.

Daisy: He says hi too.

I go to pick a photo, but none of them are right.

This isn't right.

I need to…

Do something.

I'm not sure what it is, but it's not this.

I delete the words. Turn my phone off. Find my dad at the shark exhibit.

Then I soak up my last night with my family around.

———

I KNOW, AS A NATIVE SOUTHERN CALIFORNIAN, I SHOULD hate the bay area. Find every opportunity to insult it.

I certainly shouldn't be at UCB.

Even if it's the best UC in the state.

But even as we sit in traffic all morning, I can't bring myself to complain *God, this traffic is even worse than Los Angeles.*

Because it isn't. Not really.

And even if it was—

Oliver was right.

The closer we get to Berkley, the more I remember. This town is amazing. A hippie college paradise a short ride away from a sprawling city.

Sure, it's not as warm. It's farther from the ocean. It's crowded and expensive (not that the UCs really scale their dorm rates to cost of living) and way too far from home.

But it's thrilling too.

My nerves rise with every mile.

My excitement does too.

By the time we park in the designated unloading area, I'm bursting. I grab my backpack. Skip to the dorm.

It's crowded with parents, siblings, students.

People lugging suitcases, moving small appliances, arguing over where to get dinner.

And there, leaning against the concrete railing.

Holden.

Chapter Forty-Nine

DAISY

He's as tall and broad as ever, but he looks a little worse for wear.

Like he hasn't slept in days.

Like he can't stand a single inch between us.

There's only one reason why he'd be here.

Or maybe I...

Maybe I'm not seeing something.

"Hey." He runs a hand through his shaggy hair.

"Hey." I tug on my backpack strings. This is weird. Like my daydreams have come to life.

I pinch myself.

I'm still here.

The sky is still blue. The grass is still green. Holden Ballard is still standing in front of my dorm.

"I, uh, I wanted to say goodbye." His voice is soft. Uncertain.

"Here?"

He nods.

"That's a long way to go."

"Yeah." He pushes off the wall. "I wanted to see what it was like."

Fuck, I need him closer.

"To see if it was doable."

"The?"

"Drive." He takes another step toward me. "It's pretty fucking far."

"Four hundred miles."

"And traffic."

"Yeah." I press my lips together. "There's a train too."

"That's even longer."

"Or a flight."

"Then you have the airport."

"Yeah." I swallow hard.

"It's far. But it's doable."

My breath catches in my throat.

"Fuck, I…" He looks up at the sky. "I tried to talk myself out of this. Even now, I'm not sure if this is the right move. It's selfish, coming here, asking you to consider this. To consider me." His eyes meet mine. "I should give you a few weeks. I should give you a chance to soar. Outgrow me. Meet some future venture capitalist who's gonna sell a billion-dollar company."

"Should you?"

"Yeah." He nods. "I should have stayed in the car. Stayed in my apartment. Gone to work instead of canceling my appointments." He takes another step toward me. Then another.

His fingers brush my wrists.

Then his hands are on my hands.

I look into his eyes.

He stares back at me with those gorgeous green eyes. "If I was a better person, I wouldn't be here. But I'm not a better person."

"Holden—" I don't know what I'm asking, only that I need an answer.

"I love you."

"You love me?"

"Yeah." He stares into my eyes. "I know it's not fair, dropping that on you. But I had to say it. I had to look you in the eyes and say it and know it was true."

"You love me?"

"Yeah." His breath is shaky. "I really do."

"I…" A million things run through my head. "So you… you're here to what? Say I love you and leave?"

"Maybe. I didn't really think past the first part." His laugh is soft. "I was too nervous."

"Oh."

"And I… It was fucked up. So I should go. Give you until Thanksgiving. Or Christmas. Or next year. Or maybe I should step out of the fucking way—"

"No."

"You have this big future and I—"

I press my lips to his.

He mumbles something into my mouth. Then his hands go to my hips.

He pulls my body into his.

My lips part for him.

His tongue slips into my mouth.

He kisses me like he's claiming me. Like he knows I'm his.

I am.

God, I really am.

Holden pulls back with a heavy sigh. "But we—"

"I know."

"You—"

"I know."

"You're gonna spend all your time missing me. I can't let you—"

I kiss him again. It's the only reasonable response.

"Fuck." He digs his hand into my hair. "You taste so fucking good."

"You too." Like chai. My favorite taste. Forever.

"Daisy, I—"

"Do I need to kiss you again?"

"Yeah, but you might not be prepared for what happens."

"You mean—" Oh.

His expression softens. "This is—"

"You're right. I'm going to spend my time missing you."

"So you—"

"But I will either way. Isn't it better if I get some of you?"

"Sounds like bullshit." His laugh stays soft.

"Yeah, but—"

"I can't fuck up your life."

"Then listen to me. This is what I want. What I need."

His eyes meet mine. He nods *okay*.

"I love you too."

"Yeah?"

"Yeah."

"But I—"

"I don't know what that means for next month. Or next year. Or next decade. But you're the one who… I'm still not good at living in the moment. But I'm getting there. And I… I am good at planning. And I can come up with a plan. To make this work."

His eyes stay glued to mine.

"Besides, my new roommate will think I'm super cool if I have a tattoo artist boyfriend."

"Will she?"

I nod. "Yeah. She'll probably think I made it up. So you're going to have to come in with me."

His lips curl into a smile. "And fuck you senseless?"

"In front of my roommate?"

He slides his arm around my waist. Motions to the dorm building. "You're not into that?"

"My dad and brother are here."

He makes an exaggerated *hmm*. "That might be awkward... so we'll have to do it here." He motions to the grass behind us.

"I don't think here is going to work."

"My hotel?"

"You have a hotel?" That's... interesting.

"Yeah."

"Oh... well... maybe after they leave." I clear my throat. "But only maybe."

"Maybe?"

I nod.

"Maybe after?"

"Yeah, you're here. I'm putting you to work."

"Cruel." He smiles. "I like that about you, kid. I like that you're absolutely merciless."

"Me too."

Epilogue

HOLDEN

"Holden—" Daisy tugs at my wrist. She lowers her voice to that tone that screams *I know I shouldn't, but oh my God I want to.* "I can't leave *my* party."

"Why not?"

"Well…"

"It's for you, right?"

Her blue eyes meet mine. They're lined in brown today. Her lips are painted a deep pink.

Between the red hue of her dress and the careful waves in her hair, she looks so much like the girl I kissed a year ago.

Was that really three hundred sixty-five days ago?

It feels like yesterday.

Her cheeks flush as she catches me staring.

She brushes a wisp of blond behind her ear and stammers. "I… is it something on my face?"

"Yeah."

Her eyes go wide. "What?"

"This." I pull her body into mine. Press my lips to hers.

She murmurs something against my mouth. Then her arms wrap around my waist and her lips melt into mine.

She sinks into my body as she kisses me back.

It's not the same as that first time. Not as desperate or hungry. We have plenty of that—every time I visit, every time she comes home—but, right now, we've been together all summer.

We have another week until we say goodbye.

But I'm not going there yet.

I have seven days with my girlfriend.

With my favorite person in the world.

It kills me every time she leaves. She takes a piece of me with her.

But it's worth it.

An hour with Daisy would be worth all the pain of parting. But seven days?

I'm the luckiest guy in the world.

Daisy's fingers curl into my hair. She rocks her hips against mine. Pulls me closer.

Closer.

Fuck. I force myself to pull back. To suck a breath through my teeth. To bring my eyes to hers. "You trying to bait me, kid?"

"Maybe." Her smile gets shy. It always does. Even after a year. And way too many goodbyes.

It drives me insane. The way it always does. My blood rushes south. My cock whines *pin her to the wall and fuck her now*. "Maybe?" I drop my voice an octave. To the tone I use to demand she take off her panties. Fuck, is she wearing panties?

If she's not—

She really is going to kill me. My girlfriend is way too fucking sexy. She's way too good at teasing me. At winding me so tight I'm going to—

Well, I really don't have a better word than explode.

It's not as poetic as what she deserves.

But *baby, you're gonna make me come* is beautiful in its own way.

Daisy's eyes meet mine. Her chest heaves with her inhale. "I, uh…"

"I'm going to fuck you until you can't walk straight—"

"Oh—"

"After this."

"This?"

"Yeah." I intertwine my fingers with her. Motion to my car. It's parked down the street. This neighborhood isn't as crowded as my dad's. But only because every fucking block is permit parking. And I'm hogging one of the few permits.

Not that I care.

Sure, I try to accommodate. I try to stay in touch with my generous nature.

But when it comes to Daisy, I'm a greedy motherfucker.

Even now—

Would it be so bad if I pinned her to the car and fucked her right here?

A cricket responds for me. A million of them. The high-pitched chirp mixes with the light breeze and the soft murmur of conversation.

This place may be two miles from the shop, but it's still suburban paradise. The driveway across the street proves it —a Tesla next to a luxury Soccer Mom SUV. Or maybe it's a Soccer Dad SUV. I shouldn't stereotype.

"Holden?" Daisy presses the pads of her fingertips into my skin. "Are you okay?"

No. I'm *this* close to dying of blue balls. She spends the summer at her dad's house. Which means her dad is there every night and all fucking weekend. Sure, his life is a bit more hectic now that he's—

That's a story for another time.

And all that shit with Oliver and Luna—

Fuck, I'm getting distracted. But it's good. Brings the blood back to my brain.

I need the help. I haven't fucked her properly in days. She's been busy with summer assignments. I've been working nonstop. Her dad's been home every fucking night.

So we—

Shit, blood leaving brain.

Thoughts dissolving.

"You look too good in that dress." My eyes go straight to her tits. Which does nothing to alleviate the situation. But then I'm starting to lose interest in remedies.

Her cheeks flush. "Thanks. I, uh… it's new."

"I know."

"The uh…" She swallows hard. "It's very—" She runs her fingers down the neckline. Then she pulls the top. Aside. Just barely. Just enough I see the lace of her pastel pink bra.

"You're gonna kill me, kid."

"I know."

"You know?" I bring my hand to her waist. "You want your boyfriend dead?"

"You want me to stop?"

"No."

"Seems like an impasse." She smiles.

"It does." I nod.

"Hmm…" She plays coy. "How are we going to solve it?"

"How are we?"

Her smile widens. "I do have one idea—"

I tap my key fob. "Get in the car. I'm gonna fuck you the second we're alone."

"*In* the car?"

"Alone alone." I press my hand into her lower back.

"How alone is that?"

"You want to debate? Or you want to come on my cock?"

————

Daisy's eyes go wide as she steps into Inked Love. She takes in the pink string lights. The framed art. The clear counter.

Her throat quivers as she swallows. "You… Are we… Really…" Her eyes dart around the room. "Now?"

The shades are already down. The only light is the yellow-white of the bulbs. Not fluorescent. Something fancier, that lasts longer and uses less electricity.

It's nicer too. Closer to sunlight. To true shades.

Makes it easier to judge the look of ink on someone's skin.

Not that I'm checking colors tonight. I already know she wants this in black. Even if she's not ready to admit it.

"Do you really—" She stammers. Taps her toes together. She's in wedges today. They're white. They're tall enough they bring us eye to eye.

I wrap my arm around her waist. Lead her to the counter.

"Holden—"

"Baby, you okay?"

"Do you really want to—"

"It's up to you."

She swallows hard. "I don't know."

"I do. But if you're not ready, if you're too scared, if you're not sure—"

"I'm sure. I just—"

"I'll walk you through it."

"After, right?"

"After?" This time, I play coy.

She clears her throat. Motions to the counter.

We've fucked here a million times. Sometimes she hangs out at the shop. Sometimes, I don't have the patience to wait until we're at my place.

There's something about doing it here.

It's illicit.

Sexy as fuck.

"After..." Her voice slips to that innocent tone of hers. That *Mr. Ballard, whatever do you mean* one.

It's too fucking sexy.

She really is going to kill me.

But what a way to go.

"After..." Her fingers curl into the hem of my t-shirt. Slip under it. She presses her palm flat against my stomach. "I come on your cock."

Fuck me. "Yes."

She pulls my t-shirt over my head and places it on the counter.

I push it to the floor. Switch our positions.

She groans as I pin her to the counter. "Holden—"

"Yeah, baby?"

"I'm gonna miss you."

"We have a week."

"I know, but—"

"Not yet." I drag my lips over her neck. "Nothing sad on your birthday."

"It's been a year."

"I know."

"A year since I kissed you."

"Since you gave me a fucking strip tease. Since you tried to kill me from blue balls."

Her blush spreads to her chest. "I, uh…"

"Aren't drunk enough to repeat it?"

"Well…" She presses her palm to my bare chest. For a second, she runs her fingers over my tattoo—I swear to God, she's obsessed with it—then she pushes the heel of her hand into my skin.

It's soft. A gesture. *Move so I can strip.*

I step back.

Daisy takes a deep breath as she unzips her dress.

She slides her left sleeve off her shoulder.

Then the right.

She catches the dress at her chest. Then she releases her arms.

The fabric falls to her ankles.

My gaze goes straight to her pink panties. They match her bra. Same hue. Same lace trim.

"You wear that for me, baby?" I try to hold on to conscious thought. To remember what I'm doing here.

Then she does away with her bra and my thoughts dissolve.

She stares into my eyes as she pushes her panties to her ankles.

She takes a step toward me. Runs her fingers over my tattoo one more time. Then she brings her hand lower. Lower.

Over the waistband of my jeans.

Over the cotton fabric.

She presses her palm against me, rubbing the rough denim against my cock.

It's equal parts agony and ecstasy.

But fuck if I'm going to tell her to stop.

There's nothing better than Daisy having *her* way with *me*.

She brings her lips to mine. Softly. Then harder.

My tongue slips into her mouth.

Kissing her is bliss. Everything inside me finds everything inside her.

I offer her the key that unlocks me.

She lays herself bare for me.

It's all there, in her lips, in the way she groans against me, in the way she digs her fingers into my skin.

I love her so fucking much.

I didn't know it was possible to love someone this much. But I do.

I love her more every day.

And now—

My last thought disappears as she undoes the button of my jeans. She pushes the zipper down. Cups me over my boxers.

Presses the soft fabric against my cock.

"Fuck, Holden—" She pulls back. "You always feel so good."

I press my lips to her neck.

She groans as I drag my teeth over her skin.

I bring my hands to her ass. Lift her. Set her on the counter.

She pushes my jeans to my thighs.

Then the boxers.

Her thumb skims my tip. It's feather light. I can barely feel it.

But it still makes my balls tighten.

I nip at her skin a little harder.

She wraps her hand around me.

I scrape my teeth against her skin.

She pumps me with a steady stroke.

Then another.

Harder.

I bring my hand to her wrist. "You're gonna make me

come, baby." I place her hand on my hip. "And I'm coming inside that pretty cunt."

Her lips part with a groan.

"After I taste you." It's been too fucking long.

She nods *hell yes*.

I press my lips to her belly button. Then below it.

Lower.

Lower.

My fingers curl into her thighs.

I tease her with a hot breath.

Then a cold one.

"Holden—" She says my name like it's poetry.

On her lips, it is.

I can't believe there was a time I hated my name. That I wanted to kill my parents for naming me after one of the most divisive fictional characters of all time.

"Holden," she says it again, a little lower, a little softer, a little needier.

I bring my lips to her cunt.

She groans as I lick her up and down. She tastes so fucking good. And the way she writhes against me—

If this isn't heaven, I don't know what is.

I pin her thighs to the counter as I toy with her.

When she's panting, I bring my lips to her clit. Tease her with soft flicks of my tongue.

Just enough she tugs at my hair.

Just enough she groans my name like it's a curse.

Then I lick her exactly how she needs me.

A little lower.

To the right.

Harder.

There.

"Holden—" she rocks her hips against me. "Don't stop."

I work her with steady strokes.

Again and again—

Until she's clawing at my skin.

Rocking her hips.

Curling her toes.

There.

She groans my name as she comes on my face. She gets wetter. Sweeter.

Short, choppy breaths.

The sharp pinch of her nails.

That perfect low moan.

The best thing I've ever heard.

"Fuck me." Her fingers curl into my neck. "Now."

I don't waste any time.

I hook her legs around my hips. Wrap my arms around her waist. Bring our bodies closer.

Closer.

She gasps as my tip strains against her.

I bring my eyes to hers as I shift inside her.

Fuck, there's nothing like the first moment. Our bodies joining. Every part of me tuned to every part of her.

I stay locked with her for a moment. Stay tuned into every single inch of her.

Then I pull back and drive into her with a steady stroke.

Again.

And again.

The two of us locked together, breathing together, groaning and moving together—

If this isn't the greatest thing in the world, I don't know what is.

We stay locked together until she's clawing at my skin, melting, begging me to release her.

I lay her on her back. Bring her legs to my chest. Wrap

my hands around her ankles. "Touch yourself, baby. I want to feel you come."

"Holden—" Her eyes meet mine as she slips her hand between her legs.

Then her head falls back.

Her eyes close.

I drive into her as she works herself.

Those same steady strokes.

Again and again.

She comes fast, pulsing around me, groaning my name as she pulls me closer.

It's too much.

It feels too fucking good.

A few more shifts of my hips and I come.

I wait until I've spilled every drop, then I pull back, help her upright, wrap my arms around her.

"Fuck." She collapses in my arms. "You—"

"Yeah."

"I—"

"Yeah."

She looks up at me. "I'm really going to miss you."

"Me too." I press my lips to hers. "Now, put on your panties, baby. I'm not gonna be able to do this if I'm hard."

———

"It's huge." Daisy traces the black letters with her fingertip. It's trace paper, but it looks like the real thing. "It's—"

"Perfect?"

"Yeah." She sucks in a shallow breath. "But is it too much?"

"Too much how?"

"Pretentious?" Nerves drip into her voice. "It is, isn't it?"

I shake my head.

"Are you sure?"

"Might attract the kind of guy who likes a damaged bad girl, but—"

"Really?" Her eyes go wide. She looks up at me, her expression streaked with vulnerability.

Yeah. I wish I could say otherwise, but I'm sure a Latin quote on her forearm is going to attract a certain type of guy.

Especially when the quote means *I struggle and I emerge.*

luctor et emerge

Sure, most guys aren't going to see Daisy and see *bad girl*. She owns an alarming amount of cardigans. And those adorable wrap dresses—

She's basically innocence, personified. At least at first glance.

Those guys don't know her.

The Daisy who gets lost in her favorite Lorde album every time she hears it. Who squeals *that's your mom's song* every time The Cure comes on the radio. Who steals my chai at every opportunity.

Stares at her morning latte like she's assessing it on a five point scale.

Spice, sweetness, flavor, balance.

The Daisy who lets me into her heart.

And loves me with all of it.

Even when she's scared I'll think she's broken, when she's falling and needs help getting up.

It's not always easy. Fuck knows Thanksgiving was big. She couldn't take all the attention on her plate. Everyone staring at her like their hopes and dreams rested on whether or not she ate her pumpkin pie.

It's more complicated than I expected. I try to be patient, to understand, to give her the space she needs.

I don't always succeed. Sometimes, it takes me awhile. Sometimes, we have to work through shit.

But we do.

Her trusting my love enough she'll tell me to fuck off—

Maybe it's weird that means the world.

But it does.

Fuck, now I'm getting sentimental. It's not my strong suit, but when I'm with her, it's almost natural.

Shit like *I want everything in your heart* rolls off my lips as easily as *panties off, now* does.

"Holden?" Her fingers brush my wrist. "You really think some guy at Berkeley will see this and—"

"Baby, you're the most beautiful woman I've ever seen."

"You have to say that."

I shake my head. "I'll be honest."

"It's just your honest opinion?"

"Yeah."

"Really." She arches a brow *yeah, right*. "So can you admit Luna has nicer boobs?"

"Bigger, yeah? I don't know about nicer."

"Because—"

"Can't really imagine anything better than the sound you make when I bite your nipples."

Her cheeks flush. "I was thinking more the size and shape and uh…" She clears her throat. "I really like when you do that."

"Yeah?"

"Yeah." Her smile is shy. "But you were right before."

"I was right about something?"

"We should try to keep some blood in your brain."

I can't help but laugh. She has the cutest way of teasing me. "Is that a yes?"

"Will it really attract douchebags?"

"You don't attract them now?"

She makes that *kinda* motion. "Most of the guys in school see me as a stuffy nerd."

"Probably makes them want you more."

"Maybe."

"They want to be the one who unzips those pretty wrap dresses." I bring my hand to her waist. "Who gets to peel those pretty pastel panties to your thighs."

"Yeah?" The look in her eyes is a dare.

I want to take it so fucking badly.

I'm *ready* to take it.

After this.

"You trying to distract me, kid?" Her nickname is practically a code word. It shifts my head out of *fuck me now* mode. I'm not sure why. Something about how innocent and impressionable she is.

Daisy is only a little younger than I am.

Those three and a half years are an eternity at her age.

She's only nineteen.

Hell, she turns nineteen today.

"Maybe." She smiles.

"Bad girl."

Her smile widens. "Are you going to punish me?"

Hell yes. "Are you into that?"

"We could try. Find out."

She's really going to kill me. I force my eyes to the wall. Force myself to read the Inked Love sign backward. When I have a little blood back in my brain, I bring my eyes to hers. "It's up to you, kid. I love it. I want it. But it's your body. It has to be your call."

She bites her lip. "It's so permanent. So forever."

"It is."

"How are you more okay with that than I am?"

"Less ability to consider the consequences."

"Maybe." She laughs. "It looks amazing."

"Yeah."

"And it's perfect." Her voice softens. "I…" Her eyes meet mine. "I, um, I don't really know what to say. If there's a way to say thank you. For being patient with me. For loving me even though I—"

"Baby, I don't love you even though you had an eating disorder."

She swallows hard.

"I love everything about you."

"But, I—"

"I hate that it hurts you. I hate anything that hurts you. But I don't love you in spite of your illness."

"You don't?"

"No, baby. I love you. All of you. Even the broken parts. Even though they're not as broken as you think."

"Holden—" She digs her fingers into my shirt. Pulls me into a slow, deep kiss.

All her need pours into me.

All my need pours into her.

Fuck, it's overwhelming how much I need her, how much I love her, how much I want her.

She pulls back with a sigh. "I love you too."

"I love you so fucking much, baby." I force my gaze to the trace paper. "Now, sit down. I need to do this. So I can fuck you again after."

She bites her lip.

"If you're sure. If not, I'll be devastated," I tease.

"Hey—"

A laugh falls from my lips. "You know I'm desperate to leave a permanent mark on you."

"You already have."

I melt. "Fuck… no more romantic shit. Or I'm going to take you again."

"Is that supposed to discourage me?"

"Okay. No more romantic shit. Or I'm going to drive you home. And tell your dad you said you're thinking about removing your IUD."

"Oh God no." Her nose scrunches in distaste. "He'll spend an hour talking about birth control options. Then he'll threaten to call Mom and…" Her eyes meet mine. "I'll be good."

"Well, don't say things you don't mean." I wink.

She makes a show of holding up her hands. Then pressing them to her thighs.

I help her into the chair.

She looks up at me with all the trust in the world.

I still can't believe that this beautiful, intelligent, strong woman trusts me with her heart, her body, her soul.

I can't believe how fucking cheesy I am now.

And how little I care.

Daisy fidgets as I clean her up, prep the stencil, grab a fresh pad of ink.

She stares at the tattoo gun like it's going to attack her.

I guess it is.

"Deep breath, baby," I say.

She nods *got it*. Sucks a breath through her teeth. Pushes out a shallow exhale.

Her next inhale is a little longer.

The exhale is a little smoother.

I wait until she has it. Then I turn on my gun.

"On three, okay?" I ask.

"Are you going to do that thing you always do?"

"What thing?" I play dumb.

"Where you say you'll count to three and—"

"Just count."

"One—"

I bring the needle to her skin.

She yelps. "Fuck." Her eyes go to her forearm. She stares as the ink marks her skin.

luctor et emerge

It fits her perfectly.

I know her so much better than I did last year. No matter how busy we were, we saw each other at least once a month.

Never more than twice.

I didn't want to tie her to her past, to home, to her impulses to stay in, protect herself from risk.

I didn't want to clip her wings.

Thank fuck I didn't.

In the last year, she's soared. She's still Daisy, but she has friends at school. She writes all the time. Edits the literary magazine.

She even took an art class.

Went into the city for tea a million times.

I miss her so much when she's gone. But I'm glad she gets the chance to spread her wings.

I'm so lucky that she shares that with me.

"Can you…" She forces a breath. "Tell me something."

"I love your tits."

She laughs. "Something… well, actually, that's pretty distracting."

"I love the taste of your cunt."

"Oh my God."

"I think about it when you're at school."

"You do not."

"I do. When I fuck myself. I think about your thighs against my cheeks. And the way your head falls back when you come." Shit, now I'm the one getting distracted.

Almost there.

I finish the second word.

Move to the third.

It's shorter than the first.

Just barely.

"I fuck myself to you almost every day," I say.

"You do not."

"You want me to prove it?"

"Depends…" She struggles through the words. "What does that entail?"

"Videos. Unless you prefer something else. A photo of the… end results."

"The—oh." Her laugh is pained. "Won't that be a lot of, uh, bandwidth."

"We can make it… what's that thing your friends use to send messages that disappear?"

"No one uses that anymore."

"I'm behind the times?"

"Yeah." Her eyes go to the ceiling. "I, uh…" The pain is getting to be too much.

I need to keep her mind on sex. "Unless you'll get bored of them."

"Oh?"

"The videos. Of me fucking myself."

"Oh. No way."

"Really? Every day? Twice a day?"

"Would you get bored of videos of me?"

"You have videos?"

"Not yet." She pushes a breath through her teeth. "I've thought about it."

"Baby, don't do this to me."

"What?"

"Tease me like that."

"Maybe for your birthday." She tries to make her voice flirty, but it only gets halfway there.

"Almost done."

She nods *thank God*. "It's not as bad as I thought. I can see why—fuck."

One letter to go.

"Does it get worse?"

"Why? You want to go for two right away?"

"Maybe." Her laugh is soft. "I still need *danger is sweet*."

"Next time."

"Next time." She sighs as I pull the gun away.

"Really?"

She stares at the ink. "Really."

The joy in her eyes steals my oxygen.

I gave that to her.

Fuck.

It's indescribable.

I've marked her forever. But then maybe she was right. Maybe that mark is already there.

She's sure as hell left her mark on me. She's going to be in my heart forever.

And next year—

She made me promise not to tattoo her name on my skin. She thinks it's a bad omen. A sign we're sure to break up.

But nothing is stopping me from getting a daisy right above her favorite quote.

Danger is sweet.

But loving her is sweeter than anything.

———

Want more Inked Love?

Find out what happens next with Holden and Daisy! <u>Sign up for my mailing list</u> for the exclusive extended epilogue to *The First Taste*.

Then dive into Luna and Oliver's story in *The Roomie Rulebook*, <u>now available</u>. When Luna needs a place to crash, she stays with her BFF's older brother Oliver. But it's not so easy resisting the brooding bad boy from across the hall.

Author's Note

Can you keep a secret?

I almost didn't write *The First Taste*. I certainly didn't plan to write it this way. For years, eating disorders were on my "uh-uh, no way are readers going to follow me on this" list.

That's the problem with my process—I show up at the keyboard with an idea and the characters take me in a totally different direction. They don't care what I want.

I don't know if readers will go with me on this journey. If you're here, I hope you did, and I thank you for reading something outside the "acceptable" romance themes. Or "acceptable romance heroine flaws."

Romance heroines are rarely allowed the types of "brokenness" romance heroes are allowed. They're rarely fucked up or self-destructive. They're rarely struggling with self-inflicted demons. Or demons society still deems self-inflicted: addiction, self-harm, eating disorders, suicide ideation, depression, or the self-loathing & self-destructive impulses that come with any of the above.

My readers know me as the queen of broken bad boys.

I wear the crown happily. But I want to extend my heroines the same consideration. They should get the chance to be fucked up and self-destructive too. They should be allowed to wrestle with their demons. To be in the middle of it, barely holding onto their recovery (the way Miles or Kit or Hunter or, in my next Inked Love book, Oliver is).

Daisy isn't fucked up. At least not more than any of us. But she is still far outside acceptable romance heroine flaws. And that is a scary, scary thing. Even for someone like me, an author of almost thirty books, an author known for her nuanced, three-dimensional characters and her refreshingly raw, honest take on mental health and addiction.

But then *The First Taste* is not a book about eating disorders. It's about a shy bookworm who wants to bone her brother's best friend. She happens to be in recovery for an eating disorder.

That's how I typically write. Or at least how I try to write—characters who are whole people, not mental health statuses with quirks and favorites.

If you'd like a more explicit take on eating disorders and the healing that comes after HEA, read my *Come Undone* series. Or read *Broken* for a more explicit take on depression.

Outside my catalog I can personally recommend *More Than You Can Chew* by Marnelle Tokio, *Wasted* by Marya Hornbacher, and *Unbearable Lightness* by Portia de Rossi.

Though it's been years since I've read any of those books, I am confident warning you that they're packed with triggering content.

Eating disorders have a reputation as a suburban teenage girl problem. They are prevalent in teenagers, but they often persist or start later in life. If you or someone you know has signs of an eating disorder, visit www.

nationaleatingdisorders.org or call their hotline at (800) 931-2237. If you're in the UK, visit eating-disorders.org.uk or call their hotline at 0845 838 2040. Please be kind to them. As I write this, we're still in quarantine. This is a particularly difficult time for people with eating disorders.

As always, thanks for reading. I hope I see you soon for Luna and Oliver's book, *The Roomie Rulebook*.

If you're new to the Inked universe, get to know Forest and Skye in *The Best Friend Bargain*. Or go all the way to the beginning with *Tempting*, another hot forbidden romance.

(If you're totally caught up on Inked boys, check out Sinful Serenade, starting with *Sing Your Heart Out*.)

Love,

Crystal

Acknowledgments

My first thanks goes to my husband, for his support when I'm lost in bookland and for generally being the sun in my sky. Sweetheart, you're better than all the broken bad boys in the world.

The second goes to my father, for insisting I go to the best film school in the country, everything else be damned. I wouldn't love movies, writing, or storytelling half as much if not for all our afternoon trips to the bookstore and weekends at the movies. You've always been supportive of my goals, and that means the world to me.

Thanks so much to my amazing audio narrators, Kai Kennicott and Wen Ross. You always bring my characters to life in a way that blows my mind.

A big shout out to all my beta readers. And also to my ARC readers for helping spread the word to everyone else in the world.

To all my writer friends who talk me down from the ledge, hold my hand, and tell me when my ideas are terrible and when they're brilliant, thank you.

Thanks so much to my editor Marla, my assistant Gemma, and to my designer Gel.

As always, my biggest thanks goes to my readers. Thank you for picking up *The First Taste*. I hope you'll be back for Luna and Oliver's book, *The Roomie Rulebook*.

About the Author

Crystal Kaswell writes scorching hot new adult romance. She is a USA Today and Wall Street Journal bestseller.

Dubbed "the queen of broken bad boys" by her readers, she adores flawed characters who help each other heal. Her books are the perfect mix of humor, heart, and heat.

When she isn't writing, she's chain drinking tea, practicing yoga, or debating which fictional character would be the best in bed. Originally from Southern California, she now resides in the Pacific Northwest, where she spends the rainy winters dreaming of sunny skies and balmy beaches.

Her weaknesses include dark chocolate, homemade matcha lattes, Netflix marathons, and tattooed men in skinny jeans (especially if they're wearing eyeliner). She is a diehard defender of pop-punk music, the present tense, and Katniss Everdeen.

Also by Crystal Kaswell

Inked Love

The Best Friend Bargain - Forest

The First Taste - Holden

The Roomie Rulebook - Oliver

Inked Hearts

Tempting - Brendon

Hooking Up - Walker

Pretend You're Mine - Ryan

Hating You, Loving You - Dean

Breaking the Rules - Hunter

Losing It - Wes

Accidental Husband - Griffin

The Baby Bargain - Chase

Dirty Rich

Dirty Deal - Blake

Dirty Boss - Nick

Dirty Husband - Shep

Dirty Desires - Ian

Dirty Wedding - Ty

Dirty Secret - Cam

Pierce Family

Broken Beast - Adam

Playboy Prince - Liam

Ruthless Rival - Simon - coming soon

Sinful Serenade

<u>*Sing Your Heart Out*</u> - Miles

<u>*Strum Your Heart Out*</u> - Drew

<u>*Rock Your Heart Out*</u> - Tom

<u>*Play Your Heart Out*</u> - Pete

<u>*Sinful Ever After*</u> – series sequel

<u>*Just a Taste*</u> - *Miles's POV*

Dangerous Noise

<u>*Dangerous Kiss*</u> - Ethan

<u>*Dangerous Crush*</u> – Kit

<u>*Dangerous Rock*</u> – Joel

<u>*Dangerous Fling*</u> – Mal

<u>*Dangerous Encore*</u> - series sequel

Standalones

<u>*Broken*</u> - Trent & Delilah

Come Undone Trilogy

<u>*Come Undone*</u>

<u>*Come Apart*</u>

<u>*Come To Me*</u>

<u>Sign up for the Crystal Kaswell mailing list</u>

Made in the USA
Las Vegas, NV
12 May 2024

89856028R10249